# BEYOND THE
## DARKNESS

# Beyond the Darkness

REBECCA ZIMMERMAN

Langdon Street Press
212 3rd Avenue North, Suite 570
Minneapolis, MN 55401
612-455-2293
www.langdonstreetpress.com

ISBN - 1-934938-02-5
ISBN - 978-1-934938-02-7
LCCN - 2008923118


Book sales for North America and international:
Itasca Books, 3501 Highway 100 South, Suite220
Minneapolis, MN 55416
Phone: 952.345.4488 (toll free 1.800.901.3480)
Fax: 952.920.0541; email to orders@itascabooks.com

Cover Design and typeset by James/DZYN Lab

*Printed in the United States of America*

This book is dedicated to Candy Kallio;
critic, editor, mentor, sister and friend,
without whose assistance this book
would have never become a reality.

# CHAPTER ONE

Darkness comes in many forms; the blackest pitch of night, the obscuring of the sun with the onset of roiling thunderheads, the abyss in your heart when it's broken; but, by far, the epitome of total despair is the blackness of the soul.

It seems all you can do is hang on as tenaciously as possible and hope you're not swallowed up whole by the all-encompassing nothingness.

Each day I arise to the same sweet birdsong that has been my wake-up call for the past 11 years. I make coffee, wash up as it brews, and try to avoid the old lady in the mirror, and most importantly, reconstruct my thought patterns so as not to dwell on events of recent months, for therein lies insanity. It, seems, however, I am doomed to this fate as I could no more forget the uncanniness of these occurrences then I could forget Albert.

Til' death do us part and maybe not then.

I take my coffee to the back porch, like every morning, and sit on the old handhewn bench, made by the loving hands of my husband over thirty years ago. The cabin had been built by his father and, though rustic, had most modern conveniences.

I surveyed my private domain that had meant everything when I'd had someone to share it with and now, now meant nothing really, just a place to grow old and die, alone.

Acres of woods bordered me on all sides but the back, which is right on a narrow channel with only two other houses within five miles, and those only occupied in season, which is fairly short this far north. A big lake pours into the channel 500 feet upstream.

We had relished the solitude, wildlife, and ambiance. Together we formed our own little insular world where outsiders, though not shunned, were not welcomed, either. Hunting season and high summer were usually the only times we even saw other people. On Holiday weekends, the channel could get quite busy with fishermen, canoers, campers and the occasional back-packer, but nine months or so out of the year you could almost imagine that you were living 150 years ago and the woods were full of Indians, that a herd of buffaloes were just over the next rise. These thoughts comforted me as the world as it is now scares me; not the technology, but the blatant misuse and misappropriation of it. The good-- evil thing scares me, as I fear evil may prevail.

I sip my coffee, cupping my hands around the fast evaporating warmness of the mug.

The feeders are teeming with the usual assortment of my feathered friends: Blue jay, Sparrows, Finches, Cardinals, the occasional Sapsucker. Squirrels, of course, were the rulers of the roost, spending most of their time making sure no birds could get to the feeders. Raccoons were sometime visitors, and quite pesky, really. Wolves could be heard at night, and one had been spotted standing in the road in the morning mist just last year. Also Beaver, Muskrats, Foxes, Cranes, Eagles, Owls and Hawks. Blue Herons in their royal plumage stand one-legged on our rickety dock, sunning themselves in the waning days of summer. Dozens of turtles line the logs set akimbo by Beavers and Natures fury. My cat, Judas, sat by my side as Al's dog, Sam cavorted at the waters edge.

The morning ritual was never changing and everyone knew his or her roles. For only with the complacency of normalcy could we all hope to go on without our lord and master.

Gumba, our fat, furry favorite of the squirrel persuasion, came running up the roughhewn steps to grovel at my feet, looking for peanuts, acorns or any other goodies I may have for him, but, alas, it was not meant to be, for Sam had heard his chattering and came running up to give chase to his little buddy, while Judas looked on with contempt for such doggish behavior; she had long ago grown bored with the chase, maybe because her quarry had always remained just that.

I watched this display with a silent chuckle, wondering if Albert could somehow be looking down on our morning ritual of so many years with his quiet contentment.

It was six months to the day since I had discovered his lifeless body in the woods a half a mile from our home. He had went for one of his many walks through the woods, but had not returned by supper time, nor responded to my repeated calls. I had hurriedly donned a sweater (the evenings were still quite chilly) and hurried through the thick woods in search of my errant husband, I was as familiar with these woods as he, and knew all the deer trails he frequented. It was on the third one that I found him, lying on his side, clutching his chest, staring with sightless eyes at the golden sunset, one of many that he would never see again.

I knew immediately that he was gone and fell to my knees, cradling his beloved head to my breast as the horror of this moment seared itself into my brain.

When I had, at last, pulled myself away from him, I ran and ran through the glooming twilight, getting torn and scratched in my heedless rush by grasping branches that seemed, in my panicked state, to reach out for me and keep me forever in their soulless clutches with my poor, dead husband.

The paramedics came along with the Sheriff, even though I told them there was no hope. It was fortunate for me that they had, though, as they were kind enough to sedate me when his lifeless body was finally pulled from its serene surroundings and I collapsed, uncontrollably, into a heap of trembling flesh.

They were quite kind and wanted to know about children or relatives they could contact that could come to my aid. No, no. We had never had children and any family I had I'd lost track of years ago. They finally departed in a hushed silence when I'd regained my composure, or a reasonable facsimile thereof.

I'd never bothered to clean out his side of the closet, or his bureau. In actuality, these things comforted me. The lingering smell of his aftershave permeated his clothes as well as his pillowcase, which I was uncertain whether I would ever wash again.

Now, six months after his death I took a walk through the woods, seeking solace in the familiar, calming influence of nature, feeling Albert's spirit with me, almost feeling HIM.

Leaves were starting to fall already, and I kicked through small windblown tufts as I strode along, deep in melancholy thought. All at once, my toe felt something under a small pile of freshly fallen leaves. It wasn't hard as a rock would be, but rather had a soft, mushy quality to it. My curiosity aroused, I bent to see what anachronism I may have discovered. To my shock and horror, a bloody carcass was exposed at my searching feet.

Upon closer inspection I realized that it was a squirrel carcass, skinned and thrown aside as a lifeless blob. I immediately thought of my beloved Gumba, but pushed aside this horrific thought as I had just seen him a while ago and this carcass was already decomposing and mutilated by scavenging animals.

I remembered a few years back there had been poachers, but they certainly wouldn't bother with squirrel pelts, I don't think it's even considered poaching if it's squirrel. Somewhat spooked about my grisly discovery, I quickly headed home, after disposing of the carcass, with little fanfare, under a dead log.

Back at the house, I sat and contemplated this disturbing turn of events. Who had done this, and why? I knew what few, and mostly seasonal neighbors, I had. None were the type to hunt or skin a squirrel. No teenagers were in residence this late in the year, and I didn't think there'd been any hillbillies in this area, well, ever.

Should I be frightened? Should I call the Sheriff? As I mulled these things I kept a wary eye on the surrounding trees and a watchful eye on Sam and Judas, keeping an eye, too, on Gumba's favorite tree. After some consideration I decided the cops were not the way to go. They already seemed to have gotten the impression that I was some sort of hysteric and being afraid of a dead squirrel would make me the butt of many a departmental joke, I was sure. No. I would go on as I always had, with a mind to protecting my animals and myself. I was sure I was overreacting, especially since it was so soon after Albert's unexpected demise.

The next day I had determined to walk all the familiar deer trails, looking with practiced eye for any sign of human presence. I pushed aside fallen leaves and snapping branches, some still heavy with plump red berries, searching for any sign of disturbance in the natural scheme of things. After several hours, battling fatigue and sore muscles, I abandoned my folly and headed home, calling for Sam, who had wandered off and returned several times during this excursion. I heard him snuffing through the brush to my right and hurried forward; not until I reached the clearing of our lawn did I see Sam bounding out of the woods, tail wagging furiously, clearly in possession of a treasured object. I called him in my "good boy" voice about to shower him with praise for his interesting discovery when he nearly knocked me over in his enthusiasm to bestow it upon me. I heard the "plop" of his prize hitting the ground and anxiously pushed his shaggy head aside to get a look. To my great shock another bloody carcass was laying at my feet. This one was larger than the last, and clearly had once been a rabbit.

I quickly grabbed Sam's collar and dragged him, fighting and howling, into the house.

Returning to the bloody corpse, which Judas had discovered and was now sniffing at, I gingerly picked it up and heaved it with all my might into the channel. In a couple of hours it would be miles away and irretrievable to Sam, for I knew if I buried it, he would find it.

The sun was now high in the sky and starting it's nightward descent. I decided to call it a day since I heard the distant rumbling of thunder and saw to the north dark thunderheads swiftly approaching.

Al and I had always enjoyed storms; the excitement of the booming thunder, the dazzling lightning displays, and the mist created on the water by the falling raindrops.

Now I felt only an ominous uneasiness as flocks of geese flew hurriedly by chased by roiling clouds.

I entered the coziness of my humble abode, fireplace to the left, covering a third of the 40 by 60 foot room. We hadn't used it in months and it gaped like a sooty maw, empty and forlorn. The roughhewn couch and two chairs were sumptuously upholstered in teal and red, surrounding a homemade log coffee table. Wooden end tables with pink shaded lamps flanked the coffee table and would soon cast a golden glow over the room. A large rug of muted, variant colors underscored the furniture and added a homey, comfortable feel to the room. The kitchen was more of a nook, divided by an island from the dining room, which was perhaps a third of the living room, differentiated by a yellow tile floor that ended at the larger room. Next to the outside door stood our faux elephant foot umbrella holder, standing silent sentinel in anticipation of the coming storm.

Our bedroom was down a narrow hall off the living room. It was done in soft pastels, accentuating the dark red wood of the walls. A large bed of unfinished natural oak dominated the room, dwarfing a bookshelf and writing desk, seemingly placed pell-mell in any available space. This was the only carpeted room in the house. A plush golden rug went nearly wall to wall. The Golden Hind, Al and I used to call it.

The bathroom was small and had been added, for there had been an outhouse when the house was originally built.

All and all, a quite peaceful and cozy place to dwell; but now, alone, it seemed somehow different, less inviting, devoid of the animation it had held when Albert was alive.

I sat on the couch and turned on the t.v. to track the storm, but the reception was already starting its white noise static and I quickly turned it off.

I went in the bedroom and turned on a small bedside lamp, casting an inviting glow on the disheveled bed. Picking up my half-finished book, I snuggled under the covers to read.

Sam and Judas soon joined me, Sam whining, as he did every time I went to bed and Al wasn't there. Judas purred contentedly at my feet.

Al was wearing his army uniform and looked quite young and handsome. I ran towards the disembarking train, in the rain, arms spread in welcome, a soft smile lighting my face.

I flung myself into his arms, sobbing in relief and happiness to have my husband back again, safe and sound, in my arms. I lifted my tear-stained face to kiss my beloved and recoiled in disbelief as I gazed at his face. A hideous death head, eyes wide, had displaced my young, handsome husband; his mouth twisted in a grimace of incomprehension.

I awoke with a start, sending my book and hibernating pets flying. My heart was pounding with enough force to make me think I may soon be joining Albert. Something about the vivid dream deeply disturbed me. Was Albert trying to tell me something? The thought had been nagging at me since the discovery of the first mutilated animal. If there were poachers, or mountain men (although there were no mountains in the state), and Albert had somehow stumbled onto their grisly doings, then it was murder! His heart would not have given out without severe provocation. He had a complete physical six months prior to his death and been told that he had the heart and stamina of a man half his age (he was 58).

I had to find out, somehow, what had happened out there. If others had been present when he suffered his fatal heart attack, why hadn't they gone for help? Could he have been saved with quick thinking?

I got up and went into the living room. The rain was coming done in torrents now, drumming staccato rhythms against the windowpane. Lightning flashes illuminated the darkening gloom, casting weird reflections off the churning channel.

I went into the kitchen and poured another cup of coffee, probably not a good idea with my heart trip hammering and my nerves frayed to the limit anyway, but I needed a clear head as the nightmare slowly loosened its grip on me.

Judas sat on the windowsill, occasionally batting at an unreachable bird, while Sam sprawled on the couch, still mad at me for displacing him from the bed.

I filled their food bowls and gave them fresh water. Sam immediately forgave me for my indiscretion when he realized food was at hand. I sat down in the dining room, (area, really) pushed aside the chintz curtains and gazed out at the tumultuous wrath of Mother Nature.

My memories of life with Albert came flooding back, as all-encompassing as the wind and rain. Our first meeting in high school, he a long-haired hippie, I, a flower child. We'd shared (as much of our generation did) the same hopes, fears and aspirations. We'd clung to each other from that day on, like a drowning person would cling to a life jacket in a raging ocean that was determined to pull him under. Together we'd weathered teen-age angst, vindictive parents, hypocritical authority figures, and all the other ills, real or imagined, that constituted puberty. He'd been drafted a year out of high school and went off with little fan-fare to fight someone else's war. I waited patiently, writing everyday, striving not to let him know how I worried and prayed and missed him every hour of every day. In time, he came home. The same sweet, quiet Albert; seemingly, yet I sensed the profound sadness that had inundated itself into his usual happy-go-lucky personality. The same, yet forever changed in some ethereal fashion. He'd grown-up.

We married soon after and never looked back. He'd become a somewhat successful manager at a local Taconite plant, I became a factory worker by day and an aspiring writer at night. Eleven years ago we'd decided that we'd had enough of the rat race.

We had 401ks, he had a pension, and he'd inherited this house from his father upon his death 15 years ago. We'd come here every weekend in the summer for 4 years, and then one day we decided we loved it so much here we should make it permanent. The ensuing eleven years had been heaven on earth. Rising every day together, sitting on the porch sipping our coffee, jumping in the channel for a cool-off dip, making love on a blanket in the deep woods with dappled sunlight filtering through whispering boughs.

Neither of us could have anticipated that our lives would take that fateful, irreversible turn. In actuality, I'd always assumed that I'd be the first to go; deep down, I think Albert did, too. I was the worrywart, worrying about everything from soaring insurance costs to a missing bird at the feeder.

Albert, on the other hand, let life's little (or big) problems roll off his back like a Canvasback in the rain.

Oh, how I missed him. We should have cultivated more friends over the years and tried to find displaced family; but it never occurred to us at the time. Things were perfect just the way they were. Now I would have to stew in my own juices; I had chosen my road and now must finish the journey, alone. I realized, of course, that our life together hadn't been as idyllic as I romanticised; after retirement, he had sometimes gotten on my nerves, following me around in his boredom. Yet, what wouldn't I have given to still have him there?

During the ensuing days I stuck close to home, keeping a wary eye on my pets, both wild and domesticated. I'd seen no further evidence of another human presence, but nonetheless was uneasy. Finally, when I could no longer take the boredom and anxiety, I decided to go on with my life as before, sans Albert, of course.

I arose early the next morning, which was my usual ritual, fed the animals, filled the bird feeders (they had to be filled frequently because of Gumba and his ilk), drank my coffee on the still dripping porch, and decided to take a trek once again through my beloved woods. I decided to take the most overgrown and lesser used deer trail, thinking if any others were around they would probably be laying low, what with the recent events of cop cars and hysterical old ladies.

I had brought my husband's old Saturday night special, which I hadn't fired in years, yet used to be quite proficient with. Al and I used to trek five miles to a large clearing and practice with tin cans set on an old wooden fence, that by now had been completely obliterated by time and weather.

Leaving Sam and Judas locked in the house, (ignoring Sam's pitiful howls); I started off down the path. I had on my hiking boots and Al's old red plaid jacket, on the off chance there may be out-of-season hunters prowling around. I'd determined to enjoy myself by communing with nature as I always had on these beautiful, almost fall, days.

I hadn't gone far when a rustling in the nearby trees startled me out of my reverie. I quickly jumped behind a huge oak, nearly falling in my haste at concealment, and slowly peeked my head around the rough bark, scraping my cheek in the process. I nearly fell over in fright as a large buck leaped not six inches from my face and ran off through the woods. Getting my heartbeat to a normal pace, I turned and wended my way through the trees in the direction from whence he'd come. Sure enough, in a little glade in front of me were the tell-tale signs that I'd disturbed his sleeping place. Matted down leaves and dead branches with hair still clinging to them, gave away his hidey-hole.

I turned back onto the path and continued my journey.

About half way to the clearing, I sat down to rest on a large, dead log, looking around to make sure no raccoons or other critters may be making a home in there. It looked safe enough.

I was more afraid of a sudden heart attack due to fright than any harm they might do me.

I sat on the log, trying not to think about the sad course my life had taken; basking in the weak early morning sun, watching the small, high, puffy clouds which hardly seemed to move in the non-existent breeze. The usually whispering branches were silent now, and no sound could be heard except for the occasional bird call.

When I felt sufficiently rested I continued on. I was almost there when a putrefying smell assailed my nostrils; whatever it was must be close as there was no air moving.

Perhaps a deer had died nearby and was laying there rotting in the fashion of all flesh once the essence is gone.

I covered my nose and mouth with the tail of Al's jacket and boldly rallied on. I had to find the source of that smell, whether I'd regret it or not. I trudged through the last few yards, tripping over branches, making quite a racket I'm sure, although I felt I was being quite stealthy.

I broke the clearing and stood in paralyzing disbelief at the sight I beheld. It seemed the whole clearing was filled with bodiless hides. Hides everywhere, of varying sizes. I recognized several raccoons, some muskrat, a few mink. There were even some large ones, perhaps bear, although I'd never heard of any bear around this area. Each pelt was staked out with a measured hand, all neatly a row.

Once the initial shock wore off, I turned and pummeled helter-skelter into the shelter of the woods, not slowing down for the numerous obstacles in my way. My face was torn by the clutching hands of branches, my feet stumbling every few steps over leaf covered rocks and dead limbs. The terror of that flight will be with me forever; the reverberating echo of my startled heart pounding blood through my ears, creating a buzzing that obscured my hearing, making me even more petrified. I kept thinking bullets would soon fell me, and I'd die where I stood, like Al did.

When, after seemingly endless hours, I reached the sanctuary of our lawn, I nearly collapsed. Yet even in my nearly demented state, I realized that the yard wasn't a sanctuary, no, not even the house was safe!

Once inside, I quickly made sure the house was locked up tight and hurried to phone the DNR. I knew from the previous experience that the police wanted no part of the poaching scene. Unless called on by the DNR, they would stay out of it. I went to the bathroom to tidy up, as I knew I looked like a wild woman; and, sure enough, one look in the mirror confirmed that I bore a striking resemblance to what, I imagined, Lady Macbeth looked like. I'm a small woman, five feet four, 105 pounds, with unkempt, perpetually wind-blown hair, now mousey brown with myriad streaks of gray. My eyes, though still the same bluish-gray color, had a demented cast about them. My always somewhat gaunt cheekbones seemed even more sunken, skull like.

Well, there was nothing to be done about my appearance, other than to run a brush through my hair, tie it back in a ponytail, and maybe change my clothes. I kept thinking that I'd absorbed the horrid death smell and was amazed Sam and Judas weren't all over me.

The DNR men arrived and I tried to sound sane and sensible as I recalled for them my scary adventure. They decided to go by boat down the channel and then inland from there. It was, perhaps, only a quarter of a mile to the field coming off the channel and going through the woods there. I was informed that my presence wouldn't be necessary as they knew right where I meant. I was immensely relieved, since I had no intention of returning there, probably, ever.

The wait seemed interminable, although it was probably a couple of hours. Upon their return, I ran to meet them, relief flooding me as I now would have collaboration of my bizarre tale.

I slowed to a stop as they drew nearer; it wasn't so much their disheveled appearance, clothes askew from grasping branches, leaves in their hair, it was the countenances they presented. Neither would look me in the eye, and their mouths were grim lines in their seemingly angry faces.

"What are you tryin' to pull?" The larger one said as I stared at a newly ripped sleeve in what had been an immaculate uniform shirt. I jerked my head up to face him at the question and the hostility in his voice.

"What do you mean?" I stammered, stupidly.

"Why, there's nothin' down there—you must be hallucinating" spat out the smaller, Barney Fifeish one. "We just spent half the day traipsing through woods on a wild goose chase!"

"They were there this morning!", I exclaimed, "Just like I told you-all staked out in neat rows, why, there must have been 50 or more!"

"Well, there's nothing there now." Said mister torn shirt,

staring at me now, like one might look at a lunatic.

"But the smell!" I insisted, "Surely the area reeked!"

"I didn't smell nothing", said Barney, "Didn't see nothing either, "'cept a bunch a trees pulling at me for a mile!"

I didn't point out the discrepancy in the true distance, nor the fact that I, an old lady, walked the long, five-mile way and back (actually, ran back) and wasn't too much the worse for wear.

"Well, I don't know what to tell ya', ma'am," the bigger man said. He seemed more compassionate than his scrawny compadre, and only looked at me with sadness now, not contempt.

"I don't understand!" I stuttered, still trying to hold on to a shred of my dignity, and sanity. "They obviously spotted me on the edge of the woods and quickly went about hiding their activities" I averred.

"If that's the case, ma'am, then they'd a had to work mighty fast and you'd think men in that big a hurry would have left some evidence of their havin' been there."

"But, But…" my voice trailed off. It was obvious I wasn't going to convince them of anything except that I was a crazy woman.

"Well, if ya' see anything, anyone, around your house here, you just call the Sheriff's office and they'll send someone out. And if I was you, I'd just try to stick close to home. A person could get lost or hurt running around in them woods."

With that, they turned to leave, Barney scowling at me until the bigger man shoved him along.

At that moment a song came into my head, "Alone again, naturally".

# CHAPTER TWO

I went up and sat on the porch, pondering my next move. Sam was scratching and barking at the door to be let out, so I went and got him, and put him on his rope, which of course he despised, since it curtailed his freedom. Judas ran out as well, heading immediately for the dock, one of her favorite late afternoon sunning spots.

Something kept nagging at my mind, as if I'd forgotten something. I sat and mulled over it some more, then decided to go in and walk around the house, hoping to stir up some memory; of what, I knew not.

Everything was the same as when I'd left in the living/dining area and kitchen. A thin patina of dust from rampant sunbeams coated the mantle and several other articles of furniture; I'd have to dust one of these days, I thought abstractedly.

When I entered the bedroom and spotted my discarded clothes on the floor where I'd left them in my haste to meet the DNR men, I immediately knew what had been preying on my mind; I ran to my clothes and hurriedly went through them, I bent and looked under the bed, nothing. In my haste to get away from the terrible spectacle at the edge of the woods, I had lost Al's gun!

This disturbing turn of events left me even more frightened, for now I had no means of defense against an unknown and unseen (in my mind) enemy.

Maybe I should drive up and down the rutted, muddy roads under foreboding canopies of trees, searching out any neighbors that may be in residence this late in the year and ask for their assistance and/or any info they may possess concerning strangers in the area. Then again, I hardly knew my neighbors. How was I to know if it wasn't one of them?

Several elderly people had died in the last decade and relatives now inhabited their properties, seasonally, or had sold them or rented them out. My nearest neighbor was miles away even when most of the "seasonals" were in residence.

Several smaller cabins along the lake were now perpetually empty and falling into disrepair. No, I no longer knew any "neighbors" I may have had at least a nodding acquaintance with, once.

At least I knew Sam would put up a hell of a yowl if anyone (or thing) came within a couple of miles of the property.

I got a beer from the frig, settling once more on the porch to watch over my domain.

I seldom imbibed anymore as I tended to like it a little too much, but one to calm my nerves right now seemed like a good idea.

I began to believe I was a paranoid as my mind took to strange pathways, envisioning the DNR men, and maybe the whole department being behind it. Who could I trust?

I spent a fitful night, tossing and turning and fearing further nightmares. My pets steered clear of the bed, for my discomfiture was theirs.

The next morning I was in my usual place on the porch (after having ran a Pledged soaked rag over my furniture). I hadn't been there long when I heard a car approaching.

This was indeed a rare occurrence and I had no idea how to react. Should I run back in my house? Fear got the best of me and that's exactly what I did.

I was peeking through the curtains when I saw an old Ford pull up into my yard. I watched as an old lady got out and wended her way, rather gracefully, up my pebbled walkway.

I opened the door before she even got to it, my curiosity getting the better of me.

"Hello?", I called out, "May I help you?".

"Yes, yes you can, I think", she trilled in a high, bird-like voice.

"Please come in", I implored, standing aside and gesturing toward the dark, cool rooms.

She entered, scanning me up and down as she passed, finally focusing on my face.

"I may be able to help you, too." She said as she ambled across the room and seated herself in a wing chair near the fireplace.

I seated myself on the couch, leaning in to face her. "What do you mean? Help me with what?" I queried.

"I heard about your recent, shall we say, odd, experience." She started to go on, but I interrupted . "How? How could you possibly know about that? For one thing, it was only yesterday, for another, there's not much of a grapevine around here-at least I didn't think there was."

"First, let me introduce myself" she said regally, holding out a bejeweled hand. I took it and found it remarkably strong for one who looked so frail. She made me look like a giant. She seemed to shrink inside her light jacket. She was quite well dressed, with gabardine slacks and a white blouse that looked like silk, sticking out of her open coat.

"I'm Irmaline Swensen. I live about seven miles down Willow road, toward the old mine."

She waited expectantly for my introduction, and I sputtered to answer, not used to such formality.

"Annie, Annie Woods", "I know, I know" I said at her raised eyebrows. "Would you care for some coffee?" I inquired.

"No thank you. I heard about your 'incident' from my daughter, who heard it from her husband, Irving Erickson, who happens to be a senior DNR officer."

"Oh" I stammered. What did I think, that they had some kind of a confidentiality code?

"I wanted to speak with you" she continued, "because this is not an isolated incident.

At least it didn't used to be. Let me explain. About 14 or 15 years ago the same thing, staked out furs, were spotted in several different rural areas. Irv's father, Irv Sr., investigated at that time and came to believe it was a certain, black sheep cousin of his named John Fuller. John had been in trouble all his life and had took to living in the woods. Living in a dugout hillside he survived by hunting, fishing and trapping. His cousin being with the DNR may have made him feel he could live out his life here and never be bothered. Irv never could prove it was him because he never could catch him, and every time he went to check out a sighting, the 'goods' were gone. In the end it was a moot point because some city cops eventually arrested John when he turned in his hides, on a totally unrelated matter. It seems he'd been burglarizing homes along the lake, and was hocking his ill-gotten gains. He got 15 years since he had some priors, nothing really big, but there was an assault charge from a barroom brawl."

She paused, watching to see if I was absorbing the information. "Go on," I encouraged, "please continue". She gave a little nod, satisfied that she had my full attention, and went on.

"He was paroled last month" she whispered, as if he might be right outside the window, listening.

"Is he dangerous?", I asked.

"No one knows, because no one's ever came up on him in the woods. Who's to know what he would do if he felt his livelihood was threatened."

I immediately thought of Al, remembering my earlier feelings of something not being right.

"I heard about your husband", she said, as if reading my thoughts. "I'm truly sorry. You must get quite lonely out here; although I see you do have an early warning system in that cute, little dog out there."

"It's been quite hard to adjust" I opined, feeling the hot tears straining against my eyelids. "And now with this on top of it. And my husband did die of a heart attack in these very woods, and he was as strong as a horse." I realized I was babbling and clamped my jaws shut.

"As far as my son-in-law's concerned, it never happened." she intoned, looking at her lap to avoid my sudden emotion.

" He doesn't think it's John, and if it is, he doesn't want to know. He feels he's not hurting anyone and has a right to live out his life in peace."

"But he's a DNR officer!" I expostulated. "His job is to protect the animals so there are enough for future generations."

"I quite agree, but what can I do? I'm certainly not going to go above his head and put my daughter and grandchildren in a terrible position. Surely you can see that?" she implored.

"Why yes, of course. I can certainly see your position, but what am I s'posed to do? It's quite frightening to think there's someone out there in the woods, a convict, whom no one seems to know the mental state of."

"If I were you, I'd just go on with my life as if no one were there. Just another creature in the woods. If you leave him alone, he'll undoubtedly leave you alone." She didn't seem convinced, even to herself, I thought.

"But-my husband! If he had a heart attack because of this man, then it's murder. I can hardly be expected to ignore that!" I was getting quite agitated at her blasé attitude toward my existence.

"Now dear, don't upset yourself", she cooed, placing her

parchment paper hand over mine.

"I'm always up for a good adventure. Perhaps you and I can put our heads together and come up with a solution that's palatable for all concerned." Her pale blue eyes held mine in a sympathetic moment and I actually saw a twinkle of excitement in them.

"What could we possibly do?" I queried. "I've lost my pistol and now have no protection other than my dog, who is far more bark than bite. Obviously he has guns.

If he were stealing from homes to supplement his income, what's to stop him from coming here? Not that I have much, but to someone with nothing, maybe I do."

"As far as I know, he only went into empty houses, and was never even confronted by anyone. He doesn't want any truck with people and will try to avoid them at all costs."

"I do go into town occasionally", I said. "I sure wouldn't want to come home to him lurking around!"

"There has to be a way that we can convince him to move elsewhere" she replied.

"After all, a few years down the road this will no longer be an isolated enclave like it is now, and he'll have to move along, anyway. We'll just have to come up with a way to hasten his departure."

She rose, running her hands down her slacks in a smoothing motion. I didn't quite know what to say. It seemed she, too, was looking for companionship and a purpose. Maybe this was just what I needed to get my mind out of the dark abyss of thoughts that had been churning ever since Al's death.

I walked her to the door, not knowing how to respond. She once again grasped my hand and gave it a small squeeze. "I have your number", she said, "And I've been so bold as to write mine down for you, in case you decide to join me in this venture. After all, when the law won't help what can one do but take matters into one's own hands?"

I thought about the strange encounter the rest of the day

and by bedtime could only conclude that there was no way to oust him out, but maybe we could find a way to keep him at bay.

That night as I lay in that limbo that is part awareness, part ethereal hallucinations, some-what of a plan of action came to mind.

Albert was standing on the edge of the woods, beckoning me. I called out to him, but he didn't reply; he just kept waving me forward. It was dark, but a full moon cast bright rays between witch-hand branches, that clutched and tugged at me, as if to keep me from Albert. I was sobbing and struggling as I neared his shadowed form, tripping and falling at his feet. I turned my tear-stained face up to see his beloved visage, but his face was still in darkness. He slowly turned his head and the shadows ran across his face until it was fully engulfed in moonlight. I awoke with a start and a scream caught in my throat, for even though I hadn't actually seen him, I was sure it was Albert in my dream and if I hadn't awoken I would have beheld the rictus death head that had been my last memory of him.

I finally fell back into a fitful sleep and woke at my usual time, with the aftertaste of the nightmare still clinging at the recesses of my mind.

After feeding the pets, throwing peanuts and sun-flower seeds to Gumba and the birds, and indulging my caffeine addiction for a half an hour, I made my way down to the old root cellar, it's heavy wooden doors dwarfing the side yard, and jutting out nearly to the edge of the trees. I took a flashlight and made a few quick trips down there. I didn't like going in there; it looked and smelled like a cave and there was only the one egress.

Emerging, I went to the large tool shed on the other side of the property and got Al's eight -foot ladder. Once on the roof, I sat on the apex, surveying my beautiful realm.

There were trees and water as far as you could see. A

flock of geese flew over, so close I could nearly touch them; somewhere in the distance the mournful call of a loon replied to it's equally mournful mate. Sighing, I hurried about my task, finishing in a scant couple of hours. I descended, dragging the 40-foot extension cord behind me. I plugged it in at the side of the house and actually clapped my hands in delight at the beautiful array before me. Thousands of Christmas lights amassed over decades now guarded my perimeters. Not a solution, but certainly a deterrent. All we had for light was an old, rusted yard light that only worked sporadically. He knew every house on the lake and I wanted him to know that someone was home. I also planned on calling Irmaline and asking her to look out over the lake and see if she could see my lights; they could be my warning system. If she could see them, and I thought she could, (those few houses faced the lake), and they were off, I was in trouble.

My next plan of action was to take a trip up to the hardware store (20 minutes each way if I drove my usual 60), purchase a bunch of "No Trespassing. Violators will be Prosecuted." signs, and nail them on trees at the edge of our property. We owned, perhaps, a half a mile of surrounding woods. This endeavor may take a few days as it involved a lot of walking on unfriendly terrain. I had time, too much time, on my hands, now that I was alone.

The phone was ringing as I stumbled in the house to answer it. Of course it had to be Irmaline, no one else ever called. We mainly had a phone for emergencies, not socializing.

"Hello", I gasped, falling onto the couch.

"I was just about to hang up, and then I would of had to drive over there to check on you." she said accusingly, making me feel like a child who needed mommy's permission to leave the house.

"I just got home from the hardware store. Hey, would you go out in your yard and look out over the lake and let me know if you can see my Christmas lights?" I asked.

"Your    Christmas    lights!    What    in    the    world…"
"Just let me know if you can see them, o.k?"

"Just a minute", she said, with a hint of irritation in her
voice.

I waited several minutes, hearing only birdsong in the
background. No radio, No t.v.,

No wonder she was as bored as me!

She eventually came back, sounding somewhat winded, to
inform me that she could, indeed, see my lights and at night
they'd be visible for miles across the lake.

I informed her of my plans with the signs, telling her not
to worry if I wasn't home because it would take awhile. She
wasn't happy about me "traipsing" around in the woods all by
myself, without even a weapon. "I could never find you out
there, I wouldn't even know where to look! And do you think
the Sheriff's office would look that hard?"

"Well, I would hope they would!" I exclaimed.

"You know what I mean!" she insisted.

After assuring her that I'd take a baseball bat, and Sam, and
call her as soon as I got back, I finally got off the phone.

# Chapter Three

The sun sets early this time of year up in the Northern Hemisphere, so I quickly set off. My old Subaru was trustworthy but quite the eyesore. Rusted out nearly through the floorboards in some places, it none-the-less always seemed to get me there. In an unforgiving climate that at times hit 50 degrees below zero, my main concerns were an unfailing starter and a good heater.

I drove to the edge of my property, parked, and got my signs. I put them on trees approximately 30 feet apart, their bright orange hue overshadowing the russet leaves not quite in their prime yet. I'd return to the car, drive down another thirty feet from the last sign, and start again. Then, of course, came the time when I had to leave the road and venture into the woods since only one side of our property faced the forest road.

I wasn't really frightened, although the enemy was still an unknown quantity. I didn't feel he'd give away his presence to attack me and bring the law down on his head. Still, I kept a wary eye and ear on my surroundings. Sam came along with me, continually running off through the undergrowth and returning frequently to make sure I hadn't left him.

Suddenly, the stillness of the afternoon was shattered by gunshots. It was hard to estimate the distance since the lake tended to carry sounds for a long way. I often heard shots during hunting season, and in the late spring and early summer many vacationers utilized the outdoor gun range (not much more than mounds of dirt and hay) that had been set up on the other side of the lake. This time of year, however, I never heard guns. Someone must be poaching, I thought. Though traps were used for smaller game, deer and moose and perhaps wolves, would have to be hunted with a gun or bow and arrow.

I kept about my work while Sam's ears pricked at each shot. I was turning around to return to the car when something caught my attention. Hanging from a broken branch, about chest high, was a clump of hair. It was about six inches long and an auburn color.

I gingerly picked it off the branch and examined it. I was wondering if it could have been Albert's, whose hair could take on the hue of a sun-ripened apple if the sun hit it right.

It looked like it could be, but I couldn't be sure. Was I already forgetting things about my Albert? Would I soon have trouble recalling his face?

I nonchalantly stuck it in my pocket as if someone were watching, and hurried toward the road, calling Sam.

We got in the car and turned around, heading home. I would call Irmaline and tell her of my discovery and get her take on this latest development.

The sun was riding low in the sky as we approached home. Dust motes wafted on mottled sunbeams, yet a foreboding chill was in the air, warning of the harsh winter to come.

My light bedecked house cast rainbow colors across the channel, giving an air of festivity to my humble abode.

As we turned to start up the pebbly path, Sam started

barking furiously and ran headlong toward the house. I had my baseball bat in hand (I had carried it the whole day) as I broke into a run after him. It took several seconds for my mind to comprehend what my eyes were seeing. There, nailed to my door, was the fly-covered pelt of my beloved Gumba!

I knew it was his by the short, jagged scar running down what used to be his flank, caused by a squirrel fight in his youth. The flies must have deposited their larvae judging from the grotesque movement under his once immaculate coat. I screamed, an involuntary, primal sound that erupted from some dark well within me.

I must have fainted from the sheer shock of the moment, for the next thing I was aware of was a rough, wet tongue massaging my face. Nudging and licking, Sam was diligently working on his unconscious mistress. I opened my eyes to gaze at a clear blue sky, with evenings first shadows already starting to cast eerie fingers of darkness across my visage, startling me into full wakefulness.

Remembrance came pouring back, causing me to quickly jump to my feet, throwing a whining Sam aside. I had to go in the house, past that thing befouling my door. I ran up the steps, keeping my eyes averted from the desecration before me. I deliberately turned my back to dig for my keys with numb, shaking hands. I flung the door open, Sam at my heels, sensing my fear. Once inside, I turned the deadbolt and leaned against the door, trying to slow my pounding heart. At first, I was terrified someone might be in the house, but I quickly realized that Sam was acting his normal self, immediately running to his water bowl, and then looking forlornly at me when he realized his food dish was empty.

Judas was perched on the window ledge, her multi-colored coat glimmering in the late afternoon sun. She gave me an acknowledging glance, than turned her attention back to the activity at the bird feeder.

When I had my wits about me I ran to the phone and called

the Sheriff's office; surely this was some sort of crime!

I got a beer to calm my nerves as I waited. Seating myself on the couch, I curled up as Judas would; only I was trying to crawl within myself; as if by making myself as small as possible I would become insignificant. Not succeeding in that, far too nervous for introspection, I watched through the window until the Sheriff arrived, nervously twirling my hair, my eyes in constant motion, searching for more unknown terrors.

I heard the car before I saw it and breathed a sigh or relief as the Sheriff himself appeared as the car door opened. I saw him look up and give a start as he spotted the monstrosity on my door, then he looked to the left and determinedly plodded toward my door, trying not to look at it.

I slowly opened the door, trying to appear reserved and in control, although the shaking of my hands and blanched face belied that fallacy.

He touched his hand to his hat as he entered; the action punctuated by a brusque, "Ma'am".

" Would you like some coffee or something?" I ventured, not wanting to give into the hysteria that was just under the surface.

"No thank you, ma'am. Now what exactly is goin' on here?" he queried, his face reflecting his puzzlement.

"That's what I'd like to know!" I sputtered, and proceeded to inform him of all the peculiar events of late. When I got to the part about the staked out hides, he gave me a most strange look; but just as quickly as it flitted across his face, it was gone.

"Well ma'am, you said the DNR was out in regards to that, and that is their jurisdiction.

As for this incident, as frightful as it might seem, the only crime involved is Trespassing.

Now if any more 'incidents' should occur, we may be able to instigate a search on a Terroristic threat, Stalking, or some such charge. If it's someone living in these woods it would take a lot of manpower at great expense to the County to organize a search and, frankly, this just doesn't warrant that."

"But what am I to do?" I implored in a quaking voice.

"Well, you've got a dog I see, and enough lights on your roof to light up the county.

You could always get a gun, and learn how to use it", he said, stoically.

At this point, remembering my lost pistol, I implored him to sit as I ran to the bedroom to get the registration and serial number. He said I should have came down and filled out a report immediately and implored me to do so. I saw no reason too as I had already given him the pertinent information.

On that sour note, he rose to depart, me trailing behind him like a rowboat in the wake of a cruise ship. He turned at the door to offer me his hand, his frustration with me seemingly gone as, I assumed, the full extent of my predicament hit him.

"You take care, ma'am, and give a call if anything else happens and maybe then we can be of more assistance."

I released his hand and thanked him, imploring him to keep in mind all I'd told him for future reference. For my sake, and maybe others. As he left, I saw him grab the carcass and fling it into the nearby woods, leaving a trail of flying maggots in its wake.

I called Irmaline immediately, nearly breaking down at the concern in her voice. She insisted on packing a bag and coming over for the night to squat on my couch. I didn't argue, I was more than happy for the company and we needed a chance to talk, anyway.

I took a quick shower as I waited, donning my faded flowered nightgown in preparation of the coming night.

I padded to the door as I heard her old car approaching.

Irmaline settled immediately on the couch, spreading

sheets and blankets that she had actually brought herself. I looked on in amazement as her nimble fingers made short work of her task, and her calm demeanor juxtaposed my own discomfiture. I felt better just being in her unruffled presence. She was the type of lady, I thought, that nothing would faze, and exactly the kind of friend I needed.

After she had washed up and donned her satin robe over a ruffled white nightgown, she settled herself with a sigh back on the couch.

"Now, pray tell, what is going on?"

Her hand flew to her mouth as I described the gruesome scene of my homecoming.

"What time was that?" she demanded. I wasn't quite sure, but I knew the sun was waning and darkness wasn't far behind. It was by now quite dark outside and I was glad Irmaline had arrived with the last light of day.

She explained that she'd thought she'd heard something around 4:00 or so and wondered if it might not have been my scream. "But all your lights were still blazing so I disregarded it after I heard nothing else."

"What am I to do, Irmaline?" I whined.

"He obviously wants to scare you out. Why, I don't know. I suppose he sees you as a threat since the DNR and Sheriffs office personnel have been on scene".

"I never thought of that!" I exclaimed, "I just made him angrier by bringing in the authorities."

"Well, there's nothing to be done about that, now", she said matter-of-factly, "now we have to figure out our next move. Did you finish with the signs?"

"No, I didn't, and now I don't know if I will."

The thought of wandering those woods, alone and vulnerable, was something I couldn't contemplate. Little did I know how quickly I would soon change my mind.

We talked late into the night about all manner of things. I heard the story of her life with her husband of 46 years,

George. He'd been dead for 6 years now, succumbing to a stroke while playing racquetball on a cruise. I learned she had three children, two sons besides her daughter. The sons were spread out all over the globe, one a career military man, now stationed in Afghanistan. She had 4 grandchildren, two boys from her daughter, whom she saw quite often, and a daughter and a son by her other son who lived on the East coast and she seldom saw.

We took an ice cream break around midnight, sitting at the large oaken table, now casting rosy shadows from the faux Tiffany lamp suspended above it. She had a quite good sense of humor, dry and witty, droll.

Conversing with her made me all the more aware of my isolation from humanity and the sheer loneliness I'd been enduring for so long.

Of one thing I was sure, I trusted her implicitly. She was the one who had come to me with an offer of help, defying her obstinent son-in-law, a man of considerable pull in the county. She had no ulterior motive as far as I could determine, and I sorely needed a friend, so I decided to accept her at face value.

We awoke the next morning with a plan, of sorts. There was an old deer stand on the edge of our property that Albert's dad had had the foresight to put on a small promontory. Al and I had spent many hours up there in all seasons, binoculars and camera in hand, ensuring enduring memories that would last through my lifetime.

I would once again brave the foreboding forest, baseball bat in hand, and take up watch there. I would wait until the next morning, at first light, and silently slip through the woods to my perch; with the binoculars I would have quite a good view of the open field, which had once graced me with beautiful woodland creatures, but now instilled only fear.

Irmaline left that afternoon, she was baby-sitting her grandchildren, a frequent event, I gathered.

I was nervous, yet somewhat invigorated the rest of the day, and retired early in anticipation of my adventure.

The next week had me believing my little escapade was only folly, for besides a wondrous supply of wildlife, nothing even remotely human appeared.

I had talked to Irmaline daily, describing the beauty of the vista, and the almost intolerable boredom. Even beauty gets boring after a while.

Everything else had been uneventful; although I lived in fear of opening my door one morning and being confronted by Gumba's rotting carcass. An even worse scenario would be Sam proudly dumping it at my feet like a grisly trophy .

The 8th. or 9th. day. of my stake-out, I espied a glimmering at the edge of the field on the far side. The midday sun was reflecting off something metal, I was sure.

I had two choices; I could run across the field, fully exposing myself to whatever may be watching, or sit, for God knew how long, observing the minute spot of light for any movement until the slanting of the sun obscured it entirely. I chose the former. I could go around on the backside and creep through the woods, but that entailed a good three more miles, through dense brush and grasping trees, with no assurance I'd be able to find the spot. If I went across the open field, I could keep it in my line of vision the whole time. I had somewhat marked the spot in relation to a large oak, but from any perspective but straight on I doubted I'd be able to pinpoint it.

I descended my treetop haven, trying to keep my eyes on the shining object, which may or may not, be anything. After so many days of nothing but nature, I was almost feeling confident that whoever was responsible for the atrocities had decided to move on; unfortunately, my curiosity had gotten the better of me, though I knew I would be taking my life in my own foolhardy hands if I was wrong.

After 15 minutes of trudging through the remaining

woods, I broke the open field. Taking a deep breath, I plunged headlong straight across. The grass and serge weeds were much higher than I'd anticipated, although not tall enough to hide me or hinder a determined pelt staker.

It took what seemed forever, in my vulnerable state, to cross that vast grassland, but eventually I was on the other side, and quickly slipped between the nearest trees. I was quite sure I could find the source of my interest as I'd kept my eyes more or less glued to the spot. After stumbling around for a while, I finally spotted the faint shimmering and hurried to find its origin.

My heart leapt to my throat and seemed to stop beating as my hands flew, winglike, to stifle the scream welling up from the deepest recesses of my soul. Boots were sticking out of a pair of blue jeans. A plaid shirt covered the torso; unwilling and unable to pull my eyes away, I finally discovered what had originally caught my interest: A silver watchband, inlaid with turquoise, was suspended from a wasted wrist, glinting gaily in the brilliant sun, unknowing and uncaring that it's owner would no longer be able to enjoy it's beauty, let alone ever need it's services again.

A shock of gray hair, matted with dried blood, topped this grisly tableau; thankfully, face down.

How I got back, I'll never know. The shock of the moment had rendered me mindless; an automaton going strictly on instinct.

# CHAPTER FOUR

When the Sheriff arrived, looking none too happy to once again be on the hysterics' doorstep, I blathered on about my latest gruesome discovery. I volunteered to draw up a map, but adamantly refused to return to the scene of the "crime".

"So," he injected, cutting off my redundant retelling, "You'll wander around in the woods alone when you've told me repeatedly how frightened you are, but now you refuse to go out there with law enforcement personnel?"

I was taken aback by the question and realized how foolhardy my actions must appear to him, yet I still could not bring myself to accompany him.

In the end, he departed, grumbling, because now he would have to bring in the cadaver dogs, incurring yet another expense to the county.

I could hardly wait to call Irmaline, but forced myself to drink a few beers and try to get my wits about me first. I didn't want to lose the one friend I had by appearing to be the lunatic everyone else seemed to think I was. I was sure the Sheriff thought I was hallucinating or telling tales to glean attention. Perhaps I should wait and see if the body was still there, after all, evidence seemed to disappear and I realized that the Sheriff might very well believe that I had been responsible for the squirrel pelt on my door.

Ultimately, I called Irmaline. I needed an ally, and the worst that could happen would be that she, too, would desert me and once again I would be on my own.

She arrived shortly thereafter and took me in her arms as I sobbed like a lost child, patting my back lightly with her wing-like hands.

We sat in the dining area, her with a cup of coffee, I still guzzling my beer, wishing for the first time in years that I could just lose myself in the false bravado of alcohol.

My quest for privacy and bucolic isolation had ultimately led to hours of terror that could have been somewhat alleviated if the modern world of cell-phones had been available to me; as it was, the first cell phone tower would be constructed early next year.

We were still seated at the table, each now lost in our own thoughts. I, wondering if she was now sorry she had ever set eyes on me, hoping against hope that the body was still there so my sanity would at least no longer be in question.

The sun was setting quickly now over the channel, reflecting a brilliant pink sheen over the water. Irmaline had made ham sandwiches and placed a thick, mayonnaise-covered one in front of me. She removed my half-consumed beer and replaced it with a tall glass of milk. The tears started flowing again at this silent gesture of friendship, given so taciturnly.

I was just choking down the last of the sandwich, gulping milk to facilitate its passage down my sorrow-clotted throat, when the Sheriff returned. I could hear dogs howling in the background before he ever reached my door. Fortunately, Sam and Judas were safely ensconced indoors, as they were no longer allowed outside without me. Sam, for sure.

I opened the door to the grim-faced Sheriff, hoping against

hope that he'd verify my sanity, although the alternative was equally frightening.

He entered, filling the doorway with his bulk, making me miss the presence of a man and the security that presence evoked.

"It was there, alright", he began. "We believe we know who it is, although we won't disclose this information until a positive identification has been established. Your gun was found at the scene." With this disclosure, I gave a start, considering all the implications that this entailed.

Irmaline had remained seated at the table but now rose and joined us by the door.

"Sheriff" she began tentatively, "You are aware that Annie's gun went missing weeks ago. She has given you all the pertinent information about that, thus enabling you to identify said weapon without all the searching you otherwise would have had to undertake."

"Yes, that's so ma'am, but we would have tracked it down eventually and it seems all roads lead here".

"Are you insinuating," I blurted, my face flushed, my hands wildly fanning the air, "That I may have had something to do with this mans' demise?"

"I'm not insinuating anything, ma'am. He may have found your gun in the brush. He may have committed suicide. He may have been murdered. We just don't know yet. We'll be printing the gun and doing a full investigation. I'd appreciate it if you'd come down to the station tomorrow to give your prints. It's obvious he's been dead too long for a gunpowder test to be effective. Any residue would have been washed away long ago."

Irmaline spoke up at this point. "You ARE inferring that Annie had something to do with it!" she exhorted.

"No, not at all, but a man is dead and we will explore all avenues." With a snort, Irmaline whirled, marched to the fridge, extracted my last beer and settled herself once more at the table, mentally turning her back on us.

I gave the Sheriff a sheepish look, like a child whose parent has embarrassed her, and waited to see if he had any more revelations to disclose. He didn't.

I grabbed Sam's collar as the Sheriff opened the door to leave, knowing he had heard the baying of the hounds and would run, like his mindless mistress, right into the fray, heedless of danger. Judas managed to escape but I really wasn't worried about her. It was dark out now, her environment, and she would go nowhere near the dogs. She'd be back at first light for breakfast.

I implored Irmaline to stay the night rather than face the long dark road to her house, but she declined, saying she had to baby-sit early in the morning and assuring me that I no longer had anything to fear. I wondered if she felt any kind of guilt for perhaps helping drive a man to suicide, as the thought now nagged at my conscience.

After I returned from the fingerprinting session the next day, I decided to soak in a hot tub and read a mindless novel, full of pap; no murderers lurking in shadows or bodies lying in the woods. The ink still clung to my fingertips and took some scouring to remove.

I read three pages before I gave up, realizing that my mind wasn't comprehending the contents. What if mine were the only prints on the gun? Maybe he thought he could get the last laugh by setting me up for his murder. Would someone like him really kill himself, though? Deep down in my heart, I thought not. He'd just got out after spending years in prison and once again roamed the forests and streams that he loved. If he were suicidal wouldn't he have took his life long ago while in prison? Could someone else be trying to set me up?

Early the next morning I was in my usual position on the porch. I'd let Sam off his leash and he was running happily, his tongue hanging out and tail wagging, savoring his newfound freedom. Judas was down on the dock, watching the silent water, pawing at hardy insects still clinging to their fragile lives in the late summer sun.

The phone rang about eight o'clock. Thinking it was Irmaline, I answered with a cheery "Hello". It was the Sheriff (I still didn't know his name, although it may have been on his uniform; I had never noticed). He identified himself as "Sheriff's office calling", but I immediately recognized his resonate voice. He had called to inform me that there were prints on the gun but they were too degraded to be identifiable. I guessed that was good news for me, as a murder trial was the last thing I needed right now (or ever).

The autopsy was scheduled for later that morning and he would keep me informed.

I'd watched the early morning news before dawn but had seen nothing about it. I supposed the story would break sometime today, and wondered if it would be big enough news that I would have to go into even deeper seclusion to avoid the press. The thought of the spokespeople for the real world invading my private domain was enough to make me want to hole up in the woods, taking a cue from the deer and raccoons, which thrived there.

I took a bath, biding my time until the next news broadcast.

I watched the news at noon, munching on a corn muffin and drinking my usual coffee.

I stopped mid-bite as the story came on. The body was identified as John Fuller, 58, who had only been released from prison six months previously. No foul play was suspected and no mention was made of who had discovered the body; only a local resident.

It looked like I was off the hook, and I had to learn to believe it was him who had been tormenting me so I could return to my peaceful, though solitary, existence. I hadn't been happy before all this began, not without Al, and I hadn't appreciated the great life I had before I lived with fear as my constant companion.

No sooner did the story go off when the phone rang. Nice goin' Sheriff, I thought to myself, thinking of a story I'd seen about a family who had heard on the news that a loved one had died.

I informed him that I had just seen it on the news, and he affirmed that this was where it stood. He told me to "stay in town" for a while; like I was going anywhere.

I went back out to check on Sam and Judas. I had to call Sam as he was off in the woods somewhere, but he came immediately, easing my mind further. I believed that now I could go on with my life and try to be happy, letting go, but never forgetting Albert.

I supposed I could take my lights down now, but why bother. Christmas was not quite three months away, and though usually hyper, a kind of lethargy had descended on me of late. I decided to leave them. They did cast a magnificent multi-colored mosaic across the dark channel.

The next couple of weeks were quite uneventful. I fell into a pattern of sporadic cleaning; walking in the woods with Sam, and sometimes Judas; talking to Irmaline on the phone. We had a standard Friday night movie date, alternating the picks from week to week. She preferred the old classics, which I had no problem with; I, however, preferred the mystery, murder, and action types. Sometimes she'd stay over and we'd sit together on the porch in the morning, watching the shadows run from the rising sun as we sipped our steaming mugs of coffee.

Life went by as if in a dream. The trees changed to bright red, orange and yellow hues, waving their brilliant plumage across the sky.

Late one night in the midst of the calm, Sam's furious barking awakened me. He was running from room to room, looking toward each window, continuing his din.

I leapt from the bed, nearly tripping as my foot caught in the bedcovers. I left the house in darkness as I stealthily crept to the kitchen window. I was never so glad about putting those lights up early as I was that night when I saw my gleaming lights flooding the yard in all their brilliance. I thought I saw a dark shadow pass across the periphery of my vision, but just as quickly, it was gone. Sam's barks had subsided into an occasional whimper yet he still wandered from room to room with his ears pricked in attention.

I had a hard time getting back to sleep that night and debated if I should inform the Sheriff of this latest occurrence or not. What if it was only a deer or a raccoon? Sam would bark no matter what it was, in fact had, several times over the years. Sometimes we had ferreted out the culprit (always a critter), sometimes not, yet we had never thought these disturbances anything but nature-related. The recent events had obviously frayed my nerves almost to the point of paranoia, once again. I had to get a grip or they'd be carting me off to the ha-ha Hilton.

I felt as if the Sheriff and I were at a standoff since my fingerprinting session. I'd had to give a statement, as well, and had seen the looks exchanged by the two young deputies as I'd told of my deer-stand stake-out. Irmaline had backed up my story, but the finding of the body in that remote location still cast suspicion on me. I'd been asked to repeat my story several times, for the Sheriff was a pragmatic man who didn't believe in coincidence, and my finding the body in that wilderness was a little too convenient for his sensibilities. That was where things stood in those strange autumn days, and I sincerely hoped the death of John Fuller resolved the mystery, for I felt no help would be forthcoming from the Sheriff's department.

A few days later, returning from the grocery store, I pulled up in the yard, my spiraling headlights chasing shadows in the gloaming; yet one shadow refused to recede.

I could have sworn I saw, for a millisecond, a darkened form out at the end of my dock. For some reason my mind screamed "Albert!". I don't know if it was the size of the form or the wild, unkempt hair briefly outlined in my lights, that made me feel it was he, but my heart said it was.

I flew from the car, almost tumbling on the dew-saturated grass, my still glowing Christmas lights casting an eerie rainbow across the darkening water of the channel.

I could no longer see anything there, even though my car lights were still on and added some relief to the gathering darkness. I screamed Albert's name as my rubber-soled shoes hit the rickety dock, half-rotten boards creaked threateningly underfoot. I stopped short, peering into the gloom of the woods, seeing nothing. I walked slowly to where I believed the form had been, getting on my knees to examine the boards closely. Nothing. I finally gave up and carefully wended my way back to my car, retrieved my groceries, and went in the house. Sam was sleeping in front of the fireplace, one of his favorite places. Why hadn't he barked, I wondered. He could hear things miles away and would set up a racket at the turn of a birds' wing. In my present, probably deluded, state, I immediately thought, "Well, he wouldn't bark at Albert." I also had to think that he would have given some sort of reaction if he thought Albert had returned.

Living as isolated as I did, I had come to rely on the instincts of my pets. They were early warning signals not only for prowling critters and uninvited human company, but also for storms, tornadoes and other natural phenomena.

I decided against telling Irmaline about my latest experience. I never wanted to see in her eyes the suspicious and pitying looks I'd received from the authorities.

# CHAPTER FIVE

A chilly breeze spiraled off the channel, causing whirlwinds of leaves to spin, foreshadowing the tornadoes that the season often brought. I sat in my usual position on the porch, pulling my old plaid-hunting shirt tightly around me against the seasonal chill.

The morning was eerily silent now that most of the seasonal birds had departed. Eagles, Hawks, songbirds, and the ever-raucous Redwing blackbirds had all departed for warmer climes.

Autumn had always been my favorite season, but now, without Albert, it boded the end of things; death. With all the strange events surrounding me, I longed for the newness and hope of spring. I feared the winter would be a harsh and lonely time; something I must endure, even as my world was falling apart.

I spent the rest of the day in the same retrospective mood, at some point forcing myself to do some much needed house cleaning. I then retired to the couch to stretch out and watch the news and read some more of the book that never seemed to end. Finally, tired and bored, I called it a day.

Laying in bed, listening to the wind, I wondered if somewhere, Albert could see me.

"Annie." I jolted awake from a sound sleep, my name spoken in Albert's voice reverberating through my head. I started up, blankets and sheets flying, to scan the chilly bedroom. "I know I wasn't dreaming!" I said aloud, even as I noticed Sam staring at the wall, making a strange, snarling, whining sound. "Stop it! You're scaring me!" I yelled at Sam, as if his confirmation of my dream as reality was his fault. He looked at me with sorrowful eyes, glanced back at the wall once more, then ensconced himself at my feet, staring at me dolefully. After searching all the obvious places, under the bed, the closet, even behind the headboard, I cautiously went through the rest of the house. Everything was as always, with the exception of Judas, who was cowering under the end table glancing at the bedroom door, making a hissing sound around her bared teeth. At least I knew I wasn't going crazy, but the alternative, that this was reality, made it all the more frightening.

I went into town that day, dragging Sam with me to ward off my loneliness and trepidation; he was more than happy to be in one of his favorite places, seated next to his mistress, drooling out the window, barking at each wandering cat or bawdy crow.

I intended to invite Irmaline over to spend the night, although I would say nothing of the previous night. I was hoping that she, too, would experience the phenomena without being influenced by my tale. In fact, I would like to ask her to stay for several days, weeks, or even months, until the mystery was solved. These occurrences only happened when I was alone; therefore, if I had company, whoever was tormenting me would have to surcease, eventually, for fear of exposure.

The town was unusually dead that morning. A cold wind was blowing off the lake, sending leaves spiraling down the deserted streets. The sun was playing hide-and-seek with the clouds, throwing off sporadic spurts of warmth as it skittered between them.

I spotted the Sheriff exiting his squad car in front of the police station and had a sudden urge to run to him and bare my soul. Of course, I wouldn't. I'd learned long ago that no help would be forthcoming from law-enforcement, or townspeople for that matter.

The whole town seemed to have that close-minded mentality that came from being isolated for too long, spurred by their fear of outsiders and any kind of change.

I hurriedly did my shopping, leaving Sam in the car with the window cracked. He was used to this, and raised no objections. He was with his mistress and his happiness was complete.

I saw Irmaline's son-in-law in the store with a mousey brunette in tow. With a start, I realized this must be Irmaline's daughter and searched for similarities in her demeanor.

She was small, and fragile-looking like her mother, but she had none of the fearlessness or strength of character that emanated from her mother. She seemed cowed by her husband, and I immediately wondered if she was abused. At that moment, as if he sensed my eyes upon them, he turned and saw me. A scowl crossed his face and he whispered something to his wife, ending on a spurt of derogatory laughter. She glanced at me almost surreptitiously, and quickly turned her eyes away. I'm sure she knew I was the friend her mother had been spending so much time with, and I thought for the first time what an uncomfortable position this friendship had imposed on her. I quickly finished my shopping and hurriedly left. I wondered if Irmaline was even now babysitting, as I hadn't seen any children.

As I pulled in the yard, I saw Judas watching out the window, pacing on sight of me in anticipation of a meal. I carried in the groceries, nearly tripping over Sam in his exuberance at being freed from the confines of the car.

I called Irmaline after I'd finished putting the groceries away, and wasn't surprised when she wasn't home, my babysitting assumptions must have been correct.

# CHAPTER SIX

I was finally able to get a hold of Irmaline later that afternoon and was relieved when she agreed to come over in a couple of hours.

I washed my dishes and concentrated on various mundane tasks that I'd let go too long.

I was, once again, in my usual position on the porch when Irmaline pulled up, her old car foreshadowing her arrival with its whining engine and somewhat loud muffler.

She settled herself on the porch next to me, gladly accepting my offer of fresh, though store-bought, lemonade.

"So, how are things going?" She inquired, looking at me closely to see if I was holding up now that (she thought) I no longer had anything to fear.

I made no mention of last night's weird happenings, but did mention that I had seen her daughter and son-in-law in the store earlier. I excluded the whispered aside he had made to her daughter and the derogatory look he had given me. I wasn't sure what her relationship with her son-in-law was and didn't want to appear paranoid, thinking that everyone was talking about me behind my back.

"I think I know you well enough to admit that I'm not all that fond of him." She surprised me by saying.

"I never wanted her to marry that man, but she was young, and pregnant, so I kept my misgivings to myself after that, " she confided. "And I must admit," she added as an afterthought, "they have beautiful children."

"I'd love to meet your grandchildren, sometime," I ventured. I saw a shadow cross her face and she turned away to scan the sun-dappled channel, leaving me with the impression that that wasn't going to happen.

"Well, I'd love for them to meet you, too, Annie." She graciously replied. "I'll bring them by sometime when I'm baby-sitting."

I once again realized what a classy lady she was, and that she probably would, if I persisted, disregarding her son-in-law's disapproval. I wouldn't insist, of course, as I didn't want to cause my only friend further trouble in what must already be an uncomfortable situation.

Judas chose that moment to jump in her lap (something she never does) thus effectively ending that awkward conversation with her loud purring and diligent kneading of Irmaline's stylish white sweater.

"Would you care to attend the Autumn Festival with me next week?" She inquired.

Every year the town held a late autumn festival, the last hurrah to a fading summer. There were booths set up by local merchants, trying to extract whatever money they could from the townspeople in anticipation of the long, dead winter ahead.

"Sure," I replied, surprising myself as well as her.

"Good!" She exhorted, "It's about time you got on with your life; "and," she added with a sly, sidewards glance, "there are still a few available bachelors in town."

Seeing my dismay at this announcement, she waved her delicate hand at me in a dismissive manner, adding, "Some aren't even that bad! There are a couple of farmers who are as reclusive as you and only venture out to socialize once a year, at the festival."

Not knowing what to say to that, I merely answered, "I'll go, but only with your promise that you WON'T be introducing me to them!"

She smiled a smug little smile and agreed, albeit reluctantly.

We went in the house as the waning sun cast shadows across the yard and water, my brilliant lights the only thing keeping them at bay.

The rest of the evening was quite uneventful. We watched t.v., laughing inanely at what passed for normalcy, for we knew better.

I was disappointed nothing untoward happened, as I was searching for verification of my delusions. I couldn't help but think I shouldn't be surprised. After all, Irmaline's car was plainly visible in front of the house, and it's loudness upon arriving left little doubt that I wasn't alone.

I bit my tongue a couple of times, on the verge of telling her my fears, yet fear of losing my only ally ultimately kept me silent.

The day of the festival dawned sunny and bright and an uneventful weekend had me thinking maybe all was normal and my over-fertile imagination had once again been working overtime.

I told Irmaline that I would meet her on the main street of town, under the faded awning of the local feed store, at 10:00. I actually took some interest in my appearance for the first time since Al died. I curled my hair with the ancient curling iron I'd found hidden under the sink. I donned a pair of blue jean shorts and a white, off-shoulder blouse that brought to mind my pseudo-hippie years. Not bad, I thought, for a 50-something lady, and a lunatic, to boot! I was actually looking forward to the outing, especially since

Irmaline would be accompanying me. It had been a long time since I'd taken an interest in the everyday joys of life.

I still made sure to lock everything up tight, with Sam and Judas safely ensconced inside, much to their chagrin!

After parking on the street I had to walk two blocks down Main Street to get to the feed store and I could feel the curious eyes on me as I nonchalantly strolled down the sun-dappled sidewalk, head held high.

I would not give in to rumor and innuendo; if someone were concerned about my life, they should try to get to know me before passing judgment; I wasn't interested in their friendship, otherwise.

Irmaline wasn't there yet, but I spotted her down the street, laughing and talking with a large, 60ish woman whose resonate laugh echoed down the street as Irmaline gestured wildly, discoursing on God knew what. She knows everyone, I thought, not knowing if I should feel better or worse for that knowledge; for that would mean frequent introductions and my antisocialness obstructed any chance of social success. They could, at least, see with their own eyes that I'm not a crazy woman. I'm quite rational, and they would have to recognize that.

Just then, Irmaline saw me and made a hasty farewell to her companion, who was running a booth selling pies, their smells permeating the crisp air.

I had watched the weather that morning and it was going to be warm in the afternoon, but now I felt a chill and wished I'd brought a jacket; perhaps I would find one somewhere in this jungle of booths, that were hawking everything from teeshirts inscribed with bawdy sayings, to vegetables and fruits.

Others were dressed as I was and seemed not to be bothered by the chill; but then, most of the townsfolk were of sturdy Scandinavian stock, and seemed not to be affected by even the coldest of weather. For me, however, the line was finely drawn between warm and cold; one degree seemed to affect me at times. Must be menopause, I thought abstractedly as Irmaline reached me, her smile as bright as the day.

We made small talk as we wandered from booth to booth, Irmaline introducing me to each vendor, all of whom gazed at me curiously, surprised that I'd ended my self-imposed exile and ventured forth into their midst. They were all aware of my circumstances, from Albert's untimely demise, to the bizarre events that recently plagued me.

We came upon a vegetable stand in the middle of the block, the smell of freshly picked corn hanging in the brisk, late morning air. Barney (whom I now knew was Irmaline's son-in-law, Irving) and her daughter, Sherry, were industriously sniffing ears of corn and thumping melons, trailed by two boys; one quite small, the other much larger, bearing the same scowl that seemed to be a permanent fixture on his father's face.

I felt the blood rush to my face as Irving (he'd always be "Barney" to me) spotted me and his lackadaisical smile was immediately replaced by a contemptuous sneer.

"Irv, Sherry," Irmaline intoned, "this is my good friend, Annie…oh, that's right, Irv, you've already had the pleasure!" she smirked. I couldn't help but smile at the smug look on her face as her grandchildren engulfed her; it was quite clear that they adored her. Her daughter smiled shyly and extended her work-worn hand to me.

"It's so nice to meet you, finally. I've heard so much about you." She blushed, realizing, I suppose, that I may take that the wrong way as her husband had made it clear what his opinion of me was.

I tried to allay her discomfiture by warmly pumping her rough hand, smiling as I replied, "I'm really glad to finally meet you, too. Your mother has spoken of you and the children so many times that I almost feel I already know you."

She smiled warmly as she released my hand, casting a

sidewards glance at her still scowling husband.

"This is Shawn," she said, drawing forward the older boy, who glanced questioningly at me, but said nothing.

"Hi." I managed, not quite knowing what to say, having no children of my own.

The younger child, Luke, hung back, hiding behind his mother's gingham dress, peeking shyly at me. I noticed that he resembled his mother and seemed to have the same meekness about him.

"Hi, Luke." I said, "You look just like your mom!"

He smiled sweetly, gazed lovingly at his mother, and then hid himself totally behind her full skirt.

"They're lovely children," I replied to Sherry, "I was never lucky enough to have any of my own." I added for some unknown reason.

Her face took on a beatific look as she gathered them to her.

"Thank you", she replied, "I can tell you, though, they're more devilish than their appearance suggests!"

I laughed, simply because her demeanor suggested that she would adore them if they were Satan incarnate.

Her husband had wandered away without so much as a how-de-do and I could tell she was embarrassed by his rudeness. After I had invited her and the children out to visit "anytime" she made a hasty retreat in search of the errant oaf.

Irmaline laughed derogatorily as we continued on our way.

"That man!" She exclaimed as she interlocked arms with me, "What a waste of skin! If it wasn't for my grandchildren I wouldn't even try to make an effort with him."

I wished, once again, that I could be as self-confidant as she was. I had a feeling that no self-doubts permeated her as they frequently did me.

We'd made our way nearly to the lake, where the booths

were spread sparsely, petering out all together at the weathered dock.

Suddenly, Irmaline was swept off the ground and swirled around like a whirling Dervish, engulfed completely in the arms of a large, smiling bear-man. She squealed in delight as her feet were once again planted on the dew-covered grass.

"Amos!" She shrieked, "When did you get back in town?"

His voice rumbled like thunder, perfectly suited to his overpowering presence.

"Last night. I'm home for now. No more cross-country runs for a while. I'm on vacation!" he exclaimed, happily. "Whose this little lady?" he asked, noticing me for the first time. Irmaline made introductions and I found myself stuttering as I took in the sheer power of him. He had to be 6'5", with biceps that bulged out of the blue denim shirt, which seemed barely able to contain him. His faded jeans appeared to go on forever, culminating in boots the size of Paul Bunyan's. His face was craggy, not good-looking in a conventional way, but rugged, masculine. The full, wiry beard added even more to his bear-like appearance.

I was impressed! He reminded me of the old-time wrestlers. Gorgeous George, or Vern Gaughna.

"I've known Amos since he was a child! I used to baby-sit him." Irmaline gushed.

"And what a hard taskmaster she was!" he added. "I was scared to death of making her angry, therefore I was always the perfect child around her."

"Posh!" Irmaline intoned, "That's the biggest crock I've heard in a while!"

They continued on in this playful mode, me hanging behind, basking in their sunshine.

We decided (they decided) that we'd go to the outdoor pavilion set up for dining in the center of the park in town.

The sun was now shining brightly, casting diamonds of light across the azure water.

We sat in the midst of the brightly dressed townspeople, Irmaline and Amos carrying the conversation, as I sat demurely, suddenly shy. Unfortunately, the pavilion was also set up as a beer garden with cheap pitchers of beer, and Amos made sure they kept coming.

Irmaline munched on a crisp Caesar Salad, Amos had three chili dogs, while I worked on an order of onion rings, accentuating my thirst.

My shyness diminished in proportion to the number of beers I consumed and soon I was feeling no pain. Irmaline knew of my propensity for alcohol, although she'd never seen me drunk, and would reach over occasionally and pat my hand in a consoling manner.

I learned that Amos had been divorced for several years, having caught his wife with another man when he'd returned from a cross-country trek unexpectedly. He had no children; it seems he thought it unfair to have a child when he was seldom home.

Even enshrouded in an alcoholic haze I held my tongue about the unsettling events plaguing me, still fearing questions of my sanity. Irmaline was far too circumspect to bring it up.

Boat races were starting at 2:00 and people were starting to wander down to the shore to get good vantage points. We decided to join the milling crowd and Irmaline and me started down the slightly sloping ground as Amos settled up the bill.

"Well, what do you think?" Irmaline queried the minute we were out of Amos' earshot.

"About what?" I asked, coyly.

"Amos, of course. Don't play dumb with me, I know better!" she answered.

"Oh, please, Irmaline," I said, my voice sounding whiny, even in my own ears. "I'm not ready for anything like that and don't know if I ever will be."

"Anything like what?" She queried. "I'm not suggesting you marry the man! It seems to me you can use all the friends you can get considering the circumstances."

I started to reply but clammed up as Amos caught up with us.

I was glad to see that I wasn't stumbling and gave no indication I was slightly inebriated.

We gathered on the shore with the others, watching the boats prepare for their hour in the sun.

A few water-skiers even zipped across the horizon, hoping against hope against a wipeout, as the water was already quite cold.

The dock was already full of milling people so we stayed on a small knoll overlooking the lake. Several racers had already made their runs and were waiting for the next heat as the crowd cheered and hooted, egging on their friends and relatives. More townspeople were wandering down in a continuing stream, many with plastic cups of beer still in their hands. They, too, seemed to be feeling no pain, causing me to smile in empathy.

I began to feel rather claustrophobic as the crowd pressed closer; hoping I wouldn't make a display of myself by having a panic attack. The last thing I needed was to justify the general opinion that I wasn't all there.

Talking was a moot point as the roar of the boat engines and shouting of the crowd precluded any conversation. I was glad for that, as my original shyness once more took possession of me.

Irmaline headed back to the pavilion in search of the bathrooms, leaving Amos and me alone in the crowd; others immediately filled her place.

Just then, a speeding boat skipped across the water towards shore, seemingly out of control. The crowd watched in horror as it drew nearer. Those on the dock were now turning to run, pushing and shoving as they fled. It looked now as if the boat was not going to hit the dock. It was swerving off to the right, heading towards the small hill on which we stood.

It was then that it happened, with a speed and unexpectedness that caught me totally off-guard. A hard shove sent me toppling over the edge of the low bluff, my arms pin-wheeling wildly as the water and shoreline quickly rose up to meet me. I had no time to think of anything, not even death, before I hit the water, barely missing the rock-strewn shoreline beneath the hill, the boat swiftly bearing down on me. I went under just as the boat turned sharply and for a brief instant I saw the spinning prop inches in front of my face. When I emerged, sputtering and coughing up water, I bobbed like a cork in the choppy waters created by the speeding boat. My heart pounded in my chest as I swam the few feet necessary to touch bottom, my legs shaking so badly it took me several attempts to get to my feet.

I looked up to the bluff, but caught no sight of Amos. Where had he gone? He'd been right by me when I'd been pushed. Perhaps he was even now holding (or beating up) the perpetrator, I thought.

I sat on the rocky shore, still half in the water, trying to get my wits together, breathing in great gulps of water-laden air.

After several minutes I wobbled to my feet and started the trek back to the small pathway that ascended the hill several yards away. I was shaking from head to foot, soaking wet and shivering despite the now warm day. Several people stared at me as I wended my way back, yet no offers of aid were forthcoming.

Suddenly, Amos was at my side. He swept me up in his arms, carrying me effortlessly up the occasionally steep incline, his mouth set in a grim line.

Irmaline had just returned as we reached the summit and I watched as the color drained even further from her already pallid complexion.

"Did you see him?" I asked Amos, grabbing his arm as he set me gently on the soft grass.

"See who?" he queried, looking at me tenderly.

"Whoever pushed me!" I exclaimed.

I saw him look to Irmaline questioningly, but she said nothing, except, "Let's get you home and in some dry clothes. We can talk about this later."

# Chapter Seven

A half an hour later I was home. Though still in shock, I was at least now warm and dry. Sam and Judas hadn't left my side since I'd returned, sensing that something was wrong.

Irmaline and Amos were in the yard talking softly, giving me time to compose myself. I knew Irmaline was waiting for me to enlighten Amos about my situation; I was sure he was wondering about my Christmas lights.

They met me on the porch as I went out, Irmaline with a questioning look on her face, Amos inscrutable. By now, I was totally sober and wishing I wasn't. I couldn't help but think that my inebriation had perhaps aided in the fact that I had suffered little harm since I had been quite relaxed as I went tumbling over the edge. I told myself that if I ever ventured forth in this town again I would make sure I was well fortified first, not to the point of recklessness, but enough to keep my fears at bay. I was now convinced that someone in this town wanted me dead, and I couldn't, for the life of me, figure out whom or why.

I was debating whether to confide in Amos or not; after

all, he seemed to have disappeared at a most inopportune moment for me. Then again, Irmaline seemed to trust him implicitly and he'd supposedly been out of town until recently. I decided to throw caution to the wind and tell them both everything, including my late-night visitations which I was now convinced were not from the animal kingdom.

They listened quietly as I laid it all out for them, holding nothing back, not even the questioning of my own sanity. Of course, Irmaline already was aware of most of the events, but she, too, seemed surprised when I told them of the late night voice that sounded so much like Al, the incident on the dock, and the fleeting shadows in the well-lighted yard. After I was finished, I leaned back in my chair, exhausted yet relieved to no longer have to bear it all alone.

"Well", Amos sighed. "It looks like we have a full-fledged mystery on our hands."

I watched him closely to see if he was sincere and decided he was. I informed them that I was afraid to notify the police as I had no proof, no suspects, and the lackadaisical attitude of the authorities and their belief that I was an attention-grabbing lunatic further precluded their involvement. Amos informed me that he had seen nothing. The crowd was pushing so close that he couldn't even tell me who had been behind me at the time.

He claimed he'd been there the whole time and couldn't understand why I hadn't seen him except for the fact that he was probably already headed down the incline to rescue me. I nodded, silently; as Irmaline confirmed for Amos the things she had been witness to. He had chuckled softly at my treetop vigilance story and seemed surprised at my turpitude.

"I guess there's more to you, little lady, than meets the eye." He said, shaking his head disbelievingly.

Irmaline insisted on staying with me, but Amos vetoed the idea, as then she, too, would be in harms way.

It was decided that he would set up a tent in the woods

behind my house and keep an an eye on things, discreetly. He pointed out that even if he were detected, it would be a deterrent to further incidents. He also suggested I go to the Sheriff's office and get my gun back; he thought it strange that it hadn't already been returned as the John Fuller case was now closed. He also expressed disbelief and anger at the Sheriff's office and their treatment of me.

"I've known Jim (evidently the Sheriff) my whole life and he's always been a thorough and diligent cop," he said. He wanted to go right down there and confront him, but Irmaline and me made it abundantly clear that no help would be coming from that direction and talked him out of it.

That's where things stood in that dark period of my existence and God only knew what the morrow would bring.

Irmaline stayed indoors with me while Amos ran home to get his camping gear. He returned in less than an hour, his large truck loaded with his equipment. He disembarked, striding purposefully towards the porch, a triangle in his hand. We went out to meet him, questioning looks on our faces.

"I'm going to set this up on your porch", he said, pulling a metal rod from his pocket.

"You strike the triangle with this if you need me, and I'll be able to hear it and come running". We gushed over his ingenuity at the novel idea and he blushed at our compliments, which I found quite becoming on his gruff countenance.

He affixed the triangle to the corner of my overhanging eaves, within easy reach of my porch chair, handed me the iron rod and promptly disappeared into the woods, unused to all the attention and seemingly anxious to get away from us gushing women.

Irmaline was on a roll, now, expostulating about what a perfect pair Amos and I would make, brushing aside my objections. I hated to burst her bubble by informing her that I wasn't entirely sure of his motives, as he had been quite close to me when I was pushed and had disappeared soon after, so I said nothing, vowing to myself to be wary of even my would-be rescuer.

Irmaline left shortly thereafter at my insistence, after all, according to her, my knight in shining armor was near at hand!

I put in a call to the Sheriff and was informed that I could pick up my gun at any time and I fully intended to do that before the sun went down. I would also make sure that Amos knew it was close at hand, too. Maybe I was being paranoid, but despite my isolation, I was well aware of the ways of the world and would not put my trust in anyone until I was sure it was justified.

I crept silently out of the house, taking Sam with me. I didn't want Amos going with me, as I didn't have my gun as yet.

When I returned, Amos was on the porch waiting for me. I fortified myself for the tirade I knew was coming, but felt that I didn't have to answer to anyone; nor would I.

I pulled the gun from my pocket as I ascended the porch steps, making sure he saw it.

"I went to get this", I said before he could say anything. "I figured it was better if you were here in case someone was waiting, hoping to get in the house."

He bit off whatever reply he had started to make, harrumphing instead in a desultory manner.

"Don't worry about me," I added as I pushed by him and unlocked the door, Sam right on my heels. "I have this now" I said, lifting the gun. "And I know how to use it, too."

The look he gave me spoke volumes, he knew I didn't trust him and was probably angry that I had insulted his intelligence by pretending nonchalance.

"I'll be in my tent", he said. "It's all set up now, but I don't s'pose you'd want to come see it." he added, scrutinizing me closely.

"No. That's o.k. It's enough just knowing that you're there; and I certainly do appreciate what you're doing for me. It's above and beyond the call of duty, especially since we hardly know each other." I looked him straight in the eye as I said this, my hand on the door, ready to close it.

He turned to leave, and I reached out and grabbed his arm, feeling like an ingrate, yet unwilling to be too trusting, under the circumstances.

"You're welcome to come have supper on the porch with me in an hour or so. I'll ring the triangle when it's ready."

"Thanks." He said, curtly, and went swiftly down the stairs and disappeared into the woods.

An hour later I rang the dinner bell and was surprised at how loud it was, it's resonance echoing across the channel. I brought out burgers and chips and set up t.v. trays as he came striding out of the woods, his hair like a sun-dappled halo.

He sat in Irmaline's usual place, diminishing it with his bulk.

"I certainly hope you have a gun, or some sort of protection." I ventured. I was fishing and he knew it. If he was the enemy than I wanted to know what I was up against. I almost regretted agreeing to this scheme but the thought of being alone out here was even worse. If he was the enemy, than better to have him close.

"I brought my rifle, a couple of knives, and my fists" he responded. "If that's not enough, then you're really in trouble".

We ate in silence for a while, the dog and cat now loose for the first time in days and taking full advantage of it. Judas was already sunning herself in her favorite place on the dock. Sam was snuffling at the edge of the woods, looking back at us occasionally.

"How long do you plan to stay?" I inquired, not knowing myself what I wanted his answer to be.

"How long do you want me to stay?" he asked, his burger

stopping in mid-air.

"I just feel funny asking you to waste your vacation living like a lumberjack." I answered.

"You didn't ask. I offered. I was going to spend my vacation camping and fishing, anyway. I can do those things here as well as anywhere else."

He took a big bite of his burger, the juices running down into his beard; I had to stifle the urge to reach out with my napkin and wipe it off.

I reached into the mini-cooler I'd brought out and handed him a beer. He threw back his head and finished half of it off with one swallow.

"It's beautiful out here," he said, setting the beer on his tray. "I don't blame you for not being scared off. I'd kill for my land."

"How much land do you have?" I ventured.

"Not much. About 40 acres, a mile or so from the old mine. Its mostly woods, with a couple of old farm fields here and there. A small piece of it's on the lake, so I've got it all."

"Did you know John Fuller?" I asked.

"Yeah, we went to school together." He replied. "He wasn't a bad guy, really. His dad used to beat him all the time and he was angry and rebellious, but weren't we all as youths? Only thing is-he carried that anger and resentment into his adult years. It wasn't so much that he took a wrong turn, it was more like his road was already chosen."

"That's sad" I said, and meant it.

"I don't believe he committed suicide, though." He said.

"He must have found my gun in the woods! I lost it fleeing after the hide incident!" I exclaimed.

"Well, I guess for someone like him a gun would be a good find." he said.

"Who would have killed him, and why?" I asked.

"You seem to believe someone's after you, maybe he saw something."

"What about those hides? Did he do that?"

"He may have. He was a trapper and hunter all his life, but just the scope of it would suggest more than one person." he replied.

"Maybe he had a partner and they had a falling out." I suggested.

"It's possible, but then, a lot of things are. I guess that's what I'm here to help you find out."

Just then Sam set up an ungodly howling, his mournful baying carrying across the channel like rolling thunder. He didn't venture into the woods, though, just stood on the edge, threw his head back and yowled.

Amos and I simultaneously flew off the porch. He reached Sam a few seconds before me. We stood staring into the darkened woods, shadows waving eerily like witch hands conjuring strange spells. Amos ventured forth first, breaking the tree line and stealthily weaving from tree trunk to tree trunk. I brought up the rear, my heart trip-hammering in my chest, my breathing short and ragged. We'd made our way about 50 yards in when we saw it. My hand flew to my mouth to stifle the scream welling up from the depths of my soul. Hanging from a tree, a few feet in front of us, was what at first seemed to be a body, but on closer inspection proved to be an inflatable doll; the kind used by demented men unwilling or unable to sustain real relationships. Its mouth was a perfect oval, adding to the hideousness of the surreal display. It was wearing a pair of red, frilly panties; panties that I recognized as my own.

Amos removed a large, serrated knife from the sheath attached to his belt and, reaching as high as he could, cut the rope that held the grotesque facsimile.

"Those are my panties!" I blurted out, my mind still reeling, unable to comprehend the sick tableau.

Amos cast me an unreadable look, then gingerly grabbed a rubber arm, dragging the ugly thing towards the house. I followed, still in shock, unable to draw my eyes from it. Sam was smelling it, occasionally throwing back his head to let out a mournful howl.

When we reached the yard, Amos released the arm and knelt beside it. I joined him as he closely inspected it. He slid the panties down the rubber legs, exposing a plastic squirt gun protruding obscenely from between it thighs.

"Oh my God!" I squeaked, my voice cracking. "What the fuck is going on?".

Amos looked startled at my unexpected outburst, but continued to inspect the doll.

There was nothing else to see, except that right beneath its left breast was a small dot, made with an indelible pen, it corresponded perfectly with the small mole on my own breast.

# Chapter Eight

The Sheriff (Jim) arrived 20 minutes later and seemed quite surprised to see Amos there, even though he'd been the one who called. After a cursory examination of the gruesome doll, he bagged it up in one of my garbage bags and threw it in his trunk in anticipation of a thorough fingerprinting session down at the station. He then joined us on the porch, settling on the top step with a glass of lemonade I had dutifully supplied.

Amos filled him in on the sequence of events, including my being shoved off the knoll.

"My main question is-why? Why would someone want to scare you off your land? Do you have any ideas?"

"No." I said, dejectedly, "but considering all these weird events I can't help thinking that maybe my husband was also a victim. Who knows what he may have seen that fateful day he had his heart attack; which, in essence, would make his death a murder."

He shifted uncomfortably on his precarious perch and raised his eyebrows slightly in, perhaps, an expression of disbelief. I could almost see the wheels turning in his mind.

Now the crazy lady thinks her husband was murdered.

He turned to Amos. "How long ya' planning on staying out there in the woods?" he questioned.

"As long as it takes to get to the bottom of this." He replied. "I always figured you'd make one hell of a cop, Amos, but we better figure this out soon or you're gonna need one of those artic tents."

"Well, it will certainly help if we can finally get some professional attention from your department instead of branding Annie as demented."

"I can send a car by several times a night, search the doll for fingerprints, ask around of the few neighbors you have to see if anyone's seen anything or anyone suspicious creeping around, but, other than that, what can I do?" he queried. "By the way, what's with the lights?"

I explained that if they were ever out it meant I needed help, that Irmaline and Amos were already aware of this, and wondered aloud if I should inform any other neighbors who might be able to see them of their significance.

"I reckon I can mention it as I go around and ask questions." He said.

"I'd appreciate it." I answered. "Believe me, Sheriff, I'm not a lunatic. I wasn't hallucinating those hides. I didn't mutilate my dear squirrel friend to call attention to myself, and I certainly didn't jump off that cliff and hang that grotesque doll in the woods." I nearly knocked over my glass of lemonade in my expostulations and quickly grabbed the glass and righted it. Somewhat subdued and embarrassed at my own outburst, I quickly took a drink and reached down to pet Judas, who was now curled at my feet.

The Sheriff slapped his thighs as he rose, dismissing me.

"Well, o.k. then. Looks like I have things to do. I'll keep you informed about the doll and anything of interest the neighbors might have to say."

I rose and offered my hand as I replied, "Thank you so

much, Sheriff. I feel much better knowing that you're now on the case." Even as I thought that he wouldn't be if it weren't for Amos.

I was growing to trust Amos more each day although I still was leery about allowing him in the house unless Irmaline was present. She still came over for our Friday night movie dates and Amos was always included. We even allowed him to pick his favorites, which ran along the lines of car chases and action flicks. Occasionally he demurred, going into town, feeling I was safe with my gun and Irmaline. At those times he'd call to check on us. I never saw him when he returned and often wondered if he'd stayed in town with a female friend, or maybe even brought one back with him. He always parked his truck in a woody lane a mile or so from the house and walked through the woods to get to his tent so no one would know (me included) whether he was there or not.

Irmaline trusted him implicitly and pooh-poohed any doubts I dared venture. She also gave me the impression that she thought we'd make a perfect pair and constantly tried to throw us together against my protestations.

It seemed her daughter and son-in-law was having marital problems although she didn't elaborate and I refrained from asking.

The weather had now definitely turned to late fall, although a rare Indian summer was stubbornly refusing to loosen its hold, to everyone's enjoyment. The days had shortened considerably and the townspeople were already digging in for the long, hard winter ahead. Every permanent resident could be heard either in deep woods chopping down dead trees or seen stacking piles of wood against their houses in preparation. Like the forest creatures, we, too, were at the mercy of Mother Nature. The foliage that still clung to the trees were mostly deep red hues now and my brilliant Christmas lights shimmered off them, giving my cozy abode a festive air.

No further "incidents" had occurred since the doll, making me wonder if it was because Amos was present or if, perhaps, because Amos was the perpetrator and was toying with me.

The doll had failed to yield any clues and proved to be another dead-end. I still kept my gun in the pocket of my old plaid over-shirt; if not being worn, always within easy reach.

Sam and Judas stuck close to home as if sensing the uneasiness of their mistress.

Halloween was just around the corner and Irmaline and Amos were now going all out to get me to participate in the annual party held at city hall. Irmaline thought it would be great therapy for my innate shyness, a costume insuring a semblance of anonymity.

Amos thought it would give him a chance to observe the various townsfolk and see if anyone showed me undue attention. I, for once, agreed. I was already getting "cabin fever" and winter had not yet begun. Irmaline had a sewing machine and as she worked on her grandchildren's costumes (one a Sponge Bob, one a vampire) she also worked on ours. I, of course, insisted on one that would totally obscure my identity, hoping, unrealistically, no one would know who I was.

# CHAPTER NINE

The ensuing days counting down to Halloween were uneventful, once again putting me in a complacent state of mind. Whoever my tormentor was had a way of building up my sense of ease and then the other shoe fell.

Darkness now came quite early and the shortened days had a crispness and definite chill to them. My summer clothes were once again stored away in bags on my closet shelves, while my sweaters and long jeans replaced them in my dresser drawers.

Our costumes were completed except for small details and Irmaline and I went to the drugstore in town to purchase make-up and various assorted sundries we thought may be of use. Though nervous, I was getting quite excited about the party in town. Amos and Irmaline would be there and their presence would be reassuring. I, also, planned to keep an astute eye on the various assorted "cast of characters" for any undue interest they may show me or otherwise suspicious behavior.

As Irmaline and I returned from the video store we

commented on the autumn décor displayed in each store and in most houses.

The town was decked out in black and orange and jack-o-lanterns cast eerie shadows from every stoop, while wind-whipped leaves danced in mini-tornadoes down the main street.

It was almost full dark now, though only 6:00, as we turned into my drive. My Christmas lights still shone brightly, though here and there bulbs had burned out. I'd left my two end-table lamps on and they gave a welcoming, homey feel to my cozy abode.

I heard Sam's welcoming bark greeting us through the semi-darkness and knew all was well with my beloved pets.

We put a video in, made a pot of hot cocoa and settled in for a quiet evening, wondering aloud to each other if Amos would join us tonight. Sam's exuberance always alerted him of our arrival.

Irmaline wanted me to summon him with the triangle, but I demurred, not wanting to appear anxious for his company.

"You've got to get over your silly shyness" she chided. "Amos is a good man, and God knows if you ever needed one, it's now".

I went to the kitchen and put in some microwave popcorn, unwilling to once again go through this now weekly recurring conversation.

She harrumphed and turned back to the t.v., grabbing the remote.

The knock on the door startled me as I carried a large bowl of popcorn into the living room, scattering several kernels across the floor. Sam hurriedly scarfed them up, tail wagging, as Judas batted one across the kitchen as if it was a mouse.

Irmaline let Amos in and as he filled the doorway I noticed how tired and drawn he looked. Guilt engulfed me as I once again realized how much he had done for me; someone he hardly knew. I also knew it would have to end eventually and if things weren't resolved soon I was running out of options.

He was unusually silent that evening, his usual ebullience nowhere in evidence. We tried to draw him out by extolling the virtues of Irmalines' amazing costumes, all to no avail; if anything, he seemed to withdraw even more.

With the party less than a week away, Irmaline was over nearly every day. I loved the way she'd managed to almost totally obscure my identity behind my wicked witch of the west personae. Not only was the costume perfect, but I'd also managed to find a long, curved, warty nose at a garage sale that I proceeded to spray paint green. It had a rubber band that went over the ears, around my head, and perfectly complimented the green make-up I planned to cover myself with. A long, scraggly black wig would complete the look. An old black thrift store dress that had been hanging in my closet for ages would be the finishing touch.

Amos had taken my advice and the final fitting for his Paul Bunyan outfit had been completed the previous day. Irmaline was adorable as Glenda, the good witch, and my arch adversary. Her blue, sequined cocktail dress was accessorized with a homemade wand and tiara.

I couldn't remember the last time I'd showed such enthusiasm. I'd even carved pumpkins with Irmaline (hers happy, mine morose) and proudly displayed them on my porch, although no one but Amos, Irmaline and I would ever see them.

Halloween dawned bright and sunny, though the temperature had plummeted to 30 degrees. I luxuriated in my soft, warm bed and thought about Amos out there in the cold.

I wondered if his down sleeping bag was keeping him warm or if he had found another warm body to do that. Oh, well. It was none of my concern. I was just happy to know another living being was out there and I wasn't alone.

I sat at the kitchen table and had my coffee as I ran my

bath. Maybe after I relaxed in the tub for a while I'd ring the triangle and offer Amos some hot coffee and breakfast, if he responded.

The longer things were quiet, the more I dared to think that my unknown tormentor had given up the game and moved on. Winter would soon be upon us and any telltale signs of human presence would soon be obvious in the snow. It, by now, must be abundantly clear that I wasn't going anywhere.

After my bath I gave Irmaline a quick call and smiled at her unbridled happiness as she gushed on about the party. She worried about Amos out there in the cold and insisted I should invite him in.

I sat on the porch, a cup of hot coffee warming my hands, the steam rising in the chilly air. I had donned a heavy sweater and jeans and my ever-present over-shirt, replete with gun, hung on the back of my chair. I rang the triangle, the loud clanging scaring off a murder of crows resting in the nearby trees. Their raucous cawing startled Sam out of his deep sleep next to my boot-clad feet. Judas gave him a disdaining look from her perch on the wooden railing surrounding the porch.

Amos emerged several minutes' later, remnants of leaves clinging to his bushy hair. I'd offered him the use of my shower on several occasions, but he always opted for his own facilities and usually accomplished this when Irmaline was present or when I went to town, always returning before me to check out the place. I handed him a steaming mug of coffee from the carafe I'd brought out, and he settled in the chair beside me, cupping his large hands around the warmth of the mug.

"I've been thinking", I ventured. "The weather is turning cold and there's no need for you staying out there any longer. I have to learn to be self-reliant and I do have my gun-and Sam. And my phone."

His bushy eyebrows rose as he gazed at me questioningly.

"I mean", I continued, "It's just not right. I can't help feeling guilty about you being out there in the cold, without any creature comforts, while I'm all comfy and warm".

"Ya' know", he answered slowly, setting his mug on the tray and appraising me with those flinty eyes, "I haven't just been sitting out there, watching you. I've been staking out deer trails from your stand, fishing in the channel, doing all the things I normally do on my vacations. I'm not some mamby-pamby. I'm an outdoorsman and I thrive on this kind of life. I couldn't be happy sittin' around inside all the time. I get enough of that sitting in my truck most of the year."

"Oh." I replied, not knowing what else to say, feeling even more selfish as I'd never considered that he might enjoy his circumstances.

When I thought about it, I guess I had smelled his fires as he'd cooked his catches but just attributed it to others on the lake who did a lot of burning this time of the year.

"You're certainly not inconveniencing me", he continued. "You have a great place here. Perfect for all the things I enjoy. I'm much closer to the water here than on my own land. The small piece of lake shore I own is quite a distance from my house so on my vacations I usually just camp out in my own woods."

I gazed out at the shimmering water, avoiding his scrutiny. Perhaps he thought I was afraid of him and was now dismissing him.

"Would you like some breakfast?" I offered lamely, at a loss for words.

"I"ve got a better idea" he responded. "Let's go into town, and I'll buy you breakfast. We've spent some time together, but never really talked or been alone much. Sometimes I think it's me you're afraid of."

I almost spit my mouthful of coffee out at that last statement and started to cough and sputter as it finally went down. I felt my face flaming and knew he may be closer to the truth than he knew.

"Well, alright", I answered, meekly. "Sure".

"Let me clean up a bit" he said, rising. He went in, pulling a comb out of his pocket, leaving me sitting there, feeling the fool.

The diner in town was filled with townspeople. They had an incredible breakfast buffet and most took full advantage of it, it seemed.

Conversation flowed loudly around us, punctuated by clanging silverware and rattling dishes. The air was permeated with the delicious smells of frying bacon and ham. My mouth watered as I inhaled the ambiance.

"I'm starved!" I exclaimed.

"Good." He replied. "They've got a hell of a breakfast steak here, and their hash-browns are the best in town."

We seated ourselves at a window booth, and gazed at the morning bustle on the street.

It seemed as if the whole town was out on this glorious morning, and, suddenly, I almost felt a part of it.

Amos attacked his food with a relish I hadn't seen since Al. His over-flowing plate diminished before my very eyes. He was almost done while I still struggled with the humongous mound of hash browns nestled between two sausage links.

Just then, I noticed Irmalines daughter and husband, with children in tow, entering the diner. I quickly looked away, hoping they wouldn't notice me in the milling crowd.

They seated themselves at a large corner booth, Barney (Irv) laughing and chatting congenially with everyone around him, acting the cock of the walk, I thought. His wife sat meekly at his side, fussing with the children; occasionally smiling warmly at a well-wisher stopping by their booth.

We had almost finished and they had just ordered, when Barney noticed us. He stopped addressing his oldest son in mid-sentence as he spied us, a look of surprise (or shock) dancing across his face.

"Oh no", I said, casting Amos a helpless look.

"What?" he asked, concern in his voice.

"Don't look now, but here comes the Calvary" I replied.

He looked up just as Barney approached our table.

They shook hands, Barney effusive in a phony, condescending manner. He glanced at me, trying to keep the animosity out of his look, but not quite succeeding.

"I heard you was back in town", he said, in his hillbillyish way. "Why ain't ya' been by?" Making me wonder if Amos could possibly be friends with this Neanderthal.

"I've been busy" Amos replied, noncommittally, at which Barney once again looked at me.

"I didn't know you knew Ms. Woods", (He pronounced it Mizz) he said, trying to act surprised. Like hell, I thought. I was sure everyone in town knew by now that Amos had been camping out on my property, and with Irmaline being his mother-in-law, there was no way he wasn't aware of it.

"Well, I guess you're about the only one in town who doesn't know what's been going on out there, then", Amos responded, as if reading my mind. "In fact, I believe you were one of the first ones on the scene in the now-famous pelt staking incident."

"Oh that" Barney waved his hand dismissively. "Everyone knows that was John Fuller did that, and he's dead now." He pronounced it "daid" in true hillbilly form. "Although there's a real mystery there. Everyone knows he wouldn't a killed hisself". He cast me a sly, sidelong glance as he said that.

"How can anyone ever know what's in another mans' mind?" Amos asked, narrowing his eyes in an appraising manner. I knew then that Amos considered Barney no friend of his.

"How are Sherry and the kids?" Amos asked, seeing Sherry wave shyly at us as she scowled at her husband behind his back. Her look turned to neutrality as Barney turned to look at her.

"They's fine", he answered non-committally, turning back

to us.

"Well, I believe your breakfast has arrived", Amos said, spying their waitress with a heavy tray approaching their table.

"Oh, yeh", Barney replied, gazing over his shoulder once more. "Nice seein' ya' again, Amos", he threw back in parting, deliberately ignoring me.

"Nice guy" I said watching his retreating back.

Amos smirked at the desultory tone of my voice, and then broke into a wide grin.

"I used to kick his ass on a weekly basis", he informed me happily. "He was always picking on the littler kids and couldn't seem to stop himself no matter how many times he got wholloped."

"Big surprise!" I said. He was a bully. "He hasn't changed much." I added.

"So what about you?" he inquired, changing the subject, "Are you ever going to tell me about yourself? Thus far, you've managed to remain a woman of mystery".

His eyes twinkled as he said this and I couldn't help but smile.

"Nothing much to tell", I replied. "I've lived here for what seems forever with my husband Al, as you know, and now I live here alone-except for Sam and Judas, of course."

"Well, you must have had a life before that. What was your childhood like?"

I gazed down at my empty plate and watched the remnants of the eggs congeal on the edges of the gaily-painted ceramic plate, wondering how to avoid the question.

Finally I looked up and met his questioning look. "It's something I really don't like to talk about." I replied, adding quickly, "Not that it was anything particularly horrible or anything like that; it's just that my household wasn't all that happy a one. My mom and dad both drank quite a bit, but they weren't abusive or anything like that. They were good people and did the best they could. And I loved them."

"Were? So they're both gone now?" He asked, his bushy eyebrows rising slightly.

"Yes. My mother died back in 86, my dad followed less than a year later. Drank himself to death in grief, I think. He just couldn't handle life without her."

"I'm sorry." He said, meaning it.

"So am I. I never really got a chance to tell them that I loved them and appreciated all they had done for me; they were good to us, despite their drinking."

"You said 'us'. You have siblings, then?" he asked.

"I have a brother, whom I haven't seen in maybe 20 years. I talked to him on the phone perhaps ten years ago. He said he was leaving the country. Australia, I believe, but he was always a vagabond and God knows where he ended up."

"Maybe you should try to hunt him down." He replied. "It's good to have family around, especially in times of crises."

"Maybe I will." I responded. "I would like to know if he's alright. And happy" I added.

"What about you?" I continued. "Where is your family?"

"My mom's in a nursing home over in Park City. My dad died a couple of years ago.

I have a sister in New York. She's an off-Broadway actress and quite good, really. My brother's down in Louisiana working off a dock. Stevedores' union. He has a son who's around 25 now. My sister never had any children. I saw her a few years ago when I was driving through New York on a run, but I haven't seen my brother for a while, though we do call each other a couple of times a year."

The waitress brought our check then and fussed over Amos for several minutes. It seemed they'd went to high school together. She seemed genuinely fond of him, which further eased my mind as to his character. I'd almost decided to trust him.

We walked around the lake for a while, making small talk

about the nearly naked trees and changing weather. He knew a lot about nature and named off all the species of trees we passed and discoursed about the different birds that were now gathered in large groups to migrate, although most had already left.

It was after noon when we got back to the house. I could hear the phone ringing as I exited his truck.

"Must be Irmaline", I said, running up the steps.

He followed me in and I didn't mind in the least.

He settled in a wingchair, his large feet dwarfing the small ottoman I'd recently purchased at a yard sale in one of my rare 'fixing up the house' modes.

It was, of course, Irmaline on the phone, wondering where I'd been. When I told her Amos and I had just returned from breakfast in town she was surprised and pleased.

We agreed she'd come over around 6:00 to get ready for the party. The children's party started at 6:00 and ran until 8:00, after which time they were banished to grandparents' and babysitters' so that the adults could revel. I never had trick-or-treaters at my place as I was so far out, but kids ran the streets most of the day, taking advantage of the various businesses; all of which gave out candy until they closed. Then the houses in town were descended on by hordes of sugar-hungry children. By the time the kids' party was over the parents were at their wits end with hyper kids running amok. Most were more than happy to relegate them to their charges and let their own hair down.

After Irmaline arrived, we had our final fittings, Amos watching with wonder as we transformed ourselves into mythical characters; waiting for Irmaline to put the final touches on his costume.

As I had predicted, he made a perfect Paul Bunyan. Plaid woolen shirt replete with striped suspenders covered faded jeans and large, chunky work boots. An axe flung over his shoulder and earflap hat (Irmalines' idea) and, voila, Paul

Bunyan!

We left shortly before 8:00, Irmaline carrying a covered casserole dish, I with several bags of potato chips. Amos had a couple of cases of beer stowed in the rear of his truck in a large metal trough covered in ice.

We jabbered excitedly all the way in, laughing at the groups of costumed children as we entered the town limits.

Though totally dark, lights shone everywhere and most children carried flashlights or glowing faux pumpkins to light their way, accentuating the spookiness of their costumes.

An abstract thought entered my mind as we neared the courthouse. A month ago I had thought there were no hillbillies around, somehow discounting Barney. I chuckled to myself, wondering if he'd just come as himself.

As we walked across the parking lot the doors to the City Hall swung wide, disgorging a large mob of frenetic children. Their raucous voices shattered the otherwise quiet night.

Car doors slammed as people picked them up and adults with no children arrived. Despite my witch costume, I almost felt like Cinderella entering the ball as the gaily-costumed townspeople engulfed me. This was going to be fun!

A blast of warm air hit us as Amos opened the large, heavy door. Today was the first time I had spent so much time alone with him, although he had passed out on my couch and slept a lot of the time. I now felt as though I could trust him. I had even left my gun at home, deciding to rely on him for protection and also not knowing if the City Hall was equipped with metal detectors.

Irmaline let out a squeal of delight as she was engulfed by gaily-dressed revelers. Her daughter ran to embrace her, her long Cinderella dress rustling as she approached. She looked absolutely lovely, but if Barney had come as Prince Charming I knew I wouldn't be able to contain my mirth.

Amos disappeared almost immediately to find some help to carry in his beer trough, leaving me adrift in a sea of strangers. I was glad for my disguising façade and went immediately to the orange draped table in the center of the room where the punch was located. I wasn't much of a punch person but had decided not to imbibe in alcohol tonight . I wanted to keep my wits about me. I stood, glass in hand, surveying the room around me. Someone had turned on music and "The Monster Mash" was blasting from a corner of the room, enticing people to dance. Several couples were already on the large parquet floor, it having been cleared expressly for that purpose. The lights were dimmed and a multi-colored party ball began to swirl, casting wavering shadows across the room.

I spotted Irmaline across the room, her sequined dress shimmering in the glow as she carried on an animated conversation with her daughter. I wondered who was watching her grandchildren and where Barney was.

Amos had returned with several other large men and was setting up the beer trough next to the punch table; he and several of his cronies already had beers in their hands and my mouth watered watching them. Maybe I'd have a few later on as the party wore down when there wouldn't be time for me to get drunk.

I was delighted to see a family of really short people dressed as Munchkins surrounding Irmaline and assumed that had been her idea. She seemed to be in her element and I was glad she was having such a good time, although the camaraderie only seemed to emphasize my own isolation.

Amos appeared at my side then, lightly touching my elbow and steering me onto the dance floor. Beer in hand, he stomped his huge feet and twirled like a clumsy bear, causing me to laugh delightedly. I hadn't danced in years, but watching him I found it impossible to feel awkward. My ungainly nose wobbled from side to side with my movements, bringing a smile to Amos' face.

The song ended, and we wended our way back to the table.

Chairs were set up along the walls and I slipped onto one, by breathing ragged from the unexpected exercise. Amos sat beside me after grabbing another beer. He handed me another glass of punch as he asked, breathlessly, "Having a good time?" "Yes, as a matter of fact I am!" I exclaimed, surprising myself.

Eventually, Irmaline made her way back over to me and perched herself delicately on the neighboring chair.

"How's your daughter doing?" I inquired.

"Oh, she's fine. I take it they're still having problems, but she didn't seem to want to talk about it. She's always been a secretive person. She'll get around to telling me about it when she's ready. If she decides to leave him she can come stay with me. It would be nice to have my grandchildren even closer at hand for a while. I hope she does! I can't abide that man!". She took a drink of her punch and gazed across the room to where Sherry was in deep conversation with a generic-looking witch.

"That's Debby, her best friend since grade school. I'm sure she knows much more about what's going on than I do."

She turned to me again. "I saw you dancing with Amos. You two sure do look good together," she gushed, "and you actually seemed to be enjoying yourself!"

I looked over to where Amos was drinking and bull-shitting with his friends, and blushed.

"He seems to be a great guy and I've more or less decided to trust him." I ventured.

She gave me a surprised look and snorted. "It's about time!" She responded.

Just then I noticed a ballerina coming across the room. She was tall and willowy and really DID look like a ballerina. Her long, blonde hair was twisted into an intricate braid that cascaded down her athletic back. She swooshed down on Amos like something out of "Swan Lake" as I sat there, stunned.

"Oh my God!" Irmaline exclaimed, espying her. "That's Vicky! Amos' ex-wife! I haven't seen her in years! What the hell is she doing here?"

We watched, enthralled, as Amos almost dropped his beer on noticing her. Her willowy arms enfolded him in a hug as bright lipstick stained his cheek at her too-familiar buss.

"That woman broke his heart with her whorish ways and there she is, pretty-as-you-please, just waltzing in here like nothing ever happened!" Irmaline sputtered.

I remained silent, not knowing what to make of this amazing turn of events.

Amos backed away from her effusive kiss, and, I swear, he was blushing! We couldn't hear the ensuing conversation and Amos' rocky face gave away nothing.

After perhaps five minutes of a mostly one-sided conversation, she floated away as quickly as she'd come, drifting off to a gaggle of women in the far corner, laughing and preening like the belle-of-the-ball.

I surreptitiously watched Amos and he seemed as stunned as me. What was she doing here, I wondered. I was suddenly thirsty, but no power on earth was going to get me to approach that table right now. Irmaline, however, had no such reservations. She jumped up and was gone before I had a chance to protest. I tried to keep my gaze averted from the scene but found it impossible. Irmaline's arms were waving all over the place, like a Dodo trying to take flight, as she practically had to bend over backwards to look into Amos face. I, once again, looked across the room to the intruder and saw her watching them with a bemused expression on her perfect face.

Wouldn't you know it! Just when things started to be falling into place for me, a new twist! This was exactly why I had cut myself off from people and my own emotions, the unexpectedness of life always caught me off-guard and left me powerless, a feeling I couldn't stand.

Another surprise! All of a sudden, there, talking to Vicky, was Barney. I saw he had decided to come as himself, wearing a farmer outfit; bib over-alls over a dirty tee shirt.

A big straw hat sat atop his misshapen head. The only thing missing was a sprig of Alfalfa sticking out of his mouth.

I could see him staring daggers at me, I'm sure quite happy to be informing Vicky of my involvement with Amos.

Sherry was still talking to her best friend, but upon noticing him, swept across the room, grabbed his arm, whispered something in his ear, and in an amazing show of defiance dragged him away to a remote corner, where what appeared to be a loud argument (it was hard to hear with the loud music once again blaring) began.

I did not want to be the thorn in the side of this party. It seemed my quite innocuous presence was, all of a sudden, causing problems.

Suddenly, Amos was at my side. He grabbed my arm gently but insistently, guiding me onto the dance floor once again; this time initiating a slow dance as someone had decided that "The Monster Mash" and its ilk were too exhausting for the sweating partiers. I gladly clung to his coarse shirt, although my face barely reached his chest, I was more than happy to bury my humility in it. My nose was crunched to the side, the tip practically touching my ear. I hardly noticed. I wrapped my arms around him as far as his great girth allowed, and hung on for dear life.

I replenished my punch and returned to my observation perch; Amos joined me with a new beer. I saw Irmaline across the room talking to a couple of the Munchkins; Vicky was watching us from her center position with the "beautiful" people (ex cheerleaders like herself ) and others of that privileged ilk. My head was starting to throb from the loud music and constant buzz of the crowd. I excused myself to go to the bathroom, wending my way down the stairs, bobbing and weaving to avoid a surge of laughing, brightly costumed women ascending.

The sudden coolness of the bathroom revived me somewhat. The lime green tile floor was still amazingly clean, only a paper towel crumpled here and there attesting to its use.

I was at the sink, washing up, trying not to smear my green make-up, and adjusting my now somewhat mutilated nose, when Vicky waltzed in. She leaned against the sink and held out a perfectly manicured hand to me.

"Hello", she purred, and I noticed her voice was well-modulated, fitting right in with the rest of her personae. I took her hand firmly, to assure her I was no wimp, and didn't release it until she pulled away.

"I'm Vicky Smythe", she purred.

"Is that your married name?" I innocently inquired.

"Oh, no!" she laughed throatily, "I'm getting divorced. I've decided to retain my maiden name. It makes my parents happy" she added. "I see you're keeping company with Amos." It sounded more like a question than a statement.

"We're friends, yes" I ventured.

"The way you were dancing belies that" she replied, her thin eyebrows arching slightly.

"Well, looks can be deceiving" I replied, keeping my tone light.

"We were married, you know," she said.

"So I've heard. So, what are your plans now?"

"Mummy and Daddy thought it best that I came home for a while until I decide what to do. It's very difficult, you know, trying to start over." She looked directly at me, her eyes tearing up. She's good, I thought. Perhaps I should suggest that she pursue a career in acting.

I turned, preparing to leave. The last place I wanted to be was here, having a conversation with her. "Well, good luck." I said.

She grasped my arm with her long, tapering nails, letting me know she hadn't dismissed me yet.

"And what are YOUR plans, Annie" she said, her blue eyes narrowing, all innocence gone now.

"I really don't see where that's any of your business!" I hissed, pulling my arm free and fleeing.

# CHAPTER TEN

What a bitch! I thought as I ran up the stairs. A couple of the Munchkins were coming down the stairs and I wondered where they were a few minutes ago when I needed an interruption.

Amos was still in his chair and Irmaline had taken a place next to him.

"Where were you?" she inquired, leaning over Amos.

"The bathroom" I replied, not trusting myself to say more as I was so angry I was shaking. Amos looked at me curiously, but said nothing.

I grabbed my punch glass and downed it in one swig, allaying further questions.

Just then Vicky returned. She saw her crowd watching her and twirled in ballerina fashion. Her elite group clapped and shouted as she joined them.

Smythe! I thought. A pretentious name for a pretentious bitch!

"Excuse me." I said to Amos and Irmaline as I rose and went to get a beer. The look Irmaline gave Amos wasn't lost on me as I popped the can and took a big guzzle.

As I resumed my seat, beer in hand, I noticed the tone of the party had changed. The free-flowing beer had taken its toll and, it seemed, inhibitions had been shed. The music had gotten even louder and just about everyone was on the dance floor now.

I saw Vicky pirouetting with a Prince Charming who'd probably been a football star and/or homecoming king in high school. His arrogance emanated from him, as in a drunken haze he swung her around with one hand while managing to hold onto his beer with the other.

She threw back her head and laughed delightedly and I noticed she cast a surreptitious glance at Amos as she did so.

Oh, this is great! I thought. I have a front row seat at the Vicky show.

My nose kept getting in the way as I drank and I had to push it to the side with each swig. I was beginning to regret my choice of a costume. It was like the "good cowboy, white hat, bad cowboy, black hat" thing, and it was obvious between Vicky and me, who was who.

Irmaline saw Sherry summoning her from across the room and excused herself hurriedly.

"So that's the ex, huh?" I asked Amos as the soothing alcohol started coursing through my veins.

"Yeah, that's her," he replied. "She hasn't changed a bit."

"That's too bad!" I replied sarcastically.

He turned, and looking down on me from his great height, observed me questioningly.

"Did something happen in the bathroom? You've been acting funny since you got back."

"How observant!" I replied.

Before he could answer, I jumped up and went to get another beer. All at once I was afraid it would be gone before I got my share.

I hadn't seen Vicky's crowd approach the table all night and wondered what they were imbibing in; it was quite plain they weren't entirely sober; then I noticed a silver flask circulating among them.

Of course, I thought, wending my way back to Amos' side, beer wouldn't be good enough for that crowd (except for the football jock).

"Put that beer down and let's dance." Amos said as I joined him.

I took a big swig and set it on the edge of the table. I could dance, too, I thought. We gyrated around the dance floor, bouncing off other revelers occasionally, though no one seemed to care. Someone had put on Metallica and I was surprised at the choice. Maybe this town wasn't as backwoods as I thought.

We danced the rest of the night away, except for beer-getting intervals, and it seemed by now that everyone dancing did so with a beer (or silver flask) in their hand. Every time the trough seemed to be almost empty, more beer miraculously appeared. I saw Irmaline being twirled by a silver-haired gentleman and wondered abstractly who HE was. Sherry and Barney swept by a couple of times. I noticed that he danced like the clod he was and laughed in amusement. At one point Vicky appeared and rudely got between Amos and me, her braid bouncing as she sidled up to him. I didn't care; I turned and kept dancing with a Munchkin and Vampire, who seemed quite glad to have me. I was in happy mode now. My beer besotted brain finding humor in my bizarre surroundings. At one point, I even picked the Munchkin up and swung him (or her. I wasn't sure) around as he/she squealed happily.

Eventually, I really wasn't sure when, I grabbed another beer and staggered toward the door, my head spinning. I needed some fresh air. I felt my make-up oozing down my face and my nose was, once again, askew. I'd lost track of Amos and didn't bother looking for him. Let him have that bitch Vicky.

They deserved each other. I was tired of his long-suffering act, his aloofness and reticence. I treasured my own company. I didn't need him, or anyone else!

I pushed through the heavy doors and drew in a deep breath of the chill night air. The stars were shining brightly and an almost full moon cast wavering shadows over the parking lot and surrounding trees. A few smokers were milling around, snippets of their conversations floating on the night air. I caught a cloud of smoke from one returning to the party and sucked it in, remembering the exhilaration of the nicotine and wishing I had one. I wandered around to the side of the building looking for a bench to sit on while I cleared my head. The wind was picking up now and a chill went through me as I settled on a concrete bench I managed to find. It was quieter here, the music muted and the voices of the partiers all blending together in a miasma of sounds. Halloween. Last year Albert had still been here. We'd made popcorn and sat on our porch, laughing at the antics of our pets in the moonlight. I missed him so. No, no one could ever replace Albert, and I was destined to remain alone until I could once again join him.

Thinking back, it was an insane thing to do, wandering off by myself when I'd been so paranoid just a week before. I had always been one of those people who watched horror movies and was dumbfounded at the stupidity of the characters; wandering off one by one to be slaughtered like lambs. In my state of mind then, it seemed quite reasonable. I was drunk and pissed off and had a fatalistic attitude. On the one hand I was almost hoping something would happen so I could kick someone's ass; on the other, if I should happen to lose, oh well, I'd see Al sooner than expected. Which was all the more reason that I should have quit drinking for good instead of embracing it sporadically. Perhaps I was hoping Amos would come looking for me, a reassurance that he cared.

Nonetheless, there I sat, bathed in cool moonlight,

watching and listening, and trying not to think.

I heard footsteps approaching and at the same time my head started spinning and my stomach roiled. I knew I was going to be sick and certainly didn't want anyone observing that spectacle, especially if it was Amos, looking for me. I jumped up and fought my way into the thick bushes behind the bench, inanely thinking, 'I wonder what kind of bushes these are? Amos would know.' Then purged my stomach as quietly as I could as I heard voices directly in front of me, by the bench.

"Do you think they're onto us?" one said. It sounded vaguely familiar, but I couldn't quite place it as they were whispering, my head was spinning and my mind was disengaged. I heard another voice answering but couldn't make out the hushed words.

I remembered thinking, are they talking about me? Then everything went black.

I opened my eyes to see Amos' worried face gazing down at me. Weak sunlight was filtering through the thick bushes and I realized I was shaking in the chill air.

Amos was no longer wearing his goofy earlap hat. His hair was as wild and unkempt as the bushes surrounding me. Then I noticed Irmaline peeking out from behind him, almost invisible because of his bulk.

"Is she alright?" I heard her worriedly ask. Her tiara was missing, but she still wore her sequined dress.

"Appears to be", I heard Amos answer, as if from a distance.

Everything was spinning and I couldn't seem to focus. I didn't know where I was or if this strange tableau was real.

"What kind of bushes are these, Amos?" I inquired before darkness once again overtook me.

When I awoke I was in my own bed. Sam was licking my face and Judas was at my feet.

I couldn't seem to remember anything and assumed it was

just another day, though my head was pounding furiously. I wondered why my bedroom door was closed, as I always left it open for the pets to come and go. I swung my legs over the edge of the bed and had to steady myself as the room spun.

Whoa, I thought. What's going on? Memories starting flooding back as I noticed I was green and still wearing my witch dress. My nose was missing and I no longer was wearing a wig. I thought and thought but the last thing I remembered was sitting on a cold bench in pale moonlight. I stumbled to the door, holding onto anything available.

I was surprised to see Amos and Irmaline at the kitchen table and asked stupidly,

"What are you guys doing here?"

Amos came to me then and escorted me to the table, bringing me fresh, hot coffee after settling me in the chair.

"Are you alright?" Irmaline asked, concern knitting her brows together.

"Why wouldn't I be?" I asked. "What happened? I can't seem to remember much."

Amos had seated himself to my right and looked at me questioningly.

"We found you in the bushes this morning after searching most of the night." He replied.

"Sometime during the night you disappeared and we didn't know where you went. Irmaline checked the bathroom and when you weren't there, we began looking."

"We told the Sheriff, but he was loaded and told us you'd probably decided to go home.

We didn't think you'd try to walk all the way home, alone, in the dark, but we called repeatedly, just in case." Irmaline informed me.

"What?" I replied, shocked.

They exchanged a look across the table, which infuriated me, for some reason.

"I was not drunk!" I exclaimed. "Not THAT drunk,

anyway." I realized I was almost shouting, and Sam came running in to see what was upsetting me. He sat at my feet, whining, his tail wagging half-heartedly.

I bent down and rubbed his ears, reassuring him, and giving me something else to look at besides their pitying eyes.

I shakily picked up my coffee, having to hold the mug in both hands as the tremors engulfed me.

"What were you doing back there in the bushes?" Irmaline asked.

I took a sip of coffee as I met her concerned eyes.

"I'm trying to remember." I replied, embarrassed. "I know I went out to get some air. It was so damned hot in there! Then I sat on the bench around the side. Let me think! It's coming back to me, slowly." I ended weakly.

"What the hell were you thinking, wandering around by yourself after all that's been happening?" Amos said, anger making his voice rise. Sam sidled closer to me, whining at his tone.

"I guess I wasn't." I admitted. "I wasn't afraid at the time."

"Of course not!" Amos said. "You were drunk and full of false bravado!"

"I was not!" I shouted, no longer trying to control my temper. "I've been drunk many times in my life, and believe me, this was much more than that!"

"What are you saying?" Irmaline asked.

"I don't know. I just know it was something other than alcohol. I've never felt like that before." I met her eyes sheepishly, imploring her, silently, to believe me.

"Are you saying you were drugged?" Amos inquired. I considered this possibility silently.

"It would make sense." I replied, rubbing Sam's ears, abstractedly. "I'd left my beer on the table the last time we danced, then, after I'd finished it was when I started feeling funny" and, all at once, I knew it was true.

He leaned back in the chair, eying me suspiciously.

"Oh my God!" Irmaline exclaimed, grabbing my hand and patting it. "Why didn't you come and get me?"

"Well, obviously, I didn't know at the time." I said. "I just knew I needed some air and wanted to clear my head."

"Well, it was a stupid thing to do!" Amos reprimanded.

"She wasn't thinking clearly at the time." Irmaline defended me.

"That's an understatement." Amos shot back.

"Well, maybe it's a good thing I went back in those bushes then, for whatever reason."

I said. "I was safe there. I have to remember why I went back there. I'm going to go take a bath and think."

I rose and made my way unsteadily towards the bathroom, leaving them there gaping at me.

When I emerged from the tub, feeling much better, Irmaline and Amos were still seated at the table. All conversation ceased at my arrival.

"We've been thinking" Irmaline said. "We think we should take you to get a blood test.

If you were drugged, God know's what it was!"

"I know I was drugged, but whatever it was, it's mostly gone now. I feel fine." I responded.

"Nonetheless", Amos intoned, "We'd have something to tell the authorities."

"Whoop-de-do!" I said, dripping with sarcasm. "Then they could say I was a drug addict, too. That would explain my so-called strange behavior."

"We're serious." Amos said. "It could be something poisonous."

"Well, my memory is coming back, and I puked my guts out. I'm sure you couldn't help but notice when you found me. I'm fine now, really."

They once again exchanged the "look" that I'd come to despise.

I, by now, was at the table with them, coffee in hand. Sam

and Judas were at my feet, waiting to be fed. I got up and fed them, then resumed my seat.

"I heard something last night. Not much, and it may be totally unrelated to me."

I offered. I told them what I'd heard and let them mull on that. "Also, I'd appreciate it if this didn't get out. It would only confirm the towns' opinion of me as a flake. I appreciate your concern and friendship, and you finding and bringing me home." I added. "I couldn't ask for better friends."

Irmaline went home shortly thereafter. She looked tired and, I'm sure, wanted to clean up and go to bed. Amos, for once, used my bathroom to shower, then went back out to his tent. He told me to ring my gong if I needed him. I was sure he was extremely tired also, but knew he was a light sleeper, as he'd already told me that.

I wasn't at all fearful. The light of day had a way of expelling night terrors. Besides, I didn't think anyone was trying to kill me. Just scare me. After all, when I'd been pushed off the knoll, whoever had done it had no way of knowing that the runaway boat would head for the dock.

I stuck close to home for the next several days, embarrassed about the party scene, and hoping it hadn't gotten around. I knew Amos would have to leave soon and I'd once again be on my own. I kept my gun loaded and close at hand, and watched my pets for signs of uneasiness.

The Indian summer was quickly fading and I brought in armfuls of wood from my pile against the house. I kept a fire going most of the time now, and the smell of fragrant wood smoke filled the house. Amos still came and joined me on the porch for coffee most mornings, but, much as I wanted too, I made no mention of Vicky. Even most of the geese were gone now, although some stayed all winter; the lazy ones, I guess.

Irmaline came over Friday night for our movie date, but said she had to leave later to babysit in the morning; Amos was nowhere in evidence.

"I certainly hope he isn't with that horrible Vicky!" Irmaline ventured as I set a bowl of popcorn on the coffee table. "She was a slut in high school and tricked him into marrying her to start with." This was the first I'd heard of this and I was shocked at her vehemence.

"How'd she do that?" I asked, "fake pregnancy?"

"I don't know that for a fact," she answered. "I just can't think of any other reason he'd marry that creature."

"Maybe he loved her." I said, simply.

"Bosh! What's to love? She's always been a spoiled rich brat who got anything she wanted, and she wanted Amos!"

"And she got him!" I replied.

I'd put Sam out on his leash and I heard him scratching at the door and hurried to let him in.

"Well, he was soon sorry for that!" she replied haughtily.

Sam ran to her and started scarfing up stray kernels of popcorn cascading down her slacks.

"I don't understand what's she's doing back here. She always thought she was to 'big city' for this town and constantly tried to get Amos to leave." She said this like Amos' living anywhere else was unthinkable.

"I saw her in the bathroom that night at the party, you know." I hadn't told her that before because I knew what her reaction would be. "She said 'mummy and daddy wanted her home for awhile'."

"Well, I know she got divorced," she said. "She probably cuckolded this husband as well.

She had a lot of nerve cornering you. I'd noticed her going downstairs right after you, but totally forgot after all that happened. Maybe it was her that drugged you to get you out of the way for the night so she could get next to Amos!" She surmised.

"That wouldn't make sense," I answered. "If I was sick, he'd stay by me all the more."

"Not if he thought you were drunk and passed out!" she exclaimed. "He'd want to distance himself from you."

"I'd certainly hate to think that she's out to get me, too. Besides whoever else is." I said. "I'm paranoid enough, already!"

"Nothing's going to happen to you." She said. "Amos and I will see to that!"

I didn't bother to point out that Amos would have to be leaving soon, and she wasn't exactly my idea of a protector. I turned the movie on, impeding further conversation.

Early the next morning Sam's furious barking and scratching at the door awakened me. I flew out of bed and ran to the living room window. I peeked furtively through the drapes and was shocked to see Vicky strolling out of the woods. Her hair was loose, hanging in a disheveled mop about her shoulders, pieces of leaves clinging to it. Her designer slacks were rumpled and had grass stains about the knees. She wore a heavy parka, obviously an expensive one. As she ambled through my yard towards the road she gazed at the house, and although I knew she couldn't possibly see me, gave a little wave, a look of triumph on her face.

As I sat at the kitchen table guzzling coffee, I made up my mind to tell Amos to leave.

It was humiliating to think he had the audacity to have her back there, on my land, without even consulting me. I told myself that if he had only let me know, it wouldn't have been so bad. I felt betrayed by the subterfuge. The last person I wanted on my property was her. The more I thought about it, the more infuriated I became. How dare he!

I didn't see Amos at all that day. At least he had the humility not to rub it in my face. I didn't know how I'd react when I did see him, and was glad for the reprieve. I could always inform Irmaline and let her rip him a new one, yet I figured it was up to me to speak up.

I went into town, Sam by my side, to replenish my food

supplies, hoping I wouldn't run into anyone I knew. I was glad no one knew about my episode at the party and still wondered if the snatch of conversation I'd overheard pertained to me or not. It could have been anyone, talking about anything. Small towns all had their secrets. Irmaline called as I was putting my groceries away, but I made no mention of the Vicky incident; I wanted to put it out of my mind and I knew Irmaline would grab onto it and and shake it to death, like Sam with a meaty bone.

When I finally did see Amos, a couple of days later, he was ambling nonchalantly out of the woods as I sat bundled on the porch. My gun was at the ready and a mug of steaming coffee was warming my frigid fingers.

I went and got a cup and poured him one from my ever-present carafe. He settled in on the chair next to me and gratefully accepted it.

"Bad couple of days?" I innocently inquired. "You look like hell." I added. He had black circles under his eyes and his hair was hanging in his face and sticking up in numerous cowlicks. His beard looked equally scraggly.

"Hmmph" he replied. "I have to go home for a while. You think you'll be alright here?"

"Of course!" I replied, pulling my gun out of my over-shirt and showing it to him.

We sat in silence for a while and then I ventured, "You'll have to be leaving soon, I assume?"

"After deer season," he replied noncommittally.

I got rather angry at that, feeling like he'd been using me the whole time for my deer-stand and ample wildlife. I said nothing, though; after all, his presence had made me feel safe. No matter what the reason for it.

"You should have gotten a drug test, you know," he said at last.

"You think I was just drunk, don't you?" I answered.

"I don't know what to think!" He exclaimed, and his

vehemence shocked me. "You claim you were drugged, but you don't get checked, or go to the police? After all that's been going on?"

I suddenly saw it from his point of view. I must appear demented with my laissez-faire attitude.

"Those roofies, those date-rape drugs, they don't stay in your system long." I replied calmly. "Don't you see? If I'd gotten checked, and they weren't there any longer, my credibility would be even more tainted! The Sheriff already thinks I'm a liar at best; a lunatic at worst!" I felt like crying but refused to let him see how much his distrust hurt me. Maybe this was the reason he'd sought solace with Vicky.

"I have to go." He sprang up and left, his boots clomping loudly down the wooden steps. To my ears it held the resounding echo of finality.

I went in, tying Sam to his rope leash so he wouldn't go in the woods and disturb Amos' things. Since Amos' appearance he'd gotten in the habit of snuffling around his camp, eating anything he could find.

I lay on the couch, resuming my reading that had sat untouched for days; yet my thoughts would not be still. What was I going to do? Not just with my present situation, but with my life? In my mind, endless days of nothingness stretched out before me like an eternal river, never finding the sea.

I was glad Amos had left so abruptly, despite the fact that he was angry. It had spared me the embarrassment of saying something I would later regret. Perhaps he wasn't so angry with me as he was with himself, for succumbing to Vicky's rather dubious charms. Either way, it was better that I hadn't gotten a chance to say what I was on the verge of saying when he stomped off. I would, however, tell him that I didn't want her coming on my property and he'd have to arrange his future rendezvous' elsewhere.

I was startled out of my reverie by Sam's barking. I grabbed my gun and ran out onto the porch. Sam was jumping at the end of his tether, barking at the woods. I pulled him in by his rope and shut him in the house. I wanted to remain as quiet as possible so I dared not chastise him. I strained to detect any sounds, but his caterwauling kept me from hearing anything. After standing there listening for several tense minutes, I quietly went inside and peered through the drapes. My gun at the ready, I stood like a stone statue; unable to move as I continued to stare at the empty yard.

The wind had picked up, and with every branch that danced to its tune, I felt a tremor go through me. Goosebumps formed on my arms, and still I stood, watching. Sam was sniffing at the door, but now, thankfully, silent.

Eventually I gave up my silent vigil and stoked the fire in anticipation of a cold afternoon and even colder night.

Returning occasionally to the window for another look, I paced the house like a guard dog; going through each room and peering out into the glooming darkness of the woods.

Despite my ambivalent feelings toward Amos, being alone out here was, by far, worse.

As darkness started to fall, Sam's barking preceded a pounding at the door. My heart jumped to my throat at the loud insistence of the knock. I peeked through the drapes to see Amos, looking eerie in the glow of my Christmas lights. I swung the door open,

"What is it?" I asked, fearfully.

He came in, a strange look on his face. "I need to use your phone. Someone destroyed my camp!" He replied. His voice held a mixture of anger and surprise. "Did you see anyone after I left?"

I told him about Sam's agitation shortly after his departure. "But I didn't see anything." I added. "I was scared and held onto my gun all afternoon."

We sat and waited for the Sheriff once again.

"I saw Vicky coming out of the woods a few days ago." I

offered, after he'd told me the extent of the damage and we'd sat in silence for some time.

He flushed, but I couldn't tell if it was in anger or embarrassment. Before he could answer, the Sheriff arrived.

The Sheriff got his flashlight from the squad car and they went into the woods, leaving me holding onto Sam's collar as I gazed after them. I shut and locked the door as soon as the darkness swallowed them, leaning against it and shaking. A picture of the obscene doll crept into my mind as I wondered what the hell we were dealing with. Guilt also consumed me, as now Amos was also a victim of my stalker.

# CHAPTER ELEVEN

Amos' camp, it turned out, had been pretty much annihilated. His tent had been ripped to shreds, as well as his sleeping bag, pillows, and a blanket. The bag he kept fresh foodstuffs in, which hung from a tree out of the reach of predators, was missing. His cooler was empty and smashed to pieces. His fishing rods were destroyed. Worst of all, his rifle was gone. Fortunately, whatever other guns he had were in his hidden, locked vehicle. His Coleman cook stove was no longer functional, having been smashed and thrown haphazardly into the brush; although I wasn't even aware that he had one, he usually had a campfire. Obviously, someone didn't want him there, but whom? Was it my stalker, or Vicky? It was time Amos and me had a long talk.

The next morning I rang the gong (Amos had slept in his truck that night, refusing my offer of the couch). When we were seated on the porch, both bundled against the now, ever present cold, I broached the subject of Vicky. Amos informed me that he hadn't been in his camp that morning. He claimed he'd left before sun up and was in my deer stand scoping the area. He said he'd been doing this for several days after checking my house and grounds for any signs of intruders. He knew Sam would bark at the slightest provocation and I'd ring the gong (which echoed for miles and he'd be able to hear.)

"Do you think she destroyed your camp?" I asked tentatively.

"I intend to find out. I can always tell when she's lying. I'll know if she is." He replied.

"What could she possibly have been doing here?" I inquired.

"I honestly don't know. As much as I hate to, I'm going to have to go over to her parents place and speak with her. While I'm gone, stay in the house. Put Sam out on his rope to watch the place, and keep your gun ready."

I assured him that I would. I also wanted to call Irmaline and let her know of this latest development.

When he left, I did as he'd suggested. Fear was once again my constant companion and my nerves were frayed. It was times like this that I wanted to drown myself in alcohol, but I restrained myself, memories of the ill-fated party keeping me in check. Though I still believed I'd been drugged, the alcohol was the catalyst. If I'd stayed sober it would have been obvious to all that I'd been slipped something.

I waited an hour before I called Irmaline, although I knew she was an early riser (as most elderly people tend to be). She insisted on coming over later that day when she was done babysitting her grandchildren. I would be glad for her company and no nonsense attitude.

I thought about Amos and wondered what was happening over at her parents. What would her excuse be? I'd loved to be a fly on the wall for that conversation!

Yet, when I thought about it, Amos had obviously been back to his camp after the morning I'd seen Vicky. If he hadn't seen her that morning, what was she doing back there and why hadn't she destroyed his camp then? Was she planning to and been scared off by Amos' return or something else? Then why would she wave at the house? I'd assumed at the time that she'd wanted me to think she'd been with Amos (which, of course, I did), but it also meant she was hoping she'd be seen. If she'd been planning on destroying his camp, why would she have been so blatant? I was having doubts that she was the one that did it; and if not her, who?

Irmaline's loud car announced her arrival and I went out on the porch to meet her. She was her usual elegant self in an immaculate camel coat over a beige sweater and light brown slacks. Her white hair was pulled back in a bun and a string of pearls graced her delicate neck.

"You sure look nice!" I exclaimed, descending the steps to meet her.

"Oh, I had a meeting at the church after I was done babysitting. We're trying to raise money for our missionaries in Guatemala and have to come up with an idea for a fund raiser." She replied. "You should join our church, as I've said before, but I know, I'm wasting my breath!" She raised her hand with a dismissive wave at this last statement.

"I'm not much of an organized religion type, as you know." I responded, lamely.

"Yes, yes, I know. Now fill me in on what's been happening." She answered eagerly.

We went in the house, as rain clouds were coming in and the wind was picking up, promising a cold and wet day.

When we were seated at the kitchen table I proceeded to tell her everything. I had no reason to omit the Vicky incident now that I knew Amos was not involved in her appearance. I was anxious to get her take on the course of events. When I told her my doubts as to Vicky being the perpetrator, and why, she got a puzzled look on her face.

"Now that is strange!" she said. I could tell by her furrowed brow that her acute mind was trying to grasp all the implications. "Maybe she waved just in case you did see her, but probably thought you didn't. That way it wouldn't look like she was sneaking around."

"Yes, but if she was planning on a reign of destruction, why would she make her presence know at all? She could have just crept out through the woods rather than exposing herself in my yard." I postulated.

"Well, she obviously wanted you to think she was with Amos. Perhaps after she thought about it, she came back and destroyed his camp thinking he'd suspect you because you were angry he was with her." She surmised.

"Now there's a thought!" I said, embracing the possibility. "It makes sense." I added.

"We'll have to run this by Amos when he returns." She said.

"You don't think he'll actually suspect me, do you?" I asked, suddenly afraid that Vicky's ruse might work.

"I wouldn't see why. He knows how deceptive Vicky is. You've never given him reason to distrust you." She replied.

I wasn't quite convinced. He'd been angry with me before the destruction, he may very well think I was responsible.

When Amos returned, we seated him at the table and swarmed him like a murder of crows, eager for any morsel of sustenance.

He informed us that she hadn't been home and her parents claimed not to know where she was. They told him that she'd been home all night on the night in question and that they knew this for a fact as she'd retired upstairs at precisely 10:00 p.m. and they had been up entertaining until the wee hours of the morning. She had not descended until the next day, when she joined them for brunch. Amos, of course, knew the layout of the house and if they were telling the truth there was no way they could have missed her, as a large double staircase dominated the large foyer and this was the only means of access (other than the locked servants quarters) to the rooms above. A large sitting room with wide double doors was off to the right and this was where they were regaling their company; the doors had been opened, facing the staircase, all night. Of course, there was always the possibility that they were occupied at some point and hadn't noticed her departure or return, particularly if she'd planned it that way. It would have given her the perfect alibi; Amos also believed that it wasn't beneath her parents to cover for her. Amos further theorized that she may have went through the servants quarters but thought it would be a futile effort to question them, as they knew what side their bread was buttered on. We were back to square one. Even when he confronted her, if he thought she was being less than truthful, there was no proof.

I was interested in what she would have to say about my sighting of her, however, even though it preceded the destruction. Would she admit that incident, or lie and say I was making it up?

Amos returned to the woods to reestablish his campsite. He was quite angry and set about it with a vengeance. He'd had extra sleeping bags, another rifle and even another, smaller, tent at his house and picked them up on his way back from Vicky's parents, along with more supplies and whatever else he could find that he thought he might need. He said no one was going to scare him off and I guess that was lucky for me, as now he may stay longer. He owned his own truck and worked independently, so unless he was in dire need of immediate income he could pick and choose his jobs as needed. The weather would probably be the main determinant now. But I guessed his anger would keep him warm for a while. To him, now it was personal. I was glad that I no longer had just a protector, but an ally against a common enemy.

Irmaline had run her theory of Vicky trying to put the blame on me by Amos, and I'd sighed a sigh of relief when he'd pooh-poohed any involvement by me. It was plain he wouldn't buy into that, even though he wouldn't put it past Vicky to try something so deceitful.

I went out to the woods when Irmaline left shortly thereafter, and helped Amos get things in order. I brought Sam with me. Judas tagged along, too. When the tent was set up and the non-canned edibles once again hung from a high branch, we set about starting a fire. We made coffee over the open fire as the shadows started to gather and I thought that coffee had never tasted so good. Occasionally as the wind blew the branches of the now nearly naked trees, a coruscation in colors could be seen from my Christmas bulbs. The warmth of the fire and Amos presence warmed me as the mug of coffee cooled in my hands.

We sat silently for a while, Amos across from me, seated on a freshly hewn stump made expressly for that purpose, me on a cloth camp chair that I doubted could bear his weight.

His eyes glittered in the dancing light of the fire and translucent moonbeams played in his wild hair. My heart was full and I felt a strange peace descend upon me despite the frightening circumstances. I couldn't recall the last time I'd felt so content. Judas sat and stared at the fire, thinking her strange cat thoughts, well Sam snuffled around the fire searching for stray bits of food. Loons called eerily to each other from the channel, while an owl hooted somewhere close by. I had a feeling of timelessness and imagined this must have been how our ancestors had felt over a hundred years ago. I looked up to see the stars starting to appear in between the now almost unseen clouds as they faded into the night.

"You know," Amos said, startling me out of my reverie, "I admire you. For all your foibles, you really are a brave woman."

"Thank you, I think." I replied, surprised and pleased.

"You've stood your ground when most women would have ran off at the first sign of trouble." He continued.

"I don't believe that's true." I said. "Most people, men or women, will fight for their homes and what they believe in, otherwise what do they have?"

He scrutinized me silently for a moment, then said, "I still think your brave. And gutsy," he added. A strange glint flickered in his darkened eyes as he said this.

Just when I suspected that he was on the verge of rising to come and sit by my side, lightning streaked across the sky, followed by a loud clap of thunder. I unconsciously reached into my pocket seeking the solace of my gun, it's cold steel bringing me back to reality. What was I thinking? A voice in my head, sounding very much like Al's, whispered, "Beware." I jumped up, nearly tripping in my haste, and stumbled unceremoniously towards the now black woods, muttering, "I have to go."

Fat drops of rain started falling and a cold wind picked up, blowing it into my face off the trembling branches. I never looked back, but could imagine the look of shock that must have been on Amos' face. Uncaring, I plunged on through the clutching trees and rain slicked carpet of fallen leaves in a sudden panic to get to the safety of my house.

Sam ran ahead of me and I followed his retreating form knowing he would unerringly lead me to the refuge of my yard. I didn't see Judas, but her cat sense would lead her home.

When I was safely inside, leaning against the door and struggling for breath, I couldn't help the kaleidoscope of images that played through my mind. Amos, behind me on the cliff as an unseen hand reached out and shoved me into nothingness; Amos, hurrying before me to find that dreadful doll, hanging from a tree; Amos, dancing with me, my drink in near proximity; Vicki, coming out of the woods, waving nonchalantly at a seemingly empty house. Although he'd supposedly been out of town when Gumba had been nailed to my door, did I know that for a fact? And what about the hides? He was an avid hunter, and, I assumed, would know how to trap. He'd expressed great interest in my land as a hunting and fishing paradise.

I changed into my ragged nightgown, hanging my dripping clothes over the shower rod to dry as I tried to dispel the gathering paranoia.

Could he have destroyed his own camp to compel me into a false sense of trust? After all, none of his things had been irreplaceable. Was he truly that diabolical? My own sanity came into question once again as these doubts plagued me. Who could I truly trust? I knew I could trust Irmaline, but she trusted Amos. He could make her believe it was I who was losing my grip on reality. He had shown up right when I was most vulnerable.

Did I dare tell Irmaline of my misgivings? What about the dead John Fuller? Would, or could, Amos be a murderer? Were they in cahoots and had a falling out? It was my gun that had ended his life and I'd had feelings of guilt about that; but it wasn't me who had pulled the trigger. Whatever the truth of the matter, I knew I had to adhere to that old adage, keep your friends close and your enemies, closer.

I talked to Irmaline the next day and she informed me that the church had decided to have a Bazaar to raise money for their missionaries. I agreed, under coercion, to set up a booth in the church basement with the others. It would give me a reason to clean out my "root cellar" of years of accumulated junk. I made no mention of the previous night or my growing suspicion of Amos. She agreed to come over later and assist me. The Bazaar was set up for the next week as no one wanted to contend with mounds of snow. We had hopes of beating the coming onslaught.

I did a cursory house cleaning in anticipation of Irmalines visit. She was a very fastidious woman and though I'd never been in her house, I could imagine it was immaculate. She had invited me over on several occasions but I always demurred;

my fear of running into Barney precluding a chance to satisfy my curiosity. His open hostility towards me kept me from being as close to Irmaline as I'd like; though I knew she also despised him. He was family; I was not.

I'd warned her that my cellar was cold and dirty yet was still surprised to see she had deviated from her usual natty dress and donned jeans and a sweatshirt.

"I can be as "hep" as you!" she said as she noticed my look of astonishment upon greeting her. She also wore a somewhat ratty old coat, completing her fall from aristocracy. We went around the house to the cellar and I lifted the heavy wooden doors leading down. I had a flashlight, as the overhead light didn't dispel the shadows in the corners.

"It's spooky and cold down here." I said. "I always hated coming down here and made Al come down for the Christmas decorations and lights." I added.

Years of accumulated junk were strewn about the cavern-like room. Irmaline was immediately intrigued. She managed to find old picture albums and became instantly engrossed in them.

"Why Annie!" She exclaimed. "You were beautiful!" She said, sounding surprised.

She quickly caught herself and added, "Not that you're not now, of course. Al was certainly a handsome man. It's too bad you never had children, they would have been quite fetching."

I came and joined her, tears filling my eyes as I gazed at my beloveds' young face.

"I haven't looked at these in years." I commented. "And after Al died, I just couldn't bring myself too."

Evidently, I still couldn't. I went back across the room and started moving around stacked boxes, pieces of my life. Spider webs clung to them and a moldy smell permeated the close air.

"I don't even know if they'll be anything worth selling in

here." I said.

Irmaline's cry of delight startled me and I dropped a box, nearly hitting my foot.

"Look at this!" She whooped.

She had uncovered a wooden side table that had belonged to Al's father and was probably circa 1920.

"This is probably worth a fortune! How come you never put this out in your house?"

"I'd forgotten all about that. By all means let's put it out. It may be the only thing we'll find that's salable." I responded.

I went to help her move it out for closer inspection and doubled over in a bout of sneezing as a cloud of dust was dislodged. When I recovered, I went through the drawers and discovered gold embossed dishes, all intact.

"These should be worth something." I said. "There should be a glass enclosure that attaches to the top." I said.

After several minutes of digging, we found it. It was in pretty good shape but needed a good cleaning, like the table.

"Let's ring for Amos." Irmaline said. "He can bring this stuff up for us without breaking it."

I had no desire to see Amos just yet, but held my tongue, as I didn't feel like going into my reasons with her.

"Let's look around some more first. There may be more good stuff." I said.

We were digging through a darkened corner, Irmaline armed with the flashlight as I shuffled boxes, when I heard Sam barking upstairs.

"Now what!" I exclaimed, just as the overhead light went out and a loud thud proclaimed the shutting of the cellar door.

"What in the world!" Irmaline exclaimed, fear insinuating itself into her voice.

I ran up the cold steps, bumping my head in the process. The heavy wooden doors were shut and wouldn't budge.

I jumped as Irmaline spoke from behind me. "Did the wind blow them shut?" she asked, playing the flashlight on the doors.

"No way! They're way too heavy. It would have to be a tornado!" I rejoined. "Besides, I think they're locked!"

"Oh my God!" Irmaline squealed, bypassing me on the narrow stairs and pounding ineffectually on the heavy doors.

"Save your strength." I said, dejectedly. "We'll be here for a while. Let's look for an axe or something."

Irmaline's fortitude came to the fore and she shuffled off before me in search of a prying or chopping implement.

"Now I know how you feel, Annie!" She said, digging through dusty corners, the flashlight set on the sideboard table, casting dubious light beams.

"Yes. Well, at least now I have a witness." I responded.

"But will you have a living one?" she answered, and surprised at her morbidity, I started to laugh. She joined me, and soon we were doubled over in gales of giggles, verging on hysteria, I suspected.

Eventually, we uncovered an old crowbar and I went to work on the crack between the adjoining doors.

Irmaline was at my shoulder, aiming the flashlight. The boards were old and somewhat rotted, so it wasn't as difficult as I'd thought it might be. I had managed to pry one board loose, jumping back and jostling Irmaline in the process. She dropped the flashlight at the unexpected onslaught, as the board crashed down on the steps. Weak sunlight filtered through the space, saving us from total darkness, as the now useless flashlight lay shattered on the floor. I was getting ready for my next assault when the doors were swung open.

"What's goin' on here?" I heard Amos boom, as his shadow filled the entrance. He reached down with a ham hock hand extended to me. I dropped the crowbar and placed my hand in his, scrambling up the last step as he pulled me free. Irmaline was at my heels and he grasped her hand and repeated the process, though it seemed not as aggressively.

Big shock! I thought. Amos to the rescue, once again. How fortuitous. Irmaline was thanking him profusely, explaining the situation in a breathless voice. Why had I gotten the impression that he'd been surprised at her presence? Her car was plainly visible in the yard, though it wouldn't have been if he'd come through the woods in the back.

I was reticent in my gratitude and hoped he didn't notice my less than enthusiastic demeanor.

"Maybe we should call the Sheriff." Irmaline said, brushing cobwebs and dust off her coat and jeans.

"Don't bother," I replied. "What can he do?" I cast Amos a sidelong glance as I said this, watching his face for a reaction.

"The lock wasn't in place when I got here" he said, looking at me questioningly.

"I probably knocked it loose with the crowbar. We were nearly through when you showed up."

Irmaline and I went in and cleaned up while Amos went down in the cellar and brought up our finds, though the shadows were deep and he needed more light before he could find them all.

I went back out, suddenly wondering why the overhead bulb had gone out right when the doors had slammed shut. Could the bulb have burned out right at that moment? Amos saw me looking at the bulb and came up behind me.

"The jar of the door closing must have burned it out. It looks like a really old bulb." He said, studying it. He was right about that. I couldn't remember the last time I'd put a new bulb in there. I could see by looking at it that the filaments were no longer connected. I went back in the house and returned with a new bulb. He put it in for me, and the light immediately came back on.

"See." He said. "No mystery there."

I went and gathered up some of the gold embossed dishes and carefully wended my way up the stairs.

Irmaline came out as I was laying them on the grass. A patina of frost now coated it, making for unsure footing.

"I'm going back down to see what other treasures are there," she stated, matter-of-factly, and descended into the cellar once again. Amos was still down there and when I followed Irmaline, I saw him looking through my picture books.

"I take it that's Al?," he asked, gazing at a picture of us on the porch, taken when Al's dad had still been alive and had snapped us unaware. We were gazing at each other, lovingly, Al's arm draped protectively around my shoulders as I leaned against him in the now long gone porch swing.

"Yes." I replied, simply. Not being able to bear looking at it, I went back out into the crisp air, fighting the tears that now gathered at the corners of my eyes.

Irmaline managed to find a few other things she thought might bring in some cash.

An old chair Al and his father had made from a felled tree years before. It still had the fragrant smell of fresh hewn lumber clinging to it, though cobwebs now engulfed it.

An ancient army trunk replete with old love letters, discharge papers and a few rusted mess kits was dragged unceremoniously up the steps by a now dust-covered Amos.

We spent the rest of the day cleaning and dusting. I unpacked the trunk, stashing the letters and papers in my bedroom closet in a futile attempt to avoid the memories.

Irmaline washed the dishes with her delicate hands, leaving them to dry in the sink side drainer. I would wrap them in newspaper and put them in the trunk.

Amos had retired to the porch when the cleaning began, keeping a wary eye on things.

At some point he went and got his truck and started loading it with my memories, preparing to take them to the church basement. He then fixed the door I'd broken.

Amos had implied that the cellar doors had shut without human assistance and I'd panicked. I knew this wasn't the case. Irmaline had kept uncharacteristically quiet on the matter, as if sensing the tension between Amos and me.

# CHAPTER TWELVE

In the morning the ground was coated with a sprinkle of snow. There was always the hope that it would melt and the last hurrah of greens would be visible for a while longer, but I didn't count on it. It was always thrilling to see that first snow, but, for me, it wore thin quickly. I knew the long months that it foreshadowed, when the world would be a white wasteland, drifts of snow enclosing my world completely. Sometimes they climbed the side of the house like an encompassing cocoon and a shovel was needed to get out the door. The channel froze over, the wind whipped the barren limbs of the trees and the entire world seemed to slumber under its cold, harsh blanket.

For now, it was just a prelude, but I knew the hunters that were now invading the town welcomed it. My land and most of my neighbors, were posted with "No Hunting" signs for the outsiders (mine now also boasted my "Keep Out" and "No Trespassing" ones, too) but people who were usually only up in the summer now roamed their land donned in bright orange hunting gear, rifles at the ready.

I always kept my pets in this time of year, going out with

Sam only when he insisted, for nature calls.

I was probably too paranoid since over the years we'd only had a stray bullet hit our house once (the hole was still visible on one of the outside walls), but the thought of all those people with guns wandering the woods made me adhere to the old adage "better safe than sorry."

Amos was using my deer stand and had fixed it up, as its rickety condition had been a precarious perch for his considerable weight. I was glad it was once again going to be used for its intended purpose. It had made me melancholy when I'd been up there to see how far to seed it had gone.

I figured I probably wouldn't be seeing too much of Amos for the next couple of weeks, and maybe he'd go back to his real life after hunting season. We hadn't spoken since the previous morning when he'd transported my things to the church.

I decided to spend the next few days helping Irmaline and the church ladies with the Bazaar. I hated to leave the pets alone but I needed to get away for awhile to combat the growing depression and isolation descending upon me. The weather only exacerbated it; and winter hadn't yet begun.

As I drove into town I gazed in awe at the previously bare branches now glistening in the mid-morning sun, the thin layer of snow transforming them into things of beauty.

Through a glass darkly, I thought. This must be what transcending into heaven is like.

Going from a drab, dull reality into a wondrous, magical place. Though we can't see through the pain and despair of this life, another awaits us that we can only occasionally glimpse.

There were six or seven cars in the parking lot when I arrived. I pulled in next to Irmaline's beater, going slowly as I was afraid of black ice and the repercussions that would ensue if I rammed someone's vehicle.

I had my ever-present plaid shirt on, but left my gun in the glove compartment. I realized I was breaking the law since I didn't have a permit to carry it, but if I needed it I certainly wouldn't care about any trouble I may get in for carrying it.

The church looked beautiful, with soft, shimmering snow clinging to its whitewashed exterior. The large cross on top seemingly glowing like a beacon, beseeching sinners to, "find redemption here."

Warm air hit me as I entered and smells from my childhood surrounded me, followed by thoughts of Al's funeral, which I quickly pushed away.

Brewing coffee, some kind of pastries baking, furniture polish. It seemed every church I'd ever been in always smelled the same.

I spotted Irmaline immediately. She had a polishing rag in her hand and was diligently buffing an ancient dresser at the side of the rather cavernous basement. A few other women were spread out through the room, involved in various tasks.

Long tables were set about the room, each covered with decorative cloths and laden with knickknacks for sale. I noticed that some of the tables were filled with Christmas paraphernalia; smiling Santa's, lights, fake snow, assorted miniature houses (separately and in village settings), candles, reindeer, elves. Furniture was pushed against the walls; everything from bunk beds to kitchen tables and living room ensembles.

I helped myself from the large coffee urn on the center table and went to greet Irmaline.

"Hi, Annie." She smiled brightly upon seeing me. "Aren't you cold with only that shirt on?"

I opened my shirt to reveal the heavy sweatshirt I had under it.

"No. Not at all. You've got a lot more stuff then I envisioned." I said.

"Yes. The response has been amazing." She chirped, happily.

She was once again wearing blue jeans and a cotton shirt, embroidered at the shoulders with miniature flowers. Her thin frame under the casual clothing belied the strength that I knew dwelt there.

"Where should I start?" I inquired, sipping the eye-opening coffee from the Styrofoam cup.

She handed me a can of Pledge and a soft rag and pointed to the back wall where my sideboard and trunk dominated, wedged between a delicate vanity and a rather rickety coffee table.

I crossed the freshly waxed linoleum floor, gingerly balancing the cup and cleaning supplies.

We'd done a cursory cleaning at the house, but the brass on the trunk and handles on the sideboard needed polishing; the sideboard, having only been wiped with a wet rag, needed a good wood polish applied to it.

I set about shining up the sideboard. Its dark oak gleamed under my administrations. It was beautiful! I almost wished I'd kept it for myself. I returned to Irmaline and got some window cleaner for the glass display case, which still needed to be attached. After a half hour or so, it was ready. I decided to put my dishes inside to make it complete. I'd have to ask Irmaline about pricing it, as I didn't have a clue what it might be worth.

I turned to the trunk. It was quite large and had brass bands crossing from back to front, ending in metal clasps with slots in them that closed over two brass vertical rings so that padlocks could be inserted. The brass was dull with age. The trunk itself was wooden and chipped in some places. We probably wouldn't get much for it. I was kind of ashamed for even bringing it. It wasn't even a regulation army trunk, just something Al had picked up at a garage sale to keep his memories in.

I went in the kitchen in search of brass cleaner, exchanging pleasantries with a rather rotund woman baking and washing dishes for the coming Bazaar. She dug a can out from under the sink for me and I waved my rag at her in parting.

I knelt before the trunk and lovingly began to buff the tarnished brass. It shone like new with a little bit of "elbow grease", and I was quite proud of the results. I then proceeded to apply the Pledge to the ancient wood, not expecting much. It shined up quite nicely, though, and I thought it would pass as a salable item. The inside, I knew, would be a different story. From the glimpse I'd gotten of it yesterday, as I'd packed it with dishes, I didn't have much hope of rectifying it. It had had some kind of cloth lining that was stained and discolored. With trepidation, I grasped the handles and flung it open. My trepidation turned to horror as the grisly contents were exposed. A sickly, sweet smell engulfed me, causing me to gag.

My hand flew to my face as I stared, dumbfounded, at a body curled in the fetal position, blonde hair in disarrayed tendrils covering its face. Despite the concealing cascade, I knew immediately it was Vicky. When my brain finally accepted what I was seeing, I turned away and threw up on the freshly waxed linoleum floor.

Chaos ensued. Irmaline was immediately at my side, surrounded by several screaming women. Someone finally pulled it together enough to call 911, while Irmaline and the portly woman from the kitchen hustled us all upstairs and seated us in pews while we waited for the authorities. All the women were praying as I hung my head and cried.

It was the second dead body I'd been unfortunate enough to find in as many months.

My sanity was hanging by a thread. I was afraid I might start gibbering and foaming at the mouth any minute. The only thing that held me to reality was the remembrance of the looks I'd gotten from the Sheriff and various townspeople (especially Barney). I knew the word about my questioned mental state was all over town, distorted and blown all out of proportion like a child's game of telephone.

By the time the Sheriff arrived, some semblance of peace had been restored. He sent a couple of Deputies around with paper and pad and took individual statements from everyone right there in the Church.

The one who interviewed me I recognized from my forays into town. I'd seen him, with family in tow, in the grocery store on a couple of occasions and I also recalled him at the lake the day of the town fair.

He was a stolid type, and quite professional. He was around 40 with hair graying at the temples, a slim build, and most importantly, despite his impassiveness, kind eyes.

I answered everything to the best of my recollection and came to realize through his persistence that I had probably destroyed crucial evidence with my frenetic cleaning of the trunk.

At last we were allowed to go, with assurances that we'd be kept abreast of things and perhaps sought out again for further questioning, as sometimes people remembered things after the fact. I was sure I would be one of the ones further questioned.

I saw a few of the women watching me out of the sides of their eyes as I exited the church; their glances quickly darting away as they noticed me noticing.

Irmaline wanted to follow me home but I insisted she didn't. All I wanted was to be alone to lick my wounds, even though they were only emotional.

Oh my God! I thought, as I drove the lonely road home. Amos! What would he think? What would he do when he found out about Vicky? Even more frightening was the next thought that entered my mind: What if he already knew?

Sam greeted me with his usual exuberance, barking and jumping all over me. Judas even left her observation perch at the window and rubbed against my leg, mewing. I hurriedly fed them and stoked the fire, staring into the burgeoning flames as if an answer may be found there.

I curled on the couch, worrying my bottom lip in concentration. I knew the trunk had been full of dishes when Amos had loaded it up. Had he stopped somewhere along the way and put her body in it, putting the dishes in boxes? How else could it get there? Did someone have access to the church? Someone who wanted her dead? I didn't know enough about Vicky or her friends to discern an answer to that question. How had she died? It might be a while before that answer was divulged, if indeed it was. The Sheriff's department may well keep that to themselves to thwart false confessions. I knew one thing: The town was going to have a field day with this, and I was sure my name would be on many lips.

The archrival. The competition over Amos, a man Vicky clearly was still interested in, as evidenced by her emergence from the woods on that crisp autumn morning. What about her soon-to-be ex? Her family had money, and there was probably a large life insurance policy. He had the most to gain by her death, I thought. The town was rural and small, but with the influx of hunters it wouldn't be that hard to sneak into town. It was cold, so ski masks were a common sight. No one would give a second look to someone dressed in hunting gear. Well, I told myself, quit dwelling on it. It's a police matter and I was sure they were asking the very same questions.

Irmaline called that afternoon, sounding disturbed, but not frightened. The same thoughts and hypotheses' had been running through her mind, but we ended the conversation on the same note: Leave it to the police.

I spent the rest of the day frantically cleaning, trying to keep my mind off the horrendous course of events. In the evening I put Sam out on his rope and sat on the porch, disregarding the danger any hunters may pose. Their presence now seemed, at most, a minor inconvenience.

The sun was slowly descending beyond the trees across the channel, casting a beautiful orange glow across it. My lights added to the illusion of unreality with their holiday festiveness.

Amos came striding across the lightly frosted grass around six o'clock; the now thickening darkness adding a spookiness to his visage, emerging from the blackness. He sat in his usual spot, saying nothing, and seemingly deep in thought. I, too, was at a loss for words and sat silently.

"Do you want to come in?" I asked at last. "I'm cold."

He rose, still not speaking, as I called Sam and unhooked him from his tether.

The fire was crackling as we entered and the smell of wood smoke filled the room.

He sat in the wing chair and I settled in my usual position on the couch, across from him.

We both stared at the fire lost in our own thoughts. Once in a while I'd steal a glance at him, but his demeanor was inscrutable.

"Did you still love her?" I finally dared venture.

His head jerked up, startled out of his reverie.

"Of course not. That was over a long time ago." He finally answered.

We both went back to staring at the now dying embers. At length I got up and threw more wood on, stirring it with the andiron. Judas came and parked herself in front of it, daintily licking her soft fur, apparently oblivious to the depressing emotions dominating the room.

Sam was curled on the couch waiting for his mistress to take up her vacated spot once again.

"So, who told you?" I asked, returning to my vacated spot.

He snorted contemptuously before answering.

"I was in town after sitting in the deer stand for hours, and noticed everyone looking at me strangely, and the next thing I knew, there's Jim!" His eyebrows climbed his forehead in an exclamation of surprise.

"He asked me to come down to the Sheriff's Department and informed me there."

"It must have been quite a shock!" I ventured, watching his reaction. Was I conversing with a murderer? He obviously had no alibi.

"I spent the next several hours down there being interrogated, and now, it seems, I'm the main suspect." Disbelief was evident in his voice, and I thought he might be in shock.

"I can't believe she's dead!" He said, almost whispering, and I actually saw tears forming at the corner of his eyes.

"I know she was a pain in the ass, and arrogant, and spoiled as hell, but she certainly didn't deserve that!" His hands were kneading his wild beard, (even wilder since hunting season and his time in the woods) as if he didn't quite know what to do with them.

My heart went out to him and I didn't want to believe he was a murderer, but could I bet my life on it?

"Did he say how she was killed?" I asked, softly.

"No. They're not releasing that information, at least not yet. And the worst part was, her parents came down there while I was there. They were screaming and crying and pointing accusing fingers at me. They never thought I was god enough or rich enough for their little girl, and even though she was the one who cuckolded me, it was always my fault that she wasn't happy. Nothing I ever did was good enough for them. And now they're accusing me of being a murderer. Christ! If I was going to kill her, wouldn't I have done it way back then?"

He had a point there. Why would he wait all these years? What possible motive would he have? Then again, I had seen her coming out of the woods that morning. He said he hadn't seen her, but how did I know that? Either way, whether he or someone else had done it, there was no question now that there was a killer in our midst.

I noticed myself unconsciously reaching for my shirt beside me on the couch, seeking solace in the gun. Sam whined as I pulled the shirt from beneath him. I put it around my shoulders, feeling for the gun in the pocket, for suddenly the room seemed as cold as the grave.

I sent Amos away shortly thereafter, yawning and feigning exhaustion. I needed to be alone to think. I assumed he was still staying in his tent, as he hadn't gotten a deer yet.

The next morning the story had broken. The news was statewide thus far and I had the feeling it had the potential to go nationwide. "The Beauty In The Trunk", it was dubbed in the local news; I was sure much worse headlines would follow. A picture of Vicky in a pink angora sweater, blonde hair a halo around her pixie face, was juxtaposed across a picture of her in death: Taken surreptitiously, no doubt, by some morgue attendant.

Then, the phone calls began. I learned after the first couple not to answer, and eventually turned the ringer off. My name had been mentioned as the donator of the trunk and reporters had responded. A few diligent ones had even managed to get my address and somehow find my place, even though it's just a rural route address. They were camped on my lawn, though I refused to answer their persistent knocks. How I was going to take Sam out was now my major concern. I had half a mind to pull my gun on them and order them off my property, only the thought of my picture flashing across the t.v. screen kept me in check.

We were still in the dark as to the manner of Vicky's demise, but I found solace in the fact that my gun hadn't been out of my possession.

Irmaline had been badgered, too. She had given one brief interview to the local paper and thereafter had refused to comment. She, too, was now in seclusion.

The only saving grace was that with all the publicity I didn't have to live in fear, for no one would dare come after me with reporters lurking around.

I waited until dark, after they'd all left, to put Sam on his leash. By then he was in extreme discomfort and let me know it with his constant yips and mournful looks.

I saw my house on the news that night, along with a commentary about how I'd refused to answer the door or phone. My solitary existence was all but a memory, and when at last I turned the phone back on, I jumped when it dared to ring. It was only Irmaline, calling to trade media information and town gossip. It seemed some townsfolk were sure Amos was the guilty party; while others were just as adamant that it was me.

Eventually Vicky's body was released to her family, although the authorities were still close-mouthed about what was found in the autopsy. She had been fully clothed when found, as I could attest to, but that didn't rule out sexual assault. The lack of pertinent information was frustrating, but I assumed the Sheriff knew what he was doing, though I doubted he'd ever had a case quite like this.

I hadn't seen Amos in several days and wondered if he was holed up in the woods or had decided to go back to work and get away for a while. After all, they had no evidence to hold him, as far as I knew.

The sky was as black as my mood the next morning. Thunderheads were hanging in the sky like sodden sponges just waiting to release their burgeoning loads. My Christmas lights exuded a false sense of gaiety as their colors danced across the frosted ground.

The channel had partially frozen over and black water gushed between the gathering ice formations. I kept my fire going, struggling to keep out the cold winds coming from the northeast.

I knew Vicky's funeral was the next day, and wondered if Amos was going or if he was miles away. I knew Irmaline wasn't. She'd never cared for Vicky, and the one thing I knew for sure about her was that she wasn't a hypocrite. The media hype had died down to a trickle as no new information was forthcoming, and new, even more bizarre cases were unfolding throughout the state.

The church sale had been postponed indefinitely as no one was anxious to return to the basement. The reporters and investigators were the only ones who ventured there.

I called Irmaline that day and asked her to accompany me into town as my food supply was dwindling. I dreaded that excursion, and refused to go alone. We agreed to meet at the parking lot in an hour. I kept looking behind me as I drove in; paranoia my constant companion. There was a murderer loose in our quiet town and it could be anyone. Sam was with me, of course. He was my constant companion, as I needed his eyes and ears; I also treasured his company and devotion. My gun was also an ever-present friend in those dark times.

I waited in the car until I heard Irmalines beater approaching. She pulled up next to me in the nearly empty lot. Her camelhair coat had it's collar pulled up, as if to hide her from a world that was ever more frightening. When she stepped from her car I saw the worry wrinkles around her eyes and mouth, and was shocked at how much she had seemed to age in the past week.

"Hi Annie." She said, and all the usual exuberance seemed to be gone from her demeanor. Her shoulders sagged under her coat and she seemed to have shrunk to an even more diminutive size.

"How're you holding up?" I ventured, suddenly afraid for my only friend.

"I'm alright." She said. "I just haven't been sleeping well lately, what with the reporters and the phone ringing off the hook." Her usual twinkling blue eyes seemed lifeless, scaring me further.

I cracked my window and locked my car door, leaving Sam

whining dejectedly in the front seat.

"Let's get this over with." Irmaline intoned, and I realized she was dreading this foray as much as I was.

Warm air rushed over us as the automatic doors opened. I grabbed a cart and told Irmaline we could share it. The few townspeople that were present were already staring and whispering as we started down the first aisle. The usual friendly banter that greeted Irmaline wherever she went was noticeably absent and I felt that my friendship was the cause.

We silently went about our business, ignoring the questioning and downright dirty looks.

At the checkout counter the gum-snapping teenage girl gaped openly at me, as if Ted Bundy had sidled up to her counter. I held my ground and refused to turn away from her rude stare. After all, I had done nothing, and I wasn't about to let town gossip rule my comings and goings.

Irmaline's portly friend from the church basement was entering as we were leaving, and embraced Irmaline in a big hug that I was certain would snap her frail spine. I was glad to see that she, too, had a faithful friend. I was certain that she had many, which was more than I could say. I was the outsider, never mind that I'd lived here for years. I had to admit, it was my own fault for being so reclusive; but that was my nature.

# CHAPTER THIRTEEN

When I got home the skies had opened up and big, fluffy flakes of snow were falling. I nearly slipped on the accumulating wetness as I grabbed four bags of groceries from the trunk and started toward the house. Sam was nipping at my heels, excited because I had food. After I'd finally managed to get everything on the kitchen counters, I looked around, perplexed. I had the strangest feeling that someone had been in my house. Sam was snuffling around the carpet, running from the door to the bedroom and back, nose down.

I left my groceries still in their bags and crept silently down the hall to the bedroom. I pulled my gun out of my pocket and held it out in front of me like a protecting beacon.

I rushed the bedroom like a raiding narcotics officer, swinging around, gun in front of me, covering every corner of the room. Nothing. All was just as I had left it; yet I still couldn't shake the feeling of another presence. I searched every room and closet in the house before I finally returned to my groceries and started putting them away. I fed Sam and Judas, who by now was rubbing against my legs in anticipation. I sniffed the stagnate air of the closed up house and thought I detected a faint smell of men's cologne.

It smelled like Al's cologne; or his brand, anyway. I must be losing my mind, I thought.

I seemed to be seeing, hearing, and now smelling ghosts everywhere of late. Vicky's murder really had me spooked and I was tempted to ring the gong for Amos. Instead I curled up on the couch and called Irmaline. Her phone rang and rang, making me feel even more isolated. She probably had the ringer turned off because of the press, I reasoned. I got my fire stoked to a roaring inferno and turned on the t.v., more to keep me company than for entertainment.

Where was Amos? I wondered.

A knock at the door woke me from where I had fallen asleep on the couch. It was Amos.

It seems he had been back down at the Sheriff's office, answering questions. He had taken a polygraph, with inconclusive results. I wondered if they'd next be asking me to take one. I was sure I'd fare no better than him if they did. I was a nervous wreck. His inconclusive results added to my uneasiness about him. If only he'd passed, I thought, then my mind would have once and for all been at rest. It seemed I was to get no surcease from my anxiety.

I didn't tell him about my intuition that someone had been in my house. I was starting to doubt my own feelings, although Sam seemed to verify my thoughts. I spent all too much time with my pets and not enough with human society. Sam and Judas were my best friends, and for good reason; I could trust them.

Amos slept on my couch that night and I locked my bedroom door, keeping my gun within arms reach on the night table. Terrifying, disjointed dreams kept me tossing and turning all night, disturbing my pets sleep as well as my own.

I didn't have a lot of money but I began thinking maybe I

should get away for a while.

I really had no place to go, though, and anxiety at home seemed better than anxiety in a strange place. And what about my pets? No. I would stick it out. This was my home and my stubbornness wouldn't allow someone to run me off.

The next morning I made breakfast with a side of small talk. I didn't want to talk about Vicky or the strange twists of fate now plaguing not only me, but also our peaceful little town.

Amos seemed to feel the same and remained even more reticent than usual.

Irmaline called later that morning and I filled her in on Amos' polygraph, not mentioning my feelings of intrusion after I'd returned home from the store. She had had her phone off the hook and I got the impression that Barney had been trying to warn her away from me, as if I were somehow responsible for the events of late. His affiliation with the DNR seemed to make him feel like he had an inside track to what was going on in the investigation. I took this for what it was, a little man trying to make himself seem important. He acted like Vicky had been a close friend, when I knew from Irmaline that this was not the case. She'd been way out of his league and often made fun of him behind his back, and had since high school.

Amos left shortly before noon to check on his camp. Then, I gathered, he planned on going home to see if he had any runs coming up. I guess he needed to distance himself for a while, although he was still planning on staying until the end of hunting season, or until he got a deer, though his heart didn't really seem to be in it anymore.

A couple uneventful days later, Amos came back and informed me he'd gotten his deer.

A medium sized buck, eight points. He'd gutted it and taken it to the meat market in town for butchering. As it was hunting season, it would be a week or so until he got the meat and when he did, he'd bring me some venison. He was cleaning up his camp and planning on making a short run the next day. He'd be gone five days or so. He wasn't worried about me, he said, as the Sheriff was going to be keeping an eye on my place, and deputies (some just sworn in) were all over the town, watching everyone. With such a gruesome crime weighing heavily on everyone it was speculated that the perpetrator was either lying low or long gone.

I couldn't help but wonder if Vicky had some how found out about whatever scheme was afoot and been killed because of it. Maybe ignorance was bliss and I should quit playing sleuth and get on with my so-called life.

Irmaline informed me that the Bazaar was scheduled for the following week (sans my trunk, of course) and the whole town was anxious to put this all behind them and get on with things, though the loss of their star resident weighed heavily on everyone. Suspicions made me think it was going to be hard for everyone to go on as usual. I just hoped I wouldn't have to deal with the whisperings and dirty looks that seemed to follow me every time I ventured into town. Irmaline seemed to be back to her old indefatigable self and reminded me that I had been the one who had the shock of finding the body, as if someone had planned it that way to further intimidate me. I thanked God daily for her unwavering friendship.

Vicky's funeral had been the previous day and the local news (and a few dogged outside news services) had had a field day. Her grieving family had been filmed through the whole service and followed to the gravesite. Her father had given an interview, tears streaming down his face. He'd said a private investigator had been brought in, as the town police were an inept bunch. A $250,000 reward had been offered for any information leading to the arrest and conviction of the perpetrator.

The police were still being close-mouthed as to the manner of her demise and wild speculation was rampant in our small community. For a town that wanted to put the past behind them, it seemed strange that no one was willing to let go; but having a murderer in our midst had spun a web of paranoia through the fabric of normalcy.

The Sheriff came the next day and asked me to come down to the station and bring my gun. Imagine my chagrin when it was nowhere to be found! My face was flaming when I had to inform the Sheriff and the worst part was, I'd been in possession of it after Vicky's murder! The last I remember having it was when Amos spent the night on my couch. I thought sure I'd put it in my bed table, but it was no longer there. I didn't want to implicate Amos, but what was I to do? I told the Sheriff the truth, though the look on his face was one of skepticism.

At the station I was informed that Vicky had been shot (I'd heard this rumor just this morning from Irmaline, thanks to Barneys' unwavering nosiness) but no bullet was found as it had been a through and through. They believed the weapon was the same caliber as mine, but they had no proof. I had seen no blood in the trunk, though there may have been some under the body, but it seems she had bleed out before being placed there.

I was administered a paraffin test for gunshot residue, though it had been so long it would no longer be detectable even if it was there at one time.

After a few hours of questioning I was allowed to leave, after filling out a report on my missing gun. Now I had no protection, but when I informed the Sheriff of this, he practically snorted! It was obvious that I was now the number one suspect, with Amos a close second. No one had access to my house, and if my gun was the murder weapon wouldn't it have disappeared before the murder and then have been surreptitiously returned after, to further implicate me? I expostulated all this to the Sheriff but it seemed to fall on deaf ears. To me, it said that my gun wasn't the murder weapon or it would have been returned to my possession, or left at the scene. Why take it after?

The Sheriff was also looking for Amos, not wanting to wait until he returned with this new evidence now in his possession.

When I got home I threw myself on my bed and cried. When the townspeople got wind of this latest development I'd be even more of a pariah.

The Sheriff called the next morning asking if I'd come down for a lie detector test. I called Irmaline and asked her to accompany me. My knees were shaking as I entered the Sheriffs' office with Irmaline in tow.

The smell of lemon wax, smoke and some indefinable sweaty odor permeated the stuffy atmosphere. It was one large room set up with individual cubicles placed seemingly willy-nilly throughout. The noise level was high, with conversation, FAX machines, computer printouts and occasional raucous bursts of laughter hanging heavy in the air.

The few recently hired Deputies who had no cubicles were milling around trying to look busy. They all turned to stare as I approached the receptionist's desk. Word travels fast in a small town, and suddenly I seemed to be the star attraction.

Irmaline settled on an uncomfortable looking wooden bench, mesmerized by all the activity in her usually quiet town. If she had an misgivings about being in my company she didn't show it. For that I was grateful.

The Sheriff met me personally, and immediately led me back to an inner room with one large window (two-way glass, I assumed). The polygraph technician, who was obviously a big-city import, quickly had me hooked up and began his questioning, all in a "yes" or "no" format.

Irmaline and me sat waiting patiently on the hard bench as my answers were analyzed.

I was shaking, and sweat slicked the palms of my hands. I wiped them unceremoniously on my jeans as the Sheriff approached, the Tech trailing behind him with a sheaf of papers in his hands.

"Your results were inconclusive" the Sheriff said as every ear in the room strained to hear.

"Now what happens?" Irmaline chirped before I had a chance to even process the information.

"Nothing." The Sheriff responded. "You're free to go now."

His demeanor revealed nothing as to any thoughts he had on the subject.

I nearly ran from the room, Irmaline's voice following as I approached the door.

"Your damn right it doesn't mean anything!" She hissed. "And I suggest you quit wasting time with all this foolishness and get out there and look for the murderer! I've known you your whole life, Jim, and I know you're good at your job. So do it!"

I stood trembling on the steps waiting for Irmaline to finish her outburst and come out.

Irmaline wanted me to stay in town and go window-shopping with her, and maybe have lunch. She knew I would just want to go home and hide and lick my wounds. The test seemed to have a way of making one feel guilty despite being innocent, and with the inconclusive results I knew the rumor mill would be spitting out fodder.

Irmaline camped on my couch that night. I made popcorn and we watched an old movie on television. She was worried about Amos and by the fact that I no longer had any viable means of protection. She tried to talk me into buying another gun, but with the state waiting period I didn't see much sense. By the time I got it I'd probably no longer need it.

We discussed the upcoming Bazaar (I didn't plan on going) and I finally dragged myself to bed around midnight.

When I awoke the next morning, around seven, I heard voices in the dining room. I quickly dressed and hurried out. Amos was seated at the table across from Irmaline, a steaming mug of coffee cupped in his giant hands. The smell of bacon filled the house, causing my pets to attack me in a feeding frenzy. After I'd fed them I joined my guests at the table. Amos' hair stuck up in cowlicks as if he'd just crawled out of his truck and I had to stifle a laugh.

"How was your trip?" I inquired as I jumped up to check the bacon.

"It was good to get away from all the tension for a while." He said. "Although I was rather worried about what was happening back here. Get away from that stove! I'm cooking this morning." With that, he jumped up and grabbed the spatula from my hand, shooing me back to my seat at the table.

I gratefully acquiesced, giving Irmaline a weak smile as I sipped my coffee.

"I was just filling Amos in on our little excursion yesterday." She informed me, glancing at Amos.

"Well, I guess you and I are the main suspects now, Amos." I replied. "My gun's disappeared, making me look guilty."

He filled three plates with bacon and eggs and placed them before us.

"And the thought crossed your mind that I may have taken it." He said matter-of-factly as he joined us at the table.

"Well," I answered, "That was the last time I saw it. That night you were here." I quickly shoveled a mouthful of eggs into my mouth, watching him from beneath my mussed up hair.

"For the record, I didn't take it. As you well know, I have plenty of firepower." He replied. "I can loan you one of my guns if you like."

I glanced at Irmaline, knowing this had been her idea.

"Maybe" I said, around a mouthful of bacon. "Maybe I should put up some surveillance cameras around here." I thought aloud.

"That may not be a bad idea." Amos said. "I could do it for you. They're motion sensitive so you'll get a lot of wildlife shots, if nothing else. Which may put your mind at ease. After all, a hungry bear is preferable to a murderer."

Irmaline chuckled at this, as she sipped noisily from her steaming cup.

I rose and put Sam on his leash. Judas managed to squeeze out before the door closed.

I waved abstractedly at her retreating form.

Irmaline and I decided to go into the next town for equipment, later. Our town was too small to have what we needed. Amos wrote down everything we'd need as Irmaline and me were totally in the dark about anything that technical.

They left shortly there after. Amos to get some much needed sleep, Irmaline to clean up and change so we could get going. I soaked in the tub for a half hour, than got ready.

Halfway to the next town the skies opened up, spewing flakes as large as grandma's doilies. I knew now that it had started I wouldn't see the grass again until spring, and it depressed me tremendously. The car swerved on the snow slicked road and the windshield wipers worked overtime trying to keep a clear observation patch open on the now snow-covered window.

Three hours later, we pulled back into my yard. Irmalines car sat under a blanket of snow, allowing us to see the full extent of the storm. We went in laden with our purchases, both leaning into the wind, trying to keep our balance as we plodded through the blowing drifts.

Sam immediately wanted out, as he always did after the first measurable snowfall. I indulged him, my fingers numb with cold by the time I had him tied out. Judas was content to sit in front of the now cold fireplace, beseeching me with her yellow eyes to start a fire.

I struggled back out to get wood, searching the carpet of

white for any signs of trespassers. As much as I despised winter it would work to my advantage now.

After the fire was going, Irmaline and I sat on the couch exclaiming over my purchases.

I felt like I was finally coming into the 21st century. Now if they could get that cell-phone tower up, I'd feel down right Jetsonish!

Thanksgiving was right around the corner and Irmaline thought I should invite Amos. Of course she had invited me to her house, but there was no way I was breaking bread with Barney! Amos was coming over later to decide where to put my surveillance equipment.

I was as excited as a kid on Christmas at the thought of having cameras watching my property. I was hoping to get some great wildlife shots and wanted one pointed at my bird feeders.

Amos arrived after Irmaline had left, and immediately set to work. I had two cameras for him to set up, and he wanted the whole yard covered. Evidently, they ran in a loop and would tape over themselves after the film ran out, so if I saw any tracks in the snow or suspicious activity, I would have to check them before the tape started over. Seeing as cable wasn't yet available in our rural community I had to go with old-fashioned store surveillance cameras, but that was o.k., since I probably wouldn't be able to operate anything more technologically advanced.

Amos put one in the big front window, concealed from outside view by my curtains. He wanted them inside so no one could tamper with them, and also so I wouldn't have to go out in the cold and dick with them. The second was aimed out my bedroom window into the back yard. It was also pointed at the edge of the tree line so anyone coming out of the woods would be visible.

After he had showed me how to work them we sat at the kitchen table, drinking coffee.

I broached the subject of Thanksgiving.

"If you're offering me a free meal, I'm here!" He quipped.

He left shortly thereafter to go to the Sheriff's office, upon learning that the Sheriff wanted to see him.

I sat watching out the window as the snow continued to fall. The woods looked like a fairyland with its frost covered trees. The sun reflected brightly off the now frozen channel, blindingly bright.

The voice returned that night, permeating its way into my dreams. A ghostly echo of my dear, dead husband. In the morning I didn't know if I'd dreamed it or heard a loving ghost, trying to tell me something. I drank coffee, staring at the still unbroken crust of snow, grateful that the only prints visible were clearly bird and animal.

I had to struggle through three feet of snow to get wood, deploring the trail my prints left in the pristine blanket of snow. I noticed that the coons had been in my garbage again. I usually tied it shut, particularly in the winter, when most of the vandalism took place. Their almost human looking prints surrounded the cans. The covers were thrown back and garbage was strung willy-nilly, making my footprint mess pale by comparison. I hastily cleaned it up as best I could, and tied the lids shut with the twine I kept at hand for just that purpose.

I tied Sam out on his rope and watched as he rolled happily in the snow. Judas didn't like going out much in the cold and only stayed long enough to relieve herself. When she wanted in she'd sit on the table on the porch, looking longingly at me through the window.

My sense of security had been greatly buoyed by the addition of the cameras. I almost hoped something would happen so I could show the Sheriff the proof, and dispel any doubts as to my sanity.

I decided to do some heavy duty cleaning and wash clothes. The morning flew as I threw myself into the tasks, stopping only to let Sam in when I heard his barking at the door.

My lights were still lit; the ones that hadn't burnt out, anyway. They looked quite shoddy now. The storm had knocked the strings loose in places and they hung here and there, casting brightly colored reflections across the yard. I was glad I had no close neighbors to complain, as I knew they surely would.

# CHAPTER FOURTEEN

The skies opened up again that afternoon. Large, fluffy flakes descended from the heavens like God throwing confetti. Sam was jumping towards the sky with wide-open mouth, catching the falling whiteness with a look of ecstasy on his face.

I sat at the window and watched, my mind wandering. Ever since Al's death I'd been more aware of my own mortality and wondered abstractly if this would be my last winter.

Amos called to check on me around six. He'd talked to the Sheriff, but of course, nothing had been resolved and no new clues were forthcoming.

Vicky's parents were evidently becoming permanent fixtures at the Sheriff's office and had created quite a scene when Amos had appeared. They'd had to be escorted out by the Deputies, hurling derogatory epithets at Amos over their retreating shoulders. I got the impression that Amos wanted to leave on another run as soon as possible to get away from everything, but was worried about leaving me. I tried to assuage his fears by reminding him that I now had silent witnesses in my cameras. We hung up with his misgivings still unresolved.

I called Irmaline shortly thereafter to tell her about Vicky's parents' untoward actions at the Sheriff's office. She was in the middle of working on the Church Bazaar and, once again, tried to talk me into going. It was only a few days away and, God knew, the town needed a diversion. I humbly declined. Wild horses couldn't drag me to that thing!

As I lay in bed that night, listening to the wind howling through the trees, I felt utterly and entirely alone. That surreal time between wakefulness and sleep distorting reality until I wasn't sure which side I was on. Judas lay purring in my hair and Sam kept my feet warm as I slowly drifted into total unconsciousness.

In the morning I couldn't quite drag myself out of bed and decided to get back to my long neglected book. I reached over to the bedside table and opened the drawer where I kept it.

Lo and behold, my missing gun was in its usual place, lying partially over my book! In a near panic I flew from the bed and ran to the windows of each room searching the, by now, window high snow for evidence of an intruder. It was still snowing! I ran to the living room camera and hastily yanked the tape out of it, dropping it in the process. With trembling hands, I slid it into my VCR, my heart trip-hammering in my chest. My yard appeared, though the blowing snow made me crouch close to see. My yard light cast light nearly to the road, so darkness wasn't too much of a problem. I certainly couldn't afford the night vision cameras, and I'd known that my front yard was well lighted.

Nothing! There was nothing on there! I hastily pulled out the tape and ran to retrieve the one in back.

This one was much harder to discern. I only had a bare bulb protruding from the side of the house back there and I probably should have put a stronger bulb in, but didn't think of it at the time.

As I watched the silent snow on the screen, mirroring the scene out the window, I thought I detected movement. My heart jumped in my chest at the unexpectedness of it. I bent closer, my nose nearly touching the screen. There! I rewound for ten seconds and watched again. A shadow was clearly visible on the unbroken snow. As I stared, spellbound, the shadow grew larger, only it appeared to be coming from above.

Then, in the blink of an eye, I saw what had scared the hell out of me; a Great Horned Owl swooped down on silent wings, picking something out of my sight from beneath the snow. It was gone as quickly and silently as it had appeared.

For the next two hours I sat straining my eyes, fast-forwarding and rewinding until I'd been through both tapes. I put a new tape in one camera, as I wanted to save the owl image, and returned the other to the backyard camera.

I went into the bedroom and retrieved the gun, carrying it wrapped in a dishtowel. I was sure my prints were still on it, but perhaps someone else's' were, too. Then, in a paranoid frenzy, I wiped the whole thing clean. I had no intention of turning it in or even telling anyone I was once again in possession of it. Perhaps I was breaking the law, but someone was trying to frame me and I wasn't going down for murder! All of a sudden I was afraid that the Sheriff may be getting a search warrant for my place and knew I must find a good hiding place for it. I couldn't just throw it, for my fear was such that I felt I may need it and wanted the option of having it. If it should work out that I did and I used it against the perpetrator, then it would be a moot point.

I wandered from room to room, gun clutched tightly in my hand, searching for an obscure spot to stash it. The perfect spot came to me suddenly. Behind the headboard of my bed was a place between the original logs. I didn't believe it would be big enough, but figured I could hollow it out. I ran to the bedroom and with great effort pushed the bed aside enough to look back there. Yes. There it was. It had been one of the reasons we'd positioned the bed where we did. I stood on the bed and bent over the headboard, digging with my fingers into the softness between the logs. I ran to the kitchen and returned with a hammer. I used the claw part to scrape away at the rotting grout (or whatever it was). When it was large enough, I stashed the gun in there. I got a brown shirt of Al's and covered it from the outside. I then swept up the mess and pushed the bed back in place.

It may not be that easy to get at if I needed it, but I'd worry about that if and when the time came. I breathed a sigh of relief. I didn't plan on telling anyone about this. It would be me and Al's little secret.

The rest of the day was spent doing mundane tasks. Vacuuming, scrubbing floors, and, my personal favorite, cleaning the bathroom!

Amos and Irmaline both called later in the day to check on me, and I related the story of the owl. I dared not tell any one about the discovery of the gun, for nothing had shown up on the tapes and the falling snow had covered any tracks that may have been there. Even to myself I looked guilty, with no one visible on the tape. How much could I expect anyone to believe?

That night I was once again plagued by eerie dreams and I tossed and turned, waking up several times, displacing my snoozing pets. In my disjointed dreams, I heard Al calling my name over and over. I tried to yell out to him but was totally mute. I was then running through sun-dappled woods, fear of some unknown pursuer spurring me on. As I looked back to see what was chasing me, I tripped and went down, landing on something soft.

I looked down quickly and was stunned to Al's face in a rictus of death. It was then I woke up, a scream stuck in my closed up throat.

Gazing at the clock after the initial shock wore off; I saw

it was 3:00 a.m. I lay in the dark, listening to the silence of solitude; that that I had once cherished was now my worst nightmare and I suddenly wished that I lived in New York City or some other large metropolitan area; somewhere I could lose myself in a sea of faceless humanity.

After a couple more hours of restless wakefulness, I gave up the fight for any more sleep and dragged myself out of bed.

Sam ran to meet me as I entered the kitchen, whining for breakfast. I called Judas as I fed Sam, getting a can of cat food out of the refrigerator. She didn't come. I felt the hairs at the back of my neck rise. Judas had never been late for a meal, ever. Panic rising bile ate at the back of my throat as I ran through the house, calling for Judas. Looking in  every corner.

By now, Sam was at my side. Looking at me and whining, his tail unsure of whether to wag or not. I knelt beside him and took his head in my hands.

"Where's Judas, Sam? Where is she, boy?"

He licked my face and snuffled deep in his chest, sensing my panic.

Suddenly, he looked behind him and barked. He ran from the room, me right at his heels.

As we reached the bedroom door I heard it, too; faint mewling, distant and hollow.

Sam ran straight to the middle of "The Golden Hind", our old, now well-worn rug.

He smelled a couple of times, then laid back his head and howled. I quickly flipped the rug back, wondering what the hell I was doing as no lump was visible beneath it.

There, in the center of the floor, was a wooden door, its hinges old and rusted.

Right then I heard it loud and clear. Judas was down there! I pulled the ring attached to one side of the door and pulled. I fell backwards, the door slamming open and nearly hitting me on my way down. I had pulled hard and the door, rusty hinges and all, flew open without so much as a sound. I started down the small wooden staircase; it, too, looked as if it were in good shape.

Snippets of a long ago conversation floated into my mind. Years before, when Al had first brought me here, he and his dad were talking on the porch as I was frolicking in the yard with his dads' dog: a door leading from the cellar! I had never seen it and the conversation soon evaporated from my consciousness. I had to go back and get a flashlight before I continued my search. Just as I was pulling one from beneath a pile of junk in the junk drawer, Judas was by my side, crying to be fed and seemingly none the worse for her adventure. First things first, I fed her to keep her from dogging my heels and possibly precipitating a headlong fall down the stairs.

I grabbed the flashlight and returned to the bedroom. I listened at the top of the stairs, wondering if I should dig my gun out before I entered the darkness. I decided I didn't need it and slowly wended my way down the narrow stairwell, which was completely concealed from the rest of the basement by towers of boxes and broken furniture. I pulled the chain that hung in the middle of the room. The switch was by the outside door, but the chain preceded its installation and I was glad it hadn't been removed.

Everything seemed to be as it was when we'd been down there to find stuff for the Bazaar. The cold permeated my bones as the wind whipped around the outer door.

Wisps of snow blew through cracks in the ancient wood and swirls of it danced across the earthen floor, like dust devils before the wind. I swung the flashlight too and fro, looking for any signs of intrusion. I crossed the crowded room and went up the outside steps to check the outer door. It was locked from the outside, as I'd left it. I knew I would now have to fight my way through the amassing snow and check it from the outside. I would also have to rig up some kind of inside lock or nail it shut from the inside.

So, I wasn't crazy after all! Should I call the Sheriff again? Or would he once again attribute it to my over active imagination? Should I tell Amos to gage his reaction?

After all, my gun appeared after he'd been over; he also may have somehow known about the other entrance. I tried to remember if he'd been alone down here and maybe stumbled upon it. Sam was now at the top of the steps leading to my bedroom, whining and barking for me to come back upstairs. Not being as agile as Judas, he was unable to come down the steep ladder steps that passed for stairs.

For now, I would just nail the trapdoor in my room shut. Maybe I'd hear the next time someone tried to open it and found they couldn't.

I returned upstairs and hurriedly found hammer and nails and set about closing off this means of access. I breathed a sigh of relief as I threw "The Golden Hind" back in position.

I decided I had to tell someone, and the only one I trusted was Irmaline. Unfortunately, she trusted Amos. I would have to swear her to secrecy and see how things played out.

The snow finally stopped around noon. It lay like a pristine white blanket, snuggling up to the house and nearly obscuring it from the outside world. Judas had to find a new promontory to see out the half covered window and had opted for the fireplace mantle, gaining access from the closest wing chair.

My friends the birds and squirrels (who came and went sporadically all winter, arousing themselves from hibernation to periodically eat) were digging in the feeders, covering themselves in a white mist as they frenetically searched for something edible.

I knew I would not only have to shovel out my car, but also my means of entry. I was pretty much snowed in until then. The road leading to my house was always one of the last the snowplow got to, so no visitors would be forthcoming. At least not ones I welcomed. Was someone lurking in the snow-covered trees, watching my house?

On the up side, tracks would now be visible, but what about around the side where my basement entrance was? I would to have move one of the cameras, or buy another to monitor it. This would be a monumental task. The eaves over the basement door were higher and I didn't know about putting a ladder out there in four feet of drifted snow. It would take hours to shovel all the way back there and why would I want to make access easier for my tormentor? Guess I could just leave the door down there unlocked and put the camera in my basement, but then he'd be in!

In a panic, I yanked all the nails I had just hammered in, out, and climbed back down the stairs, hammer and nails in hand, to make that door impenetrable. It was awkward and uncomfortable trying to stand on the narrow wooden step with my arms upraised, but I accomplished it, eventually. Now I would at least hear anyone trying to get in. It would give me time to get my gun.

I was shivering uncontrollably by the time I finally got back upstairs. I went for more nails and once again nailed this door shut, checking to make sure Judas was upstairs first.

Fifteen minutes later, I was relaxing in a hot tub when the phone rang. Cursing and dripping, I grabbed a towel and ran for it. With all the strange things going on, my imagination would drive me crazy if I didn't answer it.

It was Irmaline calling to assess the severity of my isolation. I convinced her (somewhat) that the snow was as much a blessing as a curse. For not only would tracks be visible, but someone would have to be wearing snowshoes to get to my place. I told her someone had been in my basement but omitted the gun part. Judas' being down there was proof enough. We decided to converse every few hours until bedtime. She informed me that my Christmas lights were still burning bright (the ones that still worked) and went on to describe the dazzling display they made at night on the frozen crust of top snow. I was heartened to hear that they were still visible to her. After swearing her to secrecy, and that meant law enforcement as well as Amos, I once again assured her of my safety and told her if my lights went out, then she would know I needed help.

After I hung up and climbed back in the rapidly cooling water, the full immensity of my predicament hit me. Someone had been right next to my bed as I slept! Where had Sam been? He may not have barked if it was someone known to him. Or had he been drugged, but functional by morning? Whoever it was, obviously didn't want to kill me, because I was to be their scapegoat; but what if I was somehow exonerated? Would my life be worth anything then? Would a convenient suicide once again implicate me?

And, of course, the main question: Why?

I spent the rest of the day on the couch, gazing at the frozen wasteland that would be my captor for the next several months. The beauty and tranquility of the scene would normally edify me, but a growing sense of hopelessness and dread engulfed me. It would be so easy to give in to despair and retreat into a state of despondency, but then they would win. They, being the majority of the townspeople, who had tried and convicted me with their cold shoulders and withering looks.

It would be futile to try to trudge through the snow to check the basement entrance, as the snow hadn't stopped until today. And what would indefinable footprints tell me anyway? That I wasn't crazy? It was a moot point since at least 6 inches had fallen last night and this morning, and according to the weather, more was on the way.

I was awakened the following morning by the loud sound of an engine straining against the dense snow cover. I ran to the window expecting to see the County snowplow, amazed that they'd gotten around to my lane so soon; it usually took several days after such an avalanche.

Instead I was surprised to see Amos' truck, complete with a snow plow attached to the front of it, slowly pushing mounds of snow in the ditch as he wended his way to my driveway. After several minutes of straining engine sounds, the ensuing silence came abruptly as he jumped nimbly from the cab, a mere 5 feet from my door.

Sam had been howling incessantly at the assault on his tender ears, but his yowls stopped as soon as the engine was cut. Once again silence engulfed my little world.

I watched as Amos, resplendent in full snow mobile regalia, trudged the last few feet to my door, snow shovel in hand. He dug out a short, narrow path to my door and I almost laughed as I caught a glimpse of his ice encrusted beard, mustache and eyebrows. He had the appearance of a demented Santa, and despite my ambivalent feelings, I was glad to see him. After all, if he intended me harm he wouldn't have left such an obvious trail.

I handed him a mug of hot coffee as he stomped his feet on the porch, dislodging big chunks of ice on the ancient doormat.

Judas was rubbing against my legs with the chance of freedom calling her, but quickly decided against it as one of Amos' stomps threw a flurry of snow in her face. Sam was already on the porch, jumping on Amos like he'd found his long-lost best friend.

"Gee thanks, buddy", I thought. If he murdered me, would Sam lick his hand?

Amos deposited his huge boots outside the door, balancing his coffee cup precariously as he struggled to disengage them. He handed the mug back to me and peeled his suit off.

"For God's sake, come in and do that!" I exclaimed. He acquiesced and came in, the suit hanging from his massive chest. I hung it by the fire, where the drops plopped against the hearth, making sizzling sounds.

After a trip to the bathroom to remove his snow cover, he

seated himself at the kitchen table, for all the world like a Lord returned to his manor. I didn't even mind. I was glad to see a familiar human being at that point, as I had been envisioning days, if not weeks, of entrapment.

"I didn't see any tracks leading into or out of the woods anywhere along the way. Of course the snow would have covered anything recent, but there were no tire tracks on the road so any visitors would have had to have come along before it quit snowing."

I held my tongue, nearly forgetting he could be the enemy. Was he trying to lure me into a false sense of security? Playing my knight in shining armor while conspiring behind my back? Once again, if I only knew the "why" of it all, I might have some perspective. I was drifting like a rudderless ship on a sea of confusion; and though it was early morning, I found myself longing for a good, stiff drink.

I thanked Amos profusely for plowing me out, and realized how easy it would be to trust him. A part of me, cynic that I am, just couldn't allow myself too. There was too much at stake, although I was in the dark as to what.

"Has anything new happened?" He inquired innocently. I hoped he didn't notice me jump involuntarily at the unexpectedness of the question.

"I want to move one of my cameras to cover the side yard." I said. "It's the only access to the root cellar, and I'd feel better if I could keep an eye on it."

The raising of his bushy brows made me wary of his response, but he said, only:

"I can see that. I can't believe we overlooked that. But I'll bring you another one. I think you should leave the other two where they are."

"Alright." I answered, meekly. "Thank you."

Wanting to change the subject, I asked if he was going to the Bazaar the next day.

"Maybe." He said. "I might go and see if I can hear any

town gossip, check out any strangers in town. You want to go? Seeing you might start the gossip mill."

Gee thanks, I felt like saying. What a nice invitation! I could just see me walking around, Amos skulking behind posts in my wake, his keen ears straining to catch idle gossip.

"No thanks!" I croaked out and was embarrassed at my unintended vehemence.

He looked at me strangely, and then threw back his head and laughed! His mirth resonated off the old beams like an echo chamber and I found myself chuckling in spite of myself. Judas had run for the bedroom at the initial shock of the booming voice, and Sam had jumped to his feet and stared at Amos anxiously. Noticing this, Amos laughed even harder, doubling over and grabbing his stomach.

I somehow felt the joke was on me and didn't know if I wanted to laugh! I grabbed his coffee mug and made a beeline for the kitchen, his unrestrained guffaws bouncing off my retreating back.

When I returned to the living room with a new steaming mug of coffee (tsp. of sugar, a little milk) Amos was on the hearth stoking the quickly dying embers. He threw a couple more logs on and the fire jumped towards the sky, accompanied by a loud roar and appealing crackling sounds.

He turned towards me, a lopsided grin still clinging to his scraggly features.

"I'm glad you find my plight so amusing." I said wryly, setting his mug on the coffee table.

He replaced the poker and ambled back to his spot in the middle of the couch while I curled in the armchair across from him. He raised his mug (which looked like a teacup in his giant hands) and stared stoically across at me as steam distorted his features, giving him a malevolent appearance. His disheveled mop of hair curled about his face as it slowly dried.

"And what would you have me do? Do you want me to

stay on your couch, shotgun in hand?" His eyebrows rose quizzically as he said this.

I felt the color and heat rising in my face under his scrutiny.

"No. Of course not! I'm just jumpy and paranoid." I managed.

"It's not paranoia if the threat is real." He replied. "Look, eventually things will resolve themselves and the truth will be revealed. We just have to be alert and wait."

"Waiting may be easy for you as a hunter, but patience is not my forte." I answered, rather coldly. "Besides, it's MY life on the line."

"If someone wanted you dead I believe you already would be." He answered, and the flames reflecting in his coal dark eyes sent a chill down my spine as I wondered if his reply had a more personal significance.

The jarring sound of the phone just then made me jump and I leapt to answer it.

It was Irmaline, calling to once again beseech me to accompany her to the Bazaar.

After declining, I hurried to tell her that Amos was here. I noticed his piercing stare as I babbled on to her about how kind it was of him to plow me out.

He knew. He knew that I suspected him.

Amos left shortly thereafter and I was left wondering if I'd alienated an ally or angered an enemy.

I spent the rest of the day puttering about the house, occasionally making trips to the woodpile (with Sam in tow). I stood in front of a roaring fire trying to get the chill out of my old bones as Judas scrutinized me from her perch atop the wingchair. I couldn't seem to stop shaking and wondered if it was physical or otherwise.

After talking to Irmaline for the third time that day, I finally dropped into bed, exhausted from the influx of emotions.

The day of the Bazaar dawned bright and sunny. I sat at

the kitchen table, a steaming cup of coffee curled in my frigid fingers. The sun's reflection off the driven snow was blinding and I had to shut the curtains against its onslaught. I tied Sam out, knowing his excursion would be brief as he, like me, had an aversion to the cold.

Irmaline called to make one last appeal for my company, citing that I had no excuse not to go since Amos had plowed me out. Her final appeal, hinting at my cowardice, finally convinced me to face my fears, those being the ostracism of the townspeople. I had already been bandying about the idea of going, anyway, as I was feeling isolated and depressed and was wavering on the edge of an alcoholic binge.

With a renewed resolve, I decided to go. I wouldn't allow the narrow-minded people of the town to curtail my activities. Irmaline wanted me to call Amos and tell him of my newfound resolve, but I refused, imploring her not to, either. It proved a moot point as I had just gotten dressed in my faded, old jeans and a plaid shirt of Al's, when I heard the whine of an approaching engine. It was Amos and I could see the determined look on his face as he trudged to the door. I decided to meet him head on and flung the door wide, coat in hand.

"I'm ready!" I trilled. I was rewarded with a look of surprise that was even more satisfying then I had hoped.

Even though I had that queasy feeling in the pit of my stomach that I always experienced when faced with something I dread, I had to marvel at the beauty outside the truck window as we made our way down the now narrow lane toward town. The pure whiteness of the day was like something out of a fairy tale. Crystal icicles weighed the limbs of the trees down like a bower of light encompassing us. Everywhere I looked twinkles of sunlight danced on billowy banks, like boles of cotton ripe for the picking.

Amos was tunelessly humming to himself and I felt that he, too, was in awe of the wonderland we called home. The drive alone would make up for any unpleasantness that may ensue. Or so I told myself.

The church came into view as we rounded a huge snow-bank. I was surprised that they had decided to still have it here. The cross on the spire shone with the new fallen snow, giving renewed hope to the weary. This place of peace could not be violated by the horror of that day not so long ago, and I knew the faithful were anxious to exorcise those bad memories. If they could face this, so could I. Irmaline's beater was parked haphazardly in the lot and I recalled her telling me that her daughter was now discouraging her from winter driving. I was glad to see that she hadn't conceded to this incursion into her independence.

# CHAPTER FIFTEEN

Amos stood outside the open truck door and stripped off his snowmobile suit. He had to sit on the edge of the seat to pull it over his humongous boots. He tossed it casually in the back and I couldn't help but notice the way his massive shoulder muscles bunched under his thick, wool shirt as he moved. He'd be a formidable enemy for the strongest of men. I hoped he was on my side. My neck would be like a twig in his huge hands.

He turned and smiled.

"You should learn to dress for the weather." He replied, as if just noticing my threadbare coat and tennis shoes.

"I don't plan on being outside much, unless that truck of yours breaks down." I responded.

He just grunted in response and grasped my elbow, propelling me across the parking lot, avoiding the slick spots shining in the morning sun.

The same feeling of déjà vu assaulted my senses as he opened the heavy door for me.

The smell of furniture polish hung in the air and bacon and egg smells emanated from the kitchen.

Breakfast was yet another offering of the Bazaar, at a nominal fee, of course.

We threw my coat in a small anteroom designated for such, and went downstairs.

The large room looked much smaller with the array of articles placed against the walls and aligned in rows in the center of the room. Furniture, bicycles, unused exercise equipment, all vied for a more prominent position. Neatly folded clothes lay on the tables, books and small kitchen appliances dispersed between them. Boxes of trinkets and ornaments were stacked against one wall with a sign saying, "$3.00 a bag". A stack of brown grocery bags lay under the sign.

Amos immediately made a beeline for a table laden with a various assortment of tools while I scanned the room for Irmaline. Though it was early, quite a few people were already present, although I only recognized a few. A strange silence hung over the scene.

I attributed it the earliness of the hour. I, for one, needed time to get into action mode in the morning and it usually took half a pot of coffee to get me there.

I spotted Irmaline looking through a pile of sweaters on a corner table and made my way to her.

"Hi." I chirped and my voice seemed to boom off the cavernous walls. She started and quickly turned.

"You made it." She said, looking around me.

"Who ya' looking for?" I inquired innocently.

She pierced me with her no-nonsense look, like a schoolmarm upbraiding a recalcitrant student.

"You know darn well!" She said, causing two portly women to turn and stare. She stared back until they turned away.

"Did you send Amos to get me?" I asked.

"Well, actually it was his idea, but I couldn't see a thing wrong with it". She answered.

"What do you guys do, have regular phone conversations

about what you're going to do with me?" I asked, amused. I could see Barney's face if he happened to be there when Amos called Irmaline. I thought theirs was a friendship he'd never understand, as he seemed to be a person in it for himself and wouldn't cultivate any relationship unless it benefited him personally. Irmaline's husband had been on the city counsel for years and wielded some political weight and I often wondered if that was one reason Barney set his sights on his daughter. As for her, I couldn't imagine what she saw in him.

"As a matter of fact, we do!" she smiled, her tiny crows feet crinkling as the smile reached her eyes.

I laughed in spite of myself and found I rather liked the idea, except for my ambiguous feelings about Amos. If only I knew I could trust him, I thought. He'd be a powerful ally.

As if sensing my thoughts, Irmaline said, "You needn't worry, dear, I'd never reveal your confidences to anyone." She patted my arm reassuringly as she said this.

"There's a rack of winter coats over there," she said, pointing across the room to a long rack replete with dresses and coats. "Let's go find you one."

I let her lead me across the room like the child she always made me feel like.

I thumbed through the assorted coats while Irmaline retrieved some bags. One bag was about big enough for the size 6 long wool coat I finally selected. $3. Not a bad deal! I wondered at the same time if I'd get looks when I ventured into town as people recognized the coat as their friends' or neighbors' and saw me as a charity case.

Irmaline was stuffing a bag with assorted sweaters and bathrobes that I couldn't picture her wearing.

"Do you wear what you buy?" I asked innocently, thinking if she did, I needn't feel like a charity case.

"I mostly buy for my daughter and grandchildren, but once in a while I'll find something I like. Why? Why wouldn't I wear it?" She said, raising her eyebrows quizzically.

"No reason", I said, coloring.

"You're feeling paranoid again, Annie." She stated matter-of-factly. "Do you really care what the townspeople think?"

"Well, I surely wouldn't want to walk around wearing Vicky's clothes!" I exclaimed, the thought just skittering across my mind.

"I doubt her family would donate anything to THIS church!" she exclaimed.

"You're right." I conceded, my shoulders slumping, "I am being paranoid. It seems to come with the territory, lately."

"Everything will work out, dear. It always does!" She answered softly.

Yeah, I thought. It didn't work out too well for Vicky or John Fuller, but I made no reply.

Since we wanted to shop more and didn't want to be burdened with our bags, we left them behind the table with the cash register being run by an elderly woman, who, evidently, Irmaline had went to school with. They chatted and laughed while I looked through baubles on an adjoining table. A homemade birdhouse caught my eye, sitting forlornly between old garden tools and ice fishing paraphernalia. It was in the shape of a pagoda, painted purple. I pictured some old codger lovingly building and painting it, the whole time thinking of exotic places he would never see. He would bring the world to him, creating an outlet for an imagination that had been stifled his whole life by a small-minded, backwater town.

I snapped myself out of my negative reverie and saw Amos returning from a trip to the truck, his huge frame filling the doorway as he descended the stairs. I'd seen him leaving earlier, straining under a load of various sized tools, none of which I recognized.

He'd gotten a few feet across the threshold when loud shouts and running footsteps could be heard above. Clattering sounds echoed off the stairs and two legs came into view as Amos turned towards the sounds. A disheveled woman appeared, a demented look on her face. She was shouting incoherently as she raised her arm, and I realized she was holding a gun! Everyone hit the floor but me. I stood, as frozen as a stone statue, unable to move or draw my eyes from the gun. I'd heard of this phenomenon, but never believed it until that moment. A bullet skidded off the floor two feet from me, ricocheting off the wall before disappearing into the ceiling tiles. I came out of my stupor and jumped behind the nearest table. I kept running, doubled over, waiting for a bullet to come whizzing by my head, or worse, hit it! When I found a large dresser to hide next to, I dared to peek.

At that moment, a giant hand swooped down on the woman's gun arm, sending the weapon flying. It landed with a loud "thunk" and slid across the floor, only stopping when it hit the wall next to Irmaline's hiding spot beneath the cash register table.

Amos had the woman subdued in his huge hands, her stick-like arms pinned behind her as she sobbed hysterically. As her uncombed mop of hair fell away from her face, I realized it was Vicky's mother!

I found out later that after the wild shot toward me, she had aimed the gun at Amos.

It was at that moment that I'd looked and seen Amos disarm her. Since her daughter's death she had descended into a deep depression and blamed Amos and, evidently, me, for the murder.

Chaos had been held at bay and the Sheriff was promptly called. Vicky's mother (I still couldn't remember her name) was taken gently into custody, her husband called.

After getting everyone's statements, we were allowed to leave. As I looked over my shoulder on the way out, I noticed Barney, standing on an old kitchen chair, digging in the tiled ceiling in search of the errant bullet. I couldn't help but wonder what a DNR guy was doing insinuating himself into a police investigation, until I remembered that the Sheriff had deputized a bunch of men in the wake of Vicky's killing. I was sure Barney was the first in line.

What next? I thought, numbly. I sat slumped in the truck seat next to Amos, both of us lost in our own thoughts.

Irmaline had run to me immediately after the horrific incident, cradling me in her arms, waiting for the tears that never came.

I think I'm in shock, I thought. I felt totally numb. My earlier giddiness at the beauty of the day was completely forgotten, replaced by the harsh reality of what had become my life.

Even though there was no correlation between the latest shooting and the others, except for the tie to Vicky, I couldn't help but feel like a Jonah: bringing misfortune to all who touched me.

Was it preordained Kismet or Karma for unknowing sins that plagued me? The only two times I had entered that church, violence or death had ensued; I was sure this fact wasn't lost on the townspeople. I was like a negative magnet or a black hole, drawing or sucking all into my void.

"I feel partly responsible." Amos suddenly blurted. "The last time I saw her, she and Vicky's dad were cussing me out in the Police station. I should have tried to talk to them, to let them know that it hurt me, too." His eyes left the road momentarily as they slanted toward me. He raised his hand in protest as he saw my mouth open to speak.

"Don't" he said forcefully. "Don't ply me with platitudes about how there was nothing I could do! I could have TRIED! I knew how close she was to her parents. They doted on her. I should have known they wouldn't just accept the fact that she was gone. Her mother has always been somewhat of a hysteric. This finally pushed her over the edge."

In the wake of his fervor, what could I say? I remained silent, eager to listen to any insight his memories might reveal into this enigmatic man. He wasn't one for small talk, and getting conversation from him most days was a chore. That was why, when he did speak, people listened. His reticence about all things personal had put me off and made me feel he was hiding something, but now that a familiarity was developing between us, I wasn't so sure my misgivings about him were justified.

When I didn't respond, he kept his eyes on the road and the only outward sign of his inner turmoil could be seen in the death grip he had on the steering wheel. I thought it might crack under the pressure of those sinewy hands: hands that looked as if they'd have no problem strangling a bull. Stop that! I told myself. No one was strangled. They were both shot. Anyone could have done it. They may not even be related. They didn't know what gun had killed Vicky as they had no bullet. Shooting someone was a cowards' crime. I didn't believe Amos would be capable of that.

None of these hypotheses changed the fact that someone was trying to scare me into leaving or drive me insane, for reasons as yet unknown to me and of no interest to the authorities, obviously. We made our way down the snow packed lane, ice-covered branches interlocking overhead like a glittering arbor; foothills of snow lining the ditches.

I felt an isolated tear roll down my cheek and wiped it away silently, turning to look out the window so Amos wouldn't notice.

When the forest gave way to my property, the Christmas lights no longer evoked the gaiety of the season. The cords hung in haphazard disarray, blown by the unforgiving wind. The remaining lights looked forlorn: small sentries among their dead comrades.

The only bright spot in the dreadful day was Judas' beautiful face gazing out the window, and the welcoming barks of my best friend as he picked up the sound of the engine.

I slid dejectedly out of the truck, not looking to see if Amos followed. He did.

I set a steaming mug of coffee in front of him. It had the consistency (and probably the taste) of mud.

We sat in silence, as there seemed nothing to say. Me, staring out the window at the busy feeders; him staring somewhere off in space, as if listening to voices from another world; the look on his face saying it was one he'd rather be in.

"Now what?" I asked, making him jump at the unexpected sound of my voice.

"Now, we get you another camera. You check the tapes every day. You watch the yard for signs of footprints. You'll probably have to talk to the cops again, as will I, before the hearing. Nothing has changed."

His air of impassivity was back in place.

"What do you mean, nothing's changed! You almost got killed today!" I half rose as the words came gushing out.

Amusement flitted across his countenance, making him almost handsome.

"You came a lot closer to buying it than I did." He replied.

I sat back down, slumping into the chair like a deflating balloon. Sam had come running over when I rose, hearing the anxiety in my voice. I patted him abstractedly, the familiar gesture calming us both. "Want to stick around for brunch? We never did get around to breakfast." I said.

"I have something I have to do." He said, abruptly.

"What's that?" I asked, sick of the pussyfooting around.

"I'll tell you about it later."

With that he made his way to the door, looking over his shoulder at me as he pulled on his boots.

"I'll get that camera for you and bring it over later. I assume you'll be here?"

"Of course. Dead or alive, I'll be here." I replied.

"Well, let's hope it's the latter." He said, slipping out the door.

My melodramatics were lost on him.

I made some toast and choked it down with coffee, the television droning in the background to give the illusion that I wasn't alone.

I sat on the couch, covered with a throw adorned with cat pictures, trying to stave off the cold that I knew was more than the weather.

I had one of the few local stations on, and watched with interest as a picture of Vicky's mother filled the screen. No mention of her intended targets was made, although an old picture of Amos was flashed on the screen as the person who disarmed her. The whole sordid Vicky murder was once again rehashed, the Sheriff reiterating that it was still top priority, as our sleepy little berg would not be a harbor for murderers.

Vicky's mother was portrayed as a sympathetic figure; her dad as the long-suffering victim; not only for losing his daughter in such a brutal fashion, but for having to endure the unraveling of his wife's sanity. He still had a Private Detective on the case, and I shivered as I realized that eventually, he'd get around to me.

Amos returned later that afternoon and set up the new camera by the side entrance to the root cellar, I knew it was no easy task and rewarded him with hot coffee and coffee cake after he'd divested himself of his wet boots and snowmobile suit.

"You'll have to fight through the snow to retrieve the tape", he informed me as he settled in one of the wing chairs, wisps of snow clinging to his beard.

I knew I could retrieve it by going through the trapdoor if I removed all the nails, but remembering the trapdoor was my secret, I bit my lip as I'd almost revealed my Trump card.

"Thanks so much!" I exclaimed. "I don't know what I'd do without you."

"I talked to that Detective earlier," he said, and I knew he meant the detective that Vicky's dad had hired. "It seems I was the number one suspect in the families eyes, but now he isn't so sure."

"Do you have an alibi for the time in question?" I queried, knowing he didn't as he'd supposedly been in my deer stand, stalking prey of the non-human variety.

"You know I don't." He leaned forward as he said this, staring at me with what I thought of as a malevolent look.

"You're not sure yourself that I didn't do it, are you?" He asked. His shaggy brows were knit together and frown lines crisscrossed his forehead.

"Put yourself in my place." I responded, leaning forward and placing my now cold coffee cup on the coffee table. "What would YOU think?"

"I'd think, why would I be wasting my time trying to keep you safe if I was the responsible party? Wouldn't I just keep my distance from you, and, if I intended you harm, just bide my time?"

"Perhaps." I said. "Or maybe by aligning yourself with me you'd deflect suspicion if anything happened to me." I felt my heart thumping in my chest as I finally vocalized what I'd been thinking. Would he now jump up and throttle me? Throw caution to the wind knowing that I could be made to disappear in this white hell and not be found 'til spring?

He stood up and I felt myself sink back into the sofa as he loomed over me. He made his way around the coffee table and stood over me, looking for all the world like Paul Bunyan, sans the axe and Babe.

"Come here." He demanded, reaching out a huge hand to me.

I held out a shaking hand, trying to buy time, my mind working a mile a minute on an escape route.

Sam was lying in front of the now cold fireplace, snoring and flicking imaginary fleas in his sleep. No help there, I thought.

He grasped my hand and yanked me into his arms. His arms encircled me and I all but disappeared into his hugeness. I held my face against his chest and heard his heart beating through the roughness of his shirt. One work roughened hand touched my face, tilting my eyes up to meet his. I could feel myself shaking uncontrollably and knew he could, too.

"You silly goose," he whispered as his lips descended on mine in a mind-blowing kiss.

Completely taken aback, I stood like a mannequin, my arms pinioned between us, my lips tingling with the forcefulness of his unexpected onslaught. A crick had developed in my neck from the height differential and I wondered if I'd be crippled when he finally decided to release me.

He studied my face and I knew my shock was obvious as he released me just as suddenly as he'd grabbed me, a lopsided grin on his face.

"Guess I caught you by surprise there." He said, and I could see the flush creeping up his neck, as he must have thought I'd rejected him.

"Y-You sure did!" I stammered, noticing that my right hand had flown to my mouth at his release. I ordered myself to lower it and grasped it demurely in my left hand.

"I just didn't expect," I faltered here, searching for words. Not finding any, I finished, lamely, "that".

The flush had now reached his cheeks and he quickly turned away, heading towards the door and his discarded snowmobile suit.

"Where are you going?" I asked in a small voice.

"It's hot in here. I need some air." He put on his boots, and not bothering to don the suit, grabbed it, and hurried out the door.

At the sound of the closing door, I burst into peals of unrestrained laughter. I tried to squelch it as I didn't wish to humiliate him further, but it flowed from me like a long dammed up river; rejoicing in its new-found freedom.

I realized that my hilarity was caused as much by relief as by seeing Amos so nonplussed, but felt no better for the knowledge. I would never deliberately hurt anyone, physically or emotionally, at least not in a sober state.

I'd heard Amos' motor and knew he was gone so I would have to wait and then do something I'd never done before-call him. He'd called me before, checking on my well being on a few occasions, but in retrospect, I realized I'd never called him, preferring to use Irmaline as an intermediary. I had to run get my pocket-sized phone directory from my bedside table and search for his number, hastily jotted down a few weeks earlier when he'd insisted. I certainly didn't want to call Irmaline for it and have to explain why I wanted it. It would make her too happy and me too embarrassed at my inexplicable reaction to something I should have seen coming.

After what I considered time enough for him to get home and a little extra to get over the embarrassment aspect, I called him. Evidently I hadn't waited long enough as I felt my own face flaming when his resonate, but restrained voice answered on the second ring.

What could I say? I should have put more thought into that before calling. I'd been hoping to lessen his humiliation; redeeming myself in the process.

"Hi." I whispered hoarsely, and then cleared my throat of the frog that had taken up residence there.

"I'm glad you found my kiss so amusing." He said, curtly.

"I didn't!" I protested. "It was quite nice! I was laughing from happiness," I ventured, "and relief." I admitted, shamefaced.

"Well, I forgive you. If the shoe was on the other foot, whose to say how I would have reacted? Although I don't think unrestrained laughter would have been my first reaction- well, second-after shock."

"I guess I don't hide my emotions very well." I said.

"On the contrary, I think you're quite adept at concealing things. I just caught you off guard."

"Is that a dig?" I asked, somewhat angrily. "And look whose talking! Mister Laconicus!"

He laughed heartily at this, forcing me to hold the phone away from my ear as the thunder rolled.

When he'd recovered, he said, "Want to go out somewhere tonight?"

"Like where?" I asked, "There's ten feet of snow, it's going to be freezing soon, and our town has about as much nightlife as Siberia."

"Don't cut Siberia short!" He replied, "I do believe they put us to shame."

"Come over here for dinner and a movie, I'll cook, of course. And you can even choose the movie, as long as you pick it up on the way!" I blurted, surprising myself.

"Should I pick up Irmaline, too?" He asked coyly, barely concealed mirth in his tone.

"It's not Friday, is it?" I asked.

"No" he responded.

"Well, just bring yourself then, and a movie, and maybe a bottle of cheap wine if you're so inclined." I said, carefully replacing the receiver as I heard him say, "But what's ..."

I knew "for dinner" was the question, but he'd just have to be surprised.

I didn't know what had gotten into me, but I found myself humming as I defrosted venison steaks in the microwave. According to protocol, enough time had passed for me to start dating again but I couldn't help but feel disloyal to Al. I'd spent so much time distrusting Amos that I'd never seen him as a romantic interest, only a possible threat. Now I was seeing him with new eyes, and I liked what I saw. I'd always told myself he'd be a good ally; well, I guess now I'd find out. I mulled through my ambivalent feelings as I went about preparing a salad and peeling potatoes. It felt good to be actually cooking again. I realized I'd been subsisting on microwavable soups and pastas for far too long.

Wait until Irmaline found out! I'd never hear the end of the "I told you so's". I could live with that. This newfound serenity was worth any crow I might have to eat.

I realized neither of us had specified a time, but being the staid Midwesterners that we were, I knew an early suppertime was the norm. In a place where in the dead of winter the sun was nearly gone by 4:30, anytime after 5 was acceptable. I'd read about how a lot of Europeans had their last meal of the day at 8 o'clock, or later, and was amazed at their patience. Also, how could they sleep on such a full stomach? Pushing my weird ruminations aside, I went about setting the table, and even dug out some spiraling red candles and holders I hadn't used in years. They would grace the table along with the vase of fake flowers from the coffee table.

I hoped I didn't give him the wrong idea; anything that might develop between us would have to do so over time. I wouldn't wear my heart on my sleeve. I hadn't been alone in years and was just getting used to it. If I could endure the disturbing events of late alone, albeit with Irmalines' and Amos' support, then being alone under normal circumstances was something I could look forward to. I didn't want to be one of those women who constantly needed a man. I had to find my own way first, then if I wanted to be with someone on an equal basis, well, that was fine.

The Amos I knew (or thought I knew) was fiercely independent, so maybe it could be a good match: as Irmaline had frequently pointed out.

Sam began barking as the crunching of snow heralded Amos appearance. Judas ran across the floor, almost tripping me, on her way to her window observation deck.

Despite the somewhat romantic setting I'd created, I'd counteracted the effect by dressing casually in my usual jeans and a fuzzy blue sweater. My hair, being its usual wild self, was caught back unceremoniously in a pink scrunchie.

I'd lit a fire, and flames roared up as I opened the door, casting dancing shadows off the rugged countenance before me.

Though the temperature was now below zero and the winds were whipping up, Amos wasn't wearing his trademark winter gear. He, too, was dressed casually. Clean blue jeans, a soft looking leather jacket, opened enough to reveal a deep red sweater. The almost wine-colored sweater, combined with the firelight, made his eyes seem to change color as pinwheels of light reflected from them in a mesmerizing kaleidoscope.

Then I noticed that a string of my Christmas lights had blown loose and was hanging directly above his head. The red lights had made his eyes look almost demonic for a minute there.

"Are you going to ask me in or stand there looking like you've seen the ghost of Christmas Future?" He asked, stamping the snow from his boots; his only concession to the weather.

Recovering, I stepped aside. I took his jacket and hung it by the door on the ancient hooks erected for that purpose decades before. He removed his boots and followed me into the kitchen.

"Venison!" He exclaimed, catching a whiff as he entered.

"You betcha!" I exclaimed, in true Scandinavian form.

He had a bag in his hand I hadn't noticed, since I'd been hypnotized by the eerie eye show. He set it on the dining room table, extracting a bottle and a movie.

He brought the bottle back in the kitchen and poured us both a glass in two fluted glasses he found in the cupboard. I gratefully accepted, surprised to find myself salivating at the thought of alcohol. Oh well, I certainly couldn't get drunk on a bottle of wine and I had no other alcohol in the house. I clinked glasses with Amos.

"To better times." I said.

"Shoal" he replied, and we both drank; a New Years toast on a cold November night.

It was strange to have someone sitting across from me at the table again. I kept expecting to see Al every time I looked up. Conflicting emotions battled within me.

All in all, it turned out to be a quite pleasant evening. Amos was a perfect gentleman.

He sat close to me on the couch and at one point draped his arm across the couch behind me as I sat with my legs curled beneath me, sipping my wine.

The movie was a light comedy, somewhat inane, but did have some amusing moments and I was glad to see he'd picked out something that didn't require total attention to the plot as my mind kept wandering, lulled into a dreamlike state by the roaring fire and the wine.

I awoke sometime later to Sam's furious barking. In that twilight between sleep and wakefulness, I struggled to remember where as I was, I knew it wasn't my bed.

Groggy from the wine, I had a hard time opening my eyes, but the intensity of the barking sent a shot of adrenalin through me. I flew off the couch, throwing off the blue blanket from my bedroom; wondering why it was there. The fire had burned down to embers and the only light was a diffused glow from the kitchen. I stood for a moment, listening, after I'd summoned Sam and silenced him. As memory returned, I looked around for Amos. I was alone.

An insistent pressure on my bladder told me I better get to the bathroom, quick, yet I stood, immobilized, Sam whining at my side.

A crunching outside the door told of approaching footsteps, but before I could react, the door flew open, a giant apparition in white filling the semi-dark threshold.

My hands flew to my face, trying to pull a scream from my paralyzed throat, at the same time that my bladder released.

Sam broke from my side and ran to greet the intruder, tail

wagging. It was then I realized it was Amos. Snow covered his thick bramble of hair and broad shoulders, the dim light from the kitchen twinkling off the flakes, giving him the ethereal appearance of a Yeti or a fallen angel.

The spell broken, I made a beeline for the bathroom, hoping that in the half-light he wouldn't notice the wet spot of shame denoting the extent of my fear.

"What's wrong?" I heard him say to my retreating back. "I heard something outside right as Sam started barking and I went out to check it out. I went around the side to get the root cellar tape and as I retrieved it a big mound of snow dislodged from the roof and landed on my head!"

He was almost yelling now as I closed the bathroom door behind me. I opened the door a crack to tell him I was going to take a shower.

When I at last emerged, hair dripping onto my old terry cloth robe, he had a fire going and was seated in a wing chair, VCR remote in hand. The television was on, a fresh-faced woman touting the effectiveness of the latest weight-loss program.

"Grab a seat." He said, barely glancing at me.

I settled on the couch, usurping Judas' throne; she let out a nasty hiss as I unceremoniously pushed her off. Sam lay at Amos' feet, his mistress seemingly forgotten.

A small puddle glistened on the hearth and I assumed that Amos had dried himself before the fire. His wet hair hung in wavy strands and I wondered why men were always the ones who got the natural curl.

"Ready?" He asked when I was settled.

"Go for it," I said.

The dark edge of the tree line came into view as the tape started rolling. A small patch of ice blocked the lower left corner of the camera, but the tape was surprisingly clear.

We watched in silence, our eyes riveted on the bucolic scene so intensely we could have been watching the horse-head scene from "The Godfather."

Amos occasionally fast-forwarded until the entire tape had been viewed. Nothing, just Amos struggling through snow as he came into view around the corner of the house, then reaching up for the tape and getting covered by an avalanche, which drew a laugh from me and a snort from him.

He then retrieved the other two tapes and, once again, we watched silently.

The living room tape showed Amos going out the front door and looking around. He then trudged out of camera range around the side of the house. The bedroom tape showed nothing but almost complete darkness. The remaining Christmas lights reflected off the wind-driven snow banks, shedding minimal light onto what appeared to be unbroken snow.

"So what did you think you heard?" I inquired as the final tape ended.

He shrugged, turning to face me. "I don't know. A big 'thunk'. It must have been a branch falling against the roof or something. I'll look around when it gets light."

I said nothing, my old paranoia welling up in the pit of my stomach. Was he fucking with me? After all, there was nothing on the tapes. Yes, Sam had started barking, but it didn't seem to me that he'd been barking that long when he'd woken me up. I pushed the negative thoughts aside. I'd been quite tired and the wine had intensified it, not to mention the roaring fire throwing off spurts of heat. I may not have heard Sam right away. I had had trouble opening my eyes and pulling reality in. 'Let it go. Give him the benefit of the doubt', I scolded myself. Yet the memory of the mind numbing fear and subsequent evacuation of my bladder clung to my consciousness like cobwebs in an attic room.

I made coffee and we sat in the kitchen awaiting the sunrise. The pets had been fed and Sam had been put on his leash to do his business. He'd wanted back in right away, the cold, the dark, and his natural love of company dictated that he be "where the action is."

He lay on the floor at Amos' feet, looking up occasionally at the sound of our voices.

The first glint of sunrise bounced off the icy channel and found it's way into my living room. I'd decided to accompany Amos on his inspection of the property. After a quick stop at his truck to retrieve his binoculars, (I assumed he used these for hunting, not stalking) we stood, the brightness of the sun ricocheting off the snow, giving the world a surreal aspect. We were blinded by the intensity of it. Not surprisingly, Amos also had sunglasses on the dash of his truck. He donned these as I shaded my eyes with my hand, Indian style.

The only disturbance we could discern in the otherwise unbroken snow was Amos' rather large trail, disappearing around the house. This was disregarding Sam's paw prints and numerous rabbit, bird, deer and unrecognizable (to me, although Amos probably knew) animal tracks.

Amos searched the roof from several different positions, but since there were several fallen branches from earlier storms laying beneath the eaves, it was impossible to tell how many were recent. The wind had blown snow helter-skelter at the side of the house, the line of trees and side of the house creating a wind tunnel; banks were drifted several feet high in some areas. My bathroom window was nearly covered.

I peered surreptitiously at Amos, looking for any hint of deception; but if he was an actor, he was a good one.

We trudged back in, Sam's jubilant barking greeting us we closed the door against the white world outside.

"It was probably a deer." Amos said, shedding his jacket.

"Yeah." I agreed, half-heartedly, drawing a glance from him.

I made breakfast as he stoked the fire, a strange melancholy overcoming me as I went about my mundane tasks.

The eggs were runny and the bacon overdone, but Amos

polished it off without comment, although he did thank me.

Conversation was limited to small talk and upcoming Thanksgiving plans. Irmaline had invited both Amos and I, but I couldn't see myself sitting down to dinner with Barney, especially on Thanksgiving. I could not stand that self-inflated little man and pitied Irmaline for having him as a son-in-law and a father to her grandchildren. Hopefully her daughter had her mothers' common sense and could counteract any narrow-minded bigotry displayed by Barney. Irmaline, too, set a fine example and I knew she was a big influence in her grandchildren's lives.

After Amos left, I locked up tight, checking all the windows and drawing the curtains shut. I dropped into bed still wearing the clothes I'd hastily donned earlier to accompany Amos' search.

Shadows were already filling the bedroom when I woke. A glance at the bedside clock showed it was after 4. I'd slept for over 7 hours. I dragged myself out of bed and went to heat up the sludge of coffee left in the pot, trailed by my hungry pets.

I sat at the kitchen table ruminating, as the shadows lengthened. I went over every incident in my mind, straining to find a common thread. Not for the first time, I wished I had a computer, but cable was as futuristic to this rural area as cell phones. Maybe when the mystery was solved I'd leave this place; too many memories were woven into every fiber of it. But deep inside, I knew I'd never leave until they carried me out in a pine box (figuratively speaking) like Al. My destiny was enveloped in this place, just as his had been.

Amos. His visage gathered in my mind, unbidden. Could I somehow learn to love him when the raw wound left by Al's death was scabbed over? Or would he turn out to be the elusive enemy who tormented me?

# Chapter Sixteen

The days had skipped by like pitched stones across a pond. Thanksgiving was two days away and I, as yet, had no plans. I felt I didn't have a lot to be thankful for this year; then felt guilty about feeling it.

Irmaline was bugging me thrice daily now to come for Thanksgiving, but I kept putting her off. Actually, I'd came right out and told her I didn't wish to attend, and why. It didn't seem to matter, she persisted.

Amos had been keeping a low profile since the other night and I wondered if my quiet perusing of him had driven him away.

I hadn't even bothered to check the tapes since the night Amos had been here, although I rewound and restarted the two in the house each night, obliterating anything that may have been on them.

All had been quiet and Sam hadn't barked. I was getting too lax, I knew, but a strange inertia had possessed me. All I wanted was to curl up on the couch in front of a roaring fire and lose myself in a book; effectively shutting out an outside world I no longer understood. I feared I was in the grip of a depression but couldn't see going to a doctor for Prozac. The townspeople would have a field day with that and my unknown enemies would believe they were succeeding in their plot to drive me over the edge.

A strange car pulled up that afternoon, setting Sam barking and me running for a butcher knife. I was loath to get the gun as no one was supposed to know it was in my possession. I sat turned on the couch, knife in hand, staring out the window at the non-nondescript vehicle now parked next to mine.

A rather portly man was struggling to excise himself from his car, his oversize parka hampering his efforts. He finally succeeded, and as he turned to stare at my house I recognized him from the news. It was the P.I. Vicky's dad had hired.

I quickly stashed the knife under a couch cushion and went toward the door, Sam's collar firmly in hand as he struggled to get free, pulling me along.

I flung the door wide just as he ascended the last step. He started at the unexpectedness of the action, and I saw him involuntarily reach under his coat. I almost laughed at the absurdity of his actions. Was he going to shoot me right on my doorstep?

"You're Mister..." My voice trailed off as I realized I couldn't remember his name, even though I'd heard it frequently enough on the news.

"Tanner." He finished for me. "Mike Tanner. You can call me Mike." He held his hand out to me as he said this, and I reluctantly embraced it.

"Come on in." I said, stepping aside.

Sam was busy sniffing him, growling low in his throat, so I attached him to his lead and shoved him out the door.

"Have a seat, I'll get some coffee." I said, playing hostess.

"Thank you, Miss Woods, that would be nice."

I took his parka and hung it by the door, then skedaddled to the kitchen for the coffee.

"Black is fine." He yelled at my back.

When we were settled in, the pleasantries behind us, I took charge.

"What can I do for you, Mike?" I asked, staring at him boldly.

He was rather on the short side for a man, but his girth gave him substance. He was of indeterminate age, but I assessed him to be in his forties. He was dressed casually in a gray sweat shirt and blue jeans, his salt and peppered hair sticking up wildly from the wind that had buffeted him on his approach. He had a kind face with large blue eyes that took in my humble home with an appraising glance. His gun was in plain view now, hanging from a shoulder holster, a cumbersome but necessary extension of himself.

His nose was rather hawk-like and his mouth large; crooked bottom teeth showed when he spoke.

"I'm sure you've heard of my involvement in this case?" He queried.

"Yes, I believe you've already talked to some of my friends." I answered.

"I've interviewed several people and will interrogate the whole town, if necessary, to get to the bottom of this untimely and violent death of a beautiful young woman." He stated,

Not so young, I thought, but didn't speak it.

"I understand you were the one who found the body, and in your trunk." His sharp eyes studied my face as he said this, and I was glad I held no guilt in my heart, as I knew he'd be able to see it.

"Yes, I did, but technically, it was no longer my trunk and hadn't been in my possession after I'd had it hauled to the church."

"By, Mr...."

"Amos." I finished for him.

"Yes. Amos" He responded, though I couldn't get a handle on his feelings about Amos and his role in all this from his non-committal tone.

"Exactly when did Amos transport said trunk and did he deliver it straightaway to the church, or stop somewhere on the way?"

"I'd have no way of knowing that, would I? He was kind enough to help Irmaline and me by offering his truck and his assistance in transporting several articles we found in my cellar." I felt a nudge of resentment at his intrusion into my little world, but knew that's what he was getting paid for, and I realized I should be thankful to him since the police seemed to be totally inept and he may be the only hope we had of finding out what really happened. When the killer was caught, I, too, would be safe.

I debated whether to tell him about all the odd occurrences I'd been subjected to over the last few months; but it turned out he was already aware of most of them, since the police had been called on those earlier incidents.

So it went, an interrogation that put the cops to shame. I only owned up to the incidents he was already aware of, wondering what Amos had told him. Irmaline had given me a blow by blow account of her interrogation, and we'd laughed together at some of his inane postulations, though it didn't seem so funny now that I was in the cross hairs of his scrutiny.

When he'd exhausted all avenues and realized I had nothing further to tell him, he rose to leave, once again extending his hand.

I decided to take a leap of faith and let him know that I, more than anyone except Vicky's parents, needed closure on this.

"You know," I ventured, "I, more than anyone except maybe her parents, need this to be over. I believe someone was trying to frame me, and was setting this up long before it happened. All the strange occurrences that preceded her death, most of which can be verified by Amos and Irmaline, were designed to make me look like a hysteric. A person who maybe was crazy enough to commit murder. Well, I can assure you, I'm on your side. More than anything, I'd like my life back. A life where I don't have to leave in fear; and to be perfectly honest with you, I'm beginning to wonder if my husband's death was natural as claimed, or the beginning of this whole plot."

He released my hand, a quizzical look on his face. Now he, too, thinks I'm not all there, I thought.

"Really!" I insisted. "It's all very strange, I admit, but Al, my late husband, had no health problems at all. For him to succumb to a heart attack for no perceptible reason doesn't sit well with me. I believe maybe it was the first blow in some elaborate scheme. Someone is trying to scare me, Mike. Trying to get me off my land, and I have no idea why. What this has to do with Vicky's death I don't know, but SOMEONE was trying to cast suspicion on me, and they succeeded. The cops still look at me with suspicion and would arrest me tomorrow if they could offer any proof as to my guilt. They even have Vicky's mother thinking I had something to do with it; hence her pot shot at me."

"Yes. Well, that poor woman has been through the wringer, and I hope you won't press charges against her as she obviously wasn't in her right mind at that time."

"How's she doing?" I inquired.

"Much better. Although I think she'll be staying in a private institution her husband picked out for her for quite a while."

"I'm not going to press charges against her." I said. Amos and I had already discussed this and even though she'd made Amos' life hell, he held no ill-will toward her; just the unsubstantiated guilt he carried for not being more supportive of her and her husband following Vicky's death.

As I opened the door and handed him his parka, I felt I had to make one last attempt to convince him I wasn't the enemy.

"We're both on the same side here," I said. "The sooner you

get to the bottom of this, the sooner I get my life back."

"Thank you for your time, Annie. I promise I'll keep you apprised of things. Have you thought about getting another gun?"

I forced myself to stay stone-faced as I answered.

"I think not. If anything else happens, I don't want to be implicated. It's bad enough my gun is still out there somewhere. I have Sam, my dog, and, as you may have noticed, several video cameras."

I surprised myself when the lie fell so glibly from my lips. I'd never been a good liar, and didn't want to make it a habit.

I called Irmaline upon Mikes' departure, relating the gist of the conversation. She once again implored me to join her family for Thanksgiving, stating that she was fairly sure Amos was going to be there, although he hadn't committed himself as yet. I knew it would be rude to keep putting her off; she was, after all, my only friend (besides Amos).

I finally allowed myself to be persuaded, telling myself that I'd never even been in Irmaline's house. She'd invited me on occasion, but I'd always demurred, afraid of running into Barney and having to endure his idiotic leers and snide remarks.

From the outside, her house was quite inviting. I'd driven by it for years, often wondering about the inhabitants of the gabled, old-fashioned-looking abode. I'd sat in the car on a few occasions when she'd had to retrieve something; admiring her large, oak-strewn yard. A small vegetable garden graced one corner of her property, a flower garden flourished on another. The house itself was white, the paint peeling in some places, but all in all, still quite attractive and homey. It was neither large nor small, but the upper floor had two bedrooms; she'd told me how she'd painted each in a different pastel color in anticipation of her precious grandchildren's visits. She'd also made it clear that her daughter would always have a home if and when Barney finally drove her away. She'd beseeched me often in the early days of our friendship to come and stay with her, but, of course, I'd declined. My home was here, with my pets.

The channel was to the rear of her house, right off the lake, wending slowly, in summer months, past her backyard. I'd seen the back before; Al and I were fishing, slowly trolling by in a pink dawn morning. A short dock jutted out into the channel, a small fishing boat was moored to it. Trees crowded close to the shoreline, their branches laden with acorns. Every breeze created a rat-a-tat sound on the dock as the acorns succumbed to the wind. I remembered wondering who dwelled in this lovely place, and if they were happy.

Immediately after talking to Irmaline, I berated myself for my spinelessness. After all, every time I'd let myself be persuaded to go out and be a part of society, something bad had happened. At the town Festival I'd been pushed off a bluff and escaped by sheer luck (the driver of the boat regaining control at the last minute). Someone had drugged me at the Halloween party, to what end I didn't know. I found Vicky's body in my trunk at the Bazaar and I'd been shot at in the same church shortly thereafter! I guess that old adage, "There's safety in numbers," didn't apply to me.

Of course, bad things had been happening to me at home, too, but I'd prefer to take my chances here, rather than exposing myself to so many others.

I told myself Irmaline's should be a fairly safe environment, even with Barney there.

It might not be a good idea to be home, alone, on a day when the whole town was closed and everyone was either out of town or with their families behind closed doors.

Al and I had lived in isolation so long that the town down the road had all but ceased to exist for us. Now I found that I may need help from said townspeople, but which ones could I trust? Now that we were embedded in winter the town's population had shrunk considerably. There were very few who stayed year round, although in the last few years (I just recently found out) an influx of young families had migrated here; despite the fact that their children had to be bussed to a school several miles away.

I guess change is a fact of life and I'd have to accept that I was no longer alone in paradise.

Amos phoned not fifteen minutes after I'd talked to Irmaline, so I knew the co-conspirators were still at it.

"Ya' heard already, huh?" I answered, upon hearing his voice.

He gave a short snort of a laugh before replying.

"Someone has to take an interest or you'd never leave those woods!" He said.

"Well, I've decided to go...if you'll accompany me." I replied blithely. "If I have to endure that horrible Barney I need lots of buffers!"

"I assume you're referring to Irv?" He chuckled.

"Of course! Who else?" I responded.

"He is inept, and an egotistical blowhard, but he's not quite the devil you make him out to be."

"I think he is!" I insisted.

"I hear the Detective was there." Amos said, changing the subject.

"Yes. And he seemed quite nice." I responded.

"Did you tell him about all the strange things that have been occurring?"

"No, he'd already been informed by the police about everything I'd made reports about, but I told him about Al's suspicious death."

"I wasn't aware that his death was suspicious." He answered.

"Neither was I! Not until all the other things started happening; then I began to wonder."

A short silence ensued before he answered.

"Have you thought about trying to get him exhumed?"

Now it was my turn to be silent; his question catching me totally off-guard.

"I never thought about that. Unfortunately, I had him cremated. We'd both decided that that was what we wanted."

"Didn't he have a heart attack?" He asked.

"Yes, but he'd never had any heart problems. I know that doesn't really mean anything, but I can't help wondering, in retrospect, if something scared him so badly that it brought on a heart attack."

"Well, I guess we'll never know, now, unless someone confesses to it when this thing is finally resolved."

Conversation ground to a halt and we hung up after agreeing he'd pick me up for Thanksgiving at Irmalines'.

The next day I spent the day cleaning and even took an hour off to go through the two house tapes. The one by the cellar (probably the one I should check) would have to wait for Amos, as I didn't think I could even reach it. He seemed to forget that everyone wasn't a giant like him! I did go out to get wood, though, and by early evening I had a roaring fire going.

I turned on the t.v., but every channel had coverage of the war. I couldn't bear to watch: memories of Viet Nam were brought back too vividly. I turned it off and retrieved my book from the bedroom. I now thought I might actually have a hope of finishing it!

I'd already picked out what I'd wear tomorrow. A slip of a black dress with spaghetti straps that I hadn't worn since the last time Al and I had went out to dinner, years ago.

I assured myself that little black dresses' never go out of style. I dug through the closet and even managed to find some low-heeled black pumps to go with the dress. If I had to face Barney, at least I could look good doing it!

I knew Sherry was spending the night at her mother's to

be able to help her with the dinner. Amos was bringing pies, and I whipped up a fruit salad from frozen berries that would have stagnated in the freezer forever if I hadn't used them. I was going to enjoy this Thanksgiving, dammit! I still did have a lot to be thankful for, and by God, I was going to be!

Thanksgiving dawned bright and sunny. I touched up my salad with cool whip, and even added some walnuts. Dinner wasn't until two so I had plenty of time to set my hair, something I hadn't done in ages. Sam and Judas watched, bewildered, as I rolled the graying strands on over-sized curlers. I held a running conversation with my pets and was glad no one was around to hear me; maybe I WAS alone too much. I rustled around in my ancient jewelry box and found a pair of diamond studs Al had given me on our 10th anniversary and put them on. I had to poke hard to get the right one in as it had been so long since I'd worn earrings my right piercing had started to grow closed. A simple gold heart necklace (another gift from Al) completed my ensemble. I was still in my robe, I didn't plan on dressing until right before Amos came so as not to wrinkle my dress too much.

I even dragged out my old make-up case and tried to turn back the clock; I didn't succeed, but it was an improvement.

Amos arrived promptly at one, as agreed. We wanted to arrive early so I could offer my help in the kitchen and Amos could watch football. That's what I'd gathered when he suggested we get an early start so I could help Irmaline and Sherry! I answered the door with coat on and salad bowl in hand.

"Jeez, are ya' ready?" Amos asked facetiously. "Oh, and you look great."

"Thanks. You look pretty good yourself" I replied, taking in his gray dress pants and blue button-down shirt, which was half visible under his good leather jacket. His beard had even been neatly trimmed and his hair brushed to resemble hair rather than a bush. I almost didn't recognize him, and it seemed out of character. But what did I know. After all, I hadn't known him that long. I should be glad that he cleaned up nicely.

To my surprise, he opened the truck door for me and helped get me settled. We made small talk on the way, him imploring me to take Barney with a grain of salt and not let him get to me; of course, this just enhanced my nervousness and made me wonder why I'd ever agreed to go.

"Can't you keep him in the living room, watching football?" I asked, hopefully.

"You'll still have to face him across the table." He reminded me.

"I know. I'll just let everyone else carry the conversation. I'm a better listener than talker, anyway. As you seem to be," I finished.

He didn't grace this with an answer and concentrated on the icy road.

Irmaline's house looked even more enchanting under its blanket of snow. The walk had been freshly shoveled and salted, which I was thankful for in my low heels. See, I thought, another thing to be thankful for! I'd hate to have to sue Irmaline! I laughed at the thought, drawing a questioning glance from Amos. He had his hand under my elbow as he guided me up the wooden steps.

I felt butterflies fluttering in my stomach as Amos rang the bell. Low chimes echoed through the house. Sounds like a death knell, I thought, and then quickly pushed the ridiculous thought aside.

Sherry answered the door and I hardly recognized her! The mousey demeanor was gone.

She was dressed in a frilly white dress that ended right above her knees, and her erstwhile brown hair had gleaming highlights in it. It was drawn on top of her head with little wisps outlining her face. Her thin body seemed fuller in white; her face was perfectly made up.

I once again found myself wondering what the hell she was doing with Barney. She ushered us in and yelled "Mom!" Irmaline appeared from another room (I assume the kitchen) and hustled over to relief us of our coats while Sherry took the pies from Amos and the salad from me and disappeared into the room Irmaline had emerged from.

Wondrous smells permeated the house and I felt myself salivating.

The living room, which we were now in, had hard wood floors, burnished to a high shine. Colorful, expensive throw rugs were interspersed throughout. A fireplace dominated the left wall; the smell of burning wood mixed with the cooking smells, creating a homey ambiance. The mantle was adorned with several pictures of Irmaline's grandchildren, a few of Sherry; Barney's ugly mug was nowhere to be seen.

My glance traveled to the long, light blue couch that sat nearly in the middle of the room, and there he was in the flesh. He rose and came towards us, arm extended to Amos.

"Hey, Buddy. How ya' doing? Welcome!"

He was wearing a gray sweater and crisp gray dress pants that accentuated his thinness.

Amos' huge hand swallowed his in a firm handshake.

"Is the game on?" Amos asked, looking beyond Barney toward the huge t.v.

Barney's glance barely flicked over me as he led Amos to the couch.

"One just started and another's on right after." He said.

Irmaline returned then from divesting herself of our coats, and came to greet me.

"You've got a beautiful home, Irmaline." I said. "It looks bigger on the inside."

She grasped my hand, propelling me forward.

"C'mon. I'll show you the house."

She jabbered non-stop as she led me through the house. The neatness of it put me to shame, and I found myself embarrassed about my lackadaisical housekeeping skills.

My mind was wandering and I just caught the end of Irmaline's running narrative.

"…and now I'm glad I got that satellite dish because it keeps Irv out of my hair.

Just like a kid, give him something inane to watch and you'll never know he's there!"

We were in the younger grandson (Luke's) room, now. The walls were full of posters of animated characters I didn't recognize.

"This is Luke's room, when he stays here." She trilled.

"I figured. How old is he?"

"Seven." She said.

"Really!" I exclaimed. "I thought he was younger than that. Although I'm not much of a judge about those things." I finished.

"He's small like me and his mom."

"Well. What do you want me to do to help?" I asked, as she led me back down the stairs.

"There's nothing to do, dear. Not until the Turkey's done. Sherry just put the potatoes on.

The yams can wait. Go sit by Amos and relax 'til dinner."

"What are you going to do?" I asked, trying to avoid Barney's presence.

We were now in the kitchen. It was a large room with muted rose-colored floor tiles. A large, double refrigerator sat next to a stainless steel sink. Sherry was sitting at a large formica table in the center of the room, puffing on a cigarette. I was surprised, but given her circumstances, it was understandable. I was salivating again. Whether it was the enticing cooking smells or the cigarette smoke, I didn't know. I hadn't been around any smokers in a while and I was surprised at the instantaneous longing I felt.

Sherry looked up from a magazine she was perusing and smiled.

"Hi, Annie. I'm so glad you could come. My mother is so fond of you, and I'm glad she's found a new friend. Sit down and let's get acquainted."

She pushed a chair opposite her out with her foot and I found myself liking her already.

I seated myself across from her and Irmaline sat next to me.

"Isn't this nice!" Irmaline exclaimed, looking from me to Sherry.

I could tell she was thrilled to have her daughter and me together, at last. As for me, I'd sit with the devil himself to avoid Barney, so seating across from this nice young woman was a pleasure.

"Where are the kids?" I asked.

"Oh. They're out back, playing in the snow." Sherry responded. "They love coming to grandmas. We have a small yard, not nearly as nice as mom's." A whiff of smoke escaped her lips and I had to consciously keep myself from leaning in to inhale it.

I found I didn't have to talk much as the conversation centered on Irmaline's family.

She and Sherry were both disappointed that Gary and Rich (Irmaline's sons) weren't going to be able to make dinner this year. Gary was still in Afghanistan and Rich and his family had decided to take a cruise. They were both planning on coming up for Christmas and it was obvious both Sherry and Irmaline were quite excited about that.

One or the other of them kept jumping up to check the turkey; poke the potatoes, put the yams on. I jumped up with them each time, hoping to be of service, but was always waved back down. Irmaline finally gave me a stack of dishes and told me to set the table.

I looked at her strangely and she laughed.

"I'm sorry Annie. I never got around to showing you the dining room! Come along."

With that she grabbed some fancy cloth napkins and opened double doors off the side of the kitchen I hadn't even noticed as they'd been designed to blend in with the walls.

The doors slid right into the walls, revealing a large room with light blue walls. Large windows graced one wall; elaborate draperies a shade darker than the walls hugged the now sun-filled windows. I saw the boys out by the dock, romping in the snow.

"What a lovely room!" I exclaimed.

The dining room table dominated the center of the room. It was polished walnut and sunbeams danced softly off its gleaming surface. Intricately carved legs bulged out at the four corners. Matching chairs with blue and gold brocade seats and backs surrounded it. A centerpiece of dried flowers sat on a colored mat in the middle; two gold candles in silver candle stands stood sentry on either side. The floor, too, was a dark wood waxed to a burnished shine.

Irmaline opened a drawer in a matching sideboard and withdrew placemats made of a brightly woven fabric.

"I guess there'll only be seven of us this year." Irmaline sighed.

Sherry, who had trailed along behind us, leaned over and kissed her cheek.

"That's o.k., mom, the boys will be here for Christmas; and the cousins!"

Sherry disappeared back into the kitchen, leaving Irmaline and I to our duties.

"I can't get over this room! And those doors that go right into the wall! I've only seen that in movies!" I gushed.

Irmaline chuckled as she opened a velvet-lined box of sterling silver flatware.

"It means I can close off this room, dirty dishes and all!" She laughed.

"As if YOU ever would. I might." I answered.

I placed the plates on the mats she'd arranged in front

of the chairs. She swiftly set out the silverware, reflections dancing off the walls as the sun caught each piece.

When we were done, we stood for a minute before the bigger middle window, watching the day unfold as if on a movie screen.

The boys were now rolling up a snowman. Childish laughter, barely audible, gave life to the tranquil scene.

"Your lights can be seen over there." Irmaline said, gesturing to the right. "But only from the corner of my yard."

Just then the boys spotted us and waved. Irmaline waved back, than gave a summoning motion, and I knew it was time to eat.

I was sent to fetch Amos and Irv. Irv's' raucous laughter assaulted my ears before I even entered the room.

"Time to eat, guys." I said, crossing the room. I took a detour to the mantle as I noticed a picture that wasn't visible from my erstwhile vantage point by the door. It showed a young couple on their wedding day. It appeared to be somewhere around the nineteen-forties, though I couldn't be sure. It was Irmaline and her new husband. Sunbeams bounced off her then-blonde hair, which was partially covered by a white veil. Her husband seemed quite tall, but Irmaline's so small it was hard to estimate. He was handsome, in the manner of a movie star of that era. Slicked back hair, a cheesy mustache; he appeared to be wearing tails.

Amos' hand on my arm startled me out of my reverie. I was about to comment about the picture when Barney shoved rudely by, knocking me into Amos. Rather than apologize, he replied, "Move it, move it. It's time to eat!" Then laughed as I hit Amos' chest.

I was about to admonish him, but he was already gone, as if someone had called "Su-ey."

Amos put his hand on my elbow and steered me toward the kitchen, whispering in my ear, "Let the games begin."

I grabbed the gravy boat off the counter as I passed through the kitchen. Sherry was in front of me with a big bowl of mashed potatoes. The turkey was already on the table, placed near the edge for easy cutting access. Barney was already seated. He'd taken the first chair to the right, next to the head of the table. Amos had stayed in the kitchen, looking for a carving knife; I heard Irmaline directing him. Sherry sat next to Irv as Irmaline and Amos came in.

"Where are those boys?" Sherry asked, turning to look out the window.

"Shawn! Luke!" Barney bellowed, nearly causing Irmaline to drop a plate of biscuits she was carrying.

"Irv!" Sherry chastised, "I could have done that!"

Thundering sounds on the stairs heralded the arrival of the boys. They burst in the room, giggling and wrestling.

Their mother summoned them over and inspected their hands. She then fussed with their shirttails and collars and brushed back their hair with her fingers.

"Get on over there and sit!" Barney barked, not waiting for Sherry to finish her ministrations.

"You boys sure do look handsome!" I gushed, hoping to alleviate the sting of their fathers' rebuke.

Shawn gave me a half-smile, while Luke sat as far away from his father as he could; in the last chair on the opposite side. Shawn sat across from him and Amos and I sat across from Irv and Sherry, Luke next to me on the far end. Irmaline would have the place of honor at the head of the table.

After we were all seated, Irmaline implored us to bow our heads for the blessing. She then proceeded to give thanks for all of us, for the food, for our comforts, etc. I could feel Barney's restless legs jiggling the table and felt like giving him a swift kick, than acting like Amos did it, just to see his reaction.

When Irmaline, at last, raised her head, Amos jumped up and went to carve the turkey.

He gave turkey-laden plates to the children first, even

though Barney sat there practically drooling; you can be sure, at home, he was first served.

Once the turkey was allotted, chaos ensued. I had to duck as arms flew pell-mell. Glasses clattered, silverware jingled. After the onslaught, things settled into a relative calm. Barney stuffed his face as if there were no tomorrow, the boys picked at their food and giggled; casting sidelong glances at their father. Sherry and Irmaline carried on a conversation between mouthfuls while I absorbed the whole scene. It had always been Al and me as long as I remembered, and the newness of family intrigued me.

Barney and Amos had cans of beer beside their plates; I had noticed in the living room that they'd been imbibing while yelling at the t.v. Great, I thought, a drunk Barney. A sober one was bad enough! Amos I didn't worry about. I'd never even seen him tipsy. He could hold his liquor.

After the main course was largely consumed and the pies were in the oven, the wine came out. I had to admit, I was glad! I could barely keep my hand from shaking as Irmaline circled the table, pouring. She even had ginger ale for the boys and poured them two wine glasses full. I was about to guzzle mine down when I realized everyone was holding their glasses out in toast mode, even the boys, who had to stand to do so.

"To health, to home, and most of all, family." Irmaline intoned. We all clinked glasses, then Amos spoke up.

"To friends, old and new," he glanced at me as he said this, and I felt myself blush.

We clinked again, but this time, everyone took a drink before the gauntlet was passed.

Sherry went next. Irv tried to speak but she raised her voice and drowned him out. This caused a spate of giggles from the boys, who gazed at her lovingly.

"To my mom, to my boys, to my friends, oh.." she gave an embarrassed laugh here, "and to my husband." I realized with chagrin that she was tipsy! She must have been guzzling wine while preparing dinner, though I hadn't noticed.

Though the rest of us (besides the boys) had remained seated, Irv stood to give his toast, causing the rest of us to have to stand, too. Wine sloshed over the rim of his glass as he gesticulated wildly.

"To my loving wife" he sneered, "who always tries to make me look bad. To her mother, who coddles her way too much, to my spoiled brat kids, who, thanks to their mother and grandmother, are total sissies. To my friend, and I say that loosely, Amos, who's willing to screw everybody over for some b..b..broad, and to that broad, who can't take a hint when it's thrown in her face…" He stared straight at me and screamed, "You're fuckin' everythin' up. GET OUT!!!"

Before he could continue, Amos' meaty fist reached across the table and grabbed his neck. Sherry screamed and the boys cowered at the end of the table. Irmalines' hands had flown to her face in shock, and she stood like a statue. Wine had flown everywhere, though the empty glass remained in Irv's shaking hand.

"Keep your mouth shut and sit down!" Amos said quietly, but with vehemence.

Barney meekly sat, setting the wine flute delicately on the table beside him.

As we all returned nervously to our seats, Irmaline remained standing. She grabbed the wine decanter and silently filled everyone's glass but Barney's'. On her way to deposit the decanter on the sideboard she snatched up two empty beer cans from in front of Irv, hissing in his ear, "You're cut off. And from now on, you'll not be drinking in my house!

After dinner we'll retire to the living room and you can explain your remarks to us. We're dying to hear exactly why Annie is 'fuckin' everything up'."

The boys' eyes were as round as saucers as their grandmother berated their father. Sherry was staring down at her plate, one hand idly twirling her glass; Amos' look, as usual, was inscrutable.

If this was what family was like at Holiday get-togethers, I was glad it had just been Al and me!

Sherry and Irmaline chose this time to get the pies and after a quick consultation quietly left the room.

Barney sat silently, apparently momentarily cowed. Even the boys had been shocked into silence and sat looking quizzically at each of us in turn.

I heard soft murmuring coming from the kitchen but couldn't make out any words. I felt totally out of place and guilty for bringing this on by my presence. I should have known better!

Amos put his hand over mine (which was clenched in a fist in my lap) and gave it a small squeeze. I felt like bawling all of a sudden, and in a deliberate gesture I grabbed my wine flute with my left hand and guzzled the last half the glass. As I finished it off, I saw Barney gazing at me with unrestrained hatred and once again wondered what I had done to arouse his wrath.

The pies were brought in unceremoniously and put in the center of the table. Irmaline retrieved small plates from the sideboard and set them next to the pies. Amos rose and cut the pies into neat pieces as Irmaline got them on plates and passed them out. I was the only one queried as to which I preferred as she knew everyone else's preference.

Sherry raised her hand signaling she didn't want any and took a huge drink of wine, peering at Barney under veiled eyes.

Barney kept his eyes on his plate until his pie was gone, then hurriedly left the table. Amos started to rise but was waved back into his seat by Irmaline.

"Let him stew in his own juices for a while. He has GOT to learn some respect! I've put up with him for years and held my tongue, but no more! For him to come into my home and insult and disrespect my friends is going too far!"

"You're right, mom." Sherry said, meekly. Looking at her sons, she said, "I'm sorry you had to see this, especially on Thanksgiving, but you know how your father is, and he needs to be put in his place."

Shawn jumped up and exuberantly yelled, "Yay, mom!" his little fist flailing in the air.

His little brother quickly followed suit, his even littler fist imitating his brothers'.

"Yay, Grandma!" Luke squealed.

"I got a better one," Shawn said, looking at his brother. "Yay, Amos!" At which we all burst into unrestrained laughter. It was moments like this that I almost wished I'd had children.

With Barney gone the oppressive feeling that had hung over the festivities was lifted. The conversation flowed as freely as the wine. At some point, the boys left and minutes later we could see them out by the dock gazing towards where my lights shone off the frozen channel. I found I really liked Sherry. Without Barney there, she seemed to emerge from her shell; the wine gave her a warm glow, enhancing an inner beauty that had been overshadowed by her husbands' dominance. Amos even seemed to shine. His subtle wit had us all in stitches as he regaled us with "on the road" stories. Sherry had been a couple of years behind him in the now non-existent little schoolhouse that used to grace the town square, and they walked down memory lane, taking Irmaline and me with them. No mention was made of how Amos used to beat Barney up for his bullying ways; but it hung over us, unsaid.

The shadows grew long across the table as the sun made its way swiftly westward. The boys came in and went upstairs to play video games. Barney had refused to let them have Game systems at home, but grandma had installed them here, further alienating her from her obnoxious son-in-law.

"That'll be the last we see of them!" Sherry had trilled as they ran up the stairs, laughing.

I wondered where Barney was. Was he in the living room, stewing? I dreaded facing him again and planned to stick close to Amos. The vehemence he'd displayed towards me was still fresh in my mind and I hoped I'd never have reason to run across him when I was alone.

Amos was the first to break the spell of camaraderie we'd been enjoying.

"Now that we're all calmed down, I think it's time for that little talk we were going to have with Irv." He said.

"Yes." Irmaline agreed. "I may be able to face him now without resorting to mayhem."

She added.

"I'm going to start cleaning up." Sherry said, removing the remaining dishes from the table.

It was obvious she didn't want to be present for the confrontation, and we didn't blame her; after all, she was the one who had to live with him.

"Let me get him." Amos said, leaving the room. "We'll meet you in the living room in a few minutes" he said, over his shoulder. Irmaline and I helped Sherry clean up and the dining room soon looked as it had when we'd arrived. Irmaline closed the doors and the room once again disappeared behind faux walls.

We left Sherry to the dishes and went into the living room. No one was there so we settled ourselves next to each other on the soft sofa. Two large lamps shone from the end tables, fighting the gathering shadows. The t.v. was off and the silence was broken only by dishes rattling in the kitchen and occasional thumps from upstairs as the boys horse played.

The gallons of wine I'd consumed gave me the false bravado I'd need to confront Barney.

"Don't be nervous, Annie." Irmaline said, patting my hand. "Maybe we'll finally get some answers, although I have no idea why Irv would be involved in any conspiracy. I really think he was just blowing his horn and the reason he wants you gone is because you, Amos and me have become friends and he's jealous. He's also afraid that Sherry may like you and then he'll have to contend with another person telling her how shabbily he treats her."

"You think that's it?" I asked, hopefully. I didn't want to think that Barney was part of whatever was going on. That would mean that maybe Government forces were behind it and there was no way I could prevail. Wow! I really was becoming paranoid! Now I was seeing shadowy Feds behind trees, conspiring against me.

Amos found Barney in Sherry's' old room, the room her mother hoped she's someday occupy again. He was sprawled across the bed, passed out. Amos' had tried to get him up, but he was out cold.

"Guess we'll have to wait to find out his part in all this" Amos said, upon returning.

Irmaline told him her theory about Barney's actions and Amos tended to agree.

Everyone in town knew Irv, and no one would trust him enough to bring him in on any thing. His propensity for edifying his own ego would preclude his involvement.

Amos was stoking the fire as Sherry entered the living room. She sat on Irmaline's other side, tucking her feet beneath her and laying her head on Irmaline's shoulder. Her earlier tipsiness seemed to have been replaced by fatigue.

"I'm SO sorry, Annie." Sherry said, peering over Irmaline's shoulder. "Irv's just jealous. He's always been like that. That's why I have few friends...only one close." Her statement echoed Amos' and Irmalines' opinions about Barney's actions. I tended to agree. Although Irv had attained a somewhat prestigious job for such a small town, it was nepotism not merit that had gotten it for him. He had, more or less, inherited it from his father. Besides his obnoxious personality, it was another reason for his co-workers not to like him.

We spent the next couple of hours watching "It's A Wonderful Life", a reminder that Christmas was right around the corner.

# Chapter Seventeen

Other than the Barney incident, Thanksgiving was enjoyable. I felt I'd made a new friend in Sherry and I'd finally seen Irmalines' home. I realized that I'd never seen Amos' house; the main reason being I wasn't sure of his alliance before and had been afraid to be alone with him in his environment. I was interested now that we'd established a relationship, of sorts. I wanted to see where he lived. Someday.

We'd driven home down the dark roads, moonbeams casting ribbons of light across the driven snow. The alcohol had embraced me in a convivial fog, leaving me feeling tired and content as I lounged against Amos' shoulder, trying to stay awake.

Barney had never reappeared and I'd have to wait for any answers he may have to my dilemma. Amos had wanted to roust him, but Irmaline and Sherry had convinced him that it was a useless endeavor.

I'd nearly nodded out by the time we reached my house. The alcohol and heat from the trucks' fan lulling me into a near-dream state. As the headlights turned onto my property and swept the front of my house in its beams, a sudden movement at the side of my house startled me. I sat up quickly, bracing myself on the dashboard as I leaned forward, straining to see out the partially snow-covered window.

Yellow eyes caught the gleam of the headlights, and with great relief I realized it was just a scavenging raccoon searching my garbage cans for food. It seemed no matter how many times and ways I'd tried to tie my cans shut, the raccoons always found a way to open them and I could only clean up their mess in the morning, marveling at their ingenuity. It had gotten to be such a constant thing that Sam rarely bothered to bark at them anymore. Fortunately, in the really cold weather they rarely ventured out, preferring periods of hibernation to the cold. Sam was, however, barking now, though I knew it was us he was barking at, his way of welcoming his mama home.

Amos practically carried me to the door, the booze and slick footing causing me to lean into him as we made our way across the snow-covered yard.

The hearth was dark and cold, no welcoming fire to greet us on this cold Thanksgiving night. Amos escorted me in and went back out to get wood. He got a nice fire going and joined me on the couch as I fought to keep my eyes open.

"Are you glad you went?" he whispered as I snuggled into him.

"Yes." I answered, truthfully. "I am glad. I feel I've made a new friend in Sherry, and the boys are a riot!"

"They'll turn out fine with Sherry and Irmaline guiding them. They're already starting to see Barney's inadequacies, as evidenced by their actions tonight." He said.

"I hope so." I replied. "They're good kids."

When I awoke, the sun hitting my eyelids and drawing me out of my dreams, I was laying on the couch, once again covered by the blanket from my room; Amos was across from me in one of the wing chairs, sound asleep. His natty clothes were now rumpled and I noticed a stain on his blue shirt. Smiling to myself, I went to make coffee. I should have been hung over, but I felt pretty good. I guess I hadn't had too much to drink, just enough.

As the wonderful smell of fresh coffee wafted through the house, I sat alternately watching the birds and squirrels at the feeders, and Amos. A horrid, yet wonderful, thought popped unbidden into my head: If I live through this, I have a future, and maybe a future with Amos! Sleeping, he was undeniably attractive in a rough, bumpkinish way.

After I managed to push off the ennui of sleep, with the help of a half a pot of coffee, I let Sam out on his leash and ran a tub of hot water.

When I emerged from the bathroom a half hour later, Amos was cooking eggs and bacon. The delicious smell filled the house and I felt my mouth watering. I went to my room and hurriedly dressed, pulling on a clean pair of jeans and a dark blue turtleneck.

Amos was setting the table as I entered the dining area.

"Mornin.'" He said as I settled into a chair.

"Hi. What a nice surprise." I exclaimed as he set a plate in front of me.

"I'm afraid you're going to have to make a trip to the store soon; you're running short on supplies." He replied, settling in across from me.

"Yeah." I answered, shoveling eggs into my mouth. "Me and Irmaline usually go together." I managed between bites.

"I have to track Irv down today." He said, after a swallowing a mouthful. "I'm really interested in finding out what he has to say when he's sober. Believe me, I WILL get answers. If there's anything other than jealousy behind his remarks, I'll find out."

He left soon afterwards, promising to call as soon as he found out anything.

I spent the next half hour or so going over the tapes I had

access to. I was pretty sure I'd find nothing on them except coons and other critters, as the snow cover was unbroken by anything other then animal tracks. Also, I knew Sam's different barks, and he'd shown no agitation lately. When he did bark, it was his usual, "there's a critter in my yard" bark. Although he usually didn't even bother anymore: he'd learned through the years that it was a losing battle, and finally resigned himself to the fact that he had to share his domain with all variety of creatures, although the presence of deer always got him going.

I reinserted the tapes in their respective machines, telling myself I'd have to have Amos retrieve the one by the cellar door that was out of my reach. I'd seen nothing on either of the tapes, not even animals. So far the most exciting thing I'd seen was the owl. Whoever was harassing me must have known about the cameras. The one in back was the only one outside and could be seen during the day if closely scrutinized. I guessed all the money I'd spent on the things went to good use if it kept my demons at bay.

Amos called later and informed me that he couldn't find Barney anywhere. He'd called Irmaline and found that Sherry, Barney and the kids had spent the night as planned, (Barney had still been passed out in Sherry's old room) but in the morning, Barney had been gone. Sherry hadn't woke up until after 10, due to the wine, I assumed; the boys had been up but had stayed in Shawn's room playing their video games. Irmaline had stayed in bed watching the news and hadn't ventured down until 9:30 or so. No one had heard him leave or had any idea where he would go. He didn't have work today and him and Sherry had planned to take the boys 200 miles to visit Barney's family, as they did every year after Thanksgiving. Barney's brother had already called, wondering when they were coming.

For some reason, I felt guilty, even though I realized it was Barney, not me, who had been out of line. Where was he? Obviously, he didn't want to face the music, and maybe he was afraid of Amos; after all, Amos admitted he'd used to kick Barney's ass. Amos and Sherry went out looking for him while Irmaline stayed with the boys. There weren't many places to go in this town, and most weren't even open today. He WAS a grown man and, therefore, could go anywhere he pleased; but still, it was out of character for him (I was told) to miss visiting his relatives. He LIKED his family. I tiptoed through the house, peeking out windows, paranoid that he may be skulking outside somewhere. I reviewed the accessible tapes: nothing.

The plot thickens, I thought. Every time it seemed everything was going back to normal and my tormentor(s) had grown tired of the game, something else weird happened. I called Irmaline and after discussing the problem at length, I suggested that if he hadn't been found in a day or so, besides the cops, we could consider hiring Vicky's parents P.I. I had thought we were jumping the gun with our panic, but after hearing Irmalines' frenzied recitation about what a creature of habit Barney was, I, too, began to wonder; thus my suggestion of hiring a P.I. I hoped it wouldn't come to that. If anyone could find him, Amos could, I told myself.

I spent the rest of the day cleaning house and shoveling snow that had blown back onto my walkway. Dark clouds moved swiftly across the face of the sun, portending a coming storm. Even though I didn't like Barney, his sudden disappearance left me with an odd feeling of foreboding. The poor boys, I thought. They'd been making fun of their father and now he was gone: Sherry, too.

He'd taken the family station wagon that was in Irmaline's driveway. His state-owned DNR vehicle was still parked in he and Sherry's driveway. Everyone in town knew their cars; so hopefully, someone had noticed the station wagon. Amos had taken his truck, of course, while Sherry drove Irmaline's old beater. They planned to hit all the open businesses in town, the restaurant, store, and any other place that may have decided to cater to the after Thanksgiving crowd.

Irmaline told me that Sherry was leery about this as she was afraid of Barney's reaction when he found out she'd been "checking up" on him, but she went, nonetheless. She was hoping they could still make the trip to his relatives house, otherwise, even though it was his fault their plans were disrupted, there'd be hell to pay.

The shadows were long on the wall as the sun made its inevitable descent. I had the fire going and sat curled up on the couch. An inane sit-com blared from the television, but my wandering mind kept me from comprehending it. The telephone rang periodically as Irmaline kept me posted on the search. Judas sat curled in the wing chair licking her luxurious coat, as Sam snored next to me. How lucky they are, I thought. The world of human understanding was as far removed from their reality as alien beings were from mine.

I retired early that night, after soaking in a hot bath for an hour. The emotional drain of the last 24 hours had taken its toll and all I wanted was my warm bed. Maybe by morning something would be resolved.

I was awakened sometime in the wee hours by Sam's furious barking. I had a hard time getting my eyes to open; the remnants of sleep clung like spider webs to my weary mind.

When I, at last, managed to fling the abyss of nothingness from me and grip reality, I flew from my bed as a shot of adrenalin pulsed through my veins. "Sam!" I screamed, but was greeted only by continued barking: muffled, far away.

I ran to the living room. Total darkness enveloped me. The fire long grown cold, the drapes, pulled closed, effectively blocking out any light from my outside lights, I stood in total darkness in the middle of the room, listening. All at once I was hit by an unseen force and knocked onto the couch. I felt a heavy weight upon me and gloved hands encircling my throat. I struggled vainly with the unseen entity, kicking out with my semi-pinned legs, grabbing handfuls of leather gloves as I tried desperately to breathe. I felt myself losing consciousness as I was pushed back into the cushions. I felt a lump in my back as the pressure increased and realized through the pain that I still had a chance. The knife! The knife I had stuffed under the cushions when the P.I. had appeared, and soon forgotten about. I managed to retrieve it and with a mighty last effort, thrust it at the invisible enemy. I was rewarded with a startled grunt as the hands around my neck were quickly removed. I heard pounding footfalls and then the door flung open and Sam rushed in as the assailant rushed out. I ran to the door as a black figure disappeared around the corner of the house. I slammed the door before Sam could give chase and put himself in harms way. I threw the bolts home and leaned against the door, sobbing, my hands rubbing my raw throat.

When I'd recovered enough to still my shaking hands, I ran to the phone. Amos. I thought. I must call Amos. His phone rang and rang. Where IS he? I wondered as I hung up and called the police.

It wasn't until the Sheriff arrived (looking like he'd just crawled out of bed and not happy) that I realized that the bolt I'd slammed home had had nothing to slam home into. The jamb had been jimmied and the part that held the bolts was hanging uselessly from the wooden door frame.

At least now I had solid proof that I wasn't imagining things. I retrieved the tape from the camera guarding the door and showed it to the Sheriff. It showed a figure, dressed all in black with a ski mask on, fiddling with the door lock. As the door was forced in, Sam could be seen running out as the intruder rushed in, pushing the door closed behind him. It was only held shut by the little tongue in the door latch, the locks no longer viable.

I informed the Sheriff that I had stabbed the intruder, and

he proceeded to look for blood droplets on the couch, floor, and snow outside the door. I gave him the knife with blood specks still clinging to it. He had me place it in a large baggy from the kitchen to avoid contamination. He then informed me that they could type it, but DNA would tell us nothing unless the perpetrators' was on file. No one in town or even the County had ever had reason to give a sample of their DNA, so he held little hope of any answers in that direction. If and when a suspect was ever found, then perhaps it could be useful. He made it clear, however, that unless charged with something; no one was required to give a sample.

He'd heard about the search for Barney and assured me that his Department would be doing a search of their own; starting in the morning. They weren't required too, by law, since Barney was an adult, but he was a State employee and the out-of-character circumstances surrounding his disappearance warranted investigation. Sherry had informed him last night of her and Amos' fruitless search, and he'd assured them he would look into it today.

He was kind enough to nail my lock plate back on the door, informing me as he did so that I should go into town and purchase a new, more secure lock. I didn't mention Amos and my unanswered phone call. After asking if I needed medical assistance, which I refused, he prepared to leave.

"Maybe you should consider getting another gun for protection." He said, causing my face to flame at the thought of my gun secreted behind the wall. I hoped he didn't notice my discomfiture with his lawman's intuition, but he didn't seem to.

"Thank you so much," I said, standing at the door as he started to leave. He had taken the tape with him to watch at the station with other law enforcement personnel, hoping someone may recognize the mannerisms of the muted figure. It would be useless to fingerprint as he'd been wearing gloves. Footprints would offer no clues as snow had once again began to fall, obscuring any that may have been visible just minutes before. Ditto for tire tread marks. I was on my own once again.

After he'd gone I tried to phone Amos again, wondering if his bedroom was so far removed from the phone that he was unable to hear it as he slept. Was he snug in his bed, totally oblivious of the drama unfolding less than 2 miles from his house?

I spent a sleepless night on the couch, jumping every time the furnace (which was in an alcove off the bathroom with my washer and dryer) kicked in. I said a silent prayer that my precious Sam hadn't been injured, as I watched him laying before the cold hearth, staring at me with questioning eyes. Judas, of course, lay unperturbed on a wing chair.

I decided to wait until dawn to call Amos again; after all, what could he do? I'd call Irmaline later, but she had enough on her plate right now and I was reticent about adding to her troubles.

I racked my brain for anything I could remember about the intruder, but it had all happened so fast, I could think of nothing to give me a clue to his identity. In the darkness and my fear, I couldn't even gage the size of the perpetrator, let alone anything of significance. Perhaps the Sheriff's department would be able to figure out how tall he was from the tapes. I was reasonably sure I'd have no further incidents tonight; but nonetheless, I dug my gun out and sat with it in my hand until the first hint of dawn peeked through the cracks in my drapes.

Amos answered when I called again at sunrise. I almost cried with relief when I, at last, heard his voice. I stumbled over my words as I gave a recitation of the disturbing events of the previous night.

"Slow down, Annie!" He implored, as I nearly lost my breath, so anxious was I to finish my story.

When I was able to finish; albeit somewhat incoherently,

he gave a long sigh and proceeded to tell me about his and Sherry's fruitless search for Barney, ending with: "Do you think it could have been Irv?"

I once again reiterated that I didn't know.

"What should I do?" I implored.

"The Sheriff has no choice now but to investigate. You have irrefutable proof with the tape. I think, perhaps, you should call the Detective investigating Vicky's murder and ask him to go to the Police station and view the tape. I'll call Jim today and ask him to please accommodate the Detective; it would be to everyone's benefit to work together on this."

"How're Sherry and the boys taking B...Irv's disappearance?" I asked.

"Well, Sherry's quite upset, obviously. They're all staying with Irmaline, which is good.

The boys don't seem to be too concerned; it's like a prolonged holiday for them. Sherry and Irmaline decided to keep them out of school for a while, in case for some reason, Irv met with foul play in his drunken flight. They don't want the boys in harms way."

"Who could possibly want Irv?" I inquired; then realized how that sounded.

He gave a chuckle before I could correct myself, replying:

"What if Irv really is aware of some conspiracy; not necessarily involved, but just aware.

He would then become a threat to whoever's behind it."

"That's a scary thought." I said.

"I'm going to continue my search today; Sherry will, too, as we can cover more territory separately, then we'll rendezvous at Irmaline's at 3:00 and compare notes."

"What can I do? I feel so useless just sitting here, and I'm still scared about last night."

"You can pack up some stuff and stay at my place, the pets can come too, of course."

"No", I answered after a moment's thought, "I'd still feel

safer here. After last night my attacker will probably avoid being seen around here for a while. Maybe he's running scared now. Also, he's injured. I know I stabbed him. It may only be a flesh wound, but he's going to have an injury."

"That's an idea, too." Amos replied. "We can check the nearest hospital and see if anyone's been in with a knife wound."

"If it isn't life threatening, I doubt he'd expose himself like that. It should be checked, though, I guess." I said.

Amos begged off then, wanting to get on with his busy day. He assured me he'd stop by later and update me. He also said that while he was in town he'd pick me up a good dead-bolt lock and install it when he got here.

I thanked him and hung up, alone with my dark thoughts once more. I'd said nothing to Amos about my earlier attempts to phone him, thinking how rude it was of me if he was sleeping to try to deprive him of his much needed rest when there was nothing he could have done in the middle of the night, anyway. I also felt I had no right to snoop into his comings and goings by asking 'where were you?' I didn't want to come off as a needy, insecure woman. Of course he'd been sleeping, or perhaps still seeking Barney. I knew he functioned well as a night person; after all, he drove truck.

I called the one motel, nestled on the edge of town, that the Detective had told me he was staying at.

"Mr. Tanner?" I asked, after being put through to his room, surprising myself that I'd remembered his name.

"Mike." He answered.

"Yes, Mike. This is Annie Woods. I'd like to speak with you about some things that have been happening around here."

"Speak away." He answered.

After I'd updated him on all that had occurred, he assured me he'd go to the Sheriff's office and try to view the tapes. As for Barney's disappearance, he'd make inquiries around town about that, as well.

"Thank you. It takes quite a bit of pressure off knowing that I'll now be taken seriously." I said before hanging up.

Amos arrived around 4:30, looking tired. I wondered if his rumpled clothes were the same ones he'd worn yesterday. He installed my new locks as he told me about the two days' search. Him and Sherry had, between them, covered every business in town. Amos had even gone to some not so savory, illegal enterprises on the outskirts of town. Of course everyone, including the Police, knew of these places but they were generally left alone; now, however, they were apparently scrambling to temporarily shut down since a visit from the authorities was inevitable. Amos was certain these characters hadn't seen Barney; he said they'd be the first to admit to seeing him, as they were afraid of the cops. They had profitable enterprises going and Amos felt they weren't involved in whatever was causing the drama in my life. He wouldn't totally rule them out, however.

Sherry was at her wits' end and resting at Irmalines'; the boys were under their mom and grandma's constant surveillance.

I wanted to invite Amos to stay for supper but was embarrassed because the cupboard was bare. I really needed to go shopping, but with all that had been going on I hadn't gotten around to it. When I told him this, he invited me to his place for steaks. How could I say 'no'? I was leery about leaving my pets; Amos told me to bring them, but I wanted Sam there to scare off intruders. He said that with my new locks and the cameras and the havoc I'd wreaked on the intruder, I shouldn't have to worry; at least not until the heat died down. I agreed, my curiosity about his home being the deciding factor.

Amos went home to shower and change, assuring me he'd be back at 7 to get me. I got cleaned up myself, donning a fresh pair of jeans and a grey turtleneck sweater that I thought, vainly, enhanced my eyes. I even added a wisp of perfume.

Despite all that had happened, I felt suddenly optimistic; a feeling quite rare, for me.

I ran out to the truck when Amos arrived; no need to make him come to the door to retrieve me. I'd locked everything up tight, my lights were blazing bright; though during the day the ramshackle way the cords hung from the eaves could be seen. They looked good in the dark, though.

Amos' beard looked neatly trimmed and his hair was combed into some semblance of order. I could see he was wearing jeans under his coat and was glad I hadn't dressed up.

It was a short ride to his house, although I didn't think I'd be able to find it myself as we'd taken so many turns down barren, snow-covered roads. The darkness obscured any landmarks that I may have recognized. As he pulled into his yard the nearly full moon peeked out from behind high flying clouds, revealing a rustic, cabin-like structure. Drifts of snow nestled next to the windows, a light from within cast dancing shadows across the  darkened landscape.

"It's beautiful!" I exclaimed, sincerely. "It looks like something out of a fairytale."

He laughed at this.

"My grandfather built this almost a century ago, when he was a young man." He said.

"My father added to it, and so did I. You'll see how rustic it really is in a minute."

I jumped out of the truck, not wanting to seem like some mamby-pamby waiting for him to open the door for me.

We met in front of the truck and he escorted me, hand on my elbow, to the door. It looked like a big log cabin. A handhewn wooden rail encircled a porch that seemed to go around the house to the right. I reached out and touched the heavy wooden door. It was oak and had been polished and lacquered to a brilliant shine, visible even in the muted moonlight.

"Wow!" was all I could manage.

He opened the door, and we went back in time. A fireplace made entirely of stone dominated the entire left wall, rising all the way to the roughhewn beamed ceiling.

The main room wasn't large, but spacious. A heavy wooden couch with large, comfortable-looking blue cushions dominated the area in front of the fireplace. Two seemingly hand-made matching chairs were on either side of it. A big, oriental looking rug spread out in front of a large roughhewn coffee table. A moose head and several antlered deer heads hung high on the wooden walls, looking down on the scene, forever destined to dwell in the land of humans.

At the back of the room, to my wonderment, was a large loft running the entire length of the room. A heavy wooden ladder with folding metal joints was positioned at a hole in the loft; 'cool', I thought, that ladder can be pulled up, if you're strong enough; which, of course, Amos was.

"This is about the coolest room I've ever seen!" I gushed.

The loft was encircled by the same rustic wood; cut in rough beams. Like a high, inside porch, I thought.

As we advanced further into the room, a hallway could be seen stretching to the left, at first unseen by the dominating fireplace.

The kitchen was on the right, partially under the loft, partitioned off from the main room by a wooden room divider.

"If you look through the fireplace, you'll see my bedroom on the other side, although I sleep in the loft often as not." He said.

I went to the fireplace wall and glanced through the waning flames. Sure enough! A room could be seen through the fireplace.

"Wow!" Once again I was momentarily struck dumb. "Where's the bathroom?" I asked.

"C'mon. I'll show you." He said, and I once again felt his hand on my elbow, guiding me. We went down the hall towards the bedroom, and there, to the right of the bedroom was a room (obviously added later). I was surprised at how modern the bathroom was compared to the rest of the house. A modern shower and gleaming porcelain sink were on opposite sides of the room. A toilet sat next to the sink. It was larger than my bathroom, but cozy.

The walls were painted a light turquoise color and were made of sheet rock. A beautiful painting of wildflowers hung above the toilet and I thought how it seemed out of character.

"My mother painted that, many years ago." Amos said behind me as he caught me looking at it.

"She was good." I said.

"C'mon, I'll show you the bedroom."

I let him guide me across the hall, beneath a log lentil. The bedroom was large; a huge, handhewn bed dominated the middle of the room, replete with giant wooden headboard. A large dresser (which also appeared hand-made) was on the wall opposite the fireplace; but the fireplace was the dominating force of the room. The entire wall, like the living room, was stone. I could look through and see the couch, chairs, and the entire room except the corners that were hidden in shadows.

"If I'd known what a paradise you live in I'd have insisted you bring me here sooner!" I exclaimed.

"I've tried, on more than one occasion." He answered dryly.

I felt myself blush at the thought of my stubborn refusals to be drawn out of my own existence.

The walls in here were knotty pine, their polished surfaces gleaming in the faint firelight. A large comforter, patched quilt-like, was thrown across the bed haphazardly.

A large picture of an elk hung above the dresser.

"Did your mother paint that, too?" I asked.

"Yes, she did. It was my 10th Birthday present, the best I ever received." He said proudly.

"It must have been great growing up here." I said.

"Well, when I was growing up, this room was just being built. I helped my dad saw and polish the wood and watched with awe as this room was formed."

We returned to the living room and he added wood from a pile in the corner to the fire.

"How come you don't have any pets?" I asked as I seated myself on a corner of the large couch.

"For years I had a Golden Retriever. He used to ride with me on my runs, and hunt with me when I was home. When he died, 5 years or so ago, I realized it wasn't fair to keep a pet in a truck for months at a time, so I figured I'd wait until I was retired. That way we could grow old together."

"You must get lonely." I ventured.

He gave me strange look.

"I'm used to being alone. I miss my dog, and when the time is right I'll get another; but until then, I treasure my own company."

"Amen to that!" I said, inducing a chuckle. "Although I think I'd go nuts without Sam and Judas." Then, looking around, I said, "Where's your t.v.?"

"I was wondering when you'd notice." He said, "This is a little luxury I set up myself," he said, stepping to the side of the fireplace. He pushed an unseen button, concealed in the stones, and two fake stone panels opened to the right of the fireplace, revealing a large t.v.

"No way!" I squealed. I marveled at his ingenuity. There was much more to Amos than met the eye.

Two small end tables, both roughhewn lumber, hugged the ends of the couch. Hurricane lamps sat atop them and Amos now lifted the chimneys and lit them. The smell of kerosene wafted into the room, making the scene all the more rustic.

"I'm gonna go start the steaks." Amos said, replacing the glass chimney on the lamp he'd just lit. "They're venison steaks," he added, heading for the kitchen.

"I'd expect nothing less." I replied. "What do you want me to do?"

"Check out the t.v. listings, I've got a satellite dish, so you may be able to find a movie or something."

"I'm gonna have to get one of those, once this is all resolved. Right now I can't even concentrate on the few measly channels I get." I yelled at his retreating back.

I nestled into the soft couch cushions, tucking my stockinged feet under me, and started channel surfing.

I managed to find an episode of 'American Justice' about some serial killer in Texas and was totally engrossed by the time the smell of venison filled the room, making my mouth water.

Amos came around the partition, two plates in hand. He set them on the coffee table and returned to the kitchen momentarily to get two beers. He settled himself a few feet from me and proceeded to stuff his face.

"Man, you must have been hungry!" I remarked, as his steak disappeared before my eyes.

"I kinda forgot to eat today," he said between mouthfuls.

I passed the remote to him as Bill Curtis summed up the episode I'd been watching by saying the perpetrator had received the death penalty.

"Let's find something a little lighter," he said, going down the listings. He found an old comedy, "Dumb and Dumber", and we spent the next couple of hours laughing at the absurdity of the characters.

By the time the movie was over, I'd downed 5 or 6 beers and Amos, twice as many.

I felt fuzzy and happy, the warm glow of the fire and the woody smells mixed with kerosene, made me feel I'd went back in time. If not for the t.v., the illusion would be complete.

I forced myself up and cleared plates and beer cans off the coffee table. I placed them in the sink and ran hot water, adding a little dish soap I'd found under the sink.

Amos appeared around the screen behind me with the remaining beer cans I'd been unable to carry, and after throwing them in a recycling bin, came up behind me and encircled me in his arms. I jumped at the unexpectedness of it, thinking 'maybe he's tipsy'.

"Leave those," he said.

"Oh. It's no problem. It's the least I can do after that delicious supper." I said, wiping a plate with a sponge.

He took the plate from my hands, placing it in the sink, and turned me around. I felt claustrophobic, my eyes were level with his chest, the screen divider cutting off the rest of the room.

I put my arms around him and laid my head on his chest. What was wrong with me? Here was a perfectly wonderful man, who'd proved to be a good friend to me, yet I froze at any hint of physical contact.

"C'mon." He said, grabbing my hand and leading me from the kitchen.

I followed docilely, allowing myself to be led up the rough wooden ladder into the loft.

I stood at the top, surveying the room from the high vantage point. A queen-sized bed was against the wall at the back of the loft. A desk and chair sat to the left of it; a lamp, with a sculpted deer base and large, beige shade, sat on a little table by the bed. This one was electric and Amos reached over and turned it on, casting a warm glow over the beamed ceiling and log walls. A multi-colored throw rug stretched from the opening in the floor up to the side of the bed.

I turned to find him staring at me with those inscrutable eyes, and was reminded of the night he'd stood outside my door, my multicolored lights dancing in his eyes, revealing a dark and dangerous glint in them.

I crossed my arms across my chest, a sudden shiver running through me. Then he smiled, and the spell was broken. He held his hand out to me, and I disentangled my arms and placed my small hand in his big one. He drew me to him and kissed me, lifting me off the floor, effortlessly. I allowed myself to be drawn into the kiss and hugged his neck, feeling the muscles bulging beneath his skin. He sat on the bed, drawing me with him, and we sprawled across the fur bedspread. I found myself wondering if we were laying on something he killed, but decided not to ask. He reached out and extinguished the bedside lamp as we lolled on the bed, making out like teenagers, exploring each other. As my hands crept under his shirt and over his massive chest, he gave a start and jumped up.

"What is it?" I asked, startled, sitting up.

"I got into a little fight at one of the shooting galleries outside of town, that's all." He said flatly.

"What do you mean, that's all? Let me see!" I insisted. "What happened?"

"It's taken care of. I've disinfected and covered the wound." He said.

"Wound?" I asked, bile crawling up my throat.

"Look. It was no big deal, and I knew you'd react like this. You have a tendency to blow things out of proportion. I'm alright."

"What, exactly, happened?"

He gave a sigh, his shoulders slumping.

"I went to one of the "establishments" outside of town, as I told you. One of the patrons took objection to my presence there. When he pushed me, I decked him. The owner of said establishment than politely asked me to leave, terrified of an altercation with the Police. As I turned to leave, I felt a sharp pain in my chest, and when I looked down, a knife was sticking out."

My blood turned to ice; the fear was so palpable.

"What's the matter, honey?" Amos said, putting his arm around my shoulder.

Then he lifted my chin with a huge finger and looked me in the eyes.

"Look, I know what you're thinking, that's another reason I didn't say anything. It's taken me this long to gain even some semblance of trust from you, and something like this, no matter how plausible the explanation, would destroy what I've tried so hard to build. You'd never trust me again; and I couldn't blame you! I wouldn't trust me again, either! But it's the truth, honey. I promise."

I pushed his arm off and stood woodenly, my legs numb. He stood too, and went to put his hands on my shoulders as he towered over me, but I flinched and his hands dropped to his sides.

"Annie, please listen to me. If I wanted to kill you, wouldn't I already have done it? What, I invite you to dinner and a movie, and then unceremoniously dispose of you? Do you know how ridiculous that is?"

I looked up into his craggy face and blurted, "Maybe you wanted to have some 'fun' with me first!"

A look of astonishment crossed his face, than he threw back his head and laughed; big, bellowing guffaws that seemed to shake the rafters. Not knowing what to do, I slipped to the ladder and began to descend, keeping my eyes on his shaking girth until the level of the floor obscured him. I jumped the last few feet to the main floor and stood looking helplessly around, for I knew not what.

He stood at the railing, over my head.

"Annie, I'll give you a ride home, if that's what you want. Please don't run out the door in the dark and try to navigate those woods. There is someone out there who DOES wish you harm; it isn't me."

I knew he was right. If it were him, he'd catch me in no

time. I had no choice but to trust him, at least until I got home. IF I got home.

"O.K." I said, defeated. "Please give me a ride home."

We were silent on the way back to my place, but when we pulled up into the yard, he said, "You said the Sheriff had taken the knife into evidence, didn't you?"

I glanced sideways at him, my right hand on the door handle, my house keys in my left hand.

He continued, "When they're done testing it they can compare it to my DNA, which I'll go down and volunteer a sample of whenever you want. Then when the results are in, maybe you'll trust me again."

"We'll see," I said, noncommittally, quickly hopping out the door and slamming it in his bewildered face.

I gave him 15 minutes to get home before I called. I had unanswered questions but I wanted to ask them from a distance, in the relative safety of my own home.

"Did you tell the Sheriff?" I asked immediately when he answered the phone.

"About the fight? No. I'd lose all credibility with those people if I did something like that. It wasn't even bad enough to go to the hospital, for God's sake. Besides, it was a drunken customer, not the proprietor who attacked me. I know who he is and I'll deal with that later. I have more important things on my mind right now."

I couldn't believe his blasé attitude, whether his story was true or not. He'd been STABBED. If it were by me, I'd think he would have somehow betrayed himself, and he was right about the dinner, movie thing; and he did bring me home safely.

If his story was true, his attitude still baffled me. Men! That machismo thing was unfathomable to anyone with a uterus, I guess.

"Look," I said. "I'm going to choose to believe you, for now. You were right about the dinner, movie thing; you have had plenty of chances to do away with me and haven't yet.

I do want to thank you for the nice dinner and…everything, though" I choked.

"I told you I didn't blame you." He said. "The coincidence is amazing, but in places like that, violence isn't all that rare. I'm sorry if I frightened you. I'd totally forgotten about it until…well, you know. Then, when I remembered, it was to late to do anything but tell you, and, of course it looked really bad for me. You were pretty brave, actually, seeing as how you thought you were in the presence of a murderer." He chuckled as he said this.

"When can I see you again?"

I was taken totally off-guard by this question. I'd been playing along and trying to act nice until I had time to think. Better to keep on his good side. I wanted to believe him, but I guess I needed proof to put my mind at ease, once and for all.

I ignored the question.

"So," I said, "Are you going to the Sheriffs office to give a DNA sample?" I asked, matter-of-factly.

"If you really want me to, I will. I'm just one of those people that are kinda squeamish about the Government knowing everything about me, including my cell make-up. I don't know; call me anarchistic, that's just how I feel. Also, the police would want to know where I got stabbed and more heat would come down on the 'business', making me yet more enemies. But yes, if you insist, if it will put your mind at ease, I'll do it tomorrow. It's gonna be embarrassing going in there and telling Jim that I want to give a sample of my DNA to compare with the blood on my girlfriends' knife, because she thinks I may have attacked her."

I realized then how hard that would be for a proud man like Amos. The whole town would know in a matter of hours how Amos' paramour didn't trust him not to kill her, yet still hung out with him; that made me look nuts, too.

"Hold off on that." I said, firmly.

"Are you sure?" He sounded relieved, I thought. But then, after all the reasons he'd enumerated for not going to the Sheriff, why wouldn't he be.

After we rang off, me still avoiding when I'd see him again, I debated on whether to call Irmaline and fill her in. Her table was already full and I didn't want to see her like she'd been after Vicky's death, pale, nervous, ill looking. It was moot, however, as she phoned shortly thereafter, demanding to know why I hadn't been in touch and what was going on.

"I know it's late," she began, "but I've been calling and calling. Where have you been?"

I felt bad, now. It was worse not knowing what was going on. I filled her in on all that had happened. When I related the intruder story, she gave an audible gasp and I knew she was thinking it was Irv. Then I told her what happened at Amos' and she remained silent so long I had to ask if she was still there.

"You know I trust Amos implicitly," she said. "If he says he got in a fight, he got in a fight, believe me! I'm glad you didn't make him go to the Sheriff's office for a DNA test. He's a very proud man, and the humiliation would make him even less inclined to socialize. You two make a good pair in that respect. You're both antisocial. You must trust him, Annie! He cares about you, and would never do anything to hurt you!" She said, emphatically.

"I'm sure you're right." I acknowledged. "I'm almost to the point of leaving for a while." I said, surprising myself as the flight or fight mode kicked in.

"You can come stay with us!' She said, excitedly. "You can bring Sam and Judas', too"

Irmaline said. She had an ancient cat; I didn't think bringing Sam over there (or Judas, for that matter) would be such a good idea.

"I don't think Wordsworth (her cat) would appreciate

that!" I said. "I'm alright, Irmaline! I promise you!" Changing the subject, I said, "I need to go grocery shopping tomorrow, do you want to meet me in town?" I asked.

"Sure, what time?"

"How about noonish?" I asked.

"Yes. Maybe we can have lunch somewhere first. I need a break from all the tension around here. Sherry's been drinking too much, the boys are running wild; I'm at my wits end!" She said, dejectedly.

I got worried then. All this might be too much for her. I didn't know what I'd do if anything happened to Irmaline; plus the guilt would be overwhelming. She'd had a nice, peaceful life before she met me.

'I'm so sorry about all this, Irmaline." I said, sincerely. "Maybe you'd be better off staying away from me for awhile."

"Bosh!" She said so loud Sam looked up and I pulled the phone from my ear. "We're in this together! Irv's being missing says I AM involved in this! I would be anyway, because you're my friend. I know you wouldn't desert me!"

I couldn't argue with simple logic like that, so I thanked her for her friendship and said I'd see her tomorrow. We'd meet at the restaurant on Main street; the one Amos and I had frequented on that, seemingly, long ago day.

After I hung up, I sat gazing out the window at the white darkness. Red, blue and green spots from my Christmas lights still glistened off the crust of snow that was now my yard. A small figure darted over it, not even breaking the crust. A mouse (perhaps running from that owl that prowled the woods) skittered away into the night.

After a restless night, I arose right before dawn and sat at the table waiting for the coffee.

I didn't feel like fighting the dark and cold to get wood, so I turned up the heat and got my heavy robe. My day had begun.

I met Irmaline at precisely 12. She'd been getting out of her car two cars from me when I saw her. We met at the door.

We settled in a booth off to one side in front of a big window. There weren't very many customers, but I supposed the lunch crowd would soon make an appearance. I wasn't looking forward to the looks and whispers I knew would ensue. Everyone in town now knew Barney was missing. I didn't know if anyone knew about my intruder, I was hoping the Sheriff and his staff were discrete. If the press found out, they'd have a field day! I could see the headlines now: "Woman who found body in trunk attacked!" I pushed the thought from my mind. The Sheriff, more than anyone, didn't want any more negative publicity in his bailiwick.

Irmaline removed her soft umber, wool coat and hung it on the hook attached to the booth. I followed suit.

We settled opposite each other and remained silent while the waitress poured us coffee, sneaking nervous glances at me while placing silverware before us.

"You look none the worse for wear after that terrifying incident the other night." She said, after the waitress left.

"I don't like to think about it." I said. My hand had unconsciously begun rubbing my neck; I placed it demurely in my lap when I realized what I was doing.

She gave me a pitying look as she blew delicately on her cup.

"And this, too, shall pass, Annie" she said, sipping her coffee.

I WISH I had her faith, I thought. Ironically, the Church loomed large in my legacy of horror. I had no desire to seek solace there.

"Yeah, it'll pass." I said, sarcastically, "but will we pass with it?"

I immediately regretted my tone and apologized.

She waved her hand in that now familiar way, and pooh-

poohed my apology.

"All you've been through the last 6 months or so, I can't believe you're still sane."

She said, patting my hand lightly as I clutched my cup.

"What's going on with Irv?" I asked.

"It's really weird. No one's seen him, or the station wagon, which stands out like a sore thumb." I knew what she meant. The front driver's side door was red, contrasting with the blue of the rest of the car. Rust encircled the wheel wells and doorframes; Barney evidently wasn't embarrassed about that. But why should he be? Sherry was the one who had to drive it. He had the almost new government vehicle at his disposal.

"Where could he be? When's he s'posed to go back to work?" I asked. I knew he got some time off for Thanksgiving.

"Not for a couple more days. He also took some vacation days to spend time with his relatives. He always really looks forward to that!" She was now mindlessly stirring her coffee, her thoughts miles away.

"I talked to Amos after I talked to you." She said. "He told me the whole story, and I must admit, some of it was comedic." She smiled wanly.

I felt my face flame as I recalled my comment to Amos about him wanting to have 'fun' with me, before he killed me. Put in context, if he was an innocent in all this, yes. I guess it would be funny. I smiled back.

"You must trust him, Annie! He's the best ally you have. I'm just an old lady. The Sheriff's more concerned about the Vicky murder, and that Detective has his own agenda."

"You're right." I found I'd been saying that a lot, lately.

Then our food arrived and conversation ceased.

By the end of the meal Irmaline had talked me into going home with her, in hopes that her daughter would pull herself together in front of company. She also hoped Sherry and I could become good friends as Barney had managed to drive off nearly everyone else she got close to. Irmaline gave me credit for having more fortitude than I actually did. But I, too, could use another friend, and I liked Sherry, so I reluctantly agreed.

# CHAPTER EIGHTEEN

I followed Irmaline home after lunch with the intention of distracting Sherry from her misery for a while. As we pulled in the drive the boys came running up; despite their warm winter coats and gloves, their cheeks were red with cold.

"Grandma, grandma." They yelled. They swarmed her as she exited her car, leaving snowy prints on her immaculate coat. I parked behind her and went up and stood next to her.

"Hi Shawn. Hi, Luke." I said.

"Hi" Shawn responded. Luke gave a little wave and ran off into the house. After disentangling herself from Shawn, Irmaline, too, headed in, Shawn following, peering at me over his shoulder.

"What's she doing here?" He asked, in a whisper loud enough for me to hear.

"Why, she's come to cheer up your mother." Irmaline answered, smiling at me over his head.

"Hi, mom." Sherry said as we removed our footwear on the mat behind the door.

"Hi, honey. Any news?" Irmaline asked, embracing her.

"No. Nothing." Sherry replied.

She was still in her robe; a large, shapeless, blue terry thing, that was half open, revealing a flannel nightgown underneath. Her hair was in disarray, her face puffy: From crying? I wondered.

"Hi, Sherry," I said.

"Hi, Annie." She answered, looking embarrassed at being caught in her nightclothes.

"Let me get dressed." She said, quickly departing.

"See," Irmaline whispered to me, "It's working already."

The boys had thrown their coats, boots and mittens haphazardly in front of the door, running off to play video games, I guessed.

I helped Irmaline gather their things, hanging them in the little closet behind the door.

We could hear Sherry upstairs chastising the boy's rowdiness as their pounding feet could be heard running up and down the hallway.

Irmaline and I settled on the couch. I could smell cigarette smoke and noticed the overflowing ashtray on the coffee table. A half empty coffee cup sat next to it.

"Poor Sherry", I said, "she must be going nuts."

"I hate to say it, but if she wasn't so upset, I'd almost be glad he's gone. It's just the not knowing what happened to him that bothers me." Irmaline said this in an undertone for fear Sherry might suddenly enter and hear. "You saw the boys," she continued, "they're always much more at ease when he's not around."

Yes, I could imagine it would be hard having Barney for a father.

Sherry appeared then, a cigarette dangling from her pallid lips.

She sat on the other end of the sofa, Irmaline between us.

"I'm sorry I'm such a mess, Annie. And I'm afraid I'm not

much help to mom, either.

Her house is totaled since we've been here. I just can't seem to find the energy to do anything." She looked totally dejected and my heart went out to her. "The boys are running wild. They don't listen to me." She looked on the verge of tears and I felt like I was intruding on her grief. I didn't know how I could help. After all, I couldn't stand her husband so how could I possibly share her sense of loss.

She'd put on a holey pair of jeans and rumpled sweater; it was obvious she didn't notice or care. It was also obvious my presence would in no way alleviate her grief.

"I wish dad was here." She said, wistfully, snubbing her cigarette out as ashes flew everywhere.

Irmaline drew her into her arms then, patting her back, as I'm sure she'd done when Sherry was a child and in pain. She murmured soft encouragement and looked about ready to cry, herself. I felt like a total voyeur being witness to such an intimate scene.

The phone rang then, causing us all to jump. Irmaline went into the kitchen to answer it,

Sherry followed behind her.

I rose and went to the mantle, scanning the old family pictures assembled there. I could hear Irmaline's voice, but couldn't make out any words. I felt myself start to shake as a chill ran down my spine.

Irmaline came back in, a solemn look on her face; Sherry trailed behind, looking like she was in shock.

"They found the car." Irmaline said, looking at me.

"Where? Where's B…Irv?" I asked.

"That's the question." She replied, cryptically.

She perched on the edge of the couch while Sherry stood, mute, in the middle of the room.

"That was the Sheriff's Office. The car was in a ditch out on Old Townsend Road, half buried in snow. Irv was nowhere to be found. The snow had covered any tracks that may have been there. The Sheriff and 2 Deputies are out there now, searching. They're calling a tow truck to take the car into the Police Impound so they can examine it."

I knew, of course, about Old Townsend road. It was about 3 miles from my house; a dirt road, nearly impassable in winter, leading to other dirt roads and another, even smaller town, 15 miles further on.

"Amos found it." Irmaline said. "He didn't touch anything, and hightailed it back to town immediately."

It was then that Sherry broke down. She fell on the couch, almost crushing Irmaline in a viselike grip as tears flowed unashamedly down her pale face. Her whole body shook in silent sobs as Irmaline tried her best to comfort her.

"Hey, c'mon." I surprised myself by saying. "That's good, isn't it? Obviously he went in the ditch and got out and started walking. Maybe he's at someone's house and they don't have a phone, or the lines are down." The lines were always down somewhere around here in the winter. Al and I had suffered through days of no electricity through the years, owing to winter storms.

Sherry sat up and looked at me over Irmaline's shoulder. "But why wouldn't they give him a ride back to town?" She asked; her tear-stained face ravaged by uncertainty.

"It is below freezing. Maybe their car wouldn't start," I said, hopefully.

"That's a lot of 'maybes'", Sherry said, breaking into sobs once more.

The phone rang again and Irmaline asked me to get it, her arms full with her distraught child.

"Hello?" I answered, tentatively.

"Hi, Annie." It was Amos. He sounded surprised to hear my voice answering. I was glad to hear his.

"What's going on?" I asked. "We just heard you found the car."

"I'd searched everywhere else so I decided to give it a shot.

I didn't think Irv would have gone that way, even in a station wagon. I have a hard time maneuvering that road in the winter even with my truck. But there it was. I probably wouldn't have even seen it if I didn't have such a high vantage point from the truck. From what I could see, without disturbing anything, was that there wasn't any blood anywhere. But I only went close enough to determine it was empty, so we'll have to wait until the Sheriff's through with it before we know anything else." He sounded as bewildered as the rest of us.

"Please come over!" I implored, whispering. "Sherry is taking it pretty hard. She hasn't told the boys, yet, she's too upset right now. I sure picked the wrong time to come over here."

"Are you sure you want me to?" He asked, coyly.

"YES. For God's sake, get over here!" I said, my voice rising.

"I'm on my way." He said, and hung up.

I poured myself a cup of coffee while I was in the kitchen, reluctant to return to the abject misery of the living room. I looked at the peaceful scene outside the window. Wordsworth was sitting on the dock, looking out over the frozen channel; wondering, perhaps, how many winters he had left.

I could hear childish laughter coming from upstairs and wondered what the boys reaction would be when they found out the car had been found, sans their dad.

I pulled myself away from the window and wearily went back to the emotional scene playing out in the other room.

I saw that Sherry had pulled herself together, somewhat, as I entered and took my original position next to Irmaline. Sherry was, once again, puffing on a cigarette, but her eyes were dry.

"Amos is on his way." I said.

"Good." Said Irmaline. "He always puts things in perspective."

A few minutes later we heard the pounding of feet coming down the stairs.

"Amos is here!" Shawn yelled, flying to the door.

"Amos! Amos!" yelled Luke.

Wow, I thought. They really like Amos! Good, at least they have some kind of decent male role model. I realized then that they must have to curb their enthusiasm for Amos' presence around their dad. They knew what a jealous, petty person he was.

When Amos entered, they were all over him. He calmed them down as he divested himself of his coat and boots, then raised them, one at a time, into the air and twirled them around, nearly knocking a picture off the mantle.

"Okay, boys" he said, setting Luke down. "That's enough for now. I have to talk to your mom and grandma. I'll come up to your room later and you can show me what level you've achieved on your game."

They left, dejectedly, casting accusing glances at their mother for depriving them of their play mate.

Sherry hung on every word as Amos described the scene he'd come upon, and his actions and reactions on finding the abandoned vehicle. He made it clear that there was nothing to do now but play the waiting game. The Sheriff's department would keep us informed of any developments.

After a while, I went in the kitchen and made chicken salad sandwiches from a Tupperware container in the refrigerator. I set the table and called the boys. They looked surprised to see me serving them as they sat at the kitchen table.

"Your mom's tired and sad and needs some rest right now. So please try to be quiet and not upset her further." I said, placing two glasses of milk next to the sandwiches.

I juggled three plates for the adults and Amos came to help me as I entered the living room. After everyone was settled, plates in hand, I returned to the kitchen and bade the boy's good-bye.

I returned to the living room and told everyone I was going home. The emotional turmoil was palpable and I needed to get away from there. I knew Amos was going to be entertaining the boys and at some point they were going to have to be told the latest developments. I didn't feel I had the right to bear witness to that scene. Nor did I want to!

Irmaline bade me to sit for a while, but I was already pulling my coat on. She rose and crossed the room to see me out, and we talked in whispers as I told her it was time for me to leave and I'd call her later.

"O.k., Annie, if that's what you want to do. Thanks for fixing the sandwiches and feeding the boys. Sherry hasn't eaten since yesterday and that was just a bite. I'm going to go now and try to force her." She retreated back to her daughter's side. Amos caught me outside the door. He closed it behind us and stood, coatless and in his stocking feet beside me on the porch.

"Why are you leaving?" He asked.

"I don't feel it's my place to be here, right now." I said, "I'm going home to take a hot bath and a nap. All this tension is physically exhausting! And I feel like a voyeur intruding on their grief."

Surprisingly, he didn't argue, just told me he'd see me later and implored me to be careful. He lifted my chin with a cold, bloodless finger and gave me a chaste kiss before disappearing back inside. He peeked back out as I descended the steps, "Call here the minute you get home." He said, than closed the door.

My little house never looked so good. I grabbed an armful of wood as I went in, intending to get a fire going. My pets greeted me noisily, letting me know, in no uncertain terms, that it was past their suppertime.

I realized, with some alarm, that I never had gone grocery shopping. Shit! And I'd been right in town, too. I searched the frig and cupboards for something to eat. I hadn't made myself a sandwich because I'd run out of the chicken salad by the time the other sandwiches were made. Besides, I really hadn't felt like eating then, with all the tension in the air. It seemed my own home was the only place I could really relax and that comfort zone was being stripped away.

The phone rang as I pulled out an ancient can of Pork and Beans. I'd forgotten to call Irmaline's to let them know I'd gotten home safely and all was well.

"I made it." I answered, on the second ring.

"You didn't call." Amos said.

"I forgot. I also forgot to go shopping and I've literally nothing to eat. I'm going to have to go to the store." I hated going shopping. Everyone I saw in town always stared and gave me questioning looks. Some were downright rude. And that was when I was with Irmaline or Amos. I shuddered to think what they'd do if I ventured out alone. Maybe I'd order a pizza. There was one place in town that delivered here.

"Don't go alone." Amos said, forcefully. "I'll come over and take you later."

I breathed a sigh of relief. "Okay." I said meekly, realizing I was once again getting sucked into Amos' world.

I lay on the couch, suddenly too tired to even take a bath, the t.v. blaring unintelligibly in the background. Eventually I nodded off to disturbing dreams without substance, but disturbing, all the same.

Pounding on the door awakened me. I forced myself to consciousness, my eyelids felt gritty and my mouth felt like I'd swallowed a dust bunny. I stumbled to the door.

"Who is it?" I called.

"It's me Annie," Amos' booming voice announced.

I hurriedly unlocked the door and let him in, quickly slamming it against the cold, winter night. It was almost 6 I noticed, glancing at the small mantle clock. In the winter I could never tell, without a clock, what time it was, once the sun went down at 5 o'clock.

Amos had stripped off his coat and boots immediately and went and perched on the edge of the couch.

"Hurry." He said, looking at me, "The news is coming on and Irv's disappearance is the lead story!"

I sat next to him just as the talking heads appeared on the screen.

"The strange disappearance of a rural Gaylord man comes on the heels of a murder investigation in the small town." The newswoman announced, looking like the cat that swallowed the canary.

A tape of a tow truck pulling Irv's snow covered car from the ditch appeared on the screen as a description of his last known movements was given. A picture of Irv was flashed on the screen with a number below it to call if you had any information.

The whole Vicky affair was rehashed, including the now famous picture of my erstwhile trunk. Amos was referred to as 'a local man who'd been out searching for the missing man' when they mentioned how and where the car was found.

Thank God my role was minor in this latest incident. The closest I came to being identified was 'a few Thanksgiving dinner guests'.

"Here we go again." I said, dejectedly.

"I saw one news truck heading into town on the way over. I'm sure there are more."

Amos replied. "Thank God they didn't mention my name." He added, mirroring my thoughts.

"God. I hate going into town, now." I said; fearing some news people may recognize me.

"Wanna pizza?" I asked.

Allies once again, I thought, when the pizza had been ordered. Amos got the smoldering fire going as I went to freshen up and get something to drink. I had to dig out the liter bottle of pop in my bottom cupboard and fight with ice cube trays before I could slake my thirst. I took a glass of ice-filled pop to Amos.

"It's warm" I said, "I had to break into my emergency stash."

"It's wet, that's all that matters." He said. "But...my emergency stash, of beer, is in the truck! I'll get it when the pizza gets here."

"It'll be frozen by then." I said.

"Nah. I just picked it up, warm, on the way over. It needs to chill for a while."

Seeing the look on my face he quickly added, "I was planning on taking it home, but I'm more than willing to share it with you."

"Right on." I said, and then felt stupid for saying it.

Amos insisted on paying for the pizza. He brought the beer in and we spent the rest of the evening eating, drinking and speculating on Barney's fate. We watched the two other tapes and, on the one showing the side yard, a blurry figure could be seen running into the woods. We decided to turn it in to the Police even though it could've been a Yeti for all you could see. I'd have to pick up some more blank tapes in town, tomorrow, as the cops still hadn't returned my living room tape.

At some point I went and took my bath and by the time I came out, Amos was fast asleep, beer can still in hand. I carefully removed the half empty can and covered him with a blanket before turning in myself.

The day dawned bright and sunny and I awoke to sunbeams dancing across my comforter. My pets were curled next to me. Judas was at my feet and Sam cuddled by my side.

I stumbled to the kitchen, nearly falling, as my long robe tripped me up. After the coffee was going I sat at the kitchen table, thinking; watching Amos' slack face as he lolled on the couch. He woke up when I let Sam out on his lead after feeding him and Judas.

I handed him a cup of coffee as he sat up.

I turned on the television to catch the morning news but they were still showing last night's video. No new news.

Amos, like me, was even more reticent in the morning and not much conversation was forthcoming.

We went to Amos' place so he would have clean clothes to put on after his shower, and I once again marveled at the uniqueness of his home. In the light I could see the front porch winding around the side of the house and thought how nice it must be to sit there in the spring, summer and fall, communing with nature. Now, however, there was about three feet of snow covering it. Bird and squirrel tracks dotted the surface everywhere. Amos gave me an unopened six-pack of blank videotapes he never used, so I mentally crossed that off my list.

We then went to town, stopping at the Sheriff's office to drop off the other tape. I stayed in the truck as Amos ran in.

The grocery store was next. Due to the earliness of the day and the cold, we were practically the only ones there, for which I was grateful. My cart was full by the time we reached the checkout counter, while Amos had only a handful of articles.

We went back to my house to have breakfast, leaving Amos' purchases in the truck.

It felt good to have someone sharing my day with me. I'd nearly forgotten how nice it was to have a man around, although the company of another woman or child would probably have had the same effect. The feeling of camaraderie was what I'd been missing.

"I hate to leave you with all that's going on, but I'm going to have to make another run. I need the money," Amos informed me as I cleared the dirty dishes after breakfast. "You can ride with me if you want." He offered.

I declined. Living in a truck for days at a time wasn't my idea of a good time, and there were my pets to consider.

Amos left shortly after breakfast. He wanted to go home

and sleep, as he had to drive all night.

He'd brought a bunch of wood in before he left and it was stacked in a neat pile on either side of the hearth; he put a new tape in my living room camera. Sam and Judas were snuffling and digging at the wood, undoubtedly smelling chipmunk or mouse spore.

I called Irmaline and asked if she could spend the night with me. I invited Sherry and the boys, too. Irmaline said she'd be happy to, Sherry's best friend (she had one that stuck by her, the one she'd been talking to at the Halloween dance. Though she was married with children and had her own life, with Barney gone, she was more than willing to visit Sherry and the boys and offer support) was going to spend the night there, so it would work out perfect, as Irmaline wouldn't leave them alone.

"Don't eat anything," I implored. "I'll make up a nice supper. Anytime you want to come, come on over."

"Debby's coming over in a couple hours. I'll leave when she gets here; I'll call first."

We had an unspoken agreement that we always let one another know when we were leaving and when we got home. With no cell phones at our disposal it was necessary to have someone know your whereabouts in winter weather. If Irv had had a cell phone, he'd probably be home right now, unless he didn't want to be found.

By the time Irmaline arrived, I had a roaring fire going; a newly purchased roast was in the oven, potatoes were boiling.

Irmaline entered like a breath of fresh air. Despite all that had happened, she'd never lost her cool. She tossed a movie to me as she divested herself of coat and boots. I looked at it: "The African Queen." Alright! Something we'll both like.

We sat at the kitchen table as we ate, discussing the latest developments. Irmaline was of the opinion that Irv had attacked me and was hiding out until he healed. I wasn't so sure. Obviously, he'd still have a scar, and disappearing would make him look guiltier. She conceded this and we both remained baffled.

She told me that a reporter and camera crew had come to her house hoping to catch Sherry and/or the boys in their grief. She hadn't answered the door and had to call the Sheriff's department and plead with them to come out and chase them away. A newly hired deputy she'd used to baby sit for finally came out as a personal favor and made them leave.

"You should have called Amos. You knew he'd be here if he wasn't home." I said.

She fluttered her bird-like hand. "I can't be calling Amos constantly. He has his own life." She gave me a knowing look as she said this.

So. She felt she was affording Amos and I some privacy.

"Still scheming, huh?" I smirked.

Her eyes went wide as she looked at me. Her hand had flown to her chest in a gesture of innocence.

"Now, Annie, I'm sure I have too many things on my mind to meddle in others' affairs."

"Sure you do." I said, laconically.

After the movie, I retrieved Irmaline's sheets and blanket from my linen closet where they now resided, and together we made up the couch. It had become a ritual of our movie nights.

In the morning, as we sipped our coffee and thought about breakfast, Sherry called.

Her friend, Debby, would be spending the day. Her kids were with their dad, but her and Sherry were going to pick them up and then they were taking all the kids to a movie in a neighboring town.

As it turned out, Debby's kids were nearly the same age as Sherry's, and loved playing together, but over the years the meetings had gotten less and less frequent as Barney curtailed Sherry and the kid's movements more and more.

Irmaline was ecstatic the friendship was being renewed and hoped, aloud, that Barney was never found; then felt guilty because the children and Sherry would suffer. Personally, I didn't think the kids would miss Barney all that much, from what I'd seen.

Sherry, too, would get over it quickly and find a new life. But being missing was a fate worse than death for a wondering family. Neither Irmaline, nor I, liked the way our thoughts were going, so the subject was changed.

Irmaline had brought a change of clothes but left them in the car, as she might have to fly for home if anything developed. She went and got them as we had decided to spend the day together. We were still discussing what we should do as I fried bacon and Irmaline shirred eggs.

Amos called and both Irmaline and I talked to him. He was leaving shortly and wanted to make sure everything was all right. He'd called and let the Sheriff's department know when he was leaving and his route. I didn't ask if he was required to because he was still a suspect in the Vicky murder, or if he just wanted to be notified, by them, if anything happened. He gave us an itinerary of his stops; complete with telephone numbers. Seems he didn't trust the police, all that much, to notify him.

We ate breakfast, than got ready to go to the Mall in a town thirty miles away. The day was bright and sunny, so driving shouldn't be a problem. We decided to take my car, as it was less of a gas hog.

I saw both Sam and Judas looking out the window at us as we got in the car. I waved, and got behind the wheel. I was excited. I hadn't been anywhere for the longest time. This was strictly a pleasure trip, and I was determined to leave my problems behind for the day.

The drive was quite scenic. Snow and ice laden branches nearly touched each other over the road, making a glimmering canopy above us. As we came over a rise in the road, the forest ended and a panorama of endless white fields nearly blinded us, their wintry crust reflecting the sun like a mirror off the windshield.

I felt my heart soar and suddenly understood the feeling Amos must get when he was on the open road. A certain sense of freedom and oneness with the world unfolding outside the window, overcame me.

Irmaline chatted casually, telling stories of times before her children were born; of how her and her husband had driven this road, then a dirt lane, and gotten stuck in thick mud from a recent rain. They'd then went into a nearby field and spread their blanket right there, and had their picnic lunch. The gushing falls they were headed to see would have to wait for another day. But they made the best of it, staring dumbfounded at a huge bull behind a barbwire fence. They fed horses in another field pieces of sugar brought for their thermos of coffee. They'd stayed all day, until finally, the farmer spied them from atop his tractor and pulled the old Ford out of the mire. Just about every mile had a different memory for her, and I listened, spellbound, to stories of life in a different time.

The fields ended abruptly at the next turn in the road. The Mall was just a strip mall, carved out of the earth less than a decade ago. It loomed large out of what used to be some farmers field: Had he been forced out by some corporate conglomerate? I knew there'd been rumors for years about the State buying up land around our town and making it into a State Park. The mall was on the outskirts of this little town, deliberately placed to utilize the traffic on the road we came in on.

The ascending sun reflected off the huge plate glass windows, giving the illusion of an alien city rising out of nowhere.

We pulled into the half-full lot. I parked as close to the

front doors as possible, for though it was sunny, a brisk wind blew across the flat land.

Once inside, we made a beeline for the nearest Starbucks. We sat on plastic chairs in a huge, open atrium area. Odors wafted in the air around us. Sounds echoed off the cavernous walls. We sipped our coffee, discussing which store to hit first. It was nice to be anonymous; there was little chance we'd run into people from our town on a weekday, especially in the morning. We chose the bookstore as our first stop. Irmaline was immediately drawn to the shelves right in front of the door where all the new releases were displayed. I wandered around, stopping to check out the magazine rack, in search of a crossword puzzle book. There was a small area set up in the middle of the store that was also a coffee shop. I met Irmaline at the checkout counter. We both had purchases. She, a new Grisham book, me, crossword magazines.

Next we hit the Neon Station, a little nook of a store with trendy neon lights, signs and statues. A rack of insulting cards for all occasions sat on one wall. Neither of us bought anything there. The prices were outrageous.

We wandered aimlessly down the intersecting walkways, pointing out things to each other in the windows as we passed by. A group of elderly mall walkers breezed past and Irmaline made a funny comment about how she should join along behind them. A few teenagers (skipping school?) were loitering outside an arcade. Which reminded me:

"Irmaline, aren't Shawn and Luke supposed to be in school, today?"

"They probably won't be going back until we know what happened to Irv. The Sheriff suggested it. Debby kept her kids out today, too, to go to the movies with Sherry and the kids."

"Wow." I said, frightened. "It's really that serious, huh?"

"They speculate that if someone's out to get Irv, his family may be in danger. That's why Debby stayed last night and they're gone today. The Police are driving by periodically, and we have a little known number to call to insure we get through right away."

"They're supposed to be watching my place, too." I said. "But I haven't seen even one of their cars go by." I added. "Nor did I get a 'special number.'"

"Well, they have to believe you, now. They have someone on tape! That's irrefutable evidence, right there!" She exclaimed. "You were attacked! You go down there tomorrow, Annie, and demand some protection!"

We had stopped in the middle of the walkway in front of a t-shirt kiosk, as the human traffic had grown heavier. The mall walkers' numbers had suddenly swelled and they assertively elbowed their way past all in their path.

I smiled as an elderly man knocked Irmalines arm and she, in schoolmarm fashion, berated him like a recalcitrant student. Everything must be getting to her, too, I thought; but it was comical, none-the-less.

"You're right Irmaline", I teased, sarcastically, "you'd fit right in with them!"

I'd effectively managed to change the subject, as there was no way I was going to the Sheriff's office unless summoned.

After another half hour of mindless wandering, we stopped at a rather upscale clothing store where Irmaline purchased a new, pale pink sweater with little pearl buttons, I, a dark blue, long-sleeved turtleneck found in the bargain bin. Cotton. We then stopped at a jewelry kiosk set up in the middle of the wide hallway. I bought some earrings and Irmaline got a faux pearl necklace to compliment her new sweater.

We decided to have lunch at the TGIF attached to the atrium, accessible by a glass door.

After we were settled, two more cups of steaming coffee sitting before us, menus perused and set aside, I asked Irmaline what Amos was like as a child. I'd broached this subject before, but somehow the conversation had turned in another direction, the query forgotten. After we'd ordered, Irmaline began her recitation.

Irmaline had watched Amos and his brother and sister as children. Amos was the oldest, his sister trailing behind him two years; his brother a year after her. Their father was an over the road trucker who had started a trucking company with 3 partners when Amos was around four. His mother was a librarian, (that explained Amos' being so articulate in a place where it was the exception rather than the rule), who traveled to different libraries in our area, as needed.

Irmaline's children were around the same ages at the time and all attended school together so Irmaline insisted it was no imposition on her to have them. They were well behaved and pleasant to be around. Amos' sister, June, was quite the little actress, even back then; raiding Irmaline's closet whenever she got the chance for outfits for the little plays and skits she wrote. Amos and the other brother, Rafe, were always a part of these little enterprises. Irmaline's husbands' hats' were also brought into play; a top hat for their rendition of "The Gettysburg Address", Amos playing a stocky Lincoln; memorizing the whole thing by the time he was 8. Rafe, now the burly stevedore, was typecast as Huckleberry Finn and various other juvenile outcasts. Peter Pan was a perennial favorite. Over the years they'd memorized nearly all the lines, this being June's favorite book. Amos was Peter, of course, June, Tinkerbelle. Sherry played the part of Wendy. Gary played John. There was no Michael as no one wanted to be 'that baby'. Rich and Rafe rounded off the cast as the Lost Boys. June also loved musicals and tried, in vain, to get everyone to do "Our Town," but unfortunately, she was the only one who could sing and dance, so these endeavors always fell flat. In high school, June put her acting talent to use and starred in nearly every play; she'd headed to New York right after graduation. By then Amos was married to Vicky and following in his dad's footsteps, driving truck. Only Rafe was still at home, finishing high school. Irmaline told me her family had been good friend's with Amos' family, especially his mother. His dad was gone a lot. She asked if I'd like to go visit her in the nursing home in Park City, and implored me to ask Amos if I could accompany him the next time he went. She tried to get over there a couple of times a year, but the early stages of Alzheimer's had besieged her friends' mind, and she never knew what to expect on her visits.

The sun was high in the sky as we exited the steel and glass conglomeration. Dark clouds were starting to form and swiftly scuttled across the face of the sun. It was going to storm. We quickly made our way to my car, hoping to get home before the snow started. We threw our packages in the back seat and pealed out of the lot, my brakes squealing as I turned onto the road. The wind had picked up and snow flew across the road in increasing intensity. I got that disorienting feeling that we were stationary and the world was moving. We were on the edge of the forest line when a loud pop, like a gunshot, startled us. The car started listing to the left and I pumped the brakes gently while turning into the skid. Great! A flat tire. When our speed was sufficiently slowed, I turned the wheel back to the right and came to rest on the edge of the small ditch. I hadn't had the pleasure of changing a tire in years and didn't look forward to doing so on a snow-covered road, with quickly diminishing visibility. Irmaline had braced herself on the dash as we slid sideways across the road. I turned on the emergency flashers and got out, keys in hand, to inspect the damage. I saw Irmaline, making her way around the front of the vehicle, clinging to the hood to avoid falling in the ditch.

The road was totally deserted as we stood next to the car, looking at the shredded left front tire.

"They better put up that cell phone tower, soon." I said. "If anyone needs them, it's us, out here in the sticks."

I noticed Irmaline was shivering beneath her camel coat.

The wind howled through the trees and the sky was now thick with black storm clouds, virtually blotting out the sun.

"You stay in the car, Irmaline!" I yelled, above the wind.

"Shit!" I screamed to an uncaring universe, stomping my foot ineffectively.

When reason returned, I sprinted to the rear of the car and opened the trunk. I didn't notice Irmaline coming up behind me as I lifted the heavy trunk lid. Before I could comprehend what I was seeing, Irmaline let loose with an ear splitting scream, causing me to jump back and cover my ears. My screams mingled with hers as I followed her wide eyes to the crumpled form stuffed in my trunk. We'd found Barney.

Then something happened that will haunt me forever; Irmaline turned and stared at me, her face as white as a sheet, her hands covering her mouth. Time seemed to stand still for a split second, and then she turned and fled down the middle of the snow-streaked road, her arms waving above her head, her screams cascading and descending in the whistling wind.

"Irmaline!" I screamed, in vain. I slowly started walking down the road; Irmaline was now a disappearing speck in the swirling snow. I was in shock. I no longer felt the cold.

A numbness had overcome me and I continued walking; I had no idea where, just walking. Irmaline was no longer visible and I hoped she was all right. I was entering the tree line when I saw headlights approaching. I put my hands up, waving frantically, as they neared. The sound of the engine intensified as it was thrown into a higher gear, and despite the now nearly blinding snow, it increased in speed and flew by me. As the dark sedan whipped past, I got a glimpse of a white face in the front passenger seat; and in the rear, eyes wide with shock, Irmaline stared at me, looking for all the world like she'd seen the Devil himself.

Despite my shock, I knew I must return to the car if I didn't want to freeze to death or get killed by a passing motorist blinded by the storm. When I reached the car, I closed the trunk and got in, immediately turning on the heat to thaw my frozen hands.

Time no longer existed and it only seemed a few minutes, but it could have been hours, when a car approached from the direction Irmaline had been headed. As it turned and pulled up behind me, I knew the Sheriff had come for me.

I was taken back to town in the rear of the Sheriff's vehicle. My car was to be towed back to the Police garage for processing.

# Chapter Nineteen

The Police station was buzzing with activity as I was brought in. I was escorted to a small, dank little room. An interrogation room, I surmised. I was read my rights and asked to sign a form saying I understood them. The charge was first-degree murder, but I'd have to wait for the arraignment to see if I'd be indicted. I assured the Sheriff I understood the legalities and I'd answer any questions he may ask. I wondered if Irmaline was somewhere in the building and how she was. I asked the Sheriff; he wouldn't tell me.

Two hours later, I was processed into the system. Fingerprinted, mug shots taken. I was then shaken down by a female officer, (brought in just for me?) and placed in a cell, downstairs in the jail. I was to be arraigned in the morning. I hadn't even made a phone call. Who would I call? I didn't have Amos' itinerary with me and I doubted the Sheriff would give it to me. I didn't know where Irmaline was, and I doubted she would talk to me, anyway.

I seemed to be the only prisoner in the few cells that were down there. Fatigue and shock had lulled me into a trance-like state and my only thought before I passed into a dreamless sleep was: who would feed my pets and let Sam out?

I was awoken in the morning by the door being opened. There stood a Deputy and a man in a suit I didn't recognize. He came in, shook my hand, and identified himself as a Criminal Attorney from the Law firm of Thomas and Spence. I'd refused one yesterday, but someone had placed a call to the Law firm in town on my behalf, and here he was. We both sat on the edge of the narrow cot that passed for a bed. I was still in the clothes I'd been wearing yesterday. The attorney, Mr. Spence, was a slim man, perhaps 40, wearing a pinstripe suit and looking quite dapper. His shock of blonde hair, just starting to recede, was neatly coiffed. He had an air of assurance about him and made me feel at ease. I hired him on the spot, the reality of my situation finally dawning on my shell-shocked brain. He had a sheaf of papers in hand, encased in a manila folder. The charges against me, I soon learned. I talked for nearly an hour straight, telling him every incident that had occurred since the beginning, even before, as I related my suspicions about Al's death. He assured me that there wasn't enough evidence to charge me with anything. Of course they still had to review Irv's autopsy results; evidently they were waiting for him to thaw out first. They still had my bloody knife; if stabbing was the cause of death it could be vital evidence. He had no idea who had called his firm, his secretary had taken a message and the caller had remained anonymous.

The Sheriff, personally, drove me to the courthouse, my attorney following behind. I was allowed to clean up in a bathroom across from the courtroom, a Deputy on guard outside.

Though I was terrified of going before the judge, I had the righteousness of innocence on my side and would stand tall.

It turned out I had no reason to worry. After the charges

were read, my attorney outlined the circumstances of my arrest, how I had made numerous calls for help from the Police Department over the past several months, how I'd filed a report about being attacked in my own home, how I had caught the perpetrator on a tape which was now in possession of the Police Department.

I was released for insufficient evidence and allowed to leave, after being cautioned that it would be in my best interest not to leave town until things were resolved to the satisfaction of the court. Outside the courtroom my Attorney informed me that should evidence be forthcoming, I could be charged. The knife was the smoking gun, but even if it was determined that Irv had been killed with the knife, it would only prove that he was the one who attacked me. It would then be a whole new ballgame, according to Mr. Spence. I would then have to go to court using a self-defense defense.

My car was released to me as nothing incriminating but Irv's body had been found. The trunk latch had a few markings on it that could have been from tampering, another plus for me. The tire had been removed and my spare put on; they'd kept the flat for examination. I was convinced that the car had been gone over with a fine-tooth comb during my incarceration. I didn't care, though my lawyer was already talking lawsuits. I just wanted to go home and lick my wounds. If it turned out I was responsible for Barney's death, I'd deal with it when the time came.

I was dreading the onslaught of reporters that would converge back on the town once news of the body being found was released. I hoped to get home without being spotted if they were already on the trail.

My lawyer escorted me to my car, which had just been brought around, with the spare donut tire now on it, and gave me his card with his home number written in pen on the back. I thanked him profusely, told him to send me his bill, and slid in the already cold car under the watchful eyes of half a dozen curious townspeople.

The storm was over, a smattering of new snow and a few downed trees the only remnants of its passing. I managed to make it home, not breaking down until I looked in the back seat and saw Irmaline's packages laying next to mine, the contents half scattered across the back seat from the search. When I saw her beautiful new pink sweater, with traces of fingerprint powder clinging to it, lying exposed on the seat, the dam broke.

Sam was going crazy as I went in. Jumping on me, whining and barking. Judas had made a beeline for her dish, and sat looking at me disdainfully. Tears coursed down my cheeks as I fed my pets. Sam scarfed his food down quickly, than ran to the door. Poor Sam! After I tied him out I looked for telltale evidence that his bladder hadn't held, but found none. Good boy!

I went in the bathroom and blew my nose as bath water ran. I let it run and went to let Sam in, as he didn't much like the cold.

After soaking in hot water for 45 minutes I donned my nightgown and robe and went to start a fire in the cold hearth. The wood Amos had brought in for me still sat there, and for some unknown reason, the sight of it started me crying again. Then I thought of Sherry and the boys, and the tears turned to wracking sobs as I buried my face in the couch cushion.

I figured someone had probably called Amos by now; if not the Sheriff, then Irmaline.

What would he think? What had he been told?

Eventually, I felt consciousness fading as I stared at the dancing flames of the now intense fire. The smell of wood smoke and crackling logs comforted me, and I dozed.

A pounding at the door roused me from sleep. The fire had died down to embers and long shadows filled the room. I stood inside the door, listening.

"Annie. It's me, Amos. Let me in!"

I swung the door wide and threw myself over the threshold and into his arms.

"Oh my God, Amos!" I said, my throat once more thickening.

He pulled me in the door with him, closing and locking it behind us.

He led me to the couch and I related the whole ordeal, breaking down on a few occasions. He waited patiently for me to finish, watching me closely with those knowing eyes.

"Who told you?" I finally asked, when I'd finished my recitation.

"Irmaline. She's the one who called the lawyer, too." He informed me.

"But… the look on her face, Amos! I've never been looked at like that before, like I'm a murderer! And by someone I love!" I choked, biting my knuckle.

He took me in his arms then and rocked me like the baby I was acting like.

"Annie," he said, softly, tilting my head up and brushing hair off my face, "Irmaline's not mad at you. She felt so bad by the time she called me, she was crying. I think she felt worse about what she did to you than about what happened to Irv!" He said.

"Really?" I asked, hopefully, my heart lifting.

The phone rang right then and I ran to answer it. It was Irmaline.

We cried and talked and talked and cried, finally ringing off when we were both exhausted from all the emotion.

I went back and joined Amos on the couch, happy, for the moment, because I hadn't lost my best friend.

"She's going to try to stop by tomorrow, but Sherry's taking it pretty hard, God knows why. I think I'd be celebrating." I bit my lip when I realized what I'd said, but Amos only smiled.

"It's alright to feel that way, Annie. You didn't really know him and the experiences you had with him weren't pleasant."

"You're right," I said, "and I didn't kill him. At least I hope I didn't. But if that was him that I stabbed, he was walking when he left here. How he got in my trunk is the real mystery. I'll find out soon enough if I'm a killer." I ended.

"You wouldn't be a killer if it were in self defense." He said. "Whoever attacked you put himself in that position, so how could it possibly be your fault?"

I knew he was right. His reassurance was something I needed right now and it felt good to have it.

The story was on the nine o'clock news. I was referred to as a "local resident". As in "A local resident, whose trunk the body was found in, was held overnight, but no charges were filed." After assuring us that they'd give periodic updates, they went on to other stories.

"It's only a matter of time now, Annie." Amos said. "The wolves will soon be at the door."

How well I knew. I remembered the faces of the townspeople who had seen me coming out of the Police Station that morning. I phoned Irmaline and told her if she called, to ring once and hang up, then call back. I also told her not to panic if I didn't answer at all, remembering the nonstop onslaught that had ensued after the Vicky murder. She told me the Doctor had given Sherry some pills and she was sleeping as we spoke. The boys had been surprisingly silent, and spent most of their time upstairs, presumably playing video games. She told me she had to help make funeral arrangements, even though she had no idea when the body would be released. Irv's family was on their way. They would stay at Irv and Sherry's house while they were in town. They'd been informed by the Sheriff's office, as Sherry was too distraught and Irmaline had no desire to be the bearer of the news. She was dreading their arrival, particularly Sherry's reaction. She wanted to shield her from them as much as possible. I gathered they weren't the couthest people: Big shock there.

I thought about my gun, once again stashed in the wall behind my bed, and wondered if the Sheriff's office would feel they had enough evidence to get a search warrant. I'd have to get rid of it. My own actions made me look guilty; of something, anyway. Lying? It didn't look good. I wondered if I should confide in my lawyer about the gun. Or Amos.

Mr. Spence called right before ten to inform me that my tire had a puncture in it, a puncture that would cause a slow leak. It looked very suspicious since the puncture went straight through and if I'd run over something, it should still be in there. I thanked him and hung up, then went to inform Amos.

I made the couch up for Amos, noticing the disappointment in his eyes as I brought out the bedclothes. Too bad! I had too much going on right now to think of romance. I wasn't in the mood. I took the phone off the hook (turned the ringer off), before going to bed, as I knew the press had no scruples and would even dare to call in the middle of the night. I kissed Amos' forehead as he settled onto the recently made couch, offering an apology when informing him I was tired and going to bed.

"O.K., Annie. I'll see you in the morning," he said, sounding dejected.

I settled in bed, my pets around me, and immediately fell asleep.

I was running through a hide-littered field, a bloody butcher knife in my hand. I was screaming, but no sound came out. I didn't know if I was chasing someone or someone was chasing me, but my fear was palpable. I could feel each blade of grass beneath my bare feet, and thought, "where's the snow?" right before I woke up. I sat up in bed, scaring Judas off. That was the first nightmare I'd had in a while; I was shaking when I woke up. My heart was trip hammering in my chest and I feared I might go the way Al did. A glance at the bedside clock told me it was 3:30 in the morning. I sat in the dark, forcing myself to breathe, my hand on my chest. Maybe I should see a shrink. I'd wait until all this was over and see if they went away. It had to be stress related.

I got up and donned my ratty robe and went to the bathroom. When I was done, I stood in the hall. From this vantage point I couldn't see the living room, but I saw flames from the fireplace reflecting off the walls and wondered if Amos was up. I went to the end of the hall and peeked around.

I could only see a lump of blankets; he must be asleep. I returned to bed and tossed and turned the rest of the night, my pets keeping their distance for fear of my flailing limbs.

When I finally dragged myself out of bed it was still dark. I got up. I smelled coffee the minute I entered the hall. Boy, I could use some!

Amos was sitting at the table, a mug of steaming coffee nearly invisible in his meaty hands. His hair was sticking up in assorted cowlicks and his beard looked even scragglier than usual. Despite my sleepless night and grogginess, I smiled. It was nice to have someone to wake up to, no disrespect to my pets.

Amos kind of grunted as he passed me on the way to the bathroom. I guessed he wasn't entirely awake yet, either.

The sun was just rising when Sam started barking. Peeking through the curtains, I saw that, indeed, the wolves were at the door. Someone in town must have alerted them about my arrest. I recognized the Channel four newswoman descending from a news van, her short, blonde hair encased in a faux fur, hooded jacket.

Her chic matching fur topped boots made crunching sounds in the snow as she approached. Amos wanted to confront them at the door, but I balked; besides the brutal questioning, I didn't want the whole town to see Amos opening my door so early in the morning.

The cold was on our side that morning as after a mere twenty minutes or so of non-stop knocking, they packed up their camera gear and left. I just hoped they'd never turned the cameras on, as I didn't want my house exposed for all to see, especially if they gave my address. I'd have to watch the noon broadcast.

Mister Tanner, the P.I., came over a little while later, as Amos and I were finishing a quick breakfast of donuts and more coffee.

"I've been trying to call," he said, stamping his feet outside the door to dislodge the snow. "I assumed the press was hounding you and decided to come over in person. I hope you don't mind."

I ushered him in and ran to get a cup of coffee for him, as he removed his boots and coat.

He seemed rather surprised to see Amos sitting at the table; nonetheless, he offered Amos his hand in greeting as he took the chair next to him.

We spent the next hour recapping all the events since Thanksgiving. He informed us that the autopsy was going to be done that day and no statements would be forthcoming by the Police until the results were released. I had told him about my nocturnal visitor and the wound I'd inflicted on him. Amos and I both got the impression that Barney loomed large on his list of suspects in the Vicky murder.

"It seems he had quite the crush on her in high school." He informed us.

"Everyone had a crush on her in High School." Amos rebutted. "If that's a motive than the whole male student body would be suspect."

With nothing resolved, he took his leave after assuring us he'd keep us informed of any developments, and imploring us to do the same for him.

I called Irmaline after he left, hoping no one would be on the other end as I gingerly lifted the receiver.

Barney's family had arrived late the night before and though they were supposed to stay at Sherry and Barney's house, they hadn't yet left Irmaline's. Sherry was practically living in the room Irmaline had kept prepared for her. Under the circumstances Irmaline didn't know how she could possibly avoid the relatives; it would be beyond rude to take Sherry and the kids and leave them there. She expected someone from the Sheriff's office would contact them soon with the autopsy results. I promised to call her periodically during the day for updates; my ringer would stay off.

"Let's go to my place." Amos said. "Then she can call us and we'll be left alone."

It was true. For some reason, the press left Amos alone. Probably because he came out looking like a hero after Vicky's mom went on her rampage: A hero, and a victim of a distraught mother. Or maybe it was fear of his wrath; either way, his place now looked like a sanctuary. I called Irmaline back and informed her of our plans.

"I wish I could go with you!" She pined.

We decided to take Sam and Judas with us. Sam sat in the back and Judas was put, protesting, into her cat carrier.

I ducked down in the truck every time another vehicle lumbered past us. Amos got a big laugh out of my discomfiture, but I didn't care. I sat up as he pulled in his yard. The sun glinting off the mounds of wind-driven snow surrounding his outwardly rustic home looked like a Norman Rockwell painting: "Winter in Rural America." I hoped I'd live long enough to enjoy that incredible porch in the summer.

"I hope you don't mind being stuck with me for a while." I said, suddenly hoping I wasn't imposing.

"If I wanted to run, I'd go back on the road. I've got plenty of work; I took a leave when I got the call about Irv." He said. Then I remembered he was a partner in the business now that his dad was gone; I supposed he could take off whenever he wanted.

Amos got a fire going as I wandered restlessly. Judas was already in the loft and I marveled that she was able to get up there. Sam was sniffing practically every inch of the living room, than continued his quest, for I knew not what, down the hall.

"Your house is so cool, Amos!" I gushed, still wandering. I kept seeing little things I hadn't noticed before. Two side-by-side pictures of Pheasants hanging beneath the high loft floor, to the left of the kitchen. There was a curved wooden table sitting against the wall under the pictures. A wedding picture sat atop it. Not Amos' and Vickys', though.

It had to be Amos' mom and dad. He looked quite a bit like his dad. The eerie thing was, I kind of looked like his mother! She was petite and had long, thick, brunette hair. They looked almost "hippyish". That would explain a lot. Amos' stoic acceptance of the way things were; bordering on fatalism, I thought. His love of nature. Although his dad took him hunting, how many hippies hunted? Maybe my assessment was totally wrong. I'd ask him more about his family later.

It was nearly time for the news. Amos had pushed the amazing little button that transformed us from the 19th. to the 21st. century as the massive t.v. came into view.

We settled on the couch, Amos had set a small ceramic coffee pot and two cups on the coffee table.

The same blonde, (this time her head uncovered, her hair neatly coiffed) who had been at my house, appeared on the screen. She was standing outside the Sheriff's office informing us that an autopsy was in progress in the basement, where the coroner was located.

"We were unsuccessful in our attempts to contact the woman whose vehicle the body was found in. She shall remain nameless as no charges were filed. When and if this case comes to trial, all parties involved will be identified."

Great! Although, of course, I wanted everything resolved, I wasn't looking forward to the circus that was sure to ensue. I knew Amos wasn't, either. If I hadn't hired that Attorney, they probably would have identified me, but now they were afraid of a lawsuit. The strange string of murders were uncharted ground for our little Sheriff's department and I knew they were concerned about procedure. I didn't know if Federal authorities were involved or not, but if they were, the Sheriff's department would have to be circumspect.

After the news, Amos disappeared shortly and returned with a long rope. We tied Sam out by the front door so he could do his business. It was dark by now, but Amos had a big floodlight mounted over the front door; I could see Sam scampering around, snuffling through the snow. Now I had to make up a litter box of some kind for Judas. Amos found an old wooden crate and filled it with wood chips, setting it in a remote corner of the room, under the loft. Judas immediately had to investigate, and realizing what it was for, promptly proceeded to do her business. Sam was barking to come in within minutes. I let him in and watched in dismay as he shook snow all over the big rug in front of the hearth, than plopped himself down in front of the fire, for all the world like he belonged there.

Amos just smiled and said, "I wish you could feel that much at home."

"I'm just jumpy. I can't stop thinking about the intruder and how he nearly killed me. If I hadn't found my forgotten knife, I wouldn't be here now." I said, forlornly.

"Well, how fortuitous is that?" He asked, sitting on the couch and patting the cushion next to him, for me to join him. "Someone, besides me, is watching out for you. Relax, whatever's going to happen, is going to happen."

Fatalist! I knew it! Yet, I had to agree. As I settled on the couch next to him, I said: "So, have I seen everything this house has to offer?"

His arm floated casually over my shoulder. I didn't flinch.

"Everything but the basement." He said.

"Basement? You have a basement?" Thinking, all I had was that spooky root cellar.

"If you want to call it that. It's not finished or anything, although I'm working on it. I hope to make it into a rec room, complete with bar." He answered.

A rec room? I thought. What does he need a rec room for? Well, I wasn't with him all the time. He probably had friends from work; drivers, his partners, or maybe, high school cronies.

"Can I see it?" I asked, jumping up.

He struggled up, standing next to me.

"Sure. C'mon." He grasped my hand and led me to the rear of the house, past his bedroom, where his furnace and laundry room were. I hadn't bothered to go in there, before. There was no door and it was obvious it was just a laundry room.

There was a door off to the side and when he opened it, an old cement staircase appeared.

When he flipped a switch at the top of the stairs, light flooded the stairs, a partially wood paneled wall the only thing visible from the top of the stairs. The same dank, musty smell that all basements seemed to possess came wafting up. At the bottom of the stairs, we took a left and a large, junk cluttered room appeared. It seemed to stretch the whole distance of the house.

"Wow." I said, "You could rent this out!"

"Are you looking to move?" He asked coyly, his eyebrows lifting and disappearing into his mop of hair.

"I just mean...it's huge!" I replied, lamely.

We wandered around as he showed me the improvements he'd already made, and told me of the ones he planned. We had to step around piles of lumber, window screens, various assorted tools, old furniture. Half the walls were already paneled in the same dark, knotty faux wood as the wall at the bottom of the stairs.

I nearly tripped over a big, tube thing, and as Amos caught my elbow to steady me, I asked, "What's that?"

"An air compressor." I then recognized it for what it was, but it looked ancient compared to any I'd ever seen.

All of a sudden an unbidden thought popped into my head; an air compressor, like one one might use to blow up a sex doll? That was insane. You could use a bicycle pump for that; or even blow it up yourself if you were desperate enough. Nonetheless, I suddenly felt beads of moisture on my forehead and the walls seemed to close in.

Amos, noticing my sudden discomfiture, grasped my arm tighter and asked what was wrong.

"Nothing. I just felt faint for a minute, there." I said, my voice weak.

"Let's go back upstairs." He said, escorting me to the steps.

Once back upstairs I fell onto the couch.

"Do you have any beer, Amos? I could use one."

He went to the kitchen and came back bearing two beers. It had never tasted so good, and I guzzled half the can in one fell swoop.

"You WERE thirsty!" He said, than downed his entire can. "Wanna have a contest?" He teased.

"No way!" I said, "I'm about ready for another one, though." I said, finishing it off.

"Me too." He answered, taking my empty can and going back to the kitchen.

I was content to sip after that, the shot of alcohol calming my nerves and forcing me to think rationally; too much more and rationality would fly out the window.

Amos had slowed down, too, and only took big gulps rather then guzzling the whole can.

Once again, we settled on the couch. The t.v. had been droning in the background, but now we focused our attention on it and Amos started channel surfing. We decided on an old favorite, "Casablanca", that was playing on the old movie channel. I hadn't seen it in years and looked forward to it. At some point, Amos got up and soon the smell of popping corn filled the room. I felt my mouth watering and went to get another beer and to see if Amos needed me to melt butter or something. I was feeling kind of tipsy now, but not drunk. In happy mode: the mode that hit before angry, then sad. One more, I told myself. Actually, I was quite proud of myself for not turning into a raging alcoholic with all that had been happening; a little rationalization there. I got another beer, anyway.

We went back to the couch, Amos with a big bowl of popcorn, me with two beers.

A knock on the door roused us both from near slumber; the movie was long over and an infomercial touting the effects of some exercise belt was droning in the background.

"Who'd be coming over this late?" Amos asked as he got up, wiping sleep from his eyes.

It was Jim, the Sheriff, standing on his doorstep.

"Is Annie Woods here?" He asked. I stepped into sight as he said this and he addressed his next statement toward me.

He had stepped over the threshold so Amos could close the door against the cold.

"I'm afraid you're going to have to come down to the Station with me, Ms. Woods." He informed me.

"What's this all about, Jim?" Amos asked, blocking me from the Sheriff's view with his girth.

"We can discuss that when we get there, Amos. This is official business and I'm not going to go into it here."

Oh, oh. I thought; does that mean he wants to get me down there and arrest me? He hadn't read me my rights yet, so I guess that was a good sign.

"Wait!" I implored as he sidestepped Amos and came towards me. "I have to get my wallet from my coat pocket, Mr. Spence's' number is in there." I started towards the hook where my coat hung, but he stopped me with an iron grip on my arm.

"I'll get that." He said. He fished my wallet out of the pocket and handed it to me. I dug through all the store receipts and I.D.'s until I found the rumpled card. The Lawyers handwritten home number on the back was now barely visible. I clung to it like a talisman. "I have to call my Attorney." I said.

"You can do that at the Station", Jim said.

"Oh come on, Jim! She can call from here, it'll give him time to get there; or is that what you're afraid of?" Amos proclaimed, indignantly.

The Sheriff relented.

"O.K., Amos. Go ahead, Ms. Woods." He motioned toward the phone.

I had no idea what time it even was as I dialed Mr. Spence's home number. He answered on the second ring, obviously he'd been roused from a sound sleep, his voice was husky and he coughed as he answered.

He agreed to meet us at the Station. I apologized profusely before I hung up, but he assured me that was his job and not to worry about it.

The Sheriff allowed me to ride with Amos and we followed his cruiser into town. No conversation passed between us in route, I was speechless in my misery.

When we arrived, I found my voice long enough to thank Amos for coming with me.

He waved me off and escorted me in behind the Sheriff.

The building was nearly silent as we entered. A few Fax machines could be heard running and I remember thinking, 'how can they run computers and fax machines, don't you need cable for that? Was it thus far only available to them, or maybe in town, or could you run computers some other way?' I was going to ask, but the thought was forgotten as he led me past a row of empty desks replete with colorful screensavers on silent computer screens, to the same small, dank room I'd been in last time.

It seemed we were the only ones there, but I knew for a fact that there was at least one Deputy on night duty. He must be on Patrol.

Amos had to wait outside, and I refused to say anything until Mr. Spence got there, so Jim left me alone in the room and I could hear him talking to Amos outside the door.

When Mr. Spence got there, we were allowed a few minutes to converse before the 'interrogation'. He advised me to keep quiet and let him speak for me. I was more than glad to. I was afraid of putting my foot in my mouth and looking guilty. I FELT guilty.

After all, I'd stabbed someone.

It turned out I HAD stabbed Barney. He had a deep gut wound, but the cause of death was listed as exsanguination AND hypothermia. That explained why there had been no blood in my trunk. He had laid somewhere, bled out, and frozen to death before he was placed in the trunk. The DNA on the knife left no doubt that I was the one who had stabbed him; my prints were all over the handle.

After repeating the same story I'd given on that fateful night (my lawyer allowed me this much) I fell silent as Mr. Spence and Jim conversed.

"But Sheriff," Mr. Spence was saying, "you were called by Miss Woods that night. You saw first hand the state she was in. She voluntarily gave you the knife, and two videotapes of the perpetrator fleeing the scene. What? She waited until you left, got a flashlight, went out in the middle of a snowstorm and found his body, waited until he'd bled out and then placed his body in the trunk? Only to take the same vehicle on an excursion with an elderly friend a day later? Does that sound plausible?"

Jim had to allow that it didn't, but still thought I should stay in jail until a Judge was available for an informal inquest.

After another hour of legal wrangling, Jim allowed me to leave, with the stipulation that I'd return when notified of the time of the inquest. I was read my rights, charged with Involuntary Manslaughter and released on my own recognizance, but only after a Judge had been contacted and agreed. It was the same Judge I'd faced before and he knew the case well. He had seemed sympathetic to me then, I guessed he figured I wasn't a flight risk. I could only surmise that protocol for such crimes were unknown territory for our small town and the Sheriff was at a loss as to what to do. Amos was, more or less, put in charge of watching me to make sure I showed up.

Personally, I'd thought I'd have to stay. I thought that was how things were done; but I could see visions of lawsuits in the Sheriff's eyes at the onslaught of my savvy lawyer.

I was no threat, it was agreed, thus my release. I had been charged, however, so it would be a matter of Public Record and the press would gnaw it like a bone. But as Mr. Spence pointed out, I was the victim, too. And even if the stab wound had solely caused Irv's death, the blame was his. In this state you were still allowed to protect yourself in your own home. Still, I had to face the charges. A man was dead, and someone had to be charged until it was sorted out, that someone being me: The murderess.

We returned to Amos' and I spent a sleepless night as the t.v. blared in the background.

He fell asleep shortly after hitting the couch; I paced back and forth. Let Sam out and back in; fed him and Judas. I studied the picture of Amos' parents and stared at the masterpieces his mother had created. I wanted to meet her and hoped I could tag along next time Amos went. I put on coffee around 5 and went to the bathroom to clean up.

My own face startled me. Big bags hung under my eyes, and my wrinkles seemed more pronounced than ever. My hair was a wild mop from the buffeting wind that had raked through it like a claw hammer on my short excursion to the police station. I washed my face and finger-combed my hair, then returned to the kitchen for a cup of coffee.

I was afraid to watch the news, but knew I would be transfixed by it, like a rubber-necker at an accident scene.

Amos was awake by six and I carried a steaming mug of coffee to him as he roused himself.

I grabbed the remote and turned up the volume as the news came on.

There was the ditzy blonde, whom I almost felt I knew by now, patting at her hair in the darkness shrouded street outside the Sheriffs department.

"Breaking news this morning, only on 4 News!" Some reporter was diligent.

"Charges have been filed in the case of the body in the trunk. A local woman, Ann Woods, was charged with Involuntary Manslaughter last night, and released on her own recognizance. Details are sketchy right now, but we'll be bringing you the latest as it's made available to us." With that, her image faded and the local weatherman started spouting his rhetoric.

The phone rang and we both jumped. It was Irmaline. She was quite agitated and demanded to know everything. As I filled her in, I wondered what Sherry thought, or did she not know, yet?

"Irmaline, what about Sherry? She's going to hate me now!" I moaned. "And the boys!"

"I'll handle that." She soothed. "The truth is always the best way."

"Oh my God. I'm so sorry!" I said.

"Annie, anyone else would have done the same. I'm just glad you remembered that knife, or it would be you dead and

Irv on trial."

"My Lawyer's assured me it won't come to that." I insisted.

"No, of course not! But if he'd killed you it would have been murder!" She said. "You just behaved in self-defense. No one can fault you for that!"

She told me to hang in there, and gave her pat 'and this too, shall pass' byline. Strangely, it gave me comfort.

Amos had been listening to my side of the conversation and gave me a quick hug on his way to the bathroom, as I was assuring Irmaline I'd keep her posted.

By the time Amos returned I was half nodded out on the couch. The coffee hadn't helped and my eyelids wouldn't stay open. He surprised me by hoisting me into his arms and carrying me to his bedroom. He gently laid me down on the bed and covered me with the heavy quilt, then gently kissed my cheek and left. I was out in seconds.

When I awoke I didn't know where I was at first. Sam and Judas were both in their usual positions next to me. Then I looked through the hearth wall and saw Amos on the other side, sitting on the couch. Flames leaped in front of him and visions of hell came to mind.

It looks like he's in hell, I thought, but then realized; it was I who was in hell.

I forced myself up and shuffled out to the living room. It was now Amos bringing me a steaming mug of coffee as I plopped onto the couch.

"Can I take a bath?" I asked, blowing on the hot liquid.

"Of course, you know you don't have to ask." He said, sitting next to me.

"What time is it?" I asked, the drapes were pulled and for all I knew, I'd slept all day.

"Almost noon." He answered.

"Turn on the news!" I implored.

"Are you sure you want to see that right now?" He

inquired.

"I have to!" I insisted.

Then, there it was, and it was worse than I could have imagined. At least two-dozen people were outside the courthouse, some with signs, protesting a murderer being released. One sign said, "Kill the B****", with the letters blurred out. I was mortified!

As the smirking newswoman signed off, I lost it, and cried like a baby.

No amount of comforting could stem the flow, and I cried until there was no emotion left.

"I may never leave here, Amos," I stuttered, drying my tears ineffectively on my sleeve.

"That's fine with me!" He said, with a crooked smile, and I immediately felt better.

The phone call came later that day. I would have to go in and face the music. I was far more afraid of the obviously hostile protesters than I was of the charges. Amos assured me we could sneak in the back, down the stairs that lead to the morgue.

It looked like a great deal of pressure was being put on the District Attorney's office to solve this whole thing. I just hoped I wasn't going to be the scapegoat. If they decided they had enough evidence to uphold the charges, I wouldn't be going home. Mr. Spence told me he didn't think they'd had enough evidence to charge me in the first place and that I should sue them as soon as I was released. Which, he said, he would personally guarantee. They had jumped the gun, he said, in their eagerness to solve the case. He would be on hand for the hearing.

I remember little of the details of that day. The sky was slate gray and matched my mood. I ducked down in Amos' truck as we drove to the rear of the building.

The room I was lead to had several people milling about outside it, and cameras flashed in my face as Amos tried, unsuccessfully, to block me from view.

The District Attorney, himself, was present; the Judge, a court stenographer, and my Attorney, were all there. Amos was asked to wait in the hall and he barricaded the door from the outside as insults were hurled at him.

Everything from the assault on up was rehashed. My Attorney had petitioned and received my videotapes and they were played for the Judge. Mr. Spence once again reiterated his tale of me waiting for Irv to bleed to death, finding him in a snowstorm, stashing him (all by myself) in the trunk, and driving my elderly friend to the mall. He also informed the court that my door had been broken into, my trunk lock tampered with, my tire punctured, so that I'd discover the body.

In the end, the charges were dropped, much to the dismay of the District Attorney and the glee of Mr. Spence; who wanted to instigate a lawsuit right then and there.

I was really afraid, now. The bloodthirsty townsfolk would not be pleased. What if they burnt my house down? I had to go home. I'd take Amos with me, if he'd go. Him and an arsenal of his guns!

My Lawyer sheltered me as we entered the hallway, then Amos took over and we rushed down the back stairs while Mr. Spence and a Deputy fended off the onlookers. They didn't yet know, I thought. I ran down the stairs, Amos at my heels.

We made it to the car unscathed and I told Amos my fears as he peeled out of the lot.

"Paranoid times call for paranoid action." That was his sage advice. We flew over the icy roads like the Devil was at our heels; in a sense, I guess he was.

We stopped at Amos' long enough to collect my pets, Amos' clothes, and almost as important as my pets, guns. Amos and I could both shoot. He'd learned at his dads' side, hunting. I'd learned at Al's side, target shooting.

On the way to my house we both calmed down a little, and he slowed down.

"You should call that news station, Annie, and tell them your side. Obviously, the Sheriffs' Department is pretty much keeping them in the dark. I guess they figure if they keep quiet no one will know that they have nothing. On anybody. And now they're back to square one, with a possible lawsuit hanging over their heads."

He glanced over at me as he said this. I relaxed my grip on the door molding as the car slowed to a reasonable speed.

"I'll have to think about it." I said, noncommittally.

Despite the charm of Amos' house, I was glad to get home.

My house sat undisturbed, as we'd left it, nestled in its' downy white coverlet. My haphazard Christmas lights, some still burning brightly, made me feel maudlin.

The unbroken crust of snow told us no unwanted visitors had invaded my domain.

My pets seemed as happy to be home as I was. They ran right to their dishes and looked at me with questioning eyes.

Amos was carrying the guns in as I fed Sam and Judas.

"You told me you can shoot." He said. "I hope that means that you know about handling guns safely." He laid the guns out on the couch. I went over to check them out. There was a rifle, a shotgun, and assorted pistols.

"Are you familiar with these guns?" He asked.

"That's a Glock," I said, pointing, "9mm, semi-automatic, 10 rounds, one in the chamber, three automatic safeties. Al subscribed to a gun magazine and used to quiz me."

"Very good!" He said, beaming at me. "What's that?" He said, pointing to another.

"Colt 45, single action, 7 and one."

Pointing at another, I said, "Smith and Wesson, 460 Magnum, 5 rounds."

Gazing at a 20-inch long gun, I said, "I don't, however, know what the heck that is."

He picked it up and handed it to me.

"Magnum Research Pistol. Semi-automatic, 17 caliber, Mach 2. Check it out."

I did. It was a scary looking thing. 10 or so inch barrel.

"None of these are loaded, of course; nor will they be, except for maybe one. At any sign of trouble, we can load the others if need be." He said matter-of-factly. "Remember, these are just precautionary measures and meant to reassure you. I've always been around guns and they hold no fear for me. It really IS the person, and not the gun, you have to fear."

"I know that, Amos. I'm not afraid of guns. I'm afraid of those nuts in town." I handed him back the big gun. He decided we'd load the Glock. Good choice, I thought. He put it, safety on, on the mantle. He retrieved boxes of ammo from his truck as I let Sam out.

"He's our early warning system." I said, as he passed me coming in.

"Yeah, well let's hope he's more helpful than he was when Irv broke in." He said, with a smirk that pissed me off.

"That's not fair!" I snipped, coming in behind him. "Sam ran out the door when it was kicked opened and Barney closed it! It was his barking that woke me up!"

"I was only kidding, Annie! His barking is definitely an asset."

He had by now dropped all the ammo on the kitchen table, he then gathered the guns and brought them over. He showed me the bullets for the "Magnum Research Pistol", the rest I knew. When he was sure I wasn't fudging on my knowledge, he went and got the cases and tenderly placed each in its place.

"Feel better, now?" He asked, when we'd stashed them in the closet in my room. "We've got enough fire power to take-over a small country."

"Yes, actually, I do." I said, and meant it. I just knew that I wished I'd had my gun in my hand when Barney broke in. I would have been spared the terror of those hands around my throat, not to mention all the trouble his disappearance and eventual reappearance had caused. If I'd just took him out right there, it would have been better for all involved. The ironic thing was, Barney was no longer a threat, but, as if he was reaching from beyond the grave, the threat had multiplied. Now I knew not who, or how many, were my enemies.

The phone had started ringing the minute we'd come in and I'd turned off the ringer immediately. Now we just had to wait for the inevitable onslaught. The anger I'd seen in those peoples' faces rivaled my own on seeing a child molester or murderer get off. That's what I was to them. A murderess. Amos was right. I'd be interviewed by that smug blonde woman and act, for all the world, like butter wouldn't melt in my mouth. I'd be honest, and real, and no one would fault me when I was done. It was my only hope; I couldn't live like this anymore.

It was by now late afternoon and, as expected, a news van pulled up in front of the house. I was going to take the tiger by the tail. As Blondie exited the van she was handed a microphone by one of her crew. I stood at the window, peeking out a crack in the curtain. When she got to the door, I would confront her. My heart was in my throat as I watched her make her way up the walk. I waited for the knock before I calmly opened the door. I had brushed my hair and put on make-up so as not to scare the viewing audience.

The look of shock on the blonde's face when I opened the door was one I wished the viewers could see, but the cameras were aimed at me.

I stepped out on the porch, closing the door behind me so Sam couldn't run out and steal my thunder. Amos had remained in the house at my insistence. This was my problem and I would deal with it.

The mike was stuck unceremoniously in my face.

"Are you Ann Woods?" The blonde inquired.

"Annie." I said. "Everyone calls me Annie."

"Annie. Could you give us your side of the recent murder and discovery of the victims' body in your trunk?"

I stood tall and looked right into the cameras as I weighed my response.

"The day Irv disappeared I was having Thanksgiving dinner with him and his family and another friend. That night, after I'd returned home, an intruder kicked in my door and attacked me. I was strangled nearly into unconsciousness when I grabbed a knife I had stashed under my couch cushion, and thrust it at the assailant."

Before I could continue, the inevitable question was asked: "Why was there a knife under your couch cushion?"

I had been anticipating this and used that as my opening to reveal all I'd been through recently, hoping the viewers would empathize with my feelings.

I described how an unknown person had been harassing me for months; how I'd had the Police out on several occasions, only to be received with skepticism. I told of my fear and isolation.

"Aren't you the same Annie who found the body of the woman in the trunk last month?"

She was getting into it now, her whole demeanor predatory. This was juicy and she had an exclusive.

"Yes, I am." I then described that whole scene, reiterating that I felt all the events were related, but that I was not the perpetrator. They didn't know I was also the one who had found John Fuller and I didn't enlighten them on that. One could only believe so much.

I described the assailant running off after I'd stabbed him, how I had videotapes showing someone running into the woods. I explained how I'd installed the camera's hoping to convince the Police that I wasn't some hysteric. The tapes were the key piece of evidence that had exonerated me. I said I had no idea why Barney (I called him 'Irv') would want to hurt me; that was for the authorities to find out. I said I hoped they would now take me seriously. I also said that I felt the authorities had done all they could, under the circumstances. I wanted to make it clear that I didn't fault them.

When the questions began to be repetitive, I begged off, saying that was all I had to say, and that I hoped to be left alone now that the truth was out. I ended by saying I was very sorry for Irv's family, but that anyone would have reacted as I did if put in that situation; the Police obviously agreed.

The blonde was still asking questions, ones I'd already answered, when I slipped back in the door, leaving her looking forlorn on my door step; but as she turned back to face the cameras, her game face was back in place. I heard her say into the microphone:

"And there you have it. That was Annie Woods, giving her version of events, exclusively for 4 news!"

I leaned my back against the door and slowly slid to the floor, emotionally exhausted.

"There." I said, when I noticed Amos' stricken look, "It's done. I did it. I faced my demons and lived to tell about it."

He knelt next to me, brushing a stray hair out of my eyes.

"You did good, Annie." He said, tenderly. He, of all people, knew how hard that had been for me, the recluse: The misanthrope.

We both felt silly about our earlier paranoia, but I could still hear those people attacking poor Amos outside the courtroom door. I knew how horrible that must have been for him.

He'd grown up here, he knew those people, and to have them turn like that because of his allegiance to me must have been extremely hard for him.

When I'd recovered enough, I forced myself up and went to call Irmaline.

Amos rummaged through my cupboards while I talked on the phone. When I hung up, the smell of canned chili was permeating the air.

"Sorry" Amos said, bringing me a bowl. "All the meat was frozen and I'm hungry. I hope this is o.k."

"It's wonderful!" I said. I felt like a great weight had been lifted from me.

I did, however, worry about Sherry's reaction to my interview. Irmaline had assured me that they'd already had several long talks and as Sherry's shock subsided, she'd started to come around. Barney's relatives were making life difficult and Irmaline had banned them to Sherry and Barney's house. I shuddered to think of their reaction to my statement. The way was now clear for Barney's funeral, so hopefully, they would be gone soon.

Later, as we snuggled on the couch waiting for the news to come on, I realized how dependent I'd become on Amos. I knew that by being my friend his whole life had changed, and not for the better. There was no way I could make it up to him; no way I could convey how important his support was to me.

When the news came on, I envisioned houses all over town settling in to watch their favorite Newswoman and get the latest juicy details on their small towns' rise to infamy.

I was startled to see the opening scene was of Amos and me coming up the steps in the courthouse. I looked haggard and Amos' mouth was set in a hard line; a trait I now knew indicated his stubbornness. His hand was out, blocking the view of one camera, which was caught on others. My lawyer then flanked me from the other side and I disappeared behind the men. The next shot was of us coming out of the courtroom and running down the stairs. Then, there it was, me, answering the door with a determined look on my face, belying the fear I felt. 'God, I look old!' I thought as I watched. Then, for some reason, it was like I was watching someone else, I detached myself.

When it was over I looked at Amos and said: "God, I look old!"

He smiled, his arm tightening around my shoulders.

"For what you've been through, you look pretty damn good."

I placed my hand over his, on my shoulder, and smiled. That was the closest to a compliment I'd ever get from him.

The phone was back on the hook and had been surprisingly silent since the news had aired. I had an unlisted number, which was the only thing that had saved me from crank calls from townspeople these last several months. Of course, the press had managed to ferret it out a long time ago. It was the media who had harassed me non-stop after the Vicky incident. When the phone rang around eleven that night I was torn from Amos' arms by the shrill ringing. I had been on the verge of finally committing to Amos and consummating our relationship so that it could move on to the next level, so I hesitated to answer it. But, of course, I must.

It was Irmaline and she was quite agitated. She had called to inform me that Barney's dad and two brothers had stopped by her house in their truck and they were drunk. She thought they might also have a shotgun on a rack in said truck. She'd made them leave. She didn't know where they were going. She wanted to know if she should call the Sheriff but Sherry was begging her not too. She was as cowed by his family as she had been by Barney. I handed the phone to Amos. This was his kind of problem.

He turned to me as he hung up.

"I'm going to find them." He said.

"Why? Call the Sheriff! They're driving around drunk!" I insisted.

It all became moot as a loud engine approached. Floodlights

glared through chinks high in the curtains and I could hear loud voices out front.

"Amos, they're here!" I whispered; though, of course, I didn't need to whisper.

I was shaking all over. I'd never met any of Barney's family but from what Irmaline had told me, they weren't big, but made up for it by being bullying drunks. Just like Barney.

His dad was a small, hillbillyish man, who ruled his roost with an iron fist. The brothers followed suit. Plenty of beatings had been meted out to them as children (that explained a lot) and now they continued the vicious cycle with their own families.

I ran to the mantle to grab the Glock. Just picking it up made me feel safer.

"Don't Annie." Amos said, coming up behind me and grabbing my wrist.

"What do you mean?" I exploded. "I'm sick of this! I'm not going to take it any more! I won't shoot them, I'll just shoot in the air to scare them. I'm not crazy!"

"Annie," Amos said calmly, "those are blanks in there."

"What?" I asked, stunned. "You brought all these guns over here for protection and no bullets?"

"I have shells for the shotgun in my shirt pocket." He said, like that would placate me.

"Annie, you insisted I bring my guns, and I did, to make you feel safe, but I'm certainly not going to bring live rounds when you're in such an emotional state. Besides, I don't need guns to protect myself. Look at me!"

Before anything further could be said, the voices out front got louder. I ran and peeked out the window. A big extended cab truck with three large floodlights on top was parked next to my car, which was in front of Amos truck, facing the house. I could see three silhouettes standing in front of the headlights; one had a long, cylindrical object in his hands.

I ran back to the phone. It was in my hand as Amos came

up behind me.

"Wait, Annie. Let me go talk to them. I've known that family since I was a boy. They won't shot me."

"No, Amos!" I said, dialing.

He turned and left the house while I was still waiting for the Sheriffs office to answer.

He didn't even take the shotgun. I'd never taken Amos for a fool, but now I wondered.

After three rings, I hung up. I had to know what was going on. I ran back to the window and peered out. I'd go out there, but that would probably endanger Amos' life further as they may start shooting.

Amos was struggling into his plaid over-shirt as he approached the men. I could hear their voices but couldn't make out the words. The one with the gun had raised it halfway up, it was pointing approximately at Amos knees.

The phone rang, causing me to bang my elbow against the windowsill. It was the Sheriff's office saying they'd received a call from my number and wanting to know if help was needed.

"Yes!" I exclaimed, rubbing my elbow and shaking. "This is Annie Woods, get out here right away!" I hung up and ran back to the window. The phone began to ring again, I ignored it, my eyes riveted on the eerie silhouettes; shimmering shadows in the headlights. The floodlights were on but were pointed high and their beams shone somewhere above my head.

I watched in fascinated horror as Amos' shadow moved swiftly forward, his big hand grasping what I assumed was the shotgun, from the smaller figure. A slight tussle ensued, but Amos quickly overpowered him. The other two figures rushed him and I saw his arm lash out, knocking down one of them. I flew to the mantle and grabbed the Glock. I was fighting with the safeties as I swung open the door. I ran, barefoot, to the porch and pointed the gun in the air and fired.

"Get away from him!" I yelled.

The fight had stopped as quickly as it had begun, at the sound of the shot. The echoes of it were still reverberating off the trees.

Just then, the Sheriff's car pulled up, lights flashing, although I heard no siren.

Jim jumped out of the car, gun drawn, pointed at me.

"Drop the gun!" He yelled.

I did. A Deputy had emerged from the passenger side, his gun on the men.

The man who'd had the gun was slowly rising to his feet, his hands behind his head in response to the Sheriff's command. The other, whom Amos had struck, got up and followed suit. Soon, they were all standing like that, including Amos. I had done the same and approached the Sheriff at his bidding. Amos related the story, being constantly interrupted by the drunken gibberings of Barney's family.

The three men were put in the back of the cruiser, handcuffed. They'd had to bring out the plastic ones as they only had one steel pair available: A testament to our small town.

The Deputy collected the Glock and the shotgun, unloading them.

"Those are blanks." Amos said, as the Glock's chamber was opened.

The Sheriff just shook his head, as if he were dealing with rebellious juveniles.

He went into the big truck and turned everything off, putting the keys in a handkerchief. He said he'd call a tow truck to come get it. He told us to come down and press charges, but we refused. The driver (who would be found out) would be charged with DWI after a test was administered at the station. The other two would probably be charged with Drunk and Disorderly.

"Please!" I implored, shivering in my bare feet, coatless. "Either keep them in jail, or process them quickly, so they can go home! To their own home." And far away, I thought.

"You can come down to the station tomorrow and fill out a Restraining Order." Jim said to me. "I'll personally have a little talk with them, I can assure you." He actually patted my shivering shoulder. "You better get inside now." He dropped his hand and went to join the Deputy in the front seat.

The Three Stooges sat cowed in the back of the Police car. One of them was staring daggers at me and I turned away, heading for the house.

Amos followed behind, the empty Glock in his hand. All his guns were registered and legal, so Jim had returned it. He'd wanted to know why it was loaded with blanks, but we had no answer for him. For the first time I wondered what effect this case was having on the Sheriff. Now, he was kind of in trouble for charging me, but he certainly didn't seem to hold a grudge. Maybe he finally realized everything I'd been through and had a modicum of empathy. I know I felt for him.

Went we got back inside, I proceeded to pout. I was angry with Amos for deceiving me. I wasn't some hysteric.

"Why wouldn't you just refuse to bring any guns?" I asked.

"You were so adamant. I don't know if you know it or not, but you can be pretty stubborn! Sometimes it's just better to go with the flow."

I knew I couldn't stay mad at him. He was right about the guns, but I'd be damned if I'd admit it to him.

He'd just risked his life for me, showing no fear. I knew he didn't think of it that way. He had played with them as children and knew them, he wasn't afraid of them. Yes, he used to beat Barney up, but so did they! Amos only did it when Barney was beating on some little kid, they did it for spite, or whatever excuse violent people used.

"Thank you, Amos." I said, in a complete about face, surprising him.

"For what? For being right about the guns?" He chided, hinting for that apology.

"No." I said, my face flaming, "for being so fearless."

I threw my arms around him, as far as they would go.

We finally took our relationship to the next level that night, and it was even better than I remembered. We lay, spent, in the predawn light, high on each other's essence. The wound in his side was nearly healed and I kissed it lovingly.

"Another time I could have lost you." I said.

He hugged me tighter, his massive chest moving up and down, still trying to catch his breath.

My pets had fled in terror at the commotion our coupling caused, and Sam now sat next to the bed, staring at me. Judas was lying on the dresser, oblivious.

Thus ensued one of the happiest periods of my life. Why I hadn't let myself succumb a long time ago, I didn't know. We decided to divide our time between his house and mine; we were now both equally at home in either place.

Irmaline had banned Irv's family from her home, and though they were still staying at Irv and Sherry's, they would be gone right after the funeral.

Amos would be attending the funeral tomorrow, but I would not. It was scheduled for the following day; bodies tended to decay rapidly after being frozen, and time was of the essence.

Irmaline was in seventh heaven that her matchmaking had worked out. It was like a dark cloud had finally lifted, and I savored every minute of my new life.

I still hadn't seen Sherry or the boys and was nervous about the time when I would have to, but I knew that with Amos by my side, I could face anything.

# Chapter Twenty

The day of the funeral dawned as gray as the mood of the mourners. Christmas was right around the corner and it was a sad state of affairs that a husband and father would be gone forever, in what should have been a celebratory time.

We were once again at Amos', and he was rummaging in his closet for his dark gray suit. When he was dressed, I tied his subdued, mauve tie for him, stretching like a child to reach his neck.

"You sure look handsome." I noted. "Too bad it's for a funeral."

"Are you sure you don't want to go?" He asked. "I'll be right by your side."

"No way!" I said, emphatically. "It's Barney's day, I won't make his funeral into a circus. It's my fault he's there."

His big arms surrounded me and he nuzzled my neck.

"It was him or you." He whispered. "And I'm glad it was him."

"Those poor boys!" I lamented.

"Sherry's a pretty woman, and sweet. She'll find someone

else. Hopefully someone who will be a real father to those boys."

"Please come home as soon as you can. I miss you already." I clung to his neck until the strain became too much for my back.

"I'll be back as soon as the funeral's over. I'm not going to the interment or the wake."

I understood. Barney's family would be invading Irmaline's house one last time and Amos didn't want another scene, especially in front of the boys.

I watched him walk to his truck under the slate sky; the sun covered by high-flying clouds. A good day for a funeral, I thought.

I went into the kitchen and washed up a few dishes, the warm water felt good on my bloodless fingers. I found Amos' vacuum cleaner and went over the large rug in front of the fireplace, my thoughts a million miles away.

When I finished, I sat before the huge hearth. Amos' had got a fire going before he left and I got up to poke the blazing logs occasionally. I pressed the magic button to expose the large t.v., and settled on the couch to watch the news.

After listening to the latest on a meeting of the School Board, the blonde newswoman appeared outside the funeral home. The funeral had already started and I didn't recognize any of the few stragglers entering in the background.

I hadn't been listening, my mind occupied with trivialities. I forced myself to focus.

"...sad ending to a strange case. Police are still trying to figure out the motive for the apparently unprovoked attack on local resident Annie Woods; and if this case is in any way related to an earlier murder."

I clicked off the set. I was afraid I'd have to face images of Sherry and the boys coming out to follow the hearse to the graveyard. I couldn't handle that. I still carried a tremendous amount of guilt over my actions; justified, or not.

I was running a dust rag over the roughhewn wood end tables when I heard Amos' truck arrive.

A gust of cold air and a few errant snowflakes entered with him. He removed his boots and hung his good leather jacket by the door.

"How was it?" I inquired.

"Depressing." He answered, as he wrapped me in his arms.

"How did Sherry and the boys take it?" I asked, putting my head against his chest.

"Luke cried. Shawn was stone-faced. Sherry held up until the eulogy, than broke down.

Irv's relatives shot daggers at me with their eyes the whole time. I talked to Irmaline a little, afterward. She wanted to know how you were doing."

"Thank God it's over!" I said, pulling away. "Do you think Barney killed Vicky?" I asked.

"I don't know, but I'm sure Jim's looking into that. I can't believe he would, but who else would have? And why?"

"And what about John Fuller? Do you think that was a suicide? I know you said before that you didn't think so."

"I just don't have any answers, Annie. We'll have to wait and see."

With that, we put the funeral behind us and I went to start supper. It was kind of early, but I was hungry and I knew Amos could always eat.

As we settled in the living room, plates in hand, Amos surprised me by saying:

"I never realized how lonely I was before I met you. I guess we all get stuck in our own little ruts and don't even realize that our lives could be a lot happier if we'd just take chances once in a while."

I set my plate on the coffee table and ran my hand over his cheek.

"How right you are, honey." I said, and smiled.

The days wore on peacefully. Barney's relatives returned home. Sherry got set up to start school in the spring. Her and Barney's' house was on the market, furnished or unfurnished. She'd sell nearly all the furniture that wasn't wanted; she'd try renting the house, if it didn't sell. The influx of city people wanting to escape the rat race had become a constant and she didn't foresee any problem finding occupants.

Amos went on a short (three day) run; I stayed at my place. I'd still rather stay at my house, if he wasn't there. My pets were equally at home in either place.

My nightmares had all but vanished; an unremembered angst clinging on nights when Amos was gone and I'd wake to the stillness of the house. On those nights, I'd wander like a ghost through the empty rooms, seeking something I couldn't find in the stillness.

Was it my loneliness, only now realized, that moved my feet to soundless music through the wee hours?

When a few weeks had elapsed and Christmas was knocking at the door, Amos had convinced Irmaline, Sherry and the kids to accompany us to the next town to do some Christmas shopping. Earlier in the week, Amos and I had trudged through thigh deep snow in search of the perfect Christmas tree. We'd found it in a small glade behind his house, a half-mile into the woods. He'd chopped it down handily, with a couple swift strokes of his Paul Bunyan axe. We'd laughed happily, dragging it over mounds of snow, our merriment echoing through the trees like water cascading down a waterfall.

I felt totally alive when I was with Amos and my former self seemed like a shadow, a wandering Nomad, looking for that elusive oasis. I couldn't remember a scene from my childhood that had held so much joy; but then, a lot of my childhood remained as blurred memories, when I tried to grasp them, they were gone.

We put the tree in Amos' living room. It spread its greenery across the whole corner of the room. Placed on the fireplace wall, its branches stretched nearly to the hearth. We spent hours decorating it with Amos' ancient ornaments, handed down from antiquity.

We threw freshly popped corn at each other, Sam snuffling it up as it fell and Judas batting kernels under the tree. At one point, she scurried up the tree in pursuit of a swinging ball, than just as quickly descended, at my admonishments. It was Rockwell, come to life, or so it seemed.

Irmaline, Sherry and the boys met us at the mall. The same mall that loomed large in my memory, from that last fateful trip. I hadn't brought my car this time, preferring the safety of Amos' truck.

They were waiting for us at a table in the wide atrium, bright sunlight shone through the glass dome overhead, creating an aura around them; bright spirits on a sunny day.

We crossed the vast space to meet them and I heard one of the boys say:

"Is she the one who killed dad?"

Then he was quickly shushed as I drew nearer. What did I expect? I didn't know how Barney's death had been explained to the boys, but the facts were out there for all to see.

I clung to the hope that their lives would be better without him.

We sat and chatted about generalities for a while, sipping freshly brewed and exotic coffees.

Sherry seemed to have blossomed since the last time I'd seen her. She seemed relaxed and at ease, something you never saw when Barney was around. I had the feeling that somewhere inside, she was happy with her new life.

We started off together, but quickly separated into little groups. Sherry went to take the boys to the video arcade for a while before she shopped. Irmaline and I followed the same route we had previously, looking through new eyes at the same wares; now we planned to buy. Amos had disappeared into a Sears store; I could see displays of chainsaws just inside. We'd all agreed to meet at 3:00 in the atrium, as we'd went our separate ways.

It was nice to be with Irmaline, again. She had all her old exuberance back now that the black cloud was no longer hanging over her. She didn't seem worried that a murderer may still be out there; but then why should she? Whatever Barney had been up to was a million miles from her life; and hopefully, Sherry and the boys'.

I had to separate from Irmaline at some point. I wanted to get her gift at a small store I'd spotted in a little niche off the main hallway. It had boasted an array of handmade jewelry and I wanted to find a broach for her new sweater and maybe a matching necklace or bracelet. I was engrossed in a display of silver and jade pins when I caught a reflection in the large mirror behind the glass display case, on the back wall. I started back at the sight of the weasel eyes that caught my glance. They were gone as soon as they'd appeared, leaving me to wonder if I'd imagined them. The pinched nostrils and narrow forehead had looked, for all the world, like Barney! Could it be one of his brothers, skulking around and following me? I'd never gotten a clear look at them, except for the one in the cop car, and that could have been his dad, for all I knew. I quickly stepped to the door and glanced down both halls: Nothing.

"Can I help you, Ma'am?" A voice behind me asked.

I turned slowly, trying to slow down my pounding heart, which I was sure she could hear. I returned to the counter and made some purchases, then cautiously emerged into the now crowded mall. I kept looking behind me as I tried to concentrate on shopping. This would probably be my last excursion before the holidays and I needed to get it done. Even if it was some kin of Barney, so what? Even hillbillies did Christmas shopping, didn't they? Maybe he'd been as shocked to see me, as I was, him. Besides, the mall was teeming with shoppers now and I could easily lose myself in the crowd. I pushed the incident to the back of my mind and carried on with my shopping.

An hour and a half later, I'd finished my shopping, and struggling with several large bags, made my way to the atrium.

I saw Sherry, sitting with the boys across the room. She rose and waved when she saw me. I was reluctant to join them, but now had no choice. Earlier, there had been buffers between us and we had had no occasion to speak one on one.

I settled on a plastic chair next to her, setting my bags on the floor at my feet.

"I'm done!" I said, triumphantly.

She pointed to the large spread of parcels at her feet, "Me, too", she said, a small smile playing at her lips.

The boys were running around the quarter-operated rides set up in the center of the atrium, leaving Sherry and me alone to talk.

"So, I hear you're set up to go to school soon." I offered.

"Yes." She replied, and her face became animated as she told she wanted to go into nursing. She was going to take Nurse's Aide Training first, and then continue on.

I told her that was great and a noble profession, etc., then conversation slowly petered out.

She went over to talk to the boys a couple times, to squelch their boyish enthusiasm. I thought that showed class, as most of the parents just screamed across the room, which had the acoustics of an amphitheater.

Amos and Irmaline appeared then, her small hand wrapped around his massive bicep, imploring him to listen as she carried on a running dialog. He was laden with so many bags, his legs were no longer visible, but he seemed to carry them with ease.

By the time all the bags were laid out, we barely had room

for our feet, but we crammed in next to the table, all seemingly exhausted, except Irmaline, who was surprisingly hyper.

Amos was kind enough to make two trips to our vehicles to deposit the gifts in his truck and Irmalines' car, so we could go have an early supper, or late lunch, however you wanted to look at it. We were all hungry and Sherry said the boys had been begging for food and sneaking candy from the machines when they thought she wasn't looking.

"You'd better eat everything you order!" She threatened as we entered the restaurant.

It turned out to be quite an enjoyable afternoon and evening was creeping in as we prepared to leave.

Sherry had a glass of wine with her dinner and her cheeks were flushed with the excitement of her new life. She was animated and witty, and I marveled that she'd kept her light under a bushel for so long. Well, the bushel was gone now!

We followed Irmaline, Sherry and the kids, in Amos' truck. Irmaline was driving and we laughed about how here head could barely be seen above the headrest, even from our vantage point!

I leaned my head on Amos' shoulder all the way home; glad I'd decided against wine with dinner. For once, I wanted my senses sharp, to savor the new goodness of my reality.

I didn't put a tree up at my house that year. I was having too much fun decorating Amos' place. With it's roughhewn interior, his home lent itself well to the bright baubles I placed throughout. I felt like we were having Christmas in the 19th Century. We invited Sherry, Irmaline and the boys over Christmas eve. The boys had several presents from me and Amos under the tree and were chomping at the bit to get at them. I'd bought them a game for their video system, after conferring with Irmaline about what they wanted. Also, some shirts with characters I'd seen on their bedroom walls. Amos had gotten them a remote control airplane that he promised to fly with them at the first sign of good weather.

A remote control car accompanied it. THAT they could play with in the house and we all had to jump aside as they took turns zooming it across the floor. While they played, we adults went about our present openings.

Irmaline was thrilled with her silver and jade broach and necklace I'd purchased. Evidently remembering my purchase of the used coat at the Bazarre she'd bought me a new coat. It was a reddish-brown suede that hugged my waist and flared out over my hips. It was beautiful, and expensive.

Amos got a plush brown sweater and leather gloves; a pocket watch and a fleece-lined cap that covered his ears rounded off his gifts from Irmaline. He gave her a beautiful antique picture frame and a generous gift certificate to a popular bookstore.

I had spent a long time speculating over what to get him and the gifts I'd purchased seemed lame, now. I'd gotten him some fur seat covers for his truck, an expensive men's Cologne, and last but not least, a new pair of binoculars. I'd remembered from his time camping in my woods that his good pair had been destroyed in the Vicky (or whoever did it) rampage. Amos and I had pitched in and bought a stylish new jacket for Sherry. It was a lightweight spring jacket, brushed, thin leather, a dark aqua color that brought out the blueness of her eyes. She'd gotten me two pairs of exquisite earrings. One with diamond chips surrounding garnets. Amos, yet another toolbox with assorted tools.

When it seemed all the presents were opened, Amos pulled a small box from some unknown hiding place and handed it to me. I felt all their eyes on me, (except the boys, who didn't seem to know we existed) as I took the little box with trembling fingers.

It was wrapped in shiny red paper with a bow bigger than the box gracing the top. I smiled. I pictured Amos' big hands struggling with little pieces of tape; picking out the big bow.

I carefully unwrapped the paper, feeling the tension

mounting. When I, at last, had unfettered the box and swung the lid open, three pairs of eyes strained to see the contents.

It was a beautiful, ruby, teardrop necklace. Two little ruby earrings sat next to it, affixed to the fuzzy blue background. I could see disappointment in Irmaline's eyes and realized that she had thought it was a ring. It had actually never entered my mind until I saw the look on her face. I loved it and was glad it wasn't a ring. I hoped even Amos wasn't that gauche! I didn't think he'd propose in front of other people! I knew that they'd cost more than all my gifts together, and mine weren't cheap! I gave him a hearty kiss right in front of everyone, and we all laughed as his face flamed.

We all got up and started putting torn wrapping paper into garbage bags I'd retrieved from the kitchen. I'd bought eggnog the last time I'd been shopping and now I went to get it and the two-dozen cookies I'd baked earlier. I laughed as I spied the saran wrapped plates of cookies on the counter. You could tell about a half a dozen were missing, but the wrap was neatly pulled back over them. No wonder the boys were so hyper!

Irmaline and Sherry had to leave by nine. Gary and Rich were coming in, Rich with his extended family. They'd meet up in Chicago. Gary had a leave from Afghanistan, but only until Jan. 3. Rich and his wife and kids were to meet Gary at O'Hare and fly up together. Irmaline couldn't wait! Not only had she not seen Gary for two years, she hadn't seen Rich and her other grandchildren in a year. Her one granddaughter was now 15, and she was excited about seeing her. Her other grandson was 17, and she was anxious to see how he looked, as last time she'd seen him, he'd had a Mohawk and several piercings. She'd laughed about it and said she always thought she'd be the one who pierced her granddaughters' ears, as she had Sherry's when she was 14, but had been mortified (but made sure she didn't show it) when her oldest GRANDSON had asked her if she'd pierce his eyebrow!

Amos and I had agreed to stay away and let the family get reacquainted. Amos said maybe the day Gary flew back we could meet him at the airport. It was about an hour's drive to our nearest BIG airport, situated on the outskirts of one of the few major cities in our state. He'd have a chance to see Rich then, too. I planned to talk to Irmaline about it after they arrived. If she agreed, we could all make a day of it in the big city.

I was still living off Al's pension and social security. I'd gotten a considerable amount from his life insurance policy, too, and thought maybe I'd make some investments or start some kind of business. I felt more upbeat and hopeful than I had since Al's death. A rudderless ship no more: I'd found my stability. Amos and me spent a quiet Christmas Eve night at his place; my pets had come out of hiding after the kids had left, and they were scampering around the tree. The next day, Christmas, Amos had come up behind me and wrapped his big arms around me. He had another small box in his hand, this one unwrapped, and as he handed it to me, he said:

"Well, will you?"

I opened it and turned in his arms to kiss him. The ring was neither large nor small, but it was beautifully faceted and had little blue stones encircling the solitaire diamond.

"Yes." I said, surprised and pleased. "But, let's make it a long engagement."

Irmaline called to wish us "Merry Christmas", and told us that her boys had made it in safe, Sherry had picked them up at the small airport that was only 20 miles away. I ran the idea of a get together by her, telling her that Amos wanted a chance to see his boyhood friends. She readily agreed as the grandchildren wanted to see the city and had already been bugging their mom and dad about going there. I asked her what Rich's wife was like and she told me that Lois was a paralegal in Boston, where they'd finally settled. She was a modern woman and Irmaline hoped Sherry would take a cue from her and find her own independence.

The next day, an unexpected knock on the door roused me from my semi-conscious state on the couch. Amos was nowhere to be seen, but I could hear power tools running in the basement and I assumed he was working on his renovation project.

I peeked out the window, a residue of paranoia still clinging in the back of my mind.

It was Mike Tanner, the P.I. I let him in with a gust of cold air and a few errant snowflakes.

"Hi." He said. "I'm sorry to bother you over the holidays, but I have a few questions that have been nagging at me and was hoping you and Amos could help me clear them up."

"Sure." I said, taking his coat and hanging it on the hook. "C'mon in. Do you want coffee?"

He said he did and I went to the kitchen to get it. While he was nestling into a chair, I went and yelled down the stairs at Amos.

Mike stood as Amos entered and they shook hands.

When we were all settled, Amos and I next to each other on the couch, he got down to business.

"Do you remember carrying the trunk into the Church?" He asked Amos.

"Of course." Amos said.

"How heavy was it?" He leaned forward, his hands on his knees, as he watched Amos' face.

"It was heavy." Amos responded. "But I knew Annie had put a set of dishes and pewter candlesticks, among other things, in there."

"And when you got to the church, did you have occasion to open it, to remove the contents?"

"No." Amos said. He, too, leaned forward. "I knew Annie would be going down there to sort through her things and get them set up."

His gaze shifted to me.

"What I can't figure out," he went on, "was when and how her body got in that trunk."

I spoke up, "When I got there, the dishes and other things that had been in the trunk, were neatly stacked on a nearby table. I assumed someone had taken them out and placed them there."

"Did you ever ask anyone if they'd done so?" He inquired.

"No. I really didn't think about it. I just set about polishing up the trunk." I replied.

"So. Sometime, probably during the night, someone went in there and removed the contents in the trunk and placed Vicky's body in there. Either that, or she was already in the trunk when Amos' carried it in."

Amos and I looked at each other. What was he trying to say?

"What are you inferring?" Amos asked, the color starting to rise in his face.

"I'm not inferring anything. I'm just trying to figure out the sequence of events. This has been nagging at me for quite some time and I believe it's worth looking into. Why the police didn't check into it further is beyond me."

"When we were still at the church, after I'd found her, I'd told the Deputy the same thing I'm telling you now. It wasn't in the trunk when it left my house. You can ask Irmaline. She was there."

"I plan on doing just that." He said, pragmatically.

He raised his cup and drank the steaming liquid in a few gulps, then stood. Once again he raised his hand to Amos.

"Thanks for your time. If you can think of anything, anything at all, whether you think it's nothing or not, please call me."

"What about Bar...Irv?" I asked. "Do you think it could have been him?"

"I'm also working that angle, though it seems unlikely."

"Well, then there's still a murderer running around out

there!" I said, too loudly.

"That's what I'm trying to find out. I'm sure the police would love to pin this on Irving and close the case, with their credibility still intact."

I escorted him to the door and handed him his coat.

"I'm sorry we weren't more helpful, Mr. Tanner." I said.

"Mike." He replied. "I'll be staying until I find out the truth." He said. "Her parents deserve to know."

"Yes, they do." I agreed. "We all want to know. Should we be afraid?" I asked.

"Who knows?" He answered, pulling on his gloves. "This is the weirdest case I've ever worked on and it's driving me crazy!"

"Let us know if you find out anything." I yelled after him as he started toward his car, his hand lifted in a backward wave as he concentrated on not slipping on the icy gravel.

"What do you make of that?" I asked, closing the door and turning to Amos.

He shrugged.

"At least he's still looking; probably more than the cops. Like he said, they'd probably like to pin it on Irv and close it."

I was glad I'd brought a large bag of dog and cat food to Amos', as the snow started coming down that afternoon and the news stations were going crazy with their dire predictions of the coming winter storm. You couldn't turn the t.v. on without seeing the blurbs running across the bottom of the screen, noting all the business closings because of it. The kids were still out of school on their Christmas vacations, so at least we were spared the constant barrage of school closings.

As I looked out the window, it seemed the icicles were now nearly touching the growing banks of snow. The windows were already partially covered, and the path Amos had recently shoveled was no longer visible. When Sam had to go out, he snuffled around in the blinding wetness for a few minutes, did his business, and came right back in. Judas had found a new perch for herself on a log windowsill that jutted out just enough for her sleek body to fit on, and she sat for hours watching the swirling flakes dance in the buffeting winds. What did she make of her winter seclusion? I wondered. She rarely wanted to go out once the weather got cold, and seemed to take her self-imposed exile stoically, patiently awaiting the first thaw.

Amos was worried about the line of stalactite-like icicles adorning the roof and wanted to go out and knock them off, but I managed to convince him to wait, at least until morning, when I promised to help him. I went to the basement with him and held pieces of the faux wood siding for the walls; as he measured and cut them on his workroom saw. I helped hold them in place as he affixed them. We worked silently, the whining of the saw the only sound in the dankness, echoing off the walls and making my eardrums tingle.

We'd accomplished quite a bit, and I complimented him on his workmanship. Only one long wall remained bare as we ascended back upstairs to make supper. I'd taken out venison steaks from the large freezer in the basement, and once upstairs, put them in the little microwave to thaw.

I waited for Amos to shower so I could soak in a hot tub. Sawdust was embedded in his dense beard and mustache, and his hair was peppered with small chips. He really WAS Paul Bunyan! I stood before the bathroom mirror, brushing chips from my own locks as steam rolled over the shower curtain and humidity filled the air. My reflection was soon lost as the mirror steamed over, and I put the brush down and wandered back out to the kitchen to marinate the steaks.

It was already dark out and I realized we'd been working in the basement for the better part of three hours. I put the steaks in marinating sauce in the refrigerator, covered by saran wrap, and waited for Amos to finish his ablutions.

His tub was bigger than mine, an ancient claw-footed

monstrosity that I could actually lay down in. I'd brought a new book with me, one I'd picked up at the mall while Christmas shopping, and I was anxious to start it. The hot water soaked the tension from my aching body. I HAD to get more exercise! The small contribution I'd made to Amos' project had worn me out, and I lolled listlessly in the steamy water. I managed to get through the first chapter before I felt myself dozing off. I quickly set the book on the toilet and forced myself out. The water was starting to cool, and I wanted to savor its heat, so I quickly dried off and put on my heavy, blue, terry cloth robe.

We ate in front of the t.v., watching the storm unfold on the wide screen. Several homes and businesses were already without power as strong winds knocked down power lines all over our part of the state. Amos pointed out that we, at least, had a fireplace, so we wouldn't freeze. He said he had an old generator somewhere in the basement and if worse came to worse, we could use that.. He hadn't needed to use it in all the time he'd lived here as an adult, but his dad had had occasion too, and he'd watched, at his side, as he'd started it up. He always kept gas in it.

The howling of the wind through the old timbers moaned like a disembodied spirit, ascending and descending in a whistling cacophony. A Banshee, come to life. I wondered about my own home and hoped I hadn't lost power. My pipes would freeze and burst without heat. Amos assured me we could check it out tomorrow.

We went to bed shortly after we'd ate, it was already past ten and we were both tired.

Despite our fatigue, we made love slowly, finding in each other a comfort that even the elements couldn't dispel. I fell asleep in Amos' arms, the ghostly howling lulling me into a dreamless sleep.

The sun shining through the window woke me up. I jumped up and ran to the window, hoping the storm was over. No such luck. High flying, dark clouds played hide and seek with the sun, and the snow was still coming down.

After a trip to the bathroom, I wandered out to the living room, my fuzzy slippers making swooshing noises on the wooden floor. I didn't see Amos anywhere, but then I heard chopping sounds outside the living room window. I pulled back the drapes and saw Amos, a little axe-like thing in hand, chopping away at the pesky icicles. I knocked on the window and he waved, shielding his eyes from the intermittent glare of the sun with his hand.

I got coffee and sat on the couch. The t.v. was already out of its hiding place, but not on.

I found the remote halfway under the couch; Judas, I thought. The early morning news was still doling out warnings about the hazards of the storm. I noticed how the talking heads' expressions could change from grave concern to hilarity as quickly as the stories they read.

'Phonies!' I thought. 'What ghouls.' After the circus surrounding the deaths of Vicky and Barney, I couldn't help but think of them that way.

Amos came in then, stomping his gigantic boots on the rug put there for that purpose.

I could see the snow falling before the door closed, big, fat flakes, swirling in vortexes like white tornadoes.

"What in the world were you doing?" I asked, stupidly. "I mean, I wanted to help you and it's still storming out there!"

He waved his hand, dismissively, as he shed his heavy coat.

"I got up early and looked outside. Those icicles were bugging me, so I decided to take care of them."

Why wasn't I surprised? He'd get a bee in his bonnet and wouldn't let it go until he'd resolved it to his satisfaction. I guessed I admired that about him.

"Sit." I said, patting the couch next to me. "I'll make breakfast as soon as I wake up, then I'll go out and help you."

"It's done now." He said, settling in next to me. Looking at the t.v., he asked "Anything on?"

"The usual. Weather, weather and weather." I said, sarcastically.

"You know what they say about the weather," he replied.

I interrupted with the punch line: "If you don't like the weather, wait a minute; or, winter and road construction?"

"I guess we're both true Northerners." He said, putting his arm around me.

New Years Eve was upon us and the storm had finally given up the ghost, leaving it as a white blanket covering the earth from horizon to horizon. The trees were no longer trees, but icy, armor-coated knights in an army of knights, standing sentinel; waiting to divest themselves of their heavy winter mail and stand naked for awhile, until their new coats sheathed them, once again, in the green finery of summer.

We donned coats, boots, hats, and gloves, and went to wage war with nature. It took a couple of hours to shovel out the cars and walkway and stairs. I dreaded the thought of returning to my house. That would be a time consuming job, as I hadn't kept up with it before the storm. I felt guilty for not keeping my feeders filled. It had been a week since I'd last fought my way through the, then knee-deep snow, and replenished their food supply. My squirrels, too, would feel abandoned. When we finally finished and went back in, Amos with an armful of wood, me, the shovels, which I left by the door, our cheeks were rosy and our muscles sore. At least, mine were.

Amos said we could go to my place anytime and shovel it out. We decided tomorrow, New Years Day, would be good. I had to get my mail, my lone mail box, guarding the end of the driveway, would probably be full by now, taken over by advertisements, flyers, and bills.

I'd talked to Irmaline a few times since the funeral, and

things were going well. Sherry was glowing with a new vitality that Irmaline hadn't seen in her in years. They'd made the boys shovel the drive and walk, but then went out and engaged in a snowball fight with them when they were done. Irmaline had then gone in to bake cookies, while Sherry and Lois stayed out with the boys and Sugar (Rich and Lois') daughter, making a snowman. Gary and Rich were visiting old school friends.

They planned to spend a quiet New Years Eve, and wanted Amos and I to come over for dinner, later. I told her I'd talk to Amos and call her back. The roads were still in bad shape, the dirt road at the end of the driveway hadn't been plowed and it appeared impassable. I knew it wouldn't be a problem for Amos, but it gave me pause. The intensity of the storm had caught us all by surprise, including the meteorologists. In the end, I won out and we decided to stay where we were. I think, even Amos knew, it was futile trying to get out until the city plow came through.

I called Irmaline and explained the situation to her. She implored us to stay home, that she would call us at midnight, if she could stay awake that long. I knew what she meant. I hadn't made it until midnight in 5 years.

My head was nodding as we watched the big ball in Time's Square descend. Amos had found an old bottle of wine in a cupboard and we toasted the New Year as the ball landed, joining the entire nation (those who had managed to stay awake) in a New Years' kiss. Then we went to bed and fell asleep immediately. It wasn't until morning that I realized Irmaline hadn't called. After I'd managed to wake up a little, I called her. I knew she was an early riser (as most older people seem to be) so I didn't worry about waking her.

She answered on the first ring.

"Happy New Year, Annie! I'm sorry I didn't call you last night, but once again, I didn't quite make it until midnight. Sherry, me, Gary, and Rich and Lois, and all the kids were waiting, with the rest of the country, for midnight. They made it, I didn't. I woke up on the couch this morning, a little note from the boys, saying, "Happy New Year, grandma" propped up on the coffee table."

"How cute!" I said. "We're kind of going stir crazy, here." I added. "God knows when that plow will get around to us."

"Well, you let me know when it does. Gary has to get to the airport and I don't think any flights are going out. I don't know what he's supposed to do if he can't get out. There must be some contingency for that. He's going to be making some calls today to find out what he's supposed to do. The teenagers have been telling me we live in the Dark Ages since we have no cell service. Their parents are glad, however, since now they have to concentrate on the family."

"Yeah, well, I guess those things are a big deal to teenagers." I replied.

"Oh, you bet they are!" She said, "Sherman, (the 17 year-old) is going crazy, not being able to talk to his girlfriend 24-7. Sugar, (the 15 year-olds' nickname) keeps picking up her phone like it's going to start working any minute."

"It's a whole different world." I lamented. "Well, let me know what Gary finds out. I know Amos wants to see them both before they leave."

"I will, Annie. They'd like to see their old friend, too."

As I hung up, Amos was donning his heavy coat, prepared to do battle with the snow; first the driveway, which, though we'd just shoveled, was rife with blown snow; then the road with his truck. I felt that was my fault, I'd distracted him.

I'd just pulled on my coat to follow Amos, when I heard the unmistakable sound of the plow. I opened the door and went onto the stoop. Amos was just getting to the end of the driveway; shovel in hand, when the plow approached. The engine sound was cut off as the driver saw Amos and stopped to talk to him.

The sun was shining that day, the snow cover an unbroken

blanket of white, covering the earth as far as the eye could see. I imagined that the Black Forest would look like this in winter, the darkness associated with it dispelled by the cover of whiteness. I FELT like I was in a fairyland.

The plow restarted and Amos headed back to the house, a smile lighting his face.

We reentered the warmness of the living room, shedding our coats.

"We can get out now." He said.

"So I see. I just talked to Irmaline, and she's worried that Gary won't be able to get back to his unit in time."

"I'm sure the airport will be all shoveled out today." He said.

We went into town and did some shopping; the store was nearly deserted in the aftermath of the storm. I'd called Irmaline before we left and she implored us to stop by.

With the groceries safely stashed in the rear, we decided to do so, so Amos could see Rich and Gary.

All the kids were in the yard as we pulled up. The teenagers had built a big wall of snow to hide behind so they could bombard the little ones with snowballs from a huge cache behind it. Shawn and Luke were working on their own wall, but it was small and lopsided compared to the bigger kids'.

Shawn and Luke came running up as Amos exited the truck.

The teenagers quit their labors and stood, staring at us.

"Uncle Rich and Uncle Gary are here!" Shawn said, his cheeks a rosy red beneath his stocking cap.

"And we're having a snowball fight with Sherm and Sugar!" Luke said, excitedly.

Amos smiled and complimented them on their snow wall.

They followed as we headed toward the house.

Sherman and Sugar came up to meet us on the porch.

I couldn't believe how big they were! Sugar, though only

15, towered over me. Sherman must have been nearly six feet tall. Not wanting to be uncool, he wore no cap and his hair stood up in short spikes, but the Mohawk was gone. He had several piercings in his ears, as did Sugar, but he also had a spike earring in his eyebrow and I saw a bright flash on his tongue as he spoke.

"Hey." He said, and I was surprised at the deepness of his voice. "Aren't you Amos?"

Amos held out a gloved hand and shook his bare one.

"I missed you when you were here last year. The last time I saw you, you were her size." He said, gesturing toward me.

"I remember you." Sugar said, "You took us to that fair in town with mom and dad and grandma."

"You're getting prettier all the time, Sugar." He answered, sincerely. "Good thing you look like your mom!"

The door opened just then, as Irmaline heard the commotion on the porch.

"You made it!" She said, happily. She was wearing gabardine slacks and her pink sweater. Her white hair was pinned up with hairpins, little tendrils falling onto her neck.

She looked happier than I could ever remember seeing her.

She herded us in and I was introduced as our coats were taken and hung in the little closet by the door.

"That's Amos' girlfriend!" Luke yelled, after Irmaline had introduced me to the teenagers.

We all laughed and Luke turned red and ran off into the kitchen, yelling for his mother.

We spent a pleasant afternoon with Irmaline's family. Gary and Rich were both handsome men, despite what Amos' teasing had led me to believe. I could see Irmaline in both of them; but they were tall, evidently like their father. Gary had dark hair, cut in short, military style, while Rich's hair was lighter, and worn longer. They were both clean-shaven and wore jeans and tee shirts. Lois was tall and willowy, with a short blonde shag cut that made her look younger than I knew her to be. She, too, was dressed casually, wearing a thick, sky-blue sweater and worn jeans.

We spent the afternoon around the kitchen table, Gary sitting on a counter, the teenagers on chairs from the dining room.

I remained silent as everyone caught up with each other's lives, and then took a trip down memory lane. Even the teenagers made occasional contributions to the conversation, mostly veiled barbs at their parents. Sherry was beaming. Wow, I thought, she's like a different person from the first time I saw her. She light-heartedly bantered with her brothers, like no time at all had passed since she'd last seen them.

Shawn and Luke were nowhere to be seen, playing video games, no doubt.

The sun was already descending westward when a distant shouting could be heard from the direction of the back yard. The front door burst open and Shawn ran in, his face wet and red, from more than the cold.

"Mom! Mom!" He screamed. "Luke fell in the channel!"

We all flew off our chairs as one and ran to the door, no one even bothering to put coats on. Gary and Rich were wearing tennis shoes, Irmaline, slippers, while Sherry and I were in our stocking feet. Amos had slipped his huge boots on with barely a hesitation in his stride. Lois was wearing some type of hiking boot and led the pack, her shoes finding more purchase on the icy snow-pack.

By the time Irmaline and I plowed our way through the snow banks to the back yard, Gary was pulling his wet nephew onto the bank. A big hole could be seen in the middle of the channel where he'd fallen through, a long line of broken ice showing where Gary had pulled him out.

He was crying, a good sign. His heavy coat had nearly pulled him down, he sobbed, brokenly. He'd been clinging to the ice when Gary had gotten to him. If he'd let go, he'd have been caught under the ice and pulled downstream.

Sherry threw herself on him, sobbing. Her brothers comforted her and Rich took him from a shivering Gary and carried him into the house, the rest of us trailing behind. The teenagers had stood taking in the whole scene, shivering in their thin tee shirts and socks.

Sherry took Luke up and stuck him in a warm tub immediately. Irmaline hovered over them. The rest of us, except Gary, who went to put on dry clothes, retired to the living room. No one spoke, the shock settling in.

After a while, Irmaline came down and told us he was fine, but Sherry had insisted he lay down, over his protestations. Seems he wanted to go back out and finish the snowball fight with his cousins. We all laughed at this and muted conversation soon resumed.

Then Sherry said something that made my blood run cold. She informed us that he'd been trying to cross the channel because he'd seen his dad on the other side. A private party owned the 'other side'. Small cabins were spread out over several acres, but there was only one rustic old cabin sitting across the channel; totally desolate in the winter, and even in summer, seldom rented out, vacationers opting for the other, well-maintained cabins.

She'd tried to explain to him that it couldn't have been his dad, but he insisted. Shawn, when asked, said he'd seen nothing.

I tuned out after that, letting the conversation flow around me without hearing a thing.

The icy feeling returned to seize my heart, and I found my hands shaking.

Amos noticed my discomfiture at some point and we made our exit soon after, Amos assuring them that we'd drive down to the city and meet them tomorrow before Gary's flight.

"What do you make of that?" I asked Amos as we drove

through the gloaming.

"It probably was the owner or one of his workers, checking the cabin out." Amos said, reasonably. "Coons and other critters get in those cabins sometimes."

"I'm sure you're right." I said, but the coldness remained.

We carried the groceries in and put them away. It was dark by now, and I was tired and hungry. We had a quick dinner of burgers, washed down with the remaining beers, and went to bed early. We both fell into an exhausted sleep almost at once.

The next day rose bright and sunny. We planned on leaving at 8 a.m., as we didn't want to drive in the dark. I'd talked to Irmaline, and they were to meet us downtown, at a block-long complex housing several stores, restaurants, a movie theater and one of the biggest video arcades in the state, complete with bowling alley. She said Luke was fine, and he acted like he'd forgotten about his brush with death, already. She thought the day in town would be a great diversion for him, and planned to spoil him a little extra.

We drove into town to fill the gas tank, as Amos had been driving on fumes for days, since before the storm. He had two big coffees in Styrofoam cups with him as he emerged from the station, and I gratefully accepted one, even though I'd already drunk two cups before we left. Fortunately, I'd emptied my bladder right before we went; I could hold it an hour.

We listened to old rock on the radio, interspersed with light banter and scathing political comments from the "Barnyard in the Morning Crew". I hadn't listened to them in ages, and laughed at the witty riposte between them.

The sun shone blindingly off the snow cover; luckily for me it was on the left side of the car and Amos' big head blocked it from my view.

The scene rushing by the window was exceedingly beautiful. Icicles clothed the bare tree limbs in celestial light as the sun refracted off them. Miles of snow-covered fields, interspersed with long stretches of forest flew by: All of it a shiny, blindingly white, world. If alien beings descended upon this scene, what would they think? They'd think, 'it's colder than hell in this god-forsaken place!' But I loved it, as did Amos.

I tried to put the scary incident of the previous day out of my mind, but I found myself going over it, again and again, in my mind.

We had to park in a ramp, as despite the recent storm, the streets were full of parked cars.

I'd forgotten how big the city was and the towering buildings gave me a feeling of claustrophobia, made worse by the blaring horns and rushing traffic. It even smelled different here, I thought. Clouds of carbon monoxide hung in the chill air and the rotten egg smell of catalytic converters assaulted my nose. Now I knew why I lived in the country. I'd never been one for crowds, either, and though it certainly wasn't New York, all the pedestrian traffic made me feel stifled.

The complex, too, was crowded, teenagers hanging out, mothers with children, men in suits (playing hooky from work?) and the ever present homeless, trying to blend in with the everyday folks, hoping to delay the inevitable ejection back out into the elements.

We waited inside by the doors, watching through the wall of windows encasing this side of the building. We saw them before I had a chance to worry, and I trotted over to Irmaline as she entered, choosing to go through the revolving door rather than fight with the humongous glass entryway door. The boys, of course, had to come through the revolving doors also, and went around three times, with Sherry trapped between them, before her voice level rose sufficiently to make them stop.

'Well, he's none the worse for wear', I thought, watching Luke laughingly emerge from between the doors.

We consulted together in the glass-enclosed foyer, everyone with his or her own agenda. It was finally decided that Sherman and Sugar would take the smaller boys to the huge video arcade on the third floor, and then we'd rendezvous in an hour, and maybe take in a movie. At first the teens had grumbled about 'having to baby-sit', but it had quickly dissipated when they saw the boys excited expressions; it was like they'd realized that they didn't get to see their cousins all that often. Also, their cells worked here!

I'd worn my jeans and a clean, red sweater, and was glad to see that everyone else had dressed casually, too. I'd insisted Amos wear his light blue sweater, and he DID look handsome in it.

Sherry wanted to spend some time with her brothers and sister-in-law, and as they were all into music, they wandered down towards a Sam Goodie's. Irmaline stayed with Amos and I, as she knew we were headed for the big bookstore in the center of the second floor. We also wanted to check out the Planet Hollywood, but soon found out that was a futile effort; there was a line halfway down the hallway, waiting to get in.

I nibbled along the way; not being able to resist the tantalizing smells. Donuts, ice cream, cookies. And that was just the sweet stuff! I limited myself to one of each treat, as I knew we were going for supper later.

As we rounded one corner, a crowd of teenagers were lounging against the wall of a Gap Store. They were playing loud Rap music, dancing in exaggerated imitation of their latest hero; mouthing loud and crude lyrics, without regard to who heard. I stepped wide to pass them, while they chuckled under their breath at the cowardly old lady. Irmaline stared straight at them, making a 'harrumphing' noise as she passed. Amos didn't even seem to notice them.

It was a rerun of our last shopping excursion only on a much grander scale. The place was huge and the prices exorbitant.

At some point we found ourselves at the arcade, and watched in awe as Shawn and Luke maneuvered stationary motorcycles and racecars along video roads. Sherman and Sugar, upon seeing us, quit their baby-sitting vigil and ran to enjoy their own pursuits; which turned out to be gory, shooting at Zombie games. Sherry, her brothers and Lois, arrived to check on the kids, and we decided it was time to eat in earnest.

After a convivial meal at an upscale steakhouse, (at which time Gary regaled us with tales of his tour of Iraq, and Rich tried to one-up him with hilarious office stories as Lois rolled her eyes in mock boredom), we decided to take in a movie. Since there was a whole complex of theaters, all beginning at approximately the same times, we split along the lines of individual interests. The teenagers made concessions to their own wants and took the boys to a movie they thought they'd all enjoy, while we adults went to a new movie with Brad Pitt, that we all wanted to see.

The kids were waiting for us in the lobby; again, the little kids were playing video games as the teenagers competed against each other in a skeet-shooting game. We gathered them up, after their games, of course, and decided what to do.

Amos and I decided to go home. It was already nearly dark and he'd gotten his chance to catch up with Gary and Rich at supper. Gary's plane was leaving at 9 p.m., so Irmaline and her extended family were going to head to the airport. She said she'd call me in the morning and we all bid our farewells. As I shook Lois' hand, I hoped I'd have more time to interact with her before they, too, left. She seemed a no-nonsense type of person, and despite her sons' somewhat unorthodox appearance, she'd raised good kids. I hoped she'd remain friends with Sherry despite the distance between them. Sherry now needed to surround herself with strong women. I didn't know if I qualified; but I was there for her and told her so.

Amos and I made our way down the sidewalk, the street side bearing mounds of black snow from the constant barrage of carbon monoxide. The parking ramp was only a block, but even that short distance brought into contrast the differences between country and city life. The streetlights had just come on, their glare only emphasizing the bleakness of the scene. Tall mountains of buildings jostled for space and the only trees were small, curbside saplings. No beautifying ice cover for their stunted branches. The pollution had melted any ice that may have settled there.

On the way home I nodded off in the warmth of the truck, my last memory of the city a crowded highway ramp and a cacophony of horns blaring as cars fought for access.

I awoke as we pulled into Amos' drive, Sam's barking startling me out of my slumber.

The snow made crunching sounds under our feet as we headed for the walkway. Despite Amos' shoveling, piles of snow still clung to the gravel, the wind designing the landscape to it's liking.

Settling before the hearth as Amos got a fire going, I pointed out the stark differences between our rural existence and that of the city folk. We laughed about the stereotype that WE were the dumb ones.

We snuggled on the couch before the fire, listening to an easy listening station Amos had put on the radio. We'd finally reached the point where we were totally at ease with each other, and could even began to hope we had a future. We'd both been hurt deeply by our marriages; me, by Al's death; him, by Vicky's philandering.

Despite all that had happened, and my continued unease, I was now, not just content, but happy. Tomorrow we would go over and shovel out my place, but tonight was for romance.

The sight of my forlorn little house appalled me as we pulled in. We had to park at the end of the drive as snow was drifted in humongous piles throughout the yard. My Christmas lights looked forlorn and tacky. A couple of strings hung off the corner of the eaves, one entangled with a huge icicle. A few bright red, blue and green bulbs still cast a subdued light on the snow-packed roof, the rest were now burned out blobs, buried in the mountain of white encasing my house. The ends of the icicles hanging from my eaves met the snow-banks climbing the walls, giving my home the appearance of a natural jail.

I moaned in dismay at the thought of all the shoveling and chopping that lay ahead.

Amos peered at me, a small smile playing at the corners of his mouth.

"Let's get to it." He said, resigned to a day spent in exhaustive labor.

We retrieved shovels, rakes, little axes, and salt from the truck and set about the cleanup.

When we finally got to the door, I apprehensively pulled my keys from the pocket of my now snow-covered jeans, and opened the door. The cold hearth and silent house gave the impression of an empty domicile, one that had been devoid of life for a long time. I retrieved wood and lit a fire, just to dispel my feelings of alienation about my home. I wandered through the house, checking for any leaks the storm may have created. I felt better when I found none. Amos was out chopping icicles off the roof and utilizing a snow rake to pull great bunches of the white stuff off the roof. After assuring myself there was no permanent damage, I went out and helped him. My electrical lines were intact, ditto the phone line.

The sun was shining and the temperature above freezing, so the task wasn't as unpleasant as it could have been. The line of icicles was melting slowly and cold water dripped on our heads as we went about our business. Amos inadvertently pulled down a string of lights with the rake, separating it from its companions by disengaging the plug from another string. He gave up the raking in frustration when it became clear that the lights were too big of a hindrance.

"There wasn't any snow yet when I put them up." I said defensively, when I saw the look on his face. "Just leave it. There's no damage inside, I looked."

He returned the rake to the truck and set about shoveling off the porch. I returned inside and checked the refrigerator for rotten food. The milk was spoiled but everything else seemed o.k. I was glad I'd frozen the bread before going to Amos'. I thawed a half a loaf in my microwave and made up some bologna sandwiches. I called Amos in and we settled in the living room, the dampness now dispelled by the burgeoning fire.

"We should come and stay here for a while." I said, between bites.

Amos took a swig of his coke, surveying the room.

"I'm going to be going back on the road in a couple days." He said, slowly. "I've been taking too much time off and it puts pressure on the other guys."

"Oh." I said, not knowing how to respond.

"Maybe you should just stay at my place 'til I get back. I'd feel better about it if you would."

"I could do that." I answered.

Before we left, I dug out another bag of dog and cat food and Amos hefted them over his shoulder and went to deposit them in the truck. I filled my feeders as one of my squirrel friends chattered at me, berating me for abandoning him.

I felt much better now that I knew my home was safe and undamaged, and was smiling as I slid in the truck beside Amos. The brightness of the day and ethereal tranquility of the scene bolstered my confidence that the worst was over. I hoped that Barney had killed Vicky, than the nightmare really would be over, although, deep in my heart, I didn't really believe that. We spent the rest of the day in what had come to be 'our routine', making a salad for supper later, me dicing vegetables, Amos cleaning and shredding lettuce. We then went down and worked on the basement some more. Later, we ate, spent a quiet evening watching t.v., and then went to bed, exhausted.

I was awakened in the middle of the night by loud, banging noises. I quickly sat up, bringing on a spell of dizziness as the blood rushed out of my head. My hand searched the other side of the big bed for Amos, but encountered only bedclothes. I reached over to turn on the lamp and nothing happened. Should I yell out for Amos? What if someone was in the house? The noises continued and then the light started flickering. I snuck out of bed and slipped on my robe. I opened the drawer to the bedside table and extracted Amos' gun. Even though I knew it was empty, whoever may be in the house, didn't.

I stealthily crept to the bedroom door and peered down the dark hallway. I couldn't see anything and wondered if I should try sneaking to the junk drawer in the kitchen and finding the flashlight I knew Amos kept there. Where was Sam? I wondered, just realizing he hadn't been in his usual position on the bed. The thumping noises continued and I realized they were coming from the basement. I snuck down the hallway, watching as the light from the bedside lamp filtered out into the hallway, then flickered off.

I wanted to call out to Amos but something made me hold my tongue. Was he in trouble?

I stood outside the door to the basement, listening. Yes, the noises were definitely coming from there. Amos wouldn't be down there working in the middle of the night, would he?

He had no tools that were that loud, except the saw, and it sure wasn't that.

Just then, the door flew open and I jumped back, holding the gun in front of me like a talisman. The light in the laundry room (where I was) came on then, and I saw a scared looking

Amos staring at the barrel of the gun.

"Oh, my God!" I sighed, lowering the gun and clutching my heart with my other hand.

"Annie! What the hell are you doing?" He demanded, reaching out and grabbing the gun, (none too gently), from my hand.

"What are YOU doing?" I said, defensively.

"For God's sake! Another storm hit last night and I was awakened by it, but once I got up I realized the lines were down, so I went down and hooked up the generator."

He was wearing his lounging sweats and his hair was in wild disarray.

"We need heat, or the pipes will freeze." He added.

I flew into his arms. "I'm sorry. I thought someone had broken in and you were in trouble."

Sam made his entrance then, entering from the hallway, his tail wagging and eyes wide, as he wondered what we were doing up.

"Sam was gone." I mumbled against his chest. "I didn't know what to think!"

He patted my back reassuringly.

"Hey, c'mon. Everything's all right. Do you want to go back to bed, or should I make coffee?"

"What time is it?" I said, pulling away and looking up at him.

"I really don't know. I'll have to go consult my watch." He said.

"Duh." I said, realizing the clocks would now be wrong.

We sat on the couch, drinking coffee; it was going on four o'clock. I was surprised that the t.v. worked, but Amos' assured me the generator had enough power to operate the necessities. He considered the t.v. a necessity as we could track the weather and find out when the power would be on again. Outside the window I could see snow falling again, big, fat flakes, swirling, beyond the drapes. Judas sat on her ledge, alternately watching the snow and us, with her green, cat eyes.

Amos called the garage as soon as it opened, notifying his partners that he was available for work. He informed me he'd be leaving the next day and would be gone about a week.

I wasn't looking forward to being alone again; I'd grown used to his presence. I told myself I could go over to Irmalines' and cultivate my friendships with Sherry and Lois.

I washed two big loads of clothes when the electricity finally came back on, around noon.

I wondered if my home had been affected, and hoped not. Though I was somewhat comfortable financially right now, burst pipes would quickly drain my bank account.

We once again had to shovel out, but it wasn't bad since we'd just done it. Amos told me he'd go check my place out on his way to the garage tomorrow.

I talked to Irmaline as I waited for the second load of clothes to dry, running back and forth between the laundry room and the bedroom, folding and putting away the laundry that was dry.

Irmaline wanted me to come and stay with her family while Amos was gone, but I demurred. Her house was crowded enough right now, and there were my pets to consider.

I'd been accustomed to being alone before Amos; I'd adjust.

Amos and I were practically inseparable the rest of the day, neither of us wanting to voice the emptiness we'd feel when we were parted.

The basement walls were nearly all paneled and we would concentrate on laying carpet when he returned from his run. I'd seen the beautiful blue carpeting rolled up in a corner of the basement and couldn't wait to see it laid out. We spent the rest of the afternoon working on finishing the paneling before he left, and only one small corner remained to be finished when we, at last, decided to quit. Amos was ecstatic with the results of our labors, and couldn't wait to finish.

I languished in a hot tub when we'd finished, washing the wood chips and plaster dust out of my bedraggled hair. Amos had already taken his shower and I could hear him on the phone with one of his partners as I entered the living room, drawing my robe over my old, flannel nightgown.

"Maybe you should stay with Irmaline while I'm gone." Amos said, hanging up the phone. "I'll worry about you being here alone."

"Just leave me some bullets for the gun, and call before you come home, so I don't shoot you accidentally." I said, half teasingly.

Amos left in the predawn morning. The first vestiges of sunlight were reflecting off the drifted snow, many-faceted diamonds portending a sunny day. We clung to each other at the door, neither wanting to be the first to relinquish our hold on the other. He promised to call periodically at various stops along the way. As I watched his truck pull out onto the snow-covered road, stray sunbeams reflecting off the windshield, I felt loneliness like I hadn't felt since Al died. I turned back into the still dark house, turning on lights to chase away the gloom. Sam and Judas seemed to sense my desolation and hovered close by, looking at me questioningly. A Cardinals' whistling song pierced the parting darkness and the sun came up with a dazzling brightness, a huge orange ball, chasing the lingering shadows of night into submission.

A feeling of anxiety spurred me into action and I began a frenzied bout of housecleaning. I hauled out the vacuum and went from one end of the house to the other. I then took a broom and went up to the loft, sweeping the rug and floor with quick strokes. I changed both beds, took out the garbage and recyclables, then got a pail full of soapy water and scrubbed the kitchen floor. I then proceeded to the bathroom and spent an hour in there, cleaning every surface. I sprayed the mirror with window cleaner, trying not to look at my aging reflection and wild hair as I rubbed at water spots.

When I finished, I went and got another cup of coffee and collapsed on the couch, grabbing up the remote and flicking on the silent set. The talking heads were midway through their morning news show; the same stories retold over and over again in the two hours allotted. I needed a job; or, at the very least, a hobby. Maybe I'd go down to the basement and do some much-needed cleaning in preparation to laying the carpet.

The storm, as usual, was the big news. Most everyone's power had now been restored and the plows were out, along with sanding trucks. No mention was made of either the Vicky or Barney murder, other stories replacing the once near-frenzied media coverage.

A teenager had frozen to death coming home from a party the night before, his body found by his father on the way to work, laying lifeless and rigid 50 feet from his driveway. The names weren't yet being released. The Police were trying to find out who had supplied him with the alcohol; charges would be filed. Big comfort to the parents, I thought. An area man and woman had been in a horrendous weather-related crash off the highway; she was killed, he was clinging to life after being airlifted to a city hospital.

I turned the set off and headed downstairs, donning a sweater to ward off the dampness of the basement.

I collected sawed off pieces of paneling and put them in a pile to be put in garbage bags.

I moved old furniture and piles of rags aside so I could sweep the floor. Sam and Judas remained upstairs, I could hear them whining and mewing, bidding me to come back up.

I was almost afraid to venture into the dark corners at the back of the big room. Mice, spiders, and God knew what else, could be hiding there, just waiting to give an old lady a heart attack. I put on big, yellow gardening gloves and stuffed the splinter-covered siding into black garbage bags. The fluorescent lights gave the room a cavernous appearance, an old mine, abandoned for years; the lode depleted.

I gathered up my courage and ventured back in the shadows at the rear of the room. A dilapidated dresser leaned against the rear wall, a broken leg left it listing to the right. Drawers were half open, years of swelling dampness precluding their ever being closed again. An ancient floor lamp, its once yellow shade now tattered and torn, resided next to the dresser. 'Why did he keep this junk?' I wondered. Maybe it reminded him of his years with Vicky? I quickly pushed the thought from my mind. I cautiously approached the dresser, curiosity getting the better of me. I pulled on the top drawer, but it was stuck fast, half open. I continued yanking and it finally gave, nearly knocking me off my feet. I staggered back as it hit the floor with a loud 'bang'. A cloud of dust emanated from it as it landed, and the side slat fell off. I knelt beside it and started looking through the ancient, rotting material of its contents. I felt guilty as I fingered through Amos' memories. I continued, nonetheless. Frilly underwear and push-up bras resided side by side in the top drawer.

The next drawer yielded sweaters and shirts, still neatly folded, as if waiting for their owner to come and utilize them once more. They were all feminine things, and had to have been Vicky's'. The bottom drawer wouldn't budge and I resorted to going through it from above, after removing the second drawer. At the very bottom of the drawer, tucked between an old pair of jeans and a holey tee-shirt, I found a pile of yellowed letters, held together with a pink piece of yarn. Feeling even more like a voyeur, I broke the string and loosed the letters, motes of dust causing me to sneeze repeatedly. They were all written in a masculine hand, the terminology and misspellings just reinforcing the feeling that they were written by a man. Amos had caught her cheating, but did he know about these?

I sat cross-legged on the dirty floor, perusing the letters one by one. Was this the man she'd lost Amos for? Or was she having several affairs? The final letter had me enthralled. In the bold script of the other letters, it described the writers undying love and implored the recipient to leave Amos and run away with him. It seemed to have an almost malevolent theme to it; veiled threats underlying the protestations of love. One paragraph in particular caught my eye:

If you don't leave him,
then I am not responsible
for what may happen.
It is all on you!
You promise to go with me
and you WILL.

They were all signed:
Your one and only

Should I give them to the Police? They sure sounded like a man obsessed. Maybe he'd been stalking her. I'd have to ask Amos. He may get mad about me snooping around, but perhaps he didn't know about them. I'd wait until he returned and tell him, then we'd decide together if we should inform the authorities.

I decided to put the letters back where I had found them; they weren't going anywhere.

There was no getting the top drawer back in the dresser; I left it where it lay.

As I shoved the second drawer back in, something rolled and thumped against the side of it. I stuck my now gloveless hand in among the sweaters and felt around. My fingers came in contact with a small, cold, hard object, and I wrapped my fingers around it and pulled it free from its soft constraints. A bullet! What was a bullet doing in this drawer? Amos kept all his guns and ammo on a top shelf in the closet upstairs. I dug around some more and came up with 4 more. Being somewhat of a gun aficionado, I recognized them as 38's, the same ammo my gun used. Amos had no 38. I thought back, trying to remember the guns Amos had stashed in the closet. I didn't remember a 38.

The old suspicions rose up, unbidden, and I threw the bullets back in the drawer. I used my hip to force it closed as far as it would go. I ran from the basement, slipping and banging my knee on the steep stairs in my haste to distance myself from a perceived truth, that I didn't want to face.

There had to be another explanation for the presence of those bullets. Amos had always had guns; so had his father. At some point in time they probably were in possession of a 38. It WAS one of the more common guns on the market. The hair on the back of my neck stood up as a creeping realization came to mind. My gun had disappeared for a while, and at the time, Amos was the first one I'd suspected. Those bullets could have been from MY gun!

I sat on the couch, unconsciously chewing my bottom lip, until the pain made me stop.

The television blared, unheard, in the background, as my mind went over every possible scenario I could think of. What should I do? Should I confide in Irmaline and ask her opinion? She always took Amos' side, I realized. He could do no wrong, as far as she was concerned. What if Amos had killed Vicky? Could I bury my head in the sand and tell myself she had it coming? Could I jeopardize any happiness I may hope for by coming right out and accusing him?

My inner anxiety continued to grow and I got up and started pacing: Back and forth, back and forth. Sam jumping at my heels as he sensed my unease. I needed to DO something!

In a frenzy, I ran to the closet and pulled the guns out one by one, doing inventory. I got a chair from the kitchen and stood on it, reaching all the way to the back of the closet shelf, pulling out boxes of ammo. No 38 gun, no 38 bullets. I tried to put everything back just the way it had been, hoping Amos wouldn't notice I'd been digging around up there.

I then went through the whole house, starting with the loft. There was nothing else incriminating, anywhere.

Returning to the living room, I plopped back down on the couch, forcing myself to take deep breathes and calm down.

Would Amos leave me alone in a house that held proof of his guilt? No. He wasn't stupid. I finally convinced myself that there was a perfectly innocent explanation for those bullets. I KNEW Amos, he wasn't a murderer, and, like he'd told me at the time of Vicky's death, if he was going to kill her, he would have done it when he caught her messing around. He had no reason to at this point in time. They had no longer been together, and hadn't been for years.

The letters had definitely NOT been written by Amos; I knew this, because some had made mention of 'her husband'; also, I'd seen Amos' script before and there was no resemblance to the script in those letters. Amos could spell, too.

I'd drive myself crazy if I kept obsessing about it.

I decided to call Irmaline and see if she was up for company. She and Lois and Sherry would get my mind off my dilemma.

I ran a brush through my hair, slipped on some jeans, a sweatshirt and my new coat, grabbed my keys and flew out the door.

The roads were slick and I had to keep my mind on driving. The brightness of the day and beauty of the pastoral scene did little to dispel my anxiety as I maneuvered the old car along. By the time I pulled in front of Irmalines', my stomach was churning and my hands were shaking. I sat behind the wheel, drawing in great gulps of air, trying to still my shaking hands.

When I'd calmed down sufficiently, I made my way up the walk, my tennis shoes gripping the concrete through the thin patina of snow.

The door opened before my finger even reached the bell. Shawn stood there, wearing one of the tee-shirts I'd bought him for Christmas, a colorful cartoon character emblazoned across the front. He had some kind of cargo pants on, and was in his stocking feet.

"Grandma!" He yelled, causing a buzzing in my ear.

Irmaline emerged from the kitchen as I entered, slipping out of my coat. She took it from my hands and hung it in her coat closet.

"What's wrong, Annie? You look like you've seen a ghost!" Her eyebrows were knitted together in concern as she scanned my face.

"Nothing." I mumbled, trying to meet her gaze. Sherry and Lois entered from the kitchen then, and greetings were exchanged, affectively ending Irmaline's scrutiny. We all went into the kitchen and Sherry brought me a cup of steaming coffee as I joined them at the table.

"Rich went into town to meet up with some old friends." Sherry said, sitting next to me.

"They're going to meet at the bar, and it's a bit too early for me." A slight smile played across her face and I realized that she was taking steps to get her drinking under control.

The maelstrom of tragic events was ended, and she no longer had the need to drown her sorrows in alcohol.

"Good for you!" I said, patting her shoulder. "When does school start?"

"Not until March." She replied, "but I'm already studying some books I got at the library. I'm going to be ahead of the game."

"She's going to be one hell of a nurse!" Irmaline trilled, a look of pride crossing her countenance.

Lois spoke up for the first time since the greetings.

"I'm so glad she's finally found her vocation. I've been telling her for years that she needs to find something that interests her and stick with it. It's just too bad that it took a tragedy to spur her on."

Sugar entered the room, hopping onto the kitchen counter and crossing her jean-clad legs in lotus position. She was wearing bright pink socks, a contrast to her worn jeans and dark blue, pullover shirt.

"Mom." She said, interrupting whatever Lois had opened her mouth to say, "Sherm and Shawn won't give me a turn. I've been up there FOREVER, waiting. They even let Luke play!" She had a pout on her face, which I was quickly learning was a mask for teenage angst.

Lois quickly rose and left the room, Sugar at her heels. We could hear yelling as they reached Shawn's room.

"I thought they each had video systems?" I said.

"Oh, they do." Irmaline answered. "Only now, all of a sudden, Luke's games are too 'babyish', and he spends most of his time bugging his brother to play his."

There was no rancor in her statement, just an acceptance of 'that's how it is with kids'.

Sherry just sat, soaking it in, the smile of a Madonna coming to her face at the mention of her sons.

"By the way, Sherry", I said, changing the subject, "you look great! You're practically glowing." Her simple shift-dress, a powdery blue, brought out the blueness of her eyes, making her a vision of loveliness.

A blush crept across her cheeks, enhancing her beauty.

"Thank you, Annie." She said, demurely.

Lois returned then, a smug look on her pert, freckled face.

"Shawn and Sherm have been sent to Luke's room, to play his 'baby games', while Sugar and Luke play Shawn's. They can switch in an hour."

She slid back into her chair, cupping a steaming mug of coffee in her well-manicured hands.

"So, Annie," she said, focusing her attention on me, "what

do you do?"

I was caught off guard, as I'd assumed my status had already been revealed.

"Do?" I asked, stupidly. "Well, I guess I'm retired. I admire Sherry for her ambition, and I suppose I should have some." I felt my face flaming, being in the presence of a career woman.

"As I think you know," Irmaline piped up, "Annie's husband died fairly recently. I've spent a lot of time, since I met her, trying to get her out of her shell. I'm the one who dogged her to death to get to know Amos. I knew they'd make a perfect pair!" She said this last statement smugly, like she alone knew a secret.

"I'm glad they're together." Sherry said, elbows on the table, the small china cup held to her lips as she blew on it. "Amos needed someone. After what that bitch Vicky did. I didn't think he'd ever get over that!" Seeing Irmaline's look, she placed her cup delicately on the table and responded, "I know, mom, don't speak ill of the dead!"

A silence fell on the room then, as I knew everyone was thinking of Barney; well, it seemed, everyone but Sherry!

Suddenly, Lois threw back her head and let loose a raucous laugh. Irmaline, Sherry and I all looked at each other, and before anyone knew what happened, we all joined in. Our laughter bounced off the kitchen walls and echoed through the house, precipitating a loud, "God, mom!" from the top of the stairway; which only made us laugh harder.

With shadows thickening on the walls, I rose to leave. We'd spent a wonderful afternoon, the best I'd had in a long time. We'd ordered pizzas, the kids stampeding down the stairs when the bell rang. They'd gotten plates from the cupboard, shoving and jostling each other in their race for the pizzas, then disappeared, as quickly as they'd descended, Sherm grabbing a whole six-pack of coke from the fridge on his way out.

"They're like locusts!" Lois observed, looking after them, and Sherry readily agreed.

On the ride home (to Amos'), I drove slowly over the snow-packed road, watching the sun setting orange in an azure sky. 'My cup runneth over' I thought, the warm communion of the day still lingering.

My pets greeted my return ecstatically, especially since their dishes were empty. I fed them (after which they quickly lost interest in me) and went to run a hot bath.

I ruminated on the afternoon as I idly ran a washcloth over my shoulders. Soapy water ran down my arms, causing gooseflesh as it dried in the air. As I watched the water bead in the chill bathroom, a memory of another place and time came back, so vividly, I might have been living it again.

My brother and I were taking turns swinging out over a small stream, a mile from our house. The rope holding him was tied high up in a giant oak that leaned out over the water. His skinny, bronzed, child's body gleaming in the afternoon sun; cutting the surface of the water like a knife. A war whoop skittered across the water like a flat stone. From my perch atop the steep bank, I grabbed for the rope, as the water sprayed up from his landing to cover me in droplets, a soothing balm to the sunburn that covered my half-naked body. I jumped on the rope and pushed off with a mighty shove, twirling and squealing in the hot, summer air.

Then, just as soon as it appeared, it was gone, lost again in the dusty past.

'Where is he?' I wondered, with a sudden feeling of nostalgia and loss.

That night I was, once again, plagued by nightmares. I awoke in a cold sweat, vestiges of long-lost memories clinging like cobwebs to my consciousness.

In the predawn darkness I packed up the belongings I had recently brought to Amos' and put them in the car. I was going home. Without Amos, his house was just another strange place; a place I cared not to inhabit alone.

The sun was just breaking the horizon as I placed Judas' cat carrier in the back seat. Sam drove shotgun, his muzzle hanging out the half open window as his ears blew in the wind.

The short drive to my place was uneventful. No other cars were on the secluded lane leading to my house and I carried on a running conversation with my anxious pets.

I pulled in the yard and turned off the engine, sitting in the half-light and stillness, listening. My birdfeeders were already starting to fill up with sparrows, chickadees and my own pair of resident cardinals. I watched as the male cardinal sat perched on a slender limb waiting for the horde of lesser birds to leave; his whistling calls an anthem to the rising sun.

I guessed it was about time to take my Christmas lights down, and smiled in the half shadows, remembering the insane feeling of paranoia that had precipitated their hanging.

After depositing my pets and belongings in the house, I wandered down to the snow-covered dock through knee-deep snow. I stood looking out over the frozen channel at the bucolic scene before me. The sun broke from the behind the trees then, the shadows running from its onslaught like vampires. I was momentarily blinded by the reflections off the channel as old Sol began his never-ending journey from east to west. The half-naked trees still clung to blankets of snow, not wanting to stand naked before the world while awaiting their summer finery. A plethora of dead cattail stems stood lonely sentinels in their frozen captivity. In the spring, Redwing blackbirds would return to create their cities on the water, their raucous cries echoing for miles down the channel.

Barn and Tree swallows would compete for the best nesting spots, on and near the house and water. Deer would once again return to grace my yard with their mute beauty, looking for food after a long, hard winter. Geese and ducks would swim by my dock in large, noisy flocks. Muskrat heads would break the surface of the water, swim for a while, than once again disappear into the nether regions they called home.

As much as Amos' house was the nicer of the two, I would have to spend the spring and summer here, and I hoped he'd be with me.

As beautiful as the winter landscape was, I longed for the renewing kiss of spring. Spring, because the earth would spring to life after the white death of winter.

The chill of the morning drove me back into my cold house. There were still a few logs on the pile Amos' had brought in for me, and I got a fire going.

My pets were exploring their home for signs of intruders in their absence, Sam going from room to room, nose to the floor, seeking the scent of unseen visitors. Judas was sniffing in corners for any mice that may have invaded while she was away.

I'd just finished making coffee when the phone rang. With a reluctance I didn't understand, I slowly put the receiver to my ear.

It was Amos. He'd called his house several times and couldn't reach me. I assured him all was well, and I'd just wanted to come home. I made no mention of the bullets, and had decided to put the whole incident of my snooping out of my mind. He worried about me being alone, but despite all that had happened, I felt I should be here, right now. I didn't mention that in his absence my nightmares had returned; maybe that was the catalyst that had propelled me home. Amos' house had been a haven from them, but it hadn't been his home that had saved me from myself, but his presence. Without it, one place was just like another, so the familiarity of my own space, and the dread of contaminating his with my night terrors, dictated that I come home. I would return to his place when he returned.

Much to my surprise, Sherry called that afternoon, inviting me to join the adults in a night on the town. Lois, Rich and their children were leaving the next day and the adults wanted a break from their kids. Sherm and Sugar were relegated to baby-sit for the two younger boys.

I found myself humming tunelessly as I dressed. I set my wild mop of hair, and dug out a pair of hip-huggers from my hippie days. I knew if I kept them long enough they'd come back in style! Even more amazing than the fact that I still had them, was the fact that they still fit! I carefully made up my aging face, thinking of the natural beauty exuded by Lois and Sherry. I found an off-white sweater I'd forgotten about, hanging in the back of the closet, and I liked the way it made me appear to have some color in my pallid skin.

Irmaline would be the designated driver, so I didn't have to worry about driving. My pets gathered around me as I slipped on my low-heeled boots; they knew I was leaving. I filled their dishes while I waited for Irmaline.

It was close to seven when they pulled into the yard. I ran out the door, grabbing my coat from its hook on the way out.

Sherry, Rich and Lois were crammed into the back seat of Irmaline's old car. I slid in next to Irmaline, greeting everyone.

Lois said she had given the kids some money for pizza before she left, and they'd practically pushed her out the door.

Conversation bubbled around me as Irmaline guided the car over the snowy roads. It was already dark, but a bright full moon hung above the darkened forest, lighting the way.

We pulled in the already crowded lot of one of the two bar/restaurants in town. I'd been here with Al before, but not for years, we usually had patronized the regular restaurant.

We tumbled from the car like schoolchildren on the last

day of classes before summer vacation.

Rich and Lois had their arms around each other like young lovers, and I felt a longing for Amos as I watched their insular intimacy.

Once inside, we struggled through a crowd that had, obviously, started celebrating quite some time ago.

A jukebox blared out Van Halen, and several of the well-oiled patrons were dancing and bumping into one another on the crowded dance floor.

I wondered how we'd be able to converse in the loud atmosphere. Clinking glasses, raucous laughter, and the underlying beat of the music seemed to build to a crescendo as we slid into a booth just being vacated by a group of young 20-somethings.

Lois and Rich slid to the middle of the booth as Irmaline, Sherry and I settled around them. We shed our coats, Sherry hanging each on the hooks attached to the booth for that purpose. I noticed Sherry was wearing a bright red sweater and jeans; Lois, khaki slacks and a button-down shirt. Irmaline had on her pink sweater and tan dress slacks. Almost at once, people started coming over to talk to Rich and Sherry, friends from their school days, whom they hadn't seen in years. Rich's best buddy from high school, (whom he'd been out with the other night), stumbled over and dragged Sherry onto the dance floor, her protestations falling on deaf ears as he clutched her wrist in a death grip.

We ordered two pitchers of beer from a harried waitress, who had to fight her way through the crowd to accommodate us.

Lois and Rich joined Sherry on the dance floor, and Irmaline and I laughed as we watched their frenzied gyrations.

Irmaline pointed out everyone to me; most being children and even grandchildren, of people she knew.

The whole room vibrated under the onslaught of sound. The beer in the pitchers seemed to dance with the patrons, and I could feel the table and floor shaking.

When the song stopped, as quickly as it'd begun, Lois and Rich made their way back to the booth, sweat beading on their foreheads. Sherry was in conversation at the bar with her high school friend, whom she'd made earlier arrangements to meet with. She returned long enough to grab a glass of beer and then disappeared in the crowd.

Irmaline nursed an iced tea that she'd had to cajole the waitress into making for her, while Lois and Rich took long drinks of beer. Rich was pointing out everyone he knew to Lois, giving a short commentary on each.

"That's George." He said, pointing to a bearded man with shoulder length hair who was in deep conversation with Sherry and her friend. "He always liked Sherry. I tried to get them together, but she always wanted to stay with that loser, Irv."

"Well," Lois intoned, "Irv's not here now!"

A slow song started then, and Lois and Rich returned to the dance floor, shuffling as one, arms entwined around each other. I nudged Irmaline and pointed out Sherry, dancing cheek to cheek with George.

She put her lips by my ear and spoke conspiratorially, "I always liked George. I used to think Sherry just hung with Irv to get my goat. I couldn't, for the life of me, see any other reason for her interest in him."

After several glasses of beer, I had to find the bathroom. I made my way, unsteadily, through the churning crowd, and was glad to see it was a real bathroom, not just a one-room thing, where you had to wait in line.

I sighed as I settled into a stall, the solid bathroom door muting the loud music, allowing me to think.

I heard the door opening and closing as I sat there, the noise level ascending and descending at each opening.

I was preparing to rise when I heard voices from the line of sinks across from the stalls.

"Did you see who's here?" A soprano voice asked.

"Yes." This one was deeper, contralto. "And her husband barely dead a month yet!"

I stayed where I was, listening. I could here the snap of purses opening and peeking through the crack in the door, I saw brushes being applied to two blonde heads.

"And that other woman!" The first voice said. "She's got a nerve! She may have killed Vicky, you know. And maybe Irv, too!"

The other voice made a harrumphing sound, followed by: "What the fuck was that Amos thinking? Vicky came back because she wanted him back. She could have had anyone she wanted-but him."

"That's probably why she wanted him!" The other voice answered.

"Rich sure looks good." The first said, changing the subject. "I used to date him, you know."

"I remember. Why don't you go dance with him?"

"He's with his wife, dipstick!"

"So what?"

The voices faded as I heard the door open, music and laughter floating in momentarily before the door shut.

Who the hell were they? I wondered. I'd never actually seen their faces.

I decided not to say anything. I wouldn't be the one to bring Sherry down just when she was coming into her own. They were just jealous, petty, small-town bitches, with nothing better to do than gossip. I couldn't blame them for their speculations about me, but Sherry didn't deserve to be maligned like that.

I slid back in next to Irmaline, looking around for Sherry and Lois. Sherry was still at the bar, leaning against it, her foot on the bar rail, in deep conversation with that George guy.

Lois and Rich were in the middle of a group of people

about their age, reminiscing, I supposed. I stared, trying to see if the women in the bathroom were among their group.

It was impossible to say with certainty unless I could hear them speak.

A casually dressed, somewhat handsome, man approached and asked me to dance. I felt my face flame as I stuttered an excuse. After he'd gone, Irmaline said, "Why don't you dance, Annie? It's only a dance. Amos would want you to enjoy yourself."

"I'm not much of a dancer." I answered, and it was true. I had no rhythm, whatsoever.

"That was Tom," Irmaline went on like I hadn't spoken, "I went to school with his dad."

"Why don't YOU dance?" I teased.

"No one's asked ME." She said.

Just then, someone did. Her son, Rich, came and drew her into the madding crowd, as Lois stood with the rest of their group, cheering her mother-in-law on.

I laughed heartily, watching as Rich swung Irmaline around the crowded floor as people tried to stumble out of the way.

I lifted my hand at a passing waitress and ordered two more pitchers of beer. Lois made her way back over and slid in next to me. He bobbed blonde hair bounced as she seated herself.

"Are you having fun, Annie?" She asked, pouring herself a glass of beer.

"Yeah. I am." I answered, truthfully.

"God. You don't know how much I needed this vacation!" She said, wiping foam off her lip.

"What's your job like?" I asked, sincerely curious.

"A rat race. A God damn rat race!"

I realized she was feeling the effects of the alcohol and smiled dumbly.

"Talk about backstabber's." She muttered. Then a lopsided smile crossed her face and she said, "I'm not talking about that anymore. I don't even want to think about it!"

"O.k." I answered, even though I knew I didn't have to say anything at this point.

"Look at Irmaline!" She said, pointing. "I love that woman."

I followed her finger to see Irmaline, being passed from one partner to another, twirling like a schoolgirl, a big grin on her face.

"So do I." I said, than repeated, "So do I."

Pulling her attention back to me, her face took on a serious expression.

"What's going on with Amos and you?" She asked, her fingers beating the side of her glass in rhythm to the music.

How do I explain that? I was at a loss for words. We hadn't, as yet, announced our engagement, and I wasn't wearing my ring. I wanted to wait until after her family had gone to tell Irmaline. I didn't want to detract from their reunion by talking about me.

"We haven't been together that long." I said, slowly. "But, so far, so good."

She raised her glass at me and I complied, raising mine to clink with hers.

"Here's to Irv, thank God he's gone. He's been a scourge on this family for way too long.

Now Sherry can have an actual life!"

I felt guilty, toasting Irv's demise, but I realized that she had Sherry's best interest at heart and knew, much better than I, the toll Irv had taken on their family; and, more importantly, on Sherry's self-esteem.

Eventually, everyone was seated back at the booth. Appetizers had been ordered and we all sat chomping on stuffed mushrooms and chicken wings. I felt like I'd found a family, something I'd never really felt. I'd had to play the role of caretaker too often in my short childhood, and I reveled in the warm feeling that enveloped me as I sat in my little group.

We finally left, a little before closing, wanting to avoid the crowd of rowdy patrons who'd be rushing the parking lot.

Once home, I rushed to divest myself of my, now too-tight pants, donning my ratty robe and sitting before the newly stoked fire. I was glad I'd went; glad I hadn't made a fool of myself, and glad I'd gotten to know Lois and Rich before their departure.

Irmaline had positively glowed all the way home and I was happy to see her happy.

I knew the town would be buzzing tomorrow, but I didn't care. I'd done nothing wrong, despite what the townspeople thought, and if they really thought I was a murderess, well, tough! Prove it then, I thought.

Someday the mystery would be solved, and a whole lot of people would be eating crow, then. I knew who my friends were, and it was their opinions I cared about, not some faceless mob of petty gossipers.

Though I'd had quite a lot to drink, I really didn't feel drunk. Maybe it was the appetizers. I should always eat if I know I'm going to be drinking, it makes all the difference, I thought.

I flicked on the t.v., knowing there was nothing on at this late hour. Unlike Amos and Irmaline, I had no satellite dish and had to be happy with the three lousy local stations, whose programming included news, weather, sports, and late at night, infomercials. Sometimes, if the weather conditions were right, I could pick up a station that played mostly old movies; it was situated in a town even further up north, and didn't have a strong signal. I got lucky tonight. It was coming in fairly clear and playing, "Giant". I hadn't seen that in so long, I could barely remember it. I settled into the couch, Sam on the other end, daring me to shoo him. I didn't. Judas was in front of the fire, lying on her well-padded back, legs in the air. She'd been lying that way since she was a kitten, but it was much easier for her to keep her balance now, since she was such a pudge.

I ruminated on the events of the evening. I would definitely relay to Amos the conversation I'd overheard in the bathroom. Well, maybe not the part about him and Vicky. He would probably have some idea of who they were; not that it mattered, as I'm sure the whole town mirrored their thoughts.

The alcohol had some benefits. I spent a blissfully dreamless night, barely making it to my bed after nodding out on the couch. Of course, the hangover made me wonder if it was worth the benefit.

When the phone rang later that morning I ran to answer, as every shrill ring echoed through my pounding head. I stubbed my big toe on the couch leg in my haste to answer, then fell onto the couch, rubbing my toe and hoping it wasn't broken.

"Hello." I said, breathlessly, trying to hide my pain.

"Annie. I tried to call last night. Where were you? I was worried." It was Amos and the sound of his voice made me feel a sense of homesickness, or something along that line.

"Hi." I said, still rubbing my foot.

I told him about my little excursion into town, describing the night and conversation. I didn't mention the bathroom dialog. I'd wait until he returned to get into that.

"Good." He said, sounding like he meant it. "I'm glad you're making friends and socializing, you're alone way too much."

"Yes. It was fun. I really like Lois. She's a breath of fresh air in this stifling town. I hope she keeps in touch with Sherry; she's the perfect role model for her. Strong, independent, funny."

He agreed. He said he'd be coming home in a few days and suggested I could stay at Irmaline's now that her company had left.

I told him I hadn't thought of that, and if I became too

paranoid, I'd do that.

I could hear loud P.A. noises in the background, and knew he was at his destination and unloading his cargo. He was to load up again and drop that load on the way home.

I spent the next couple of hours catching up on my cleaning. I washed clothes, smiling when I found a large pair of men's briefs under the bed.

It was, by now, early afternoon; the sun was shining bright and I could see icicles melting on the eaves outside the window. I let Sam out and wiped snow off my porch bench so I could sit for a while, pretending it was spring. The wood was cold beneath my thin denim jeans, but I barely noticed, I was so happy to be outside. I had a hot mug of coffee in my hands as I sat and watched Sam gamboling in the snow. The cardinals were chasing the chickadees and sparrows off the feeders; then they were in turn, chased off by the squirrels.

My thoughts went to my old friend Gumba, but I quickly pushed the unbidden thought from my mind as I felt the hot welling of tears behind my eyelids. Maybe Gumba was gone, but his offspring still haunted the feeders. Life goes on, I thought, spring was right around the corner, and with it, rebirth. Al was gone, too, though in my heart, he would always live on.

I set my quickly cooling mug on the snow-covered table and brushed an errant tear from my cheek. I'd think ahead, not behind. Let the dead bury their own dead. I rose and walked to the dock through drifted snow, my shoes and the bottom of my jeans getting wet. I stood in the afternoon sun, surveying my insulated little world. Soon, the ice would be breaking up on the channel, it was already melting under the onslaught of the sun, though I knew it would freeze, yet again, before winter was over.

I headed back to the house, grabbing Sam on the way in. I had to believe the worst was over, yet my thoughts kept returning to the thought: Who put Barney in my trunk? The why was easy; I was to be the scapegoat. My gun disappearing and reappearing had convinced me of that. With my cellar door nailed shut, no one would any longer have access to my house. Was the perpetrator still in town, or was he now miles away, gloating that he'd gotten away with murder? I hoped it was the latter. Though I wanted some resolution, I could live with the unknowing, as long as nothing else happened. Besides, what could I do?

It took a minute for my eyes to adjust as I entered the shady living room. I opened the drapes to let the sunbeams dance across the floor, Judas chasing the motes in the air.

I should be happy, I thought, and I guessed I was. I just had to let go and live in the moment.

Irmaline called then and my dark thoughts were put back in the musty recesses of my mind, as I listened to her bubbling chatter. Rich and Lois had just left, and Irmaline was lamenting the stillness of her house in their absence. She relayed that Sherry had just gotten up and was making promises of abstinence as she nursed a major hangover. The boys were surprisingly quiet with their cousins gone, or maybe it was just that the number of kids had been halved. Mirroring Amos' thoughts, she invited me to come and stay until he returned. I was fine, I assured her, and she understood my need for solitude.

I spent the days waiting for Amos' return doing the mundane things that constantly needed doing, but that I rarely did. My house was now cleaner than, perhaps, it had ever been. The pets dogged my every step as I climbed the footstool to reach the curtains so I could wash them. I'd just noticed this morning how yellowed with age and gray with dust they'd become. I was embarrassed for never noticing it before. I dragged the footstool through the house with me until I'd gathered all the curtains. By the time I'd washed, dried, ironed and rehung them, the sun was making a hasty retreat behind the tree line.

Amos would be home tomorrow, and he would be coming here, after trading the large company truck for his own, which he'd left at the lot.

I collapsed on the couch, exhausted after my massive cleanup. The floors shone from beneath my scattered rugs, glossy from the recent waxing. Judas skittered across the floor, landing on a throw rug and sliding across the slippery floor, than she ran off in a panic, leaving wisps of hair and claw marks on my newly waxed floor. Oh, well, I thought; Sam's toenails constantly clicked across the floor, leaving his own marks. If I wanted pets, I'd have to put up with the inevitable.

I eventually found my way into a hot tub, slipping beneath the frothy water and sighing as the tension drained from my battered body. A big bruise still graced my toe, and it was painful to bend it. The phone rang as I languished in the healing font; I couldn't bring myself to get out and answer it.

I was so cold. Running through the woods in knee-deep snow, getting nowhere. All at once, a trail of blood appeared in my wake, and suddenly, I was transported deeper into the woods, the trail getting broader as I progressed, unbidden, along it. I wanted to close my eyes, but they wouldn't close. I was unable to stop the grisly images from assaulting me. Quicker and quicker I flew, towards an unknown destination. Was I dead? I thought abstractly. My forward movement stopped as quickly as it had started, ending in a macabre tableau, not meant for the eyes of mortals.

Vicky and Barney were hanging from the trees, gutted like deer, while a large figure stood before them, a knife moving in its hand. Blood dripped from the mortal wounds, creating the path I'd been drawn down. The face of the figure was unseen, as I stood in imaginary shadows and watched. My heart constricted in my chest and I thought I must have had a heart attack and died, and I was now in some demented purgatory, paying for my sins.

As I stood, frozen as if by rigor, the unknown hunter of men turned to face me, he'd heard my heart pounding in my chest and knew more prey was at hand. The bushy mustache and beard, covered in blood, left no doubt as to the identity of the killer. I stared into Amos' eyes, and saw the soul of the devil.

I awoke sputtering. I'd slipped beneath the surface of the ice-cold water and breathed in a mouthful, waking me. Wow! What a nightmare, I thought, coughing.

I didn't really believe Amos was the killer, did I? No. It was just the recent finding of the 38 bullets that had once again made me doubt Amos. If I was going to spend my life with this man, I had to quit turning perfectly plausible things into sinister ones.

I leaped from the tub, shivering in the brisk air of the now cold bathroom. I dried off and slipped on my heavy robe, tying it tightly around my still shaking body.

The phone rang again as I entered the living room. It was now 9:30 p.m.

"Sorry to call so late," Irmaline said, as soon as I'd picked up, "I tried to call earlier and no one answered."

"I was in the tub, and just couldn't bring myself to get out." I said, making no mention of my nightmare.

"Turn on the news, Annie." She implored.

"Why? What's going on?" I asked, feeling goose bumps rising on my arms.

"Just turn it on." She insisted, than hung up.

I hurriedly turned on the t.v., and settled on the couch.

There was blondie, her hair being buffeted in the wind outside the Sheriff's department. Huge klieg lights had been set up to dispel the darkness, and her skin looked sallow in the dazzling brightness.

"A press conference was called by the Sheriff's department earlier today, and if you missed it, we'll be playing it again in a few minutes."

A commercial then came on, leaving me on tenterhooks, waiting for the latest revelations. The program came back on, at last, and the Sheriff was standing on the steps of the building.

"After an exhaustive investigation, we've come to the conclusion that the death of the young woman known as 'the body in the trunk,' was probably caused by an obsession on the part of a local man, who, himself, was later found dead, coincidentally, in a trunk, the car trunk of a local resident, Annie Woods." The Sheriff paused here, looking at the camera, his eyes squinting under the unforgiving Kleig lights.

"Though his death was partially caused by the wound received from Miss Woods, it is still unknown how his body came to be in her trunk. We will continue with our investigation, but for all intents and purposes, the death of Vicky will be marked 'closed'. There is no reason to believe that there is any danger to the general populace. We think that whoever put the body in the car trunk was trying to set up the local woman, for reasons unknown, as she has been cleared of any involvement."

An onslaught of questions were than hurled at him, as he stood stoically, looking like he wanted to flee.

The blonde was the first to speak up, the hand microphone she held glinting under the lights.

"Why would someone want to set someone else up, if, in fact, there was no foul play, but rather, self-defense, involved in the death of Irving?"

"We don't know at this point; all we know is, there is no reason to suspect that a murderer is loose among us. We know why and how Irving died; his being placed in the trunk is the mystery. Tampering with a body is a crime, but not a felony. There are no bogey men in our town, just a misguided soul who, obviously, had a grudge against an innocent woman, and for his own reasons, tried to set her up on a murder charge."

An older man, whom I recognized as the news anchor of another local station, spoke up then, talking over the ambitious blonde.

"Why was this woman attacked in the first place; Ms. Woods, the woman who was partially responsible for his death?"

"We don't, as yet, know that either." The Sheriff responded, curtly. "Perhaps she knew something she wasn't even aware of, that could have connected the deceased to Vicky's death."

A few more questions were fielded before Jim abruptly turned on his heel and entered the building, the cameras following his retreating back.

Cut to the present; the blonde on the steps, recapping the press conference.

"So it seems there are still just as many unanswered questions as before. The Sheriffs Department is adamant in their belief that there is no reason for fear. The death of Vicky has been officially closed; the secreting of the killers body in a car trunk may never be solved. The exact time and place of his death is unknown, as there was a blinding snow storm the night he ran into the woods, bleeding profusely from the wound inflicted by a woman who was attacked in her own home, for reasons unknown."

Although I wasn't happy about being once again thrust into the limelight, I was just happy that I'd been absolved of any culpability in Barney's death.

I sat pondering the Sheriffs remarks about me unknowingly knowing something. What did I know? I'd seen Vicky sneaking out of the woods from the direction of Amos' camp that long ago morning. A couple of days before his camp had been trashed. But she had waved towards the window, like she was hoping I'd seen her. It was all so complicated; it hurt my head to think too much about it.

The only thing I got out of the press conference was the

uneasy feeling that no one had any reason to fear, except for maybe, me.

The blonde was finishing up her segment and I forced my attention back to the screen.

"It is known that a 38 was the caliber of the weapon used in the commission of the crime and that the suspect had access to such a weapon in his capacity as a DNR official. He was also a newly sworn-in Deputy in the aftermath of the Vicky murder. There may be some egg on the faces of officials in this small town, as so many questions remain unanswered."

I switched off the set. So, they were going to pin it on Barney. I wanted to believe their version; it would certainly simplify my life. I couldn't, however, forget the fact that someone had tried to frame me. Why? Would they even bother to look anymore? They obviously wanted to put this behind them; their embarrassment at having hired the very murderer they were seeking was a blot on the whole department.

What about poor Sherry and the boys? Life would be rough for them, now that Sherry's husband and the boys' father had been officially declared a murderer.

# CHAPTER TWENTY-ONE

The letters! Sherry would know Irv's writing. Irmaline may even recognize the author's penmanship or style. She'd lived here all her life, and probably babysat every kid in town at one time or another; maybe something in those letters would jog a distant memory.

Something told me I shouldn't wait for Amos. A niggling feeling at the periphery of my psyche told me I must retrieve those letters. The broken drawer would alert Amos immediately of my discovery. If Amos was aware of there existence, and Barney was the author, it would be a motive; a motive for BOTH murders; still, I couldn't picture Vicky with Barney. Maybe Barney had been back-mailing her. The conversation I'd overheard had implied she'd returned to get Amos back. Maybe he knew she'd trashed Amos' camp, or about some trickery she had planned.

I quickly went and retrieved my gun from its hiding place. I could see it had bullets in it. I didn't bother to count how many, and I couldn't remember, but I knew there were two or more, and that should be enough for any contingency.

I hurriedly put my shoes on and grabbed my coat on the

way out. Amos was coming tomorrow. Though it was getting late, I planned to go to Irmaline's as soon as I got the letters. They would, of course, have to be turned over to the police, but I thought I should get copies first. The way the police were handling it, the letters may just disappear, especially if they pointed to someone other than Irv. If Amos got to them first, they might disappear.

I slipped and fell in my haste to get to the car, soaking the butt of my jeans. Swearing, I picked myself up and made it to the car.

The moon was playing hide and seek with fast flying clouds, high above the silent forest.

I kept my eyes on the road, which appeared and disappeared through blowing snow. It was a short trip and I pulled in his drive shortly. I stared at the darkened hulk, looming black, amid a forest of blackness. The tree's leafless limbs, visible in the diffused porch light, waved spiny limbs in the buffeting winds; ancient idols worshiping themselves and each other.

I doused the headlights and sat in almost total darkness, the porch light and glimpses of moonlight between clouds the only illumination. The wind had picked up and it howled around the car, whining like wind in a wind tunnel.

After searching the shadows for any movement not connected to the wind, I was satisfied that I was alone. I gingerly stepped out of the car, my feet crunching on the packed snow cover. My hair whipped across my face, acting as a spur on my sudden inertia. I made a mad dash for the door, slipping and sliding all the way.

I stood on the porch, fumbling with the keys, wishing Amos still had a dog. I released the lock and quickly went inside. I leaned against the door as I threw the bolts home, my heart thumping like a trip-hammer in my chest. My hands were shaking and I took deep breaths, trying to gain some control of my emotions. There was nothing to fear; not only did I have my gun, Amos had a whole closet full. Someone would have to be crazy to come after me in this setting.

When my breathing returned to normal, I pulled my gun from my pocket and pointed it in front of me like a flashlight. I lit the lamp on the end table, the smell of kerosene filling the room as the wick caught. The fireplace wall stood dark and cold, Amos' bedroom unseen behind it in the darkness. My paranoia had me seeing eyes watching me from the dark hearth. I went down the hall, turning on lights as I went, my gun at the ready. Of course there was no one present. Amos' huge bed sat, unmade, as we'd left it, the giant quilt half on the floor. I fought a sudden desire to make it and continued through the house. The wind swept through the giant chimney, howling like a banshee, a portent of death. When I was satisfied that I was alone, I proceeded to the basement. Everything was as I'd left it. The broken drawer sat, untouched, on the dank floor. I carefully picked my way across the floor, fearing injury from the clutter that I'd left in my earlier haste.

The letters were right where I'd left them, beneath various articles of moldy clothing.

I breathed a sigh of relief when they were, at last, in my hand. I unceremoniously stuffed them in my coat pocket and turned to leave.

Just then, the lights went out and I was left in total darkness. A loud bang followed, it shook the house and my heart leapt into my throat. I forced myself to remain calm and found my way to the wall, following it back in the direction of the stairway. I walked with shuffling steps, kicking things across the floor in the darkness. When I came to the stairs, I practically crawled up them, my gun glued to my hand in a death grip. The door was closed. That had been the 'bang' I'd heard. My hand found the cold doorknob and turned it. Nothing happened. In a near panic, I shoved against it with my weight, but it didn't budge. As far as I knew, there wasn't a lock on this door, although I'd never paid much attention.

The wind whipping down the fireplace must have created a vortex and slammed the door shut. I really didn't think there was anyone else in the house; I'd checked every room. It was my own stupidity, in my haste to retrieve the letters, which had kept me from checking to ensure I had a means of egress.

What a fool I felt! I had visions of sitting here in the dark until Amos finally rescued me when he found me gone from my house. I had a whole lot of 'plaining' to do. I sat on the cold steps in the inky blackness, tears welling behind my eyelids, my throat constricting as I held back sobs of frustration.

That the brewing storm had knocked the lights out was a foregone conclusion, but I'd nearly forgotten about Amos' generator. Could I, in the total blackness, get it started?

I shuffled back down the stairs, clinging to the damp wall, visions of Amos finding my lifeless body at the bottom of the stairs, neck broken, jumping unbidden into my mind.

I found the generator, stubbing my toe on it as I miscalculated its whereabouts. I couldn't see the knobs so I'd have to hope I got it right the first time. I knew there was a switch to turn it on, then a lever for the gas adjustment, then a cord like on a lawn mower. I'd have only once chance at this in the dark because I couldn't see the switches. I carefully ran my hands over the hulking tank and hoped I could remember the sequence.

When I thought I had it right, I grabbed the cord and pulled. It sputtered, but didn't catch.

God. What if it was out of gas? I tried again. And again. I remembered how I'd always had trouble just starting our lawn mower, and how Al had always had to do it.

Al's not here, I told myself. I have to do it myself, or sit here in the dark until Amos found me, probably gibbering in a corner, my mind gone.

With a mighty pull that sent me reeling, the engine caught. I landed on the hard floor, my tailbone taking the brunt of my fall, as the lights flickered and held. The loud thumping noises were now music to my ears. I rubbed my throbbing tailbone as I slowly rose, picking up a letter that had fallen from my pocket.

Once again I maneuvered the steep staircase. I'd set my gun aside in my struggles with the generator, but it was now once more nestled in my hand. At the top of the stairs, I fumbled with the knob, shouldering the door. I'd shoot the damn thing if I had to.

With a final mighty shove the door gave, spilling me across the threshold. I lay there in the semi-darkness, my heart pounding, my breath coming in short, ragged gasps. I could see muted light flickering across the ceiling from the kerosene lamps in the living room.

When, at last, I'd calmed my fluttering heart, I rose to my feet, my tailbone still throbbing.

Though there was no need to, I crept silently down the hall, my gun pointing the way. I may be a paranoid, but it might save my life. Better to be safe than sorry! Visions of all the horror movies I'd ever seen swirled through my head, making me grasp the gun even tighter.

The light from the bedroom, which I'd turned on before going in the basement, cast wavering shadows across the hallway. Combined with the kerosene lamplight, an eerie half-twilight enveloped the house.

I made my way to the living room. I had to call Irmaline and let her know I was on my way. I grabbed the phone with a feeling of relief. It was short-lived, however. No comforting dial tone greeted me. The phone lines were down. Shit! I replaced the receiver and went to peek out the curtains before making my escape. Snow was now falling, big, fluffy flakes, swirling in white tornado shapes across the barren yard.

I blew out the kerosene lamps, but left the other lights on. The thumping from the generator continued, dulled by the closed basement door. I'd leave it on so Amos' pipes wouldn't freeze. The heat tape Amos had wrapped around them needed electricity.

I was just about to open the door when a shadow crossed the yard, barely perceptible in the blinding whiteness. Had I imagined it in my paranoid state? Or was it merely an animal seeking cover in the shelter of the looming forest? Dare I leave?

I was fully aware that a murderer was loose. Someone had put Barney's body in my trunk, even though that fact seemed to be of no interest to the Police (maybe they really believed I'd done it, trying to hide my guilt in stabbing him). I stood behind the thick door, craning my head around to peer through a crack in the curtained windows. I realized that my hand had become numb from clutching the gun so tightly and forced myself to relax my grip on it.

I strained to see my car through the white on black bleakness. So close but yet so far, I thought. Should I make a run for it? I stood, indecisive, my tailbone throbbing, my gun hand still numb. Maybe this hadn't been such a good idea after all. I should have let someone know before I'd left; now I was truly on my own. My supposed epiphany may have been a foolish whim; one any thinking person would have considered more carefully.

I could stay until morning, arming myself with a plethora of guns, and wait for Amos.

I wouldn't have to show him the letters. I could take my leave and go to Irmalines'. I could say I came over when the electricity went out to start his generator so his pipes wouldn't freeze.

I'd have to decide soon. I wouldn't be able to get my car out if I waited too long. Amos, with his truck, should have no problem.

The shadow could have been anything from a deer to a swooping owl.

I made up my mind. Tearing the door open, I ran pell-mell

through the gathering snow cover, sliding with every step. If anyone had seen me, I'd have been quite a sight; my arms pin-wheeling like windmill blades in an effort to stay erect; the gun waving erratically in my numb fingers.

The snowflakes clung to my eyelashes in soggy clumps, further obstructing my vision.

I could see a dark hulk on the otherwise white landscape and knew I was nearly there.

How could such a short distance seem so long?

I reached the car and lost my footing as I reached for the door handle, sliding partially beneath it. I could feel the cold wetness seeping through my thin jeans. I scrabbled on the frozen ground searching for a foothold on the slick, snow-encrusted gravel.

The wind howled around me, causing a whistling sound in my ears. I kept waiting for a hand to reach out of the swirling whiteness and grab me.

When I'd finally found my footing, I leaned against the now ice-encrusted vehicle as I grabbed the door handle. Locked. Or course. Either out of habit or the deep-seated memory of tales of strangers lurking in back seats, I'd locked it. Fortunately, my keys were still in my coat pocket and it took me only seconds to enter the snow covered car.

As I languished behind the wheel, breathing in short, shallow spurts, my heart pounded in my throat. I locked all the doors immediately upon entering, and checked the back seat. The locked doors would, of course, afford me no protection from a bullet, so I quickly fumbled the key into the ignition, my hand numb and shaking. I was rewarded with a metallic click; not even the droning sound of a battery being overtaxed, just a click.

My God, I thought, my paranoid mind working overtime, he's disabled my car!

I strained to see through the snow-covered windows but it was a useless effort.

I jumped from the car, yelling into the wind, "I've got a gun!"

My reverse flight began. I slipped and fell, picked myself up, and ran on, as if all the hounds of hell were after me. And one of them was, I told myself.

I felt exposed in the dim porch light as I fumbled once more with the keys, keys now colder than my frigid hands.

Inside at last, I leaned against the heavy door as I drove the bolts home. I slid to the floor, my heart was now fluttering in my chest like a wounded bird.

"I'm comin' to join ya' 'Lizbeth," I said aloud, my hand clutching my chest. Fred Sanford, that's who it was that spoke those immortal lines. Then I laughed dementedly at the absurdity of my situation.

I had no choice but to wait out the storm, now: The storm outside, and the metaphoric one raging inside me.

I dejectedly picked myself up off the floor. My wet jeans left a wet spot on the polished wooden floor. I didn't want to get his Oriental rug wet, so I hurriedly crossed to the hallway. I was sure I had a few things of mine here. In the bedroom, I found a pair of my jeans in the hamper and opted for somewhat grimy over wet. My gun was never more than a few feet from me.

When I returned to the living room, I picked up the few logs remaining indoors, and set about starting a fire.

I then went and checked the phone again. No luck.

The generator was still thumping away, the house practically shaking at its onslaught.

I'd have no way of knowing if the electricity was back on with the generator running.

Oh well. I'd put up with the irritating noises; I wasn't about to shut it off and take the chance of not getting it on again. Then a scary thought occurred to me, how much gas was in the generator? I pushed the unwanted thought aside and settled on the couch. I knew from before that the generator was powerful enough to run most everything. I wouldn't test it by washing clothes or anything, though!

I flicked on the t.v. and was happy to see the picture pop on, unimpeded. The tail end of the nightly news was on. As usual, it was all weather related. For once, I actually watched, telling myself to take their dire warnings with a grain of salt and not get roped into their auguries of gloom and doom. As I well knew, the minute a snowflake fell, they were like Chicken Little. If I were from another state, I would be living in my basement if I were to believe the talking heads and their seasonal scare tactics. Unfortunately, EVERY season presented a reason to cower in your basement, according to them: Thunderstorms and tornadoes, blizzards. It seemed to be a never-ending fight against the elements to them. It made one wonder why ANYONE would choose to live here. Or maybe having lived more than a half a century in the eye of the never-ending storm, I'd become inured to the danger.

I knew sleep wouldn't find me tonight, and though my eyes burned with fatigue, my trembling innards would afford me no rest.

I lounged on the couch, gun next to me on the plush cushions, ready for any contingency.

The thumping from the basement had a cathartic effect on me, like a mothers heartbeat: I being the fetus, entombed in the womb of the house.

I'd lift the receiver periodically, hoping against hope to here the welcoming dial tone. I knew from experience, however, that it could be up to two or three days after a storm before service would be restored.

Amos' doors were thick and sturdy, his locks deadbolts. If someone wanted in, they would have to break a window, alerting me.

I wished I'd brought Sam with me, but I wasn't planning on staying.

Despite my earlier conviction that sleep would elude me, I

found myself nodding off to the constant dull thumping and the talking heads droning in the background.

I jerked myself into consciousness, reaching for my gun. This wouldn't do. I had to get some rest. After some consideration, I decided the loft would be the ideal place to hole up for the night. The heavy wooden ladder could be pulled up and a lock could be slid into place on the heavy wooden trapdoor. It offered a vantage point of the entire living room and a portion of the hallway. No one outside of Spiderman could scale those steep wooden walls, and if they could, I had a distinct advantage. My gun would be at the ready. With the lights off I couldn't be seen, especially if I stayed low to the floor.

I checked the phone one more time, turned off the t.v. and climbed, tiredly, into the loft.

I struggled with the heavy steps for five minutes, but finally managed to get them up.

I stood and surveyed the living room, dancing shadows from the dying light of the fire played on the walls like lingering specters, seeking the light, yet formed in darkness.

I'd left a small lamp next to the kitchen on, but it's beam barely reached the edge of the loft. I knew there was a big flashlight in the bottom door of the bedside table. I checked it to make sure the batteries still worked.

With nothing else to do but wait, I fell onto the bed; the emotional strain far more exhausting than physical labor.

The human mind is an amazing thing. When the tribulations of life are closing in and fear is your constant companion, your mind creates elaborate, albeit bizarre, dreams to help you cope. To help you work through your fears, and release the tension that plagues your waking life.

Despite my protestations of insomnia, I found myself drifting off to the steady thrum of the generator. The trees made scurrying sounds as they swept against the roof and walls, like squirrels scratching to get in, or giant brooms sweeping the snow cover from the house.

A muted light went on in the living room and I looked up to see a figure standing stock still in the middle of the Oriental rug, surveying the room with eyes that seemed somehow familiar to me.

I watched in silence from my dark cubbyhole, unseen in the thick shadows of the loft.

The smell of kerosene reached my nostrils and I realized he was holding the lamp from the living room table, slowly turning, searching dark corners.

The dancing light from the lamp shone off his hair and gave the appearance of a halo encircling his head. His light hair gave off shimmers of light as he basked in the lamplight.

He slowly turned my way and, with sinking heart, I waited for his glance to discern the the loft resting among the shadows.

I lay frozen, unable to move and hardly breathing. My fear was such that I felt he would hear my shallow breath and I tried to not even breathe.

The lamp was suddenly raised and he came forward.

Though I knew he couldn't possible see me, my heart jumped to my throat and I covered my mouth with my hand to stifle a scream.

He had stopped about five feet from the edge of the loft, the lamp still held high.

As the halo encrusted head turned up, I felt our eyes lock, and I realized with a sense of wonder, and horror, that I was staring at the face of my long dead father.

I started awake and heard the gun go scuffling across the floor as I knocked it off the bed in my night terrors. I sat up, my breath coming in ragged streams, my heart pounding, and scanned the room below. No light, no lurking dead.

I'd hardly given a thought to my father in years. Was he trying to warn me, through dreams, of a coming Armageddon? Or was it simply my unconscious mind telling me everything would be alright, I had guardian angels from a higher realm watching out for me? I pondered the strange dream and thought about my long dead father.

I retrieved my gun from where it had come to rest against the rail, and returned to sit on the big bed, surrounded by darkness and the constant pounding of the generator. Its eerie cadence took on an ominous tone in my unsettled thoughts. Jungle drums beating as a prelude to an imminent attack.

I lay back down on the big bed, snuggling beneath the heavy quilt. Once again, my exhaustion overcame me and I drifted into an uneasy sleep. I was snowbound until Amos rescued me, like it or not.

Stray sunbeams leaking over the curtains in the living room awakened me. Their trajectory was such that light bounced off the metal rod and came to rest on my face. Another strange and wonderful anomaly that Amos' house boasted.

I sat up and surveyed the room below. It was still encased in shadows but the furniture was clearly visible.

I forced myself up, the need for the bathroom and caffeine spurring me on. After a brief struggle with the ladder, I descended.

I went to the window and peeked through the curtains. Snow was still coming down, though it seemed to have petered off to a normal snowfall; the storm was over.

Before going to the kitchen I turned the T.V. on. I wanted to catch the news, and the background drone was comforting, making me feel I wasn't alone.

As I crossed the carpet, my bare feet felt something wet. I bent down and peered at the spot, reaching down to touch it. It was water. I retraced my steps and stood beside the door, inspecting the wooden floor. Yes, there were definitely water spots visible. I tried the door. It was still securely locked.

What was going on? Yes, I'd seen my father last night, but neither dreams (nor ghosts) left physical evidence of their passing.

I once again tried the phone, but it was still out.

I had put my gun in the waistband of my jeans, in back, to leave both my hands free to descend the ladder. I now pulled it out and held it before me. My bladder would have to wait while I searched the house.

When I was convinced I was alone, I took care of business. I waited impatiently by the coffee maker. The interrupted sleep of the night before had left me groggy and listless.

Finally, with mug in hand, I retired to the couch, turning the volume up on the T.V. to hear the news.

As expected, the storm was still the big news. Phone service was out all over the area, giving rise to a sigh of relief on my part; I now knew the outside lines hadn't been cut.

A map of impassable roads now graced the screen, and I prayed Amos would be able to get home.

I tried not to think about the minute water spots, even now reflecting the morning light in rainbows across the floor. Therein lies madness, I thought. I'd wait for Amos and let his rationality and strength sustain me.

It bothered me that I still had doubts about him, but the question of the letters had to be answered before I could totally exonerate his culpability in events. Then maybe I could totally put my faith in him and together we could face the future, no matter what it held.

I hardly heard the background beat of the generator anymore, so inured to the sound had I become. I hadn't really gone in the basement, just turned on the light and glanced in the dark corners from the top of the stairs. Someone could be lurking down there, I thought.

In my paranoia I jumped up and ran to get a chair from the kitchen. When the chair was firmly in place under the knob of the basement door, I returned to the couch.

The wind had picked up again and rattled the windowpanes as it swirled relentlessly around the house.

No matter how I tried, I couldn't get my fathers face out

of my mind. It had been the face I remembered from my childhood, not the drink ravaged countenance of his latter years. Perhaps that's how I chose to remember him. The memories were bittersweet, like an old photograph, yellow and curled around the edges.

My father going off to work, swinging me around in his strong arms, a smile lighting his eyes, my brother hanging on his leg as he struggled to disengage himself. Why were these memories coming back now, after so many years of blankness? Maybe I should see someone when this thing had finally been resolved.

I tried the phone again, though I knew it was useless. I silently cursed the hick town I had chosen to make my home in. Why was it that something as common as a cell phone would be considered a luxury here, where its services were needed most? Farmers having accidents in the fields would be in dire need of one. Children vacationing with their parents, losing their way in the woods, could use one. And stupid women alone in a snowbound cabin, with only guns for company could, most assuredly, use one.

I wanted to start a fire but balked at leaving the house for the short trip to the woodpile.

Snow would have enveloped the wood and I'd have to disengage the frozen limbs from one another, slipping and sliding the whole time. I settled for sweeping the remaining chips and small limbs from the floor, getting the broom Amos kept in the closet by the door. I managed to get a small fire going, but it wouldn't last long.

Amos kept the heat low as he always had a blazing fire going in cold weather; I, however, preferred a balmy 80 degrees. Now, there would be no heat, except the fire.

I settled on the couch once more, noticing that the news had been replaced by a popular talk show, though trailers continued to roll across the bottom of the screen, warning of closed roads and informing parents of school closings.

My coffee had grown cold sitting on the big wooden coffee table. As I was refilling the cup in the kitchen, a shudder passed through the house and the lights went out.

The heartbeat of the house had ceased with the dying of the generator and a total silence engulfed me.

Since it was daylight, the house was diffused in a strange half-light. I could draw the curtains and have light, but I'd better find some warm clothes, for the cold would soon find my old bones. I went through the house, opening drapes and curtains, allowing the brightness in to dispel the gloom; not only of the house, but also of my soul. Somehow sunlight always had the feeling of optimism accompanying it. When you dwelt in a place where winters were long and days short, sunlight was a definite mood elevator.

I hesitated to return to the basement. My paranoia was still such that I imagined someone locked down there by the chair I'd placed against the knob. Someone who'd deliberately shut the generator down and was, even now, in the total darkness of the basement, waiting. Even though I had the gun, I had no desire to face an unseen assailant in a darkened basement. No. I would wait for Amos.

Having no mindless television to occupy my mind, I retrieved the letters from my coat pocket, and fresh cup of coffee in hand, (it would be the last hot one), settled in my spot on the couch again.

The tableau out the window, now stripped bare of their coverings, was an adventurers dream. A stark white landscape, unbroken by the colors of summer, surrounded the house. The trees were no longer spindly gray spiders, but snow and frost covered adjuncts of the earth, so packed with hoar that no spaces could be seen between them: Big, white, mountains, encasing me in the house. I was alone in a white wilderness.

I thought idly about Irmaline, and wondered if she'd tried to call me at home and was, even now, sitting at her cozy kitchen table, wondering what had happened to her high-strung friend.

It wouldn't be long; I consoled myself, until someone came.

The letters were all of the same theme and in the same hand. The writing looked familiar to me somehow, but I knew that couldn't be. I really knew no one in town and wouldn't have had occasion to see anyone's writing style. The postmarks on the envelopes spanned a period of a year. There were no return addresses and none of them were signed; at least not with a name. Endearments like, "your love" and "me" were the closings.

I put the letters aside when I'd finished and sat musing the significance of them. The fire was dying and soon the cold would insinuate itself into my bones. I put on one of Amos' big lumberjack flannel shirts, rolling up the sleeves to have use of my hands.

I stood before the living room window, arms wrapped around myself, watching the blowing snow. My car was only a white lump now, hardly visible as mounds piled against it.

I couldn't see the road and heard no plows straining against the onslaught.

Where had those water spots come from? I once again wondered. Was I alone? Did Amos have a pair of snowshoes anywhere? The thought of leaving, despite the rawness of the weather, weighed on my mind. Well, if he did have snowshoes, they'd probably be in the basement, so forget that, I decided.

Without the thumping of the generator and sound of the t.v., I could almost hear my heartbeat. Strange how the sound I'd found so irritating now took on the memory of a comfort.

I went and stood by the basement door, creeping silently in stocking feet to stand before it, listening. The gun was hanging limply in my hand as I put my ear to the door.

I could hear nothing behind the thick door and gave up

my vigil shortly. If someone were down there, they'd soon realize I wasn't coming down and would try to get out. I didn't feel like sitting on the floor, before the door, for God knew how long, waiting for rescue.

On an impulse I padded to the kitchen and returned with an armful of plates. I placed them on the tilted chair, the sturdy back holding them at an angle on the polished seat.

Surveying my handiwork, I was satisfied that if the door moved, I'd be aware of it.

My stomach was growling, but I had no desire to eat, my nerves getting worse with the silence and my suspicion that I wasn't alone.

I longed to go soak in a hot tub before the water cooled down, but the vulnerability of that position didn't appeal to me.

I wandered aimlessly through the house, making the messy bed as I entered Amos' room.

As I, once more, went to check the basement door, a movement behind the looming hot-water heater, beside the door, caught my eye. I started to bring my gun up and was in the middle of turning, when a strong arm encircled my neck and a rag was placed over my face.

The thought that popped into my head at that moment was, "Oh no, I'm going to be killed with my own gun".

I struggled to bring it up with the arm piniored at my side by his other arm. The pressure of his arm around me caused me to pull the trigger and a loud pop preceded the appearance of a bullet hole in the heavy basement door. His grip had loosened somewhat from the unexpected shot and I took advantage by turning, ducking, and slithering out of his grip. Just like a character in a horror movie, I felt my heart thudding in my chest and my ears ringing. Whatever had been on the rag had made me feel woozy, although I'd tried to hold my breathe when it was placed there.

I stumbled toward the hallway, but he was on me before I'd

gone a foot. I fell face down on the threshold of the hallway, my cheek brushing against the rough wooden floor.

I still hadn't seen my assailant and thought maybe I'd be better off if I didn't.

"Please," I gasped, "I haven't seen you. I don't know who you are. Please, just leave!"

The rag was once again placed against my face and I felt the gun being removed from my hand. I turned my head in a futile attempt to escape the fumes, and as I did, over the rag, I caught a glimpse of the unknown attacker, the one who had tormented me for so long, for reasons I didn't understand.

In that moment, any hope I had of understanding was dashed, as I recognized a face from the past; a dead face. My father had somehow come back from the grave to put me in mine.

Whether from the drug or the shock, all thoughts left my mind as darkness descended.

# CHAPTER TWENTY-TWO

When I came to myself, it was well into February: Although "myself" may not be completely accurate. I could tell I was under the influence of some drug. I knew I was in a hospital; what I didn't know at that time, was that it was the State Mental Hospital.

Amos had found me on the floor, where I'd fell. I could only assume that his coming had scared off the dangerous apparition. When I'd finally come around to consciousness, I was hysterical and totally incoherent. It seems I'd had a "Psychotic Break". It also seemed that no one believed there'd ever been an intruder. It being my dead father, I couldn't really blame them, and eventually, I stopped trying to convince them.

Amos and Irmaline were constant visitors when I finally came around, but they, too, got that blank look in their eyes when I tried to relate what had happened.

Amos had been taking care of Sam and Judas, who had been frantic by the time he'd gotten around to them.

He'd taken me directly to the County Hospital where I languished for a few days before it was obvious I wasn't going to connect with reality any time soon. They, in turn, had transferred me to the mental facility, where I'd finally connected after several weeks had passed.

I was taken from my isolation cell and put in with the general populace, where the management of the establishment seemed to think I belonged.

In the two weeks since I'd "come back", I'd come to realize that I was now at the mercy of the State, and that the Sheriff's Department was taking a much closer look into my comings and goings, as I was now, being a mental patient, the main suspect in more than one murder. Also, they now had my gun and doubted my story about it suddenly "appearing" again.

I'd gleaned this little tidbit of information from two bored Nurses' Aides working the night shift. They hadn't seen me sneaking into the Nurses lounge in the middle of the night, seeking coffee to counteract the constant lethargy of Thorazine. They seemed to have quite a bit of time on their hands as they discussed the patients, in a not too professional way. They sat in the cafeteria and their voices could be clearly heard from my unseen position behind the Nurses' lounge door.

I'd hung my head in shame as they'd tittered about my antics when I was out of it.

It seemed I was already a convicted murderess in their eyes.

And so, I'd come to realize that if I didn't play my cards right I'd never get out of here.

Thus, I never mentioned the attack, and when the Psychiatrists questioned me about it, or my father, I clammed up and refused to say anything.

I shared a room with a woman named Rose, who insisted on being called 'Her Majesty', and believed that any day William and Harry were going to come for her and restore her throne. She was of indeterminate age, she could have been anywhere from 35 to 50, and skinny as a rail. Her hair hung in matted white plaits over her bony shoulders.

I tried to spend most of my time in the day room, staring out the big window on the third floor at the freedom I had once enjoyed, but never appreciated.

The cacophony was constant, day and night, never ceasing. If you weren't truly crazy when you came in, you certainly would be before long. That's why no one ever gets out, I thought dejectedly.

Sunday was visiting day, and one sunny Sunday I was surprised and pleased to see Sherry perched on a chair in the visitor's lounge.

We were allowed to wander the grounds, though since it was winter, few did. We decided too. A few hardy souls were wandering the neatly shoveled paths, Orderlies close by, smoking cigarettes and laughing at private jokes.

We skirted the outside of the Gothic looking building, her arm hooked through mine in a gesture that had surprised me.

She stopped at a stone bench and gingerly brushed snow from it. She gathered her coat beneath her and perched on the edge. I followed suit.

"Annie." She began, looking at me earnestly, "I heard something and I think you should know."

"What?" I implored, impatiently grasping her mittened hand.

"You know my best friend, Debby?" She asked, looking me straight in the eyes, like I was a sane person.

"Her husband is a Real Estate Developer, and she overheard a phone conversation of his pertaining to some big Real Estate deal."

"And?" I prompted.

"And, from what I could hear, it seemed like some investors have had an idea in the works for some time about opening a big Casino."

"And?" I repeated, anxiously.

"Annie!" She exclaimed, her eyes bright in the cold afternoon sun. She grasped my hands with both of hers and I could feel her shaking.

"The land they want is yours!"

"What?" I jumped to my feet, drawing the attention of a lingering Orderly.

"What?" I whispered.

"Don't you see?" She exclaimed. "Your land would be worth millions! Well, a lot, anyway." She amended.

"Why wouldn't someone just come and ask me then?" I said, disbelievingly.

"Do you remember when Al died? Mother told me that you had to see a lawyer then about the estate. Do you remember that?" She asked sincerely, as if maybe I didn't in my demented state.

"Of course I remember, Sherry. What about it?"

"Did he ask you if you wanted to sell?"

She was standing next to me now, her breath touching my face as it wafted on the winter air.

"Well, or course, that's to be expected." I said, still not getting it.

"And? What did you say?"

The light dawned slowly on my Thorazine besotted brain, but it dawned.

"I said," I replied, remembering, "They'll have to carry me off like they did Al!"

We stared at each other mutely for a couple of minutes, the wails of the dangerously ill surrounding us from their locked ward on the fourth floor.

"Thank you, Sherry! Thank you so much! I KNEW I wasn't crazy; and this proves it!

Does Amos know?"

"No. He had to go on the road again, remember?"

I vaguely remembered, but the drugs did nothing to enhance my memory. If I didn't get out of here soon, I'd be a zombie like the other poor souls, who wandered the halls in their drug induced, comatose states.

Irmaline came later that day. Amos had given her the key to my house and she was taking care of my pets while he was gone.

She hadn't known what to think when I'd been placed here in a psychotic state. I'm sure the memory of Barney in my trunk passed through her mind as I'd raved incoherently.

She also seemed to think I'd been vindicated by Sherry's' revelations.

"I never really thought you were a murderess, Annie," she said before she left.

I didn't mention her running down the country road, a look of horror on her face, after the discovery of Barney in the trunk.

I tried to "cheek" the pills they gave me twice a day, and spit them into the toilet as soon as I could without arousing suspicion. I then had to do the "Thorazine shuffle" and force my eyes not to focus when anyone was looking. I thought perhaps a career as a Thespian may await me if I ever got out. But then, how hard is it to act crazy and drugged? All I had to do was watch my fellow inmates and follow suit.

The antics of "Her Majesty" would have been a source of mirth if they hadn't been so heartbreaking. I played along with her even though the staff didn't think it advisable to play into her fantasies. It didn't matter, I was crazy too, and so it was understandable that I believed her.

Most of the others were beyond even small talk. I kept my own counsel and, wearing my gray inmates' uniform, tried to blend in.

I saw the "Shrink" once a week and had decided on my next visit I would disavow all knowledge of having seen my father, although I couldn't bring myself to lie about the intruder. I would not say I'd imagined it.

I couldn't wait to see Amos and find out what he thought

of the new revelations. I was hoping the news had been relayed to the Sheriff's department (Irmaline told me she'd been in touch with the Private Detective and was having him take care of things). In fact, he was due to visit next Sunday and I planned to tell him everything. Maybe my "father" was actually someone wearing make-up to look like him; reinforcing the idea that I was crazy. After all, it had worked!

I was sitting on my bed, gazing out the mesh-covered window at the bucolic winter scene outside as "Her Majesty" instructed the orderlies that she wanted Pheasant under glass for dinner, when I was called to the Nurses' station for a phone call. I was surprised, as we weren't allowed to have phone calls until Saturday.

It was Mike, the Detective, and he'd somehow managed to convince the nurse to let me talk to him.

He informed me that he'd managed to uncover quite a bit of information about the land deal. It seems that some Native American organization had managed to uncover an old treaty that specified my land as Indian land. Since my property had been owned by Al's family for so long, it was "grandfathered" in. Meaning, I couldn't be forced off just by the fact that it was now Indian land. Of course, the Government could keep it bound up in the court system as long as possible, but Mike seemed to think they had a different agenda. He was of the mind that the Government wanted their piece of the pie and would strike a deal with the Indian leaders. The State would pay for the development of the land and the building of the Casino, the roads, etc., for a cut of the profits once it was running.

I was the only one standing in the way.

I told him of my conversation with the Attorney after Al's demise, and wondered aloud if he could have known about the plans being secretly devised. Mike seemed to think it was a pretty good possibility as no one had approached me about selling.

Hanging up the phone, I felt a stab of fear at the enormity of it. I must remain crazy or be "taken out". If I remained crazy, however, the State would come in and take over my land, as I had no heirs, and Al's family was long dead. I didn't want to lose my land, but was I willing to die for it? Maybe I should take the money and run. Although I'd have to prove my sanity first, and than 'the powers that be' would become a threat and I might not live long enough to let them know I'd sell. They'd certainly never let me get out of here.

The last thing Mike said to me before hanging up was, "Watch your back."

I bit back a laugh as I softly thanked him for calling.

Watch my back? I was in a Mental Hospital; I'd be mental if I didn't!

I was due to have a hearing in three weeks. I could be released if the "Shrinks" agreed I wasn't a threat to myself, or others. I though of "Her Majesty", and wondered why they didn't let her out. She certainly was no threat. I guess it was hard to take care of yourself if you were used to servants. She wouldn't eat unless her meal was served on a silver platter (which was actually a cheap pewter tray painted with silver paint, the nurse's had allowed this only because she wouldn't eat, otherwise) maybe it was a matter of being independent, and having people that cared. I could see how people could "fall through the cracks" and be left to languish here while the State picked up the tab.

I just had to be halfway coherent, though not too, considering my daily dosage of drugs.

I'd lie in bed at night and wonder if this nightmare would ever end, the desperate cries of lost souls surrounding me, a keening that my own soul understood only too well.

Amos came the next Sunday, looking tired. His hair was it's usual wind-blown mop and his beard looked scruffy.

He had talked to Mike and was up to speed on the new

developments. He'd brought my pets to his house, and I was glad. I didn't want them alone in that house.

He'd called the Attorney I'd had before and he was going to accompany me to my competency hearing, further insuring my release. Most patients had no such luxury, and most wouldn't know, anyway.

Amos hugged me tightly and I realized what he must have been through. Finding me on the floor, babbling incoherently. Maybe he actually believed I was a murderess for a while there; but I'd never ask him and besmirch the faithfulness he'd always displayed.

We walked the grounds arm in arm, discussing the course of action we should take.

Amos thought the only way I'd be safe was to get the press involved.

We didn't talk about what he thought were my delusions, but I made sure I told him of the idea I'd had that someone had disguised himself. After all, I never really got a close look at him.

I asked him about the Police and their investigation into who had attacked me and about Barney's placement in my trunk, for now I wondered if they weren't all related. I knew they blamed me. I also knew John and Vicky's deaths were marked closed. He said they were looking at me closely, but since I was innocent, I had nothing to worry about. I bit my tongue as visions of falsely imprisoned death row inmates flashed through my mind.

After Amos left I wandered into the day room, swerving to avoid the patients who danced to unheard music, their arms pin-wheeling like demented conductors.

I stood staring out the window, thinking. The vista was still as cold and lifeless as it had been for months, but spring wasn't that far off now: Two to three more months, depending on the vagaries of Mother Nature. Where would I be then? Sitting with Amos in the old rocker on my porch, sipping coffee and watching early tourists in canoes floating by? I refused to think of any other scenario.

I tried not to dwell on the severity of the situation. I'd rather it had been some demented person than an unseen government conglomerate that I knew nothing about. There was a lot of money involved, and therefore a lot of power.

I shuddered in the late afternoon sun, shining through the dusty, streaked windows that probably hadn't been washed in years.

I lay in bed that night, listening to the moans of the inmates and the wind whipping around the corners of the ancient building.

"Her Majesty" had been unusually difficult that day, insisting that the same people that had killed Princess Di were now after her, to keep her from her rightful legacy.

It wasn't just her, the mood of the place had taken on an ominous tone; usually passive patients were being unusually difficult, and the Orderlies were running to and fro as one crisis after another popped up.

The long winter had taken a toll on them. Being cooped up for months at a time with others who had as tenuous a grip on reality as they did, was wearing them down.

As I finally drifted off among the screams and hysterical laughter, a bass voice from somewhere in the bowels of the place lulled me to sleep with a poignant rendition of "Amazing Grace".

Mr. Spence (my Attorney) came the next day. He was allowed in as it was in an official capacity.

We went over everything from the time of the attack until the present. The hearing was just around the corner and he wanted to reassure me that there was no doubt that I'd be released, barring another psychotic episode. I took his hand and thanked him profusely for coming. His reassurances had put me in an unusually happy mood, and I had to force myself to shuffle and unfocus my eyes for the rest of the day.

The day of my hearing dawned bright and sunny and I sat nervously on the edge of my bed until an Orderly came to escort me down to the room my hearing would be held in.

A whole plethora of Doctors greeted my arrival by rising from their chairs as I was seated across a long table from them.

The questions were fast and furious and I answered in a meek voice; even admitting, when asked, that the intruder was not my father and, yes, perhaps I'd imagined him as my assailant because of childhood trauma.

My lawyer sat beside me, having already been there when I'd been brought in. Though he never spoke, his presence was reassuring, and I could tell by the Doctor's faces that they were surprised and impressed that I had an Attorney. Crazy people didn't call lawyers.

Although it seemed like hours, the hearing lasted under a half an hour, and I left the room with Mr. Spence and proceeded to the dayroom to consult.

"You're free to go Annie." He said, smiling. "I came prepared to drive you wherever you wish to go, any time your ready."

I grasped his hand and informed him that I was ready, now.

He stayed in the dayroom, observing the other patients, perhaps trolling for any that may have the wherewithal to hire an attorney, as I went to pack up the few meager possessions I had with me.

When "Her Majesty" saw me packing up, she began to cry. It seemed I was her most trusted "lady in waiting" and now I was deserting her.

There was no doubt in my mind where I wanted to go. Amos', of course, that's where he and my pets resided, and therefore, my heart, also.

Mr. Spence didn't have to drive me, as it turned out. As the elevator doors opened, Amos, Irmaline and Sherry, who all started clapping excitedly as the doors opened to reveal my lawyer and me, greeted me.

After much hugging and laughter, I shrugged into my coat and accompanied them to the snowy parking lot.

Mr. Spence waved and gave me the victory sign from across the parking lot as I slid into Amos' truck. Irmlaine and Sherry followed behind us until we reached Amos' turnoff, and I gave them a wave as we turned off.

I scooted across the seat and put my head on Amos' shoulder, a contented sigh escaping me. His big arm went around me, and I knew I was home.

When I'd settled myself on Amos' couch, he slipped a tape into the recorder.

"Look at this", he said, settling next to me.

As I watched, my darkened yard came into view, snow nestling all the way up to the windowsills.

A shadowy figure skulked into view, face unseen under a large, furred hood.

"Notice the date." Amos said, pointing to the corner of the screen.

It was the night I'd been attacked at Amos'. Though there was no sound, I could imagine Sam's ferocious barking at the intrusion into his domain.

The figure lingered at the window for a moment, then disappeared as silently as he had come, going around the side of the house.

I was touched by Amos' diligence, as I'd long ago given up watching the tapes. The snowy landscape, never changing, held all the excitement of an empty aquarium, and the monotony of it held no interest for me.

"Do the Police know?" I asked, anxiously.

"I took them a copy the same day I saw it." He said. "That's the only thing that showed up on any of them."

I hugged him, leaning into his big chest until I could hear his heartbeat.

"Thank you so much, Amos," I said. "I gave up watching those long ago."

"I know," he said, amusement in his voice, "but you got them for a reason, and now they've paid off."

"You were stranded at my house that night, so it couldn't possibly be you." He said, tilting my chin up to gaze into my eyes.

"Do they know about the land deal?" I asked.

"Yes. Mr. Tanner informed them as soon as he'd gleaned the information. He also said not to expect too much from the authorities, as it's anyone's guess how far up the interest in this project goes."

"What do we do?" I asked, the knot of dread once again welling up in my stomach.

"We call the newspaper," he replied, reiterating what he'd told me in the hospital.

"Going public is the only way to insure your safety." He said, seriously.

"And yours, as well." I said, suddenly afraid for him.

Sam had been lying at my feet from the minute I'd returned, and now raised his head to look questioningly at me, as if sensing my fear.

Judas was draped over the back of the couch and I could feel her whiskers brush my face as I turned my head.

Now, as Amos gazed into my eyes so trustingly, I had to bite back the question I wanted to ask, but dared not. "Did you really think it was me?"

We decided to go to the Newspaper Office early the next morning. The phones and electricity had come back on a day after I'd been committed, but Amos didn't want to have them come to us as other media might get wind of it and bombard the house. I agreed.

For now, all I wanted to do was relax and enjoy my pets and Amos, putting all thoughts of my dilemma aside until tomorrow.

I awoke the next morning expecting to hear "Her Majesties" demands assaulting my ears, and was pleasantly surprised as the realization of my freedom dawned on me.

The smell of coffee wafted down the hall as I sat up and stretched in the big bed, Judas watching me, Sam nowhere in sight.

I glanced towards the hot water heater as I started down the hall. Amos had already checked every access to the house, trying to discover where the intruder had entered, to no avail.

"Hi." I said, yawning, as I seated myself at the table, across from Amos. I could hear Sam, outside barking, and Amos went to let him in.

I was wearing one of Amos' shirts and it hung down below my knees, but had ridden up to expose half my thigh as I'd sat down. Amos ogled me as he retook his seat, and I chuckled at the lewd look on his face.

"I'm sure glad your back." He said, sincerely.

"Yes. I gathered that, after last night." I said, smirking.

I had my elbows on the table, my hands cupped around the steaming mug, as we gazed at each other, lovingly, across the table. Pulling his gaze away, Amos said, "Back to reality, little lady."

I felt my spirits plummet and wished he'd allowed me a little more time to dwell in my newfound freedom, without the truth of reality.

Amos also informed me that we had to stop at the Sheriff's Office. Jim (the Sheriff) had been going to come to the Mental hospital after I'd come around, but Amos had talked him into waiting until I got out, assuring him that he would, personally, bring me down to give a statement. It would also give us a chance to ask him about his take on the tape; which would, hopefully, help convince him of my innocence. Could we trust him? Was he, somehow, in on the land deal?

Amos didn't think so. He said, "Jim is as honest as the day

is long."

"Yeah." I said, sarcastically, "Well, the days aren't too long right now!"

He just looked at me and shook his head, his wild mop becoming even more disheveled in the process.

"Sorry." I said, contritely. "You know him a lot better than I do, so I'll have to take your word for it."

We took turns cleaning up in the bathroom, and prepared to leave.

Most of the roads were passable, despite several storms while I'd been away. We drove in silence, each lost in our own thoughts; mine weren't pleasant.

The building the paper was housed in was only a block from the Sheriffs office, a sprawling, one-story building made of faux brick. Amos took me around to the back so we could avoid the curious stares of the reporters. We used the service door and had only to traverse a short hallway to reach the editor's office. Amos had specifically wanted to talk to him, as they'd went through school together and had, at one time, been good friends. Amos knocked softly and a booming voice yelled, "Come in!"

The office was cluttered, with stacks of newspapers everywhere. A large desk dominated the middle of the room; it too, was cluttered.

The man behind the desk stood and reached his hand out to Amos, a smile lighting his face. He was rather short and very slender. A shock of pure white hair encircled his skull.

He must have the same barber as Amos, I thought, noting the unruliness of his mane.

Amos shook his hand profusely, evoking a slight wince from the little man.

"Annie, this is Tommy Winkleman, but we call him 'Ink,'" Amos said, seating himself.

"Ink, this is Annie."

I shook his hand and he smiled warmly.

When we were both seated in the rather shabby chairs, he turned to his computer screen, nearly unseen under the piles of paper, and pushed a few keys.

"Here's everything we have on you," he said, swinging the screen in our direction, "now, tell me what I don't know." I liked him immediately and proceeded to tell him the whole sordid tale, leaving nothing out.

"So you think by going public you'll be safe, huh?"

I looked to Amos, who shrugged and said, "Well, she can't be any less safe then she is now."

"I'm sure you remember the siege of reporters who practically stalked you not too long ago. Be prepared to go through it again. Hang-up calls, threats, hate mail. Every nut in the country will be coming out of the woodwork."

"The country?" I asked.

"Of course. There's always some reporter who's hoping to latch onto a story and pump it for all it's worth. With CNN, it'll probably be seen internationally. Also, computer coverage."

Totally going off the wall, I said, "How come you have computers? I can't get service."

He laughed heartily, like I'd said something really funny.

"Well, sweetie, the town's had service for quite some time. The cops and the hospital, even the school, would be lost without it. The library. Out where you are, there's not much demand for it. It could be years before you get cable. You got a dish? Well, I know you do, Amos; you've got about everything out there at your place. Quite the place."

Amos cleared his throat, and the conversation got back on track.

"I just want to make sure you know what you're getting into. Being a newspaperman, I should jump on this and not consider your feelings at all. But Amos and me go way back, and I wouldn't, in all good conscience, be able to do that."

"I know that, Ink," Amos said, "that's why I came to you."

We ended up telling him we wanted to think about it a little longer and see if anything developed through the Sheriff's investigation. There was a lot of new evidence, so maybe we wouldn't have to wait long for a resolution.

Ink locked his lips with a childish motion and I knew our information was safe with him. He wouldn't publish until we gave him the go-ahead.

The Sheriff's office parking lot was nearly empty when Amos pulled the truck in. The lot had been recently plowed and was nearly devoid of snow.

I wondered if their were still townspeople acting as deputies, or had the expense been too big a strain on the budget?

With the new information, some Government Corruption committee, or something, should be called in. I wanted to ask the Sheriff about that.

I was glad when I wasn't taken to an interrogation room, but rather, seated at the Sheriff's desk. He silently passed my gun across the table, I put it in my pocket.

I went over all the events of that night. When it came to the part about my father, I told him it had to be someone wearing a mask. I no longer feared the Mental Hospital; I'd been declared sane.

A slight twitch of his eyelid made me think he still wasn't sure about me, and now I was armed, but he covered it well.

When we got into the land scheme, he raised his hand and vehemently denied that any such deal was in the works.

"It's just a rumor." He said, his voice broaching no argument. "Believe me, I've looked into it and there's nothing to it. If someone is after you, that isn't the reason."

My spirits dropped considerably at his statement. It made so much sense. It would explain everything. I looked at him, disbelievingly.

"Now don't go looking at me like that, Miss Woods. There is NO conspiracy, so, therefore, I am not involved in any conspiracy."

Not knowing what to say, I remained silent.

"Now look here, Jim," Amos intoned, "All the pieces fit. Maybe you just didn't look in the right places."

I could see the redness creeping up Amos neck, the muscles tensing in his shoulders.

The Sheriff held his ground and insisted it was rumor.

"Mr. Tanner said he gave you everything he dug up." I insisted, stubbornly.

"And I checked into all of it. There was no prove, nor even taint of anything untoward going on."

Amos stood, dwarfing the room, his bulk bringing an ominous ambiance to it.

Jim started to rise from behind his desk, but Amos waved him back, grabbing my elbow and turning toward the door.

Curious stares followed us as we quickly wound our way through the maze of desks. Eyes followed us, and whispers echoed off the walls.

I felt my face flaming as Amos pulled the big door open; right before it closed, I heard a loud laugh and a voice called to our backs, "Go back to the loony bin, ya' psycho."

I looked at Amos, sheepishly. "I guess we won't be getting much help here." I said, laconically.

"We should have asked the Sheriff for a copy of Mike's report." I said, as we pulled onto the road, tires squealing.

"It wouldn't have done any good. He won't show it to you. It's official Police business."

He snorted the last part.

"Mike will give us a copy, though." I said.

Another squeal of tires pierced the still air as Amos made a u-turn in the middle of the street and headed for the motel on the edge of town.

"He was going to bring me a copy." He said. "I'll bet he came when I was out of town and didn't want to leave it on the doorstep." Neither of us could remember what room he was in so we went to the office.

The smell of burnt coffee and cigarettes assaulted our noses as we entered. An ancient man sat behind the counter, and his red eyes lifted above the rim of his glasses and the paper he was reading, as we entered. He was stooped over like a crone, his back bent with Osteoporosis.

"Ain't seen him in a couple days." He said, when queried.

"Well, isn't that unusual? Isn't he usually here at night?" I asked.

"Ain't no business of mine what he does. He pays a month in advance, so's as long as he comes back before the rent's due, his business is his own."

Amos had to grease his palm with a fifty to get him to let us into Mike's room.

Everything was neat and tidy. His clothes hung in the closet; a suit jacket behind the door.

We searched the dresser and desk drawers, but there was nothing. His briefcase was missing, though. We couldn't find it anywhere.

Where had he gone?

The poor man had been living here for months, at the request of Vicky's father, neglecting his family. Although I think he had said something about spending weekends with them.

"Amos. I think he stays with his family on the weekends."

It was a Saturday. I'd have to try to find his home number. I didn't even know if I had it.

Neither Amos nor I would get any information out of Vicky' parents, I was sure. It was a scene I didn't want to participate in.

"We'll just have to wait." I said.

"Well, that was a productive day." I said, when we were once again in the truck.

"Every door slammed in our face." Amos answered. "It's strange, Annie. Something is going on."

"I know." I replied, meekly, than turned to scan the bleak

landscape.

When Monday arrived and Mike was still nowhere to be found, Amos went back down to the Sheriff's office. I refused to subject myself to that humiliation again, so I stayed home (at Amos').

I wandered nervously through the house, afraid for Mike. What could have happened to him? I didn't want to think about that, and where was his briefcase? Had he put Amos' copy in a safety deposit box somewhere? I really wanted to see what he'd discovered, regardless of what the Sheriff said.

When Amos returned, I ran out to meet him, falling on my ass in the slick driveway. He helped me up and ushered me back inside.

"Calm down, Annie", he admonished. "Jim's going out to talk to Vicky's parents and see if they know anything. If not, then he'll have to talk to Mike's family. There's nothing we can do."

"Shit!" I said, exasperated. "We have to get a copy of his report." I added.

"I've been thinking," Amos, said, "maybe someone got a hold of that report before the Sheriff got it. We know important people have an interest in it, maybe things were removed, or redone, before Jim got it."

I mulled this over.

"Yes." I said, excitement overtaking me, "that would make sense. Then Jim really would be just as much in the dark as we are; it would also make me look like the paranoid everyone thinks I am. But where is your copy, Amos? It has to be somewhere.

Maybe a safety deposit box?"

"Then we'd have to wait for his family to claim it and hope they'd let us see it."

"What should we do?" I asked, frustrated.

"We wait." Amos said. "If there is a deal in the works, it's got to come out eventually; they're not going to give up the idea because you don't want to leave."

"That's just it. Maybe I should let it be known around town that I'm ready to sell. Put the house on the market and see who crawls out of the woodwork. After all, I wouldn't have to sell."

"That's a thought." He said, his brow furrowing in concentration.

We decided to go outside and shovel and gather firewood, putting the nagging problems behind us, at least for the afternoon.

The day was bright and sunny, and I felt my spirits lifting as I pried frozen logs off the woodpile. Sam was snuffling around my ankles, chasing a chipmunk I'd evidently disturbed.

Amos was wielding a snow shovel, making a path to the woodpile so the going would be easier. When we were back inside, our faces red and our hands cold, we stood before the fireplace, warming them.

"Amos, what was Jim's response to my tape? The one showing the figure by the window."

He snorted.

"That could have been anybody, was his response; A Fed Ex employee, a stranded motorist, a long lost friend of yours looking for you."

Amos thought I should move in with him, since we were always together anyway, either at my house or his. He just wanted me out of 'harms' way.' And of course it would be the sensible thing to do.

"It's the principle of the thing!" I said, self righteously, but the truth of the matter went much deeper. I'd lived the last decade of my married life in that house. All my memories of Al were tied up there. It was the first 'real' home I'd known. I also wasn't one to be chased off my own land. I had the feeling that if I quietly sold and moved in with Amos, the casino would be built and the mystery never solved, because no one would be bugging the cops and it would just be forgotten.

They had tried to convince Vicky's parents that it had been Barney who killed her, and I had killed Barney: End of case. No one cared about John Fuller, mountain man, ex-con.

If I remained steadfast and refused to sell, events would accelerate and, hopefully, a conclusion eventually reached.

I didn't want to put myself in harms way, but I didn't know if I could live with always wondering which of my fellow townsfolk had been willing to off me.

We invited Irmaline, Sherry and the boys over Friday night for a movie. Sherry was planning on going to bed early. She was in nursing school now, and she and Debby had early morning shopping plans. It seems she needed some kind of special shoes, so they'd have to drive to the mall. The shoe store in town had a limited selection.

Sherry felt Irmaline could use a night out by herself, away from the constant roughhousing of the boys.

I'd missed Irmaline. I hadn't seen her since I'd been out, and the short Sunday visits at the hospital didn't really count, as I'd been constantly on guard against other patients, and had had to play act like a Zombie around the Orderlies. I was quite looking forward to her visit.

She arrived with much fanfare, her hands laden with packages. Amos took them from her cold hands as I helped her off with her coat. She was wearing her favorite beige, khaki pants and a pale, pink sweater that accentuated the redness of her cold cheeks.

"Annie, you are in dire need of a new wardrobe."

She went to the couch where Amos had placed the bags and started rummaging through them.

"Ta-da!" She said, pulling a soft, blue Cashmere sweater out of the bag.

"It's beautiful, Irmaline, but what's up?"

"Oh, I just felt in a generous mood that day." She said, holding it up in front of me.

"There's more. Oh, and Amos, there's a little something for

you in here, too."

She pulled out a small box with the logo of a saddle shop in town printed on it.

Amos' face flamed as he reluctantly accepted the unexpected gift.

His huge hands fumbled with the cover as he murmured thank you.

It was a belt buckle. Though I'd never seen Amos wear one, it suited him. It was toled in silver and had some kind of Retriever on point worked into the middle of it. It was beautifully hand crafted, and I'm sure, not cheap.

"Wow," was all he could manage as I ran to place it over his belt.

"Actually," Irmaline informed us, "Sherry just received some insurance money and insisted on paying me back some of the money Barney finagled out of me through the years. I didn't want to accept it, but there it was in my Jewelry box one day after she'd went to school."

There was also a white blouse and a pair of gray dress pants for me. I hugged her affectionately and thanked her sincerely.

We settled on the huge couch. I was in the middle with Irmaline on my left and Amos on my right. Judas was curled behind Irmalines' head on the back of the couch. Sam lay in front of the fire, an occasional twitch signifying he was dreaming.

The ambiance was such that I forgot my troubles and fear for a while; ensconced in the warmth of the people I loved most.

Amos and I downed a few beers, while Irmaline had her usual glass of Sherry, which she'd brought with; but only one, she had to drive, she reminded us primly.

We watched, "Some Like It Hot", laughing at how old-fashioned it seemed, though we'd all been alive then. We lamented the loss of Marilyn at such a young age and then got into conspiracy theories.

It was a great evening and I was disappointed when Irmaline got up to leave.

"Stay, Irmaline." I implored.

"No. I must go. I'm watching the boys in the morning so Sherry doesn't have to drag them with."

I helped her into her coat and Amos escorted her to her car, above her protestations, while I watched from the window.

Amos had to make another run in a couple of days, so we decided to change the locks. At least that meant he believed me about the intruder; or, at least, didn't want to take any chances. We'd go to the hardware store in the morning.

There was still no sign of Mike as far as we knew, and the Police were being closed mouthed about it. If we wanted to question his family, we'd have to go to Vicky's parents for the information. I doubted they'd even see either one of us.

We went to town in the morning, stopping at the restaurant for breakfast. We got the usual stares and whispers from the few other patrons, but nothing more. We had the same waitress who was Amos' friend in high school and she beseeched us to ignore the "small minded hicks," lamenting her choice to stay in town rather than leave after high school.

The sun was shining as we exited the restaurant, my arm entwined in Amos'. The town seemed nearly deserted and I wondered if it was the cold, or the thought of a murderer running amok, that was keeping the townspeople at bay.

I feared someone may try to burn my house down to get rid of it, and informed Amos' that I wanted to stay at my place while he was gone. He, as anticipated, had a fit, but I stood firm. He thought I should, at least, have Irmaline stay with me, but I refused. I didn't want to put her at risk. Sam would alert me to anyone lurking around, and I had my gun. I also informed him that we'd be staying at my place for a while when he got back; I needed to protect it.

After the locks were changed, we got in the truck to drive

to my place and check it out.

Amos removed the tapes and we fast-forwarded through hours of monotonous footage.

He returned them to the players as he once again carped about my stupidity and pigheadedness.

"Please, Amos. Just drop it. You know I'm not changing my mind. In fact, I'd like to stay here tonight, as well. Besides, I was no safer at your house! Less safe, 'cause I didn't have Sam."

He really flipped then. We'd been arguing about it and I hadn't dared bring it up earlier, so now we had to go retrieve my pets and some clothes.

By evening he'd settled down, and after several hours of the silent treatment, started speaking to me again.

My car was running again, as all it had needed was a battery, which Amos' had installed while I was in the hospital; my paranoia about someone disabling it was just that: Paranoia.

Tomorrow (Sunday) was our last day together before his run. The sky was clouding up again and I feared another storm. I needed my phone and prayed the lines would hold if an ice storm hit.

"Maybe you should have brought another gun." Amos said before we went to bed.

"Mine's perfectly functional." I said, haughtily.

I was still rather angry with him for calling me pigheaded, when he was the most stubborn person I'd ever met! I talked to Irmaline in the morning; she was concerned about the weather and me being alone.

"There's nothing to be done about it," I informed her. "No matter where I am, if someone wants to get me bad enough, they either will, or die trying!" I said, more bravely than I felt.

We had to go into town for groceries since whatever was left in the fridge was rotten. This, of course, brought on another barrage from Amos, "there's plenty of food at my house!" I ignored him and wandered the aisles of the supermarket, in search of chocolate.

When we got home I was surprised at how happy I was to see my own house; sagging, mostly burnt out Christmas lights, not withstanding.

I made a light lunch of ham sandwiches, fresh from the package. We ate in silence, Amos' disappearing within seconds.

I spent the afternoon cleaning the accumulated dust off of everything, while Amos languished in front of the television, nodding in and out, as weather reports droned in the background.

We spent the evening cuddled on the couch, watching our favorite network dramas. Amos was hiding his misgivings about me being alone. He was kind and attentive and I had to point out to him that I worried equally about him.

"It isn't just about me," I ranted. "I don't like you driving on those icy roads! It goes both ways, Mister!"

He laughed at my vehemence, and the subject wasn't brought up again.

I woke in the morning to Amos getting dressed.

"Weren't you going to wake me?" I asked, hurt.

"Why? You need your sleep," he said buttoning his shirt.

That really steamed me, but I said nothing. If that wasn't just like a man!

As he turned towards me, I saw Irmaline's buckle gleaming in the stray sunbeam that shone in through a gap in the curtains.

"I really like that buckle," I said. "How thoughtful of Irmaline; and my clothes, too!"

"She's one of a kind." He agreed, wholeheartedly.

I got up and donned my natty old robe, than we went to make coffee.

I sure was going to miss Amos, even though, barring really bad weather, he'd only be gone a few days: Neither one of us made mention of the fear that nibbled at the edges of our psyches. We'd each be strong for the other.

# CHAPTER TWENTY-THREE

The minute Amos pulled out I ran to my underwear drawer and pulled out the letters secreted there. They had been in my coat pocket the whole time I'd been in the hospital and I hadn't even discovered them until I'd gotten to Amos' after the hospital released me. I'd kept them there and stashed them in my drawer the minute I'd gotten home. I don't know what kept me from showing them to Amos, except maybe a deep-seated fear that he might recognize the handwriting and go off half-cocked.

I hurried threw on jeans and the white blouse Irmaline had given me and ran to the car.

I silently blessed Amos as the ignition turned right over.

Irmaline was surprised to see me, and even more surprised when I whipped the letters onto the coffee table. After I'd explained about finding them and my reticence to show them to Amos, she slowly went through them.

"No." She said, at last, "I don't believe I can identify that writing. Over the years I've probably gotten cards from everyone in town, and I've assisted at the school on numerous occasions, as a kind-of teacher's assistant. I'm sorry, Annie. I wish I could help. Does Amos know about these?"

"I don't know." I said, honestly. "I guess that's why I was afraid of showing them to him."

We went in the kitchen and had coffee while the boys dawdled over bowls of cereal, getting more on the table than in their mouths. They had a snow day and therefore would be home all day. At our arrival, they suddenly had no trouble finishing and made a hasty retreat, their footfalls and voices bouncing off the enclosed walls of the stairway as they went to play their video games.

Sherry was at school and Irmaline filled me in on her progress.

"I've never seen her so happy and excited!" She gushed.

The guilt about being the one who killed Barney abated slightly on hearing this. I'd learn to live with it. I couldn't help thinking that I'd done them all a favor, and then chastised myself for thinking it.

We had a pleasant morning catching up on all the gossip and pondering the Private Detective's whereabouts. I took my leave about noon as Irmaline was making soup for lunch. I declined her offer to stay, and stuffing the letters back in my coat pocket, made my exit.

Why did the writing seem familiar to me, but not Irmaline? It was another imponderable.

Sam and Judas greeted me at the door, probably fearing I would leave them again. More likely, fearing that I wouldn't be there to feed them when they demanded it. Regardless, I was happy to be back in my own home. I'd take Al's ghost over the ones at Amos', anytime.

I spent the next couple of days doing a more thorough job of cleaning, and washing clothes. The nights were tough, though Amos called whenever he got a chance, and I made my voice light and didn't mention anything that would worry him. I passed on some gossip from Irmaline about some childhood friends of his, eliciting a laugh.

He was due back the next day, and I had to restrain myself from breathing a sigh or relief. Not yet, I told myself. I had one more lonely night to get through.

God. Would I have to spend years waiting and wondering? Would I feel my knees shake every time Amos had to leave?

I wallowed on the couch, beer in hand, just one, to take the edge off my fear.

The shadows of late afternoon were crowding in, and I started a fire. My pets were sprawled contentedly on the hearth; I think they, too, had missed their home.

One more night became my mantra, as I jumped at shadows.

I had my gun strategically placed on the coffee table before me, never more than a second away.

My floors gleamed in the flickering firelight and I was proud of the cleaning job I'd done.

The t.v. droned in the background; I wanted to be able to hear the sounds of the night around me.

An owl hooted loudly outside the window, and I started, remembering the old wives' tale that said death was to follow.

I wanted to go to the window and peer through the drapes, but a groundless fear kept me rooted to the couch. The phone rang just then and my beer flew from my hand, spilling across my clean floor and making a stain on the rug. My pets jumped up at the sound, Judas hissing and licking herself as beer spattered on her.

"Sorry," I said, as I flew to answer.

It was Amos, and I felt like crying in relief as I heard his gruff voice.

"What's wrong?" He asked immediately, hearing something in my voice.

"Nothing." I stammered, "nothing at all. I'm just jumpy. I can't wait until you get home."

"Hopefully, it will be early. As usual, it depends on the

weather." He said, stoically.

"Well, don't worry about me. I'll be fine. Wait until you see how clean the house is!" I said, proudly, glancing around the tidy room.

"Maybe I should leave more often." He teased.

"Don't you dare!" I admonished.

I felt better having talked to him and decided to actually try to concentrate on a t.v. program.

The promised storm had never appeared, hitting, instead, the southern part of the state. They were now buried under several feet of snow. We could be next, so I could take no comfort in their misfortune.

I flipped through the channels and finally settled on an old sit-com. I needed light comedy to get me through; the mysteries hit too close to home.

I remembered the beer spill as my bare foot stepped on a sticky spot, and hurried to clean it up, scrubbing at the spot on the rug, fearing it would stain.

That accomplished, I settled back on the couch just as the commercial was ending.

The wind picked up as the news came on at ten. I could hear it howling around the house, the fire blazed up and wavered from side to side, grasping at the oxygen that blew down the chimney.

Will this winter never end? I wondered. Each year they seemed to get longer.

Could I leave this house? I asked myself. The same answer came back to me. It wouldn't matter, if I never found out the cause of all the trouble. I had to know!

Irmaline called then, apologizing for the lateness of the hour, but worried about me.

I told her I doubted I'd get any sleep that night, and she agreed, telling me to call, no matter how late, if I needed to talk. I assured her I would and hung up, reluctantly. I went back to the couch, and fell into a half doze.

Sam started barking, he was clawing at the door and growling. I started at the sudden cacophony. I automatically glanced at my mantel clock, 2 a.m.

I dragged him back by his collar and firmly admonished him. I couldn't hear anything with his wailing.

I turned all the lights out and surreptitiously peaked through the curtains. Blowing snow made visibility impossible. If someone was out there, maybe I'd get lucky and they'd freeze to death.

I had my gun firmly in hand as I made the rounds of the house, looking through each window. Sam followed me from room to room, whining and jumping at shadows.

Eventually, I returned to the couch and sat in the dark, listening. I turned the t.v. off and almost total darkness engulfed the room. The fire was just dying embers now, Judas' still form barely visible on the hearth where she slept. Sam settled nervously at my feet, his ears pricked.

Suddenly, a loud noise came from the back of the house, toward my bedroom.

I silently slipped off the couch and ran through the shadows, gun at the ready. Sam had already taken off to investigate; I could hear his toenails clicking on the hall floor, a low growl coming from his throat.

I'd just entered the hall when I heard Sam whine and a door slammed closed, almost simultaneously. I hesitated at the end of the hall, peering around the corner, trying to see in the deep shadows of the hallway. I wanted to call out to Sam, but resisted the impulse, biting my lip.

I could see the bathroom door was still open by a weak shaft of moonlight that spilled into the hallway through the open door. So it must have been my bedroom door that slammed. I could hear Sam now, barking and scratching at the bedroom door. Should I let him out? I didn't want to put him in harm's way. He'd go after the intruder and I didn't know if he had a gun. No. I'd leave him in the bedroom. I had my gun; if that wasn't enough, then I don't know what Sam could do. His neck could be broken easily enough by a strong man.

I could go into the bedroom with him, but I was afraid he'd escape before I could get the door closed.

I quickly ran the short distance to the bathroom door and turned to face the room, my legs spread, my arms out in front of me, pointing the gun. I quickly flicked the light switch with my left hand, feeling along the wall until I found it. It was empty, but the window was wide open; snow was blowing in as the curtains billowed inward.

I ran and closed and locked the window, noticing the displacement of the mound of snow beneath it, than turned to go and get Sam.

I'd just reentered the hallway when a flash of light caught my eye. My gun was at the ready and I was starting to press on the trigger, when I recognized the pointing dog design on Amos' belt buckle, it had caught some beam of light, enabling me to recognize it. I lowered my arms and breathed a big sigh of relief.

"My God, Amos, I could have killed you! He was just here. He went out the bathroom window!" My voice bounced off the narrow hallway walls as I realized I was shouting.

Watching his approaching form in the near darkness, I couldn't help notice something odd. He didn't move like Amos. I felt the hair on the back of my neck stand up and started to bring the gun up again; simultaneously, a sharp pain and a loud noise swirled in my head; then, blackness.

When I came to, the first thing I heard was Sam barking and still clawing at the bedroom door. I unconsciously raised my hand to my head, further hurting the swelling lump growing there with the gun, which was still clutched in my hand.

I staggered to my feet, leaning against the wall. I walked, half crouched over, my head throbbing, toward the living room.

A scream escaped my throat as I saw an inert form sprawled across the living room floor, next to the door.

"Amos!" I cried, noticing the plaid shirt and the belt buckle, still reflecting light from an unseen source. As I ran toward the prostate form, a voice from the couch, still crouched in darkness, called out.

"No, Annie. It's not me. I'm here."

I ran to the figure reclining on the couch. "Oh Amos. What happened?"

He let out a groan as my weight pressed down next to him; it was then I noticed the stickiness beneath my fingers as I held him.

"Turn on the light, Annie." He croaked in a barely audible whisper.

I ran to the small table lamp and turned it on, bathing the living room in a warm glow.

I went to the phone, expecting to hear nothing as I raised the receiver. To my amazement and relief, the dial tone buzzed welcomingly in my ear. 911 calls in our town were dispatched directly to the Sheriff. I told him to get an ambulance out to my place immediately, that I had a dead man on my floor, as well as a wounded hero.

I went back to examine Amos' wound while I waited. He was still conscious and I implored him not to speak.

"Save your strength, Amos. They're on their way."

His wound was just beneath his shoulder, but not being a nurse, I had no idea how serious it was. It didn't seem to be bleeding much now, but I didn't know how long I'd been out or how long he'd been here.

I wanted to go look at the dead man on the floor, but couldn't bring myself too. I kept a wary eye on his limp body from the corner of my eye; on the off chance he was still alive and may act.

Time seemed to stand still as I sat holding Amos, my gun

still at the ready, my eyes peering sideways at the body on the floor.

Who was it? I knew better than to disturb the crime scene, and I guess I'd find out soon enough.

The wail of sirens could be heard approaching; yet it seemed to take forever for them to arrive.

The ambulance attendants entered first, followed by the Sheriff and a Deputy. I could hear more people outside, talking in muted voices. They hurriedly put Amos on a gurney. The EMT kneeling by the body on the floor screamed, "This one's still alive," as he dropped the limp wrist and went into rescue mode.

The Sheriff gently guided me to the kitchen area and made me sit down. He motioned for an EMT to come over and check me out.

I insisted I be allowed to go to the hospital with Amos, but I could hear the wail of the siren leaving even as I wobbled towards the door.

The Sheriff assured me he'd give me a ride shortly. He thought I should spend the night there as well, under observation.

"I'll stay there with Amos." I said, "Not as a patient."

I told him all I knew as we headed for the hospital.

We were informed that Amos was in surgery to remove the bullet that was lodged somewhere in his massive body. I sat in the surgery waiting room, jumping each time the doors opened, looking for a doctor that would be looking for me.

When they told me that Amos wouldn't be allowed to see anyone even when he came out of surgery, I went to find a phone.

Irmaline was on her way. I noticed the large clock on the wall across from the phone. It read 4 a.m. She'd answered the phone on the first ring, though her voice sounded like someone's who's been pulled out of a deep sleep. She'd nearly dropped the phone when I told her and I could hear hollow fumbling sounds as she fought with it. Then a strange calm seemed to overcome her and she told me she was on her way.

When I returned to the waiting room, the Sheriff was in the chair next to the one I'd vacated.

"Any word?" I asked, hesitantly, bracing for the worst.

"No. He's still in surgery."

I settled in the chair next to him and bombarded him with questions: "Who is the intruder, Sheriff? Why was he after me? Why did he shoot Amos?"

"We don't know the answers to any of those questions, yet." He said, raising his hand, palm up, as if silently shushing me.

"In fact," he continued, "we won't even know if he's the one who shot Amos until Amos wakes up…if…" he trailed off and the implication brought a chill to my heart.

"What do you mean? Who else would have shot him?" I demanded, indignantly.

"Miss Woods, I should inform you that Amos was shot with your gun. The gun I only recently returned to you, the gun you had in your hand when you awoke from your supposed 'concussion'."

"What?" I exclaimed, jumping up and facing him with clenched fists.

"The doctor came out while you were gone." He pulled a plastic baggy from his pocket. "This is the bullet they pulled out of Amos." He held it up for me to see. "As you can see, it's the same caliber as your weapon. The other guy was shot by Amos and we have Amos' gun in our possession, too." They'd taken my gun at the scene, depositing it in a larger baggy, holding the trigger guard with a pencil.

"Miss Woods," he said this sternly, and something in his voice made me draw my eyes from the bullet to his face, "the intruder had no gun. At least not that we could find."

My hands unclenched and I fell back into the chair.

"Well," I said, "that would mean Amos shot an unarmed man. And who shot Amos?"

He just looked at me, a probing look, like one might give to a mental patient who had no conscious memory of a misdeed.

"I was knocked out!" I insisted. "When I came too and went into the living room, I found Amos shot and the other man on the floor. I didn't touch anything, except Amos."

Right then a nurse came in and insisted I go with her to be examined by a doctor.

"We've been looking all over for you!" She exclaimed. "I was here earlier and you weren't."

"I'll talk more to you later, Miss Woods," the Sheriff said as I was led away. I looked back to see him, still seated, with an inscrutable look on his face.

By the time my head had been looked at and I'd been asked stupid questions, like what day of the week it was, Amos was in the recovery room. He'd be allowed no visitors until, at least, tomorrow.

I went down to the main waiting room and saw Irmaline, pacing in front of the reception desk, her hands fluttering like captive sparrows. She really needs to take up smoking, I thought inanely.

I ran to her and we embraced, her questions coming before I could even catch my breath.

After talking to the nurse, we found an all-night hospital lunchroom and sat, coffee in hand, me fielding her questions, answering as honestly as possible.

"Amos wouldn't shoot an unarmed man!" She said, vehemently.

"I know. None of it makes sense. I still don't know who that guy is!"

"Well, then we should go find out." Irmaline said, and I could tell by the set of her jaw, that that's what we were going to do; but not until I'd finished my coffee. My head throbbed as I stood up too fast, and I had to sink back into the chair momentarily. Irmaline tried to convince me to check myself in overnight, but I refused.

We didn't want to find the Sheriff, knowing he'd probably tell us nothing, so we wandered down to the emergency room and grilled the employees until we found one willing to give us the time of day. He informed us that the unknown party was still in surgery, that it was a very serious wound, and that they had no idea of the prognosis.

There was nothing we could do but wait.

We spent the night in the uncomfortable plastic chairs that littered the waiting room.

After several coffee runs, we went to the desk and inquired about Amos' condition.

The nurse told us that a doctor would be with us shortly. We resumed waiting.

I was worried about my pets not having their breakfast. I'd let Sam out of the bedroom before the Sheriff had rushed me to the hospital.

Another hour went by before the doors swung open and a white-coated figure appeared.

After introductions and handshakes, he seated himself on the rim of one of the uncomfortable chairs.

"He'll fully recover," he informed us with a smile. "He lost a lot of blood, but the bullet missed any major arteries. He'll need to take it easy for a few weeks, but he should be able to go home in a couple of days, barring complications. I don't foresee any. He's a big, strong man."

After he explained any complications that could occur, I beamed. Amos was too strong to be affected by any "complications"; I knew he'd be fine.

"Thank God!" Irmaline said in a breathy whisper.

He suggested we go home and get some rest and come back that afternoon, when he was fairly certain Amos would be up to visitors.

We hugged and laughed excitedly. We'd just been given a precious gift: A second chance for Amos.

When we got to the elevators, the Sheriff approached us.

"Miss Woods, Irmaline." He said, nodding a greeting.

"We're going home, Jim. We're tired. So don't give us any guff!" Irmaline said, heatedly.

In the garish lights of the corridor, her skin looked like parchment pulled over a frame.

Blue veins stood out on her forehead and cheeks. She looked really tired. I knew I looked just as spent. I stood silently, waiting for the Sheriff to get to the point.

"I assume you'll be here this afternoon." He asked.

When I told him I would, he continued, "I'd like to show you some pictures of the perp, er, perpetrator. They won't allow me to take any right now because he's in Intensive Care, but they figure he'll be moved to a private room, with a guard, sometime this afternoon, if his vital signs hold. Then I'll be allowed to take a picture of him, so we can get the ball rolling. We have to identify him before we do anything."

"I understand." I answered. "I can't wait to get a look at the person who's been tormenting me for so long!"

Irmaline came home with me; we took my car. When we got there, she pulled her bedding from the linen closet and made up the couch.

I fed my ravenous pets and washed up. I went back in to the living room to tell Irmaline I'd see her when I woke up, but she was already sound asleep, her favorite sweater wrapped tightly around her as she clung to the light blanket.

Sometime later, a knocking at the door roused me. I had a hard time wiping the remnants of an indecipherable dream from my mind as I forced myself into a sitting position.

"What is it?" I called, still half in another reality.

Irmaline's head popped around the corner of the door as it opened.

"I'm sorry to bother you, Annie. Amos is on the phone."

I flew from the bed, grabbing my tatty robe and knotting it around me as I ran down the hall.

"Amos!" I yelled, realizing, too late, I'd probably ruptured his eardrum.

"Hi, Annie." He said, weakly.

I could tell he was under the influence of some drug, probably Morphine, by the faraway sound of his voice, and the way the words seemed slightly slurred.

I told him we'd be there soon. He said he was glad Irmaline was with me, even though the guy'd been caught. I said we'd discuss everything when I got there. He said Jim had already been there and taken his statement.

"Amos," I started, timidly, "who shot you?"

"I don't know, Annie. It was dark. We'll talk when you get here."

I hung up, once again feeling a weight descend on my heart. Irmaline and me discussed it on the way to the hospital.

"Don't even think it!" She admonished. "Who is that man, and why was he there? How long have you been getting not-to-veiled threats?"

"You're right, of course, Irmaline, but Jim has a way of making me feel guilty just by looking at me."

"That's his job, Annie. You're innocent, you have nothing to worry about."

I wished everything in my world were so black and white.

I hugged Amos, being careful not to touch his injured shoulder, now wrapped in white bandages, with an accompanying sling. Irmaline had opted to wait in the hall, not wanting to invade our privacy.

I settled in a chair, this one upholstered, and more accommodating to the human body than the plastic monstrosities in the waiting room.

I went through what had happened from the time I realized there was an intruder in the house, up until I was knocked out. Then I continued with what had transpired when I woke up and went into the living room, mistakenly thinking Amos was the man on the floor.

"You know the rest." I finished.

He told me he had come back early, because he had a "bad feeling." As soon as he entered the house, a shot rang out and he felt a burning pain in his shoulder. Realizing he'd been hit, he fell to the couch, not visibly moving in the darkness, but surreptitiously drawing his gun with his good hand (fortunately he'd been hit in the left shoulder). Whoever it was had run off down the hall. Amos stayed put, bleeding profusely and feeling weaker by the minute. A few minutes later he heard footsteps pounding down the hall, coming toward the living room. A figure bent over him, reaching out. He knew it wasn't me, whoever it was, was dressed like him. He, too, had seen the glimmer of the belt buckle. It was then he'd pulled the trigger. The man had fell heavily to the floor and Amos had remained on the couch, unable to move. I had come out shortly thereafter.

We pondered each other's versions trying to figure it out. It was Amos who hit on it. After Amos had been shot, the man went down the hallway. He'd had the gun then, but not when he came back.

Of course! It was so obvious now that that missing piece had been filled in. He'd planted the gun in my lifeless hand.

Amos grabbed the phone and left a message for the Sheriff, even though we knew he'd be here soon.

I went and called Irmaline in, and Amos, once again, outlined the events.

"But who is he?" Irmaline implored.

"We'll find out this afternoon. One of us is bound to recognize him." I said.

When Jim got there, Irmaline and I crowded close, Irmaline ignoring the pointed looks the Sheriff cast her way.

The Sheriff took the comfy chair I'd been in, pulling it even closer to the bed. I motioned Irmaline to the other, less upholstered one, while I poised on the edge of Amos' bed.

The Sheriff pulled a large manila envelope from under his large jacket; the Sheriff's insignia on the shoulders gleamed in the garish hospital lighting, heightening his authority.

"I took these just a couple of hours ago." He said, pulling three five by seven photos out.

He passed them to Amos, but from my vantage point we could both see them quite clearly.

Irmaline had jumped up the moment the photos had appeared and leaned over the bed, blocking the Sheriff's view. He stood, towering over her.

I looked down at the picture and felt a scream rising in my throat. The room began to spin and I lost my rein on consciousness and would have fallen to the floor if Amos hadn't grabbed me with his good arm.

A horrid smell brought me to my senses, and I opened my eyes to see a nurse standing over me (I was now in the comfy chair) holding a little bottle of horrid smelling liquid under my nose. I could see Irmaline behind her, a worried look on her face. The nurse blocked my view of Amos, but I could feel the Sheriff standing behind me.

The nurse moved, pulling her bottle hurriedly back as I flailed out against it.

I looked up into Amos' eyes.

"Who is it, Annie?" He demanded.

I swallowed quickly, my mouth suddenly dry.

"It's…it's my father!" I said softly, and then collapsed in a fit of weeping.

He went by the name of Forrest Taylor, but the police believed it was an alias and were, even now, running his prints.

I didn't know that name, but I knew that face, as did Amos. He was the one Amos had caught in bed with Vicky all those years ago! My father? No way!

"I must speak to him!" I insisted. "He's dead, you know." I

added, stupidly.

"It can't be him, Annie," Amos said soothingly, "remember your idea about the make-up?"

"I must speak to him." I said, again.

The Sheriff told me it could be arranged, as a part of the investigation; after all, it was obvious I was at the heart of it. I would, however, have to wait as Taylor, or whoever he was, was still unconscious, and would be for a while. We didn't know if he would speak to me, even if he were able.

I practically lived at Amos' bedside the next few days. He was now ready to be discharged, and chomping at the bit!

"Taylor" was still in a drug-induced coma, to give him time to heal. They would start weaning him off the drugs soon, and he should then wake up.

Irmaline had spent a good deal of time at the hospital, but had to baby-sit while Sherry went to school.

Sherry had been up a couple of evenings, as had the waitress from the diner and several other childhood friends of Amos'. The story was all over the news and everyone in town was talking about it. Amos and me had attempted to watch one of the earlier newscasts, but found we didn't want to.

The reporters weren't allowed to see Amos; another good reason for me to camp out there.

As Amos packed up the few things I'd brought for him, the Sheriff came in and told us that "Taylor" had come around. He would be with me when I talked to "Taylor", but, of course, Amos would not.

Amos waited in the hall, talking to the Deputy on guard duty, who was the son of another of his childhood friends.

The room smelled of sickness and drugs as the Sheriff held the door for me. My eyes were glued to the figure in the bed. Tubes were coming out of everywhere and an oxygen tube was taped to his nose.

His eyes were closed under an unruly mop of blonde hair, and I, once again, felt a tug of recognition.

"Mr. Taylor," the Sheriff prompted in a soft voice, "there's someone here to see you. I think you should speak to her."

His eyes slowly opened and focused on me. Recognition dawned in them and he spoke.

"Hello, Annie. Long time, no see."

At the sound of the voice I realized it wasn't my father at all, it was my brother, whom I hadn't seen in over three decades.

No wonder he'd looked like my father, and no wonder the handwriting had been so familiar. He and Vicky must have had a falling out after Amos discovered them, and that was when Paul had retreated to Australia. How long had he been back? Quite a while, evidently.

"Why, Paul? Why did you do it?"

"Do what?" He said, innocently, and the years fell away as I remembered the same cavalier attitude as when my parents had asked him why he'd taken the car without permission.

My heart tugged at me to go and wrap my arms around him, but I stayed rooted to the spot, standing next to the Sheriff, by the door.

"I was just coming to see you, Annie, and I got shot for my trouble!"

Despite the tube attached to his nose, he still managed, what I considered to be, a smirk.

A trace of an accent could be heard and it made the meeting even more surreal. "You stop it right now, Paul!" I shouted, and the Sheriff touched my arm.

"You own up to what you did. I want to know why. Why did you shoot Amos and try to frame me? Why did you kill Vicky and put Irv in my trunk?"

His eyes got big and round and he started to sit up, but a wince of pain forced him back onto the pillow.

"I swear to you, I didn't kill anyone!" He insisted. "You know me! I could never kill anyone!" The accent was even more pronounced when his anger flared. What was it?

Australian?

"You almost killed Amos." I said, softly.

"But I didn't do that, Annie, you did!"

Looking at the Sheriff I said, "this is getting us nowhere, I'd like to leave now."

He opened the door for me, but he remained. I heard a chair scraping across the floor as the door closed behind me.

I filled Amos in on the unproductive conversation, and the shock I felt at seeing my long lost brother, as I drove home.

His arm was still in a sling, but his color had returned, and he looked his usual robust self.

"Well, they've got him now, and they know who he is, so we can put it behind us and let Jim take care of it now."

"What if he's just a cog in the Casino machine? Won't other's take his place?"

"We'll just have to wait and see. I doubt anyone will take a chance now that he's in custody; if anything, they'll go after him."

"Yeah, but HE'S protected!" I said, huffily.

"So are you, Annie." He said, reaching for my knee, and then pulling back as the pain returned.

I looked at him and smiled.

"I know, Amos. You saved my life as far as I'm concerned. If you'd died, I'd be sitting in prison right now. Just like he planned. Or back in the nut house."

Sam and Judas swarmed Amos as I helped him disregard his coat. He reached down and played with Sam's ears as Judas rubbed against his legs.

He groaned as he sat on my couch.

"Man, it's good to be out of that hospital! You have any beer?"

"Amos, you shouldn't…" I let my voice trail off as I went to the kitchen and pulled out a cold one from the back of the refrigerator, where a few bottles still sat.

Reporters showed up later, but after several hours of

unfruitful waiting, gave up their ghoulish vigil.

Weeks went by, but the winter weather still clung, like cobwebs in an your grandmother's attic. The phone had just recently been returned to its cradle, after non-stop ringing for weeks.

Irmaline had been bringing us supplies, as neither of us wanted to face the onslaught; when it came on the news, we turned it off. The Sheriff called and told us Law Enforcements' theory of events. They hypothesized that Vicky had been in contact with Paul. He returned, whether to see her or because he'd already heard about the scam was unknown. He didn't want to kill his sister to get the land, but framing me or getting me put in a mental facility would be sufficient. Then he'd killed Vicky, either because she hadn't known and had found out about the scam, or there'd been some kind of falling out. Barney may, or may not, have been in on it. We'd never really know unless Paul decided to confess.

Amos was almost as good as new; only some stiffness in his arm bespoke his ordeal.

Everything had been quiet, besides the media attention, and we went on with our lives. For the first time since we'd met, our relationship wasn't marred by murders and accusations. It was heaven!

More details had come out since my brother's arrest, but it didn't seem to be coming from him. It was speculated that he'd dressed like Amos on the (correct) assumption that I wouldn't shoot when I the saw the buckle, which he'd picked up at the same saddle shop Irmaline had purchased Amos' at.

Mike had never been found: Another mystery. He had, however, left the information he'd uncovered with his lawyer, who had turned it over to the Sheriff when it became obvious Mike wasn't returning on his own.

There was a plan for a casino in the works. Indian lobbyists and greedy white men were making plans, and had been for a long time.

A few low-level politicians took the brunt of the uncovering of the cover-up, and were expected to receive minimal prison terms.

My brother was yet to go to trial, and neither Amos, nor I, were looking forward to testifying.

No one had ever been charged with either the murder of Vicky (though the cops were trying, even now, to prove it was Paul); at least Barney's name would be cleared, or Barney's appearance in the trunk; John Fuller's death went unnoticed, though it was speculated that he had seen something on 'his land', perhaps people surveying, and had done something to try to stop it.

I didn't want to believe my brother was a murderer, but his attack on Amos was hard to get past. They'd found burglary tools in the shabby room he'd been renting; that explained the easy access to both my, and Amos' house. That explained my appearing and disappearing gun. Ditto for Barney in my trunk. He must have been outside when Barney ran out, and followed him. It must have fit right into his plans when he'd found him dying. Then he simply jimmied my trunk open and thrown him in. He'd been right under our noses all along.

When I thought back on everything that had happened, it all made sense if Paul had done it. Who else knew about the mole, which had been so accurately positioned on the sex doll?

How he'd gotten Vicky's body in the trunk was still debatable. The Sheriff believed he'd put it in there in my root cellar and Amos had unwittingly taken it to the church. He believed that the trunk packed with dishes had been someone else's and Irmaline had been confused.

Amos had taken down my sagging, half-dead Christmas bulbs, another of my bright ideas that didn't pay off. I'd run and turned them off the night Amos got attacked, after I'd called 911. Irmaline, sound asleep, had never noticed. Time went on, and our lives took on an easy casualness.

Slowly the winter released its grip on the land. The smell of spring was in the air. The snow melted, and trees started budding. The ice on the channel started breaking up, and migrating birds returned, their birdsong a welcome sound after the dead silence of a northern winter. We sat on either Amos', or my, porch in the mornings, sipping coffee from steaming mugs; our winter coats replaced with light, spring jackets. The nightmare of the last nine months or so seemed just that, a nightmare. Irmaline, Sherry, and the boys were frequent visitors. It was nice to hear childish voices and laughter coming from the dock. Sherry absolutely glowed in her new life. Her self-confidence had grown with each new thing she learned; and she'd met another student, who may, or may not, be more than a friend.

My happiness was complete. I looked forward to all the days ahead, Amos by my side.

Together we'd enjoy all the days of spring, the fish slicing through the water like shimmering knives, occasionally leaping high above their watery worlds; for a split second becoming a part of ours.

Then summer, fall, and winter would follow, and, like the seasons, we'd change; only we'd grow older, our spring long gone, our summer waning.

Though now we could only view things through a glass darkly, one day, when our time was nigh, all things would become crystal clear.

# AFTERWORD

I'd always enjoyed writing, and after everything that happened, I felt I now had something to write about. The story is complete, except for my afterword, which will remain under lock and key in a nameless hiding place; perhaps to come to light long after I'm gone.

My book had done well in the Midwest, where everyone was all too aware of the puzzling case. This is the true ending, known only to me.

I now had everything I'd sought. I'd gotten really lucky when the land scheme came to light; it worked out better than I ever could have imagined.

The last six months of his life, Al had been talking about selling the house and moving to the city. I couldn't let that happen! He'd also been dogging my every step for months and driving me crazy.

The day Al died, we'd went on a picnic. He'd been delighted when I suggested it and packed our old picnic basket with thick ham sandwiches and homemade Cole slaw.

We'd settled in a small clearing not far from the trail. I pulled out the old thermos Al had used when he was working, and filled his glass with the freshly squeezed lemonade I'd made that morning.

It hadn't taken long before Al was doubling over in agony, the Terro ant killer was working better than I could have hoped. When his spasmodic death throes had finally abated, I dragged him back to the trail, taking a branch and erasing the trail I'd left.

John Fuller had appeared at my door a few months later. It seemed he'd expected me to vacate the premises when my insurance money came through. When he found I was planning on staying, he sprung the news on me that he had seen what I'd done in the woods that day, and was going to turn me in if I didn't vacate 'his' land.

Too bad for him. I managed to get to my gun and forced him, at gunpoint, to get in my car and drive. When we'd gotten as close as we could to the large clearing, we got out and walked. I shot him right where I'd "pretended" to find him. Then placed my gun in his hand. I'd later told the Sheriff that my gun had been lost, but I hadn't realized it immediately.

Vicky sealed her own fate that day when I'd seen her coming out of the woods. Amos was nearly mine by then, she wasn't going to come between us. I had been the one who'd trashed his camp, knowing the blame would fall on Vicky.

When she'd emerged from the woods, I beckoned her in. I quickly dispatched her, making sure to pocket the offending bullet from where it lay by the fireplace. I'd pulled the nails from my bedroom trap door and unceremoniously thrown her down the stairs.

Her parents had unwittingly aided me by lying and covering for her. She'd never come home that night. When they'd later tried to change their story, the cops hadn't believed them.

The day Irmaline came over to help go through things for the church Bazaar, Vicky'd been secreted beneath boxes and piles of moldy clothes in the root cellar. After the heavy door

I'd rigged slammed closed (blowing the old light bulb, as I knew it would, otherwise I'd have managed to unscrew it when Irmaline wasn't looking) I stuffed Vicky in the trunk as Irmaline had searched for the crowbar to open the door. The dishes were later stashed and never got to the church. No one noticed, as I'd "discovered" Vicky before the Bazaar even started.

Barney had been just as easy. He'd come over to question me after the Vicky murder, and I'd simply dispatched him and invented the intruder story, and then I'd broken the lock. He'd been getting too close and had caught me in a lie; he wasn't quite as dumb as he seemed. I'd been the one seen running out on the tape. I'd donned his jacket, stuffing a couch pillow in the hood to make me appear taller. He'd been bleeding out in my bathtub. Later, I'd simply turned the camera off while I stashed him, then turned it back on afterward. No one noticed because I'd moved him to the trunk several hours later, with the cameras off. They'd quit watching about a half an hour after they saw the figure run out. The Sheriff had been in my house while Barney had lain in my tub. I'd planned on dumping his body later, but the flat tire had foiled that plan when Irmaline had seen him. I'd had to improvise. I'd scraped the trunk with my key to make it appear to have been tampered with. His car probably wouldn't have been found until spring if I hadn't gotten it stuck in the ditch. I'd had to walk the three miles home in the freezing cold.

My feigning of fear of Amos just enhanced my role as victim.

Yes, the whole land scheme had been quite fortuitous for me.

My poor brother was the scapegoat; what did I care? He'd knocked me out and almost killed Amos. He deserved to be in prison. He must have been the one who'd pushed me off the bluff. He may have even been at the Halloween party.

How would I know? Everyone was in costume.

It was presumed that he'd met Vicky some years previously, probably on a trip to see me. I'd never seen him, so either me and Al hadn't been home, or he abandoned plans to visit after Amos had caught him with Vicky; after which he'd hightailed it back to Australia, or wherever.

I had nothing to do with the Private Detective's disappearance. After all, his theory about the land scheme worked right in with my plans. I was sure that was why he'd disappeared; he'd stepped on some big toes.

I learned long ago, you have to go after what you want, make things happen, don't let anyone get in your way; and that was what I'd done.

I could now enjoy the fruits of my labor. I had Amos, the house, and the land. Good friends.

Yes, life was good.